Dear Reader,

Lovers Dark and Dangerous, the third annual Shadows collection, is tempting...tantalizing... terrifying! But beware—dark and dangerous lovers are the ones who haunt your nights...just as they haunt the pages of these three scary, sensual novellas by some of the best writers in the genre.

Lindsay McKenna's "Seeing Is Believing" will lure you to the most mysterious of places, where secrets— and love—wait to be revealed.

In Lee Karr's "Storm-Tossed," a handsome stranger who appears from out of nowhere is—literally!—the stuff haunting legends are made of.

And lastly, in Rachel Lee's "The Ancient One," a woman's desperate quest leads her to the very edge of desire...and danger.

Three dark and dangerous lovers are waiting for you. So lock your doors, turn on all the lights and prepare for a passionate good time as you take a walk on the dark side of love, with Shadows as your only guide.

Happy Hauntings!

Leslie Wainger
Senior Editor and Editorial Coordi

LINDSAY McKENNA

spent three years serving her country as a meteorologist in the U.S. Navy, so much of her knowledge comes from direct experience. In addition, she spends a great deal of time researching each book, whether it be at the Pentagon or at military bases, extensively interviewing key personnel. Lindsay is also a pilot. She and her husband of fifteen years, both avid "rock hounds" and hikers, live in Arizona.

LEE KARR

is a multipublished author of Gothic romances and suspense novels. An avid reader, Lee especially loves books that make her heart pound and bring a dry lump of fear to her throat. When she isn't reading and writing, the author enjoys visiting her four children and traveling into the Colorado mountains with her husband, Marshall.

RACHEL LEE

has lived all over the United States, on both the East and West coasts, and now resides in Florida. Having held jobs as a waitress, real estate agent, optician and military wife—"Yes, that's a job!"—she uses these, as well as her natural flair for creativity, to write stories that are undeniably romantic. "After all, life is the biggest romantic adventure of all—and if you're open and aware, the most marvelous things are just waiting to be discovered."

Lovers
DARK AND
DANGEROUS

Lindsay McKenna
Lee Karr • Rachel Lee

Silhouette Books

Published by Silhouette Books
America's Publisher of Contemporary Romance

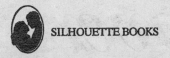 SILHOUETTE BOOKS

LOVERS DARK AND DANGEROUS
Copyright © 1994 by Harlequin Enterprises B.V.

ISBN 0-373-48310-4

The publisher acknowledges the copyright holders of the individual works as follows:

SEEING IS BELIEVING
Copyright © 1994 by Lindsay McKenna

STORM-TOSSED
Copyright © 1994 by Leona Karr

THE ANCIENT ONE
Copyright © 1994 by Susan Civil

Printed in U.S.A.

CONTENTS

SEEING IS BELIEVING

Lindsay McKenna

CHAPTER ONE

Wes McDonald remained impervious to the beauty of the Great Smoky Mountains. As he drove along the two-lane North Carolina road toward Quallah, the Eastern Cherokee Reservation, his scowl deepened. Renting and driving this automobile and catching the flight from Washington, D.C. had all been effortless tasks. *Too* effortless. Why couldn't Morgan have picked someone else for this stupid assignment? He snorted out loud and glared at the brilliant fall colors swathing the thickly wooded mountains that lined the highway.

If this weren't an assignment, he would be enjoying this scenery. The fog was rising from the woodlands in ethereal sheets—like huge, thin veils—moving silently in an almost dreamlike effect as it disappeared into the pale blue, early-morning sky. His hand tightened on the wheel for a moment. This assignment was pure malarkey—some science fiction someone had cooked up in a moment of absolute boredom.

But then again, Morgan had seemed deadly serious as he'd gone through the assignment step-by-step with Wes. And he was privy to some of the government's most top-secret information.

With a ragged sigh, Wes shook his head. Morgan couldn't have picked anyone more at odds with this particular mission. Wes didn't believe in psychic ability in any form. He knew what his own eyes told him, what he could smell or hear or touch. Everything else was bunkum, pure and simple. And now, here he was in the middle of North Carolina, on his way to fetch some psychic from the Native American reservation, to drag her along on this already preposterous mission.

Rubbing his recently shaved jaw, Wes felt exhaustion creeping through him. Morgan's company, Perseus, was just too damned popular with the federal government these days. They were piling on assignments faster than Perseus had employees to fill them. So Wes had gotten off a plane from the Middle East, been driven to the Perseus office—and handed another mission.

What he wanted was downtime. He needed some rest. Morgan had told him this assignment was low risk. *Stupid* and low risk, Wes corrected himself, disgruntled. He slowed the car down and made a turn onto another well-paved road marked by a sign that read Welcome to the Eastern Cherokee Reservation. Now, to hunt up this Diana Wolf, the supposed psychic he was to convince to come along on this mission. Too bad Morgan didn't have a psychic on his payroll; it would certainly save time. *Useless time.*

Wes caught a glimpse of the small town of Cherokee coming into view, noting how clean and well kept it looked. He'd been on reservations before, and while many of them were in sad, disheveled condition, others, like this one, would make any community proud. The basic layout of this town looked like any other, with restaurants, hotels and grocery stores—all of it, he knew, Cherokee owned. Spotting a sign for the museum, he turned left off the main highway. According to the directions he'd been given, Diana Wolf worked at the Cherokee museum as a translator.

The riot of colorful red, yellow and orange leaves stood out dramatically against the cobalt sky. The fog, referred to as "smoke" in these mountains, had burned off as the bright October sun rose. Suddenly Wes had the urge to pull his car off the road, make his way down to the clear-looking creek that wound alongside it and sit. *Sit and do what?* Ordinarily, Wes didn't like a lot of quiet time, because it meant having to think—and remember. There was plenty he chose not to recall.

His mouth tightened, one corner quirking inward. The museum was just ahead, a modern, two-story structure that looked as if an architect had designed it. On the passenger seat next to Wes lay the small file of information that had been amassed on Diana Wolf. He had already memorized what little was there. Diana Wolf was a thirty-year-old divorcée with no children. She lived with her mother, a powerful medicine woman of the Cherokee nation and worked daily at the museum, going through artifacts and translating old texts; the research noted that the Cherokee were the only Native Americans ever to have their own alphabet and written language. The Wolf woman also taught the children growing up on the reservation their native tongue. Wes had to applaud those efforts.

Pulling into a parking spot, he turned off the engine and sat for a moment, feeling the warmth of the sun coming through the window. Ahead of him was the museum, which he knew opened at 0800. Glancing down at his watch, he saw he'd arrived right on time. Taking a deep breath, he gathered up the thin dossier, which hadn't included a photo, and placed it in his black leather briefcase. Suits weren't his thing. As usual, he was dressed casually, in a plaid short-sleeved shirt, khaki chinos and brown loafers. The informal dress helped him blend in, rather than stand out, although Wes knew that his six-foot-five-inch, two-hundred-forty-pound frame was anything but inconspicuous, no matter what he wore.

What would Diana Wolf think of him? Not that he really cared. He'd rather be heading home to his farm in Vermont. Maybe if this Wolf woman refused to go with him, he *could* head for home. After all, a so-called psychic was necessary to this mission. No psychic, no mission. Wes grinned a little at the thought. It wouldn't break his heart if he had to call Morgan and tell him Diana Wolf refused to go along. *End of mission.*

With that cheering thought in mind, Wes unwound his lanky frame from the car. As always he carried a pistol in a shoulder holster. Now he shrugged into a lightweight, beige cotton jacket, adjusting it over the gun, then retrieved his black baseball cap and settled it on his short dark hair. There, he was ready to face the world. Wes knew the image he presented was disarming. He looked like some kind of baseball fan—if a big one—not a hired mercenary with a high-tech handgun under his coat. Picking up his briefcase, he shut and locked the car door and set the alarm. One could never be too careful.

Looking around, his hearing already keyed for unusual sounds, Wes tested the air, much like a dog. His life had hung precariously on his senses too many times for him not to automatically go through the routine: observing and categorizing sights, sounds, smells. Everything—anything—could be crucial. Anything out of place, not quite right, put him on immediate guard. Being part of Delta Force for ten years had earned him a lot of enemies on foreign soil, and he never let down his guard. He couldn't afford to. Any one of those enemies could send a hit man over to U.S. soil to blow him away.

The sun was warm, coaxing him to relax, but he pushed that desire aside. First things first. He had to find this Diana Wolf. Striding with studied casualness toward the entrance to the museum, Wes hoped like hell that the lady would say no.

Diana felt an energy disturbance. Nothing obvious—it was a subtle shift of energy in the main area of the museum, not here in her office. Looking up from her paperwork, she narrowed her gaze on the door, which stood ajar. From her desk, she could look out into the museum, and she noticed that a few people had wandered in as soon as the doors had been unlocked for business. No, it wasn't them. So what had aroused her peripheral senses?

Her hand was poised above the paper she was translating. It was an old text that Chief Sequoyah had written. Shaking her head, Diana refocused on the document. Whatever had caught her attention wasn't there—at least, not in the physical sense. Her mother, Walks with Wolves, would smile and tell her she'd probably felt a spirit passing through.

Maybe. Diana tried to concentrate, but it was impossible. She twisted the end of one of her two long braids, which hung down the front of her bright red blouse. Her gaze dropped to the buzzard pattern woven into her beaded belt. Buzzards were as sacred to the Cherokee as the eagle was to the Plains Indian tribes—admired and respected. Smoothing her light blue denim skirt, Diana shrugged. Sometimes she picked up on a foreign energy and that was all it was: just some unique vibration passing through.

But this energy wasn't leaving. It was getting stronger. And closer. Frowning, Diana looked up again. Her eyes widened slightly, and her heart started to pound slowly. A man, a very tall, large man, was standing no more than thirty feet from her office door. Her hand froze. Her breath caught. This was no ordinary man, her intuition warned.

Her gaze riveted on him, focusing on the power that swirled and eddied around him. Diana felt his strength, an indomitable, almost frightening strength. Who was this man? He was dressed in old, well-worn clothes, the baseball cap settled low on his head, so she could catch only a glimpse of his eyes. She thought they were a fiery blue, narrowed and searching. *Searching for what? For whom?* She had no answers.

Slowly, Diana released her held breath. She laid the pen aside and folded her hands over the text. A magnetic quality radiated from the stranger as he slowly looked around the spacious museum. Diana picked up a warning of danger, and her heartbeat raced in response. Although he appeared relaxed, she knew he wasn't. It was something in the way he looked around the museum—missing nothing, as if he were absorbing everything his gaze touched.

An eerie sensation hit her stomach. Automatically, Diana's hand dropped to cover that part of her body. Violence surrounded him, and it frightened her. Indeed, his face appeared to be ruggedly chiseled out of the gray granite of the Great Smoky Mountains she loved so much. His nose was prominent and obviously had been broken a number of times. His cheekbones were high, his flesh darkly tanned. Nothing about him looked forgiving, Diana decided—certainly not his thinned mouth, like a dark slash across his face. *Warrior.* The word burned into her head, her heart. This man was a modern-day warrior. Or was he a criminal about to hold them up?

The thought was there, and Diana knew that with her psychic impressions, she had to be careful. Sometimes her own creative imagination got in the way of the purity of the initial sensation she received, changing it into something it was not meant to be. Was he a warrior or a would-be robber? No one had ever robbed the museum. But *he* could, her brain told her. Yes, he could. Such violence and barely controlled energy surrounded him that Diana had a tough time sorting reality from her own flighty imagination. Being a psychic wasn't necessarily a blessing. Often it was a curse of sorts, too.

At age thirty, she was all too familiar with both sides of her unique abilities, so she didn't push the panic button. At least, not yet. Diana automatically tensed as she saw him slowly turn in her direction, those merciless blue eyes scanning like some long-range radar in her direction. Her heart thudded hard to underscore the sensation pulsing through her. This man was dangerous! The feeling rippled through her like tiny fire alarms going off.

Diana didn't know what to do next. His scanning gaze would meet her eyes at any moment. She felt helpless—an unusual feeling for her. Suddenly, she knew what a deer felt like under the cross hairs of a hunter's rifle. Her hands clenched. Her palms grew damp. And then their eyes met.

A riveting shock bolted through Diana, as if lightning had struck her—as if one of the mighty Thunder Beings who trod the sky, creating storms, had hurled a thunderbolt in her direction, leaving her stunned in the aftermath. The connection made, those blue, narrowed eyes were merciless in their probing. The man's scalpel-like assessment cut into her with an invasive brutality.

Her lips parted and the air left her lungs. Diana felt trapped. Helpless. A long time ago she'd experienced those feelings for real, and she'd taken steps to escape. She didn't like having them return. Her eyes widened enormously as the man slowly moved forward—toward her office. Toward *her.* Her mouth going dry, Diana could only sit, unmoving, as he made his way across the light gray carpeting to her office. She felt her pulse bounding, her heart beating triple-time like a wild drum in her chest.

In her mind, Diana worked to calm the turmoil of emotions that had exploded in her at the stranger's stare. Despite his height and bulk, he walked lightly, as if he were tightly sprung, ready to leap in any direction. And she was his target. It had been years since Diana had felt this kind of tension, this fear coupled with a mesmerizing fascination. It was like watching a hooded cobra sway and dance before her, within easy striking distance, knowing that if she dared move a muscle, the snake could strike and bite to kill.

Trying to rein in her wild imagination, Diana forced herself to break the stranger's fiery, monopolizing stare. She stood—albeit on weakening knees—and rested her trembling hands lightly on the reassuringly firm surface of her desk. This man was a warrior; there was no doubt. His hair was cut military short, his strong jaw was clean shaven. Although his clothes appeared disarming in comparison to the energy swirling around him, they did not fool Diana.

Even as her psychic self trembled in fearful anticipation, another part of her, the woman, was powerfully drawn to him. He was a virile man, a throwback to the days that Diana would just as soon leave behind. Such confidence and authority filled every nuance of his walk, his bearing, that she began to question her own confidence and authority. This man could rattle the most formidable of opponents, she thought haphazardly as her fingertips tensed against the edge of her maple desk.

Wes saw the woman looking at him. Actually, staring at him, her dark brown eyes doelike. For a moment he thought about the intrinsic beauty of deer and their helplessness against a man's rifle. This woman, with her thick black braids and heart-shaped face with high cheekbones, was like a deer, he decided. Because of his past, because of who he was, Wes realized the power he held over her. But then, with his skills and experience, he met few who could be counted as worthy rivals.

This woman was tall, her breasts and hips ample. She was no pencil-thin magazine model, but Wes appreciated her generous curves. He liked, too, her large, liquid brown eyes framed by thick black lashes. As he soundlessly drew closer, he saw them widen enormously, revealing flecks of gold in their depths. She reminded him of the Old Masters' paintings—the Rubenesque women whose full figures evoked the symbology of a ripe, fertile Mother Earth. She wasn't overweight, just wonderfully rounded in all the right places.

Her bright red blouse brought out the golden duskiness of her skin and emphasized her soft, full mouth. Wes smiled a little to himself. She was one hell of a looker, in his book. His gaze swept to her left hand. No ring. Then he caught himself. Why was he looking in the first place? He had no business doing that.

Undoubtedly she was Cherokee. And proud of it. Wes saw her slowly rise, as if waiting for him. He saw the tension in her proudly held shoulders and the defiance in the tilt of her chin. This woman had not only confidence, but pride in who and what she was. He liked that. He even applauded it. She blended modern woman with ancient culture in one appealing package. The watch on her right wrist spoke of the twentieth century, while her agate necklace with the wolf carving hanging below it spoke of her ancestry, her people's way of life. Old and new. Was she a throwback to another era? Or a modern-day woman? A feminist, perhaps? She could be all those things, Wes thought, enjoying the process of discovering her.

As he entered her office, his head barely clearing the doorway, Wes took off his baseball cap. He wasn't one to smile. He wasn't one of those people who said, "Have a nice day." There wasn't much humor in what he did for a living, and he wasn't apologetic about it. He was very clear about the fact that he had been on the front lines of protecting his country.

"I'm looking for a Diana Wolf. Could you tell me where her office is?"

Diana's heart thudded in her breast. Her fingers went flat against her desk. The man's eyes were unforgiving, icy and without any hint of what he wanted from her. For a moment, she wanted to lie.

She squared her shoulders. "I'm Diana Wolf. Who are you?" The best defense was a good offense, and she heard the uncharacteristic edge of challenge in her voice. Every possible alarm was going off inside her. Who was this man?

Wes swallowed the glimmer of a smile. He could see the distrust in her eyes—along with a lot of defiance and grit. He liked what he saw. "My name is Wes McDonald," he growled, "and I'm from Perseus, a security company out of Washington, D.C." He turned and shut the door. As he looked over at her, he said, "We have business to discuss." Then, uninvited, he took a seat.

Shocked, Diana froze. With the door shut, she felt claustrophobic. Again. Always. "Would you please open the door?"

Wes frowned. He heard a faint wobble in her low, husky voice. Further, he saw a spark of real fear in her eyes. "What I have to say is for your ears only, Ms. Wolf. It's a security matter."

"I don't care what it is, Mr. McDonald. Open that door. Please."

Ruffled, Wes got up and pulled the door open. He'd heard the unmistakable panic in her tone, and he wondered why it was there. As he turned to look at her, he saw that her skin had gone ashen beneath the gold. He frowned. Something else was going on—something he didn't fully grasp. Digging in his back pocket, he pulled out his identification.

"I'm from Perseus, Ms. Wolf, and what I have to talk to you about can't be overheard. That's why I closed the door."

Shaken, Diana scrutinized the professional-looking ID. "I don't know you. I don't know Perseus."

"I realize that." Wes tried to use a gentler tone of voice with her, seeing that she was truly shaken. "Look, if you're claustrophobic or something, can we go outdoors and talk?"

An excellent compromise, Diana realized with relief. "Yes, let's do that," she suggested briskly and quickly came around the desk, handing him back the identification card and slipping out the door before he could even get to his feet. Walking fast, she headed for the information booth, where Kathy Black Bear was sitting.

"Kathy, I'm going to be outside, sitting on the bench near the entrance, talking with that man. It'll take just a few minutes. If you need me, come and get me." Diana didn't want to leave with this dangerous-looking stranger without alerting someone—just in case.

Kathy looked up. "Sure, Diana."

Diana sensed him approaching. It was such a powerful sensation that she felt the queasiness resume in her solar plexus. *Large, powerful and dangerous.* She gripped the counter for a moment, trying to steady her reeling emotions as her past was triggered again. Pressing one hand against her blouse over her heart, Diana took a deep, calming breath. Her imagination was in full flight, and she had to get it under control.

It was obvious that Wes McDonald didn't like her and didn't want to be here. That much Diana had picked up psychically. He hadn't smiled when he'd introduced himself. He hadn't even held out his hand to shake hers. Social obligations didn't count with him, and that made her deeply suspicious of him.

Diana didn't want him getting too close to her, so she turned.

"Follow me," she ordered.

Wes followed this unusual woman at a respectful distance. It was obvious she didn't trust him any further than she could throw him. Part of him was overjoyed by the knowledge. After all, if Ms. Wolf didn't like him now, there was every chance of her turning down the assignment. But a more sensitive part of him, a part he rarely showed even to himself, lamented her response. He knew he wasn't handsome in the conventional sense, but he wasn't an ogre, either—and she was treating him as if he were. Further, as Wes followed her out into the warm October sunlight, he felt himself wishing he could somehow apologize for scaring the hell out of her.

Laughing at himself, he wondered what kind of magic Diana Wolf had woven around him. It had been a long time since he'd been genuinely interested in a woman, and to have her looking at him as if he were some kind of monster was a little tough to swallow.

The dew was still on the short, neatly cut grass as Wes followed her to a stone bench not far from the spreading arms of an oak tree now turned scarlet for autumn. He saw that she wore deerskin moccasins, prettily beaded and darkening from the wet grass. Her hands were clenched, he noted, frowning. Why was she so frightened of him?

Wes took a seat at one end of the long bench. She sat at the other end, staring darkly at him. Tension was apparent in every line of her body, and as he set his briefcase down beside him, he sighed.

"Look, I'm not going to bite you, okay?" The words came out sarcastically, and Wes flinched inwardly. He hadn't meant it quite that way, but it hurt him to think she saw him as such a threat.

Diana gulped at his insight. His dark brown eyebrows were drawn straight across his narrowed eyes. His mouth never seemed to relent from its thinned control. Did he *ever* smile? Probably not. "The energy around you is scaring me," she admitted.

"Energy?" Wes lifted his eyes from the papers he'd pulled from his briefcase.

With a wave of her hand, Diana said, "Yes, everyone has energy around them. An electromagnetic aura. Your energy is overwhelming to me."

"I scare you?"

Diana nodded and watched as his large, long hands, marked by numerous scars, brought a sheaf of papers together. "If you'd smile, it might help."

"In my business," he told her in a clipped tone, "smiles don't get it."

Rebuffed, Diana wondered why she was sitting here with this stranger. Curiosity more than anything else made her stay. "Just what is your business?" she demanded testily.

"I'm a mercenary, Ms. Wolf, and I work for an organization called Perseus." He lifted his head and held her frightened brown gaze. "I'm on an assignment, and it concerns you."

"Me?" The word came out strangled. Diana's world upended for a moment. Wes McDonald was a mercenary. A man who fought battles for pay. Her first impression had been correct: he was a warrior—not a thief, as her silly imagination had suggested. She didn't know whether to be relieved or not. Men with such violence around them scared her more deeply than anything else in her world. Knowing that about herself, she tried not to allow it to color her assessment of McDonald. He was here on an assignment—not to hurt her.

Clearing his throat, Wes said, "Look, everything I have to tell you is top secret. Do you understand that?"

"Does that mean I can't tell anyone what I hear?"

"Yes. Once I tell you about the mission, regardless of whether you decide to come along with me and help, you're to say nothing to anyone."

Shaken, Diana stared at his rugged, unforgiving face. Despite the harshness, the glitter in his shadowed blue eyes, she sensed a deep sadness in Wes. Just knowing that took the edge off her fear. And the more she probed his intense gaze, the more she allowed her frightened senses to open up and feel that all-pervading sorrow he wore like a heavy, smothering coat.

"I—I see."

Wes saw her blanch, but also felt her warmth. It wasn't just the sun's rays on his back. For an instant, he actually *felt* her warmth; then just as quickly, he pooh-poohed the sensation. The only things that could save his hide during danger were those he could hear, see, smell, taste or touch. Still, he thought, disgruntled, it was as if he'd actually felt her warmth move through him, like a soft hand briefly touching his closed, hardened heart. The feeling had been electric, freeing and, just as suddenly, frightening. Wes had made decisions long ago that would affect the rest of his life. He knew the pros and cons of such decisions and had made them with a clear head and a good dose of realism. But that didn't mean he didn't sometimes feel a certain sadness—and it was funny how keenly he felt it now. What was this woman? A witch? A magician capable of tapping his darkest secrets, the things he never wanted to think about again?

Violently rejecting the whole train of thought, Wes thrust a color photo of an older woman into her hands. "The woman is Ruth Horner. She works at Psi-Lab, an arm of the government devoted strictly to undertakings such as reading minds, astral travel and that sort of thing."

Surprised, Diana carefully held the large color photo. Ruth Horner was about fifty, her ginger hair mixed with strands of silver. She had watery-looking green eyes, a thin, narrow face and an exhausted expression. Her hair was knotted in a chignon, and she wore a white lab coat over a nondescript beige dress. Everything about her looked bland, Diana thought. Her hands tingled, and she closed her eyes, waiting to receive impressions.

"This woman is *so* unhappy," she offered in a whisper. "My heart goes out to her." She opened her eyes and felt tears. Embarrassed, she handed the photo back to Wes and wiped her eyes.

Stunned, Wes stared at her. Then he remembered that supposedly, Diana Wolf was a psychometrist—someone who could touch an object and tell him about the person who owned it. That was why Morgan had chosen her. Scowling deeply, he slipped the photo beneath the papers he had.

"I don't know about that."

"I do." Diana pointed to the papers. "She's very unhappy."

"She shouldn't be," Wes growled. "The federal government has paid her very highly for her skills."

Tilting her head, Diana saw the mockery in his eyes and heard it in his voice. "Why don't you just start at the beginning, Mr. McDonald? Why are you here? What do you want from me?"

He managed a grimace with one corner of his mouth. "Let me tell you something up-front, Ms. Wolf: if I had my way about this, I wouldn't be here at all, and I sure as hell wouldn't be talking to you."

Stunned, Diana glared at him. "Under the circumstances, I'd guess you didn't have a choice, Mr. McDonald. So let's cut to the chase on this, shall we? You're completely lacking in manners, and I'm not about to sit here and be insulted by you or anyone."

Wes cursed softly to himself. When she stood up, her eyes blazing, her hands at her sides, he muttered, "I'm not angry with you. I'm angry with my boss, Morgan Trayhern. I didn't want this assignment. It has nothing to do with you. All right?" He was genuinely sorry he'd hurt her feelings. Once again, Wes realized that his anger was being projected onto someone who hadn't earned it. It was a terrible weakness he had, and he'd been working to change that particular habit for a long time.

When he lowered his voice, his tone genuine, Diana hesitated. She was ready to walk back to the museum and tell him to go on his way. But for an instant, she saw contrition in his eyes, saw the persistent gleam of fire in them diminish. In that moment she saw the man, not the warrior, and it was a breathtaking discovery. Even his customary clipped tone of voice had disappeared. She gripped the back of the bench to steady herself.

"All right, I accept your apology, Mr. McDonald. Get on with the reason why you're here—whether you want to be or not."

Wes opened his mouth to explain, seeing the hurt in her eyes, the soft set of her mouth with the corners drawn inward in response to the pain he'd launched at her. Life was such a bitch. Utterly a bitch. He knew he wasn't the kind of person many people wanted to have around. Hell, he had a lot of rough edges, and he wasn't worth sticking around for any length of time. That's why his army career had fitted him so perfectly. He was a loner in a loner's job. But now he had to take a partner. And he didn't like it. A woman, at that. A soft, compassionate woman who'd mysteriously tugged feelings from his hardened heart that he thought had died long ago.

Lifting his hand, Wes rasped, "I know I'm a bastard. I'm hard on people. That's about as close to an apology as you're going to get from me."

Diana relaxed slightly, her fingers loosening from their position on the granite bench. She could feel Wes wrestling with so many feelings, even see them in his eyes, if only for a split second. As a psychic, her forte was picking up on subtleties, and she was glad this once that she could ferret out such things, because they painted a less violent and aggressive picture of him.

"Fair enough," she whispered, her voice softening in compromise. "Just tell me why you came here."

CHAPTER TWO

Wes put the papers aside. "Ruth Horner is a psychic," he began, retrieving the information from his memory. "When she was ten years old, the Psi-Lab, a top-secret branch of the federal government, tested her."

"What do you mean, 'tested'?"

"They tested her for her psychic skills," Wes said. "This lab's whole reason for being was to develop a team of psychics to use in the Cold War and any other hot spot around the world. They used psychics to ferret out top-secret information. If they could get access without putting one of our spies in danger, they did it."

Diana grimaced. "What a terrible use of psychic gifts."

Wes shrugged. "If you believe in that sort of stuff."

She felt rebuffed. "Obviously, you don't."

"Nope." He pointed to his eyes. "I believe in my own five senses. Beyond that, nothing is real."

The flat statement came out hard, uncompromising. Diana curbed her reaction—one of anger. "Okay, so poor Ruth Horner was tested when she was only ten. And they used her? At that age? I think that's terrible."

"It's worse than you can imagine," Wes said. "Ruth Horner's skills were so high on their index that they brought her to Washington, D.C., and she worked in their lab facilities five days a week."

"How awful! What did her parents say?"

"She didn't have any. She was an orphan."

"Oh, dear..."

Wes smarted beneath her softly spoken words and the glistening of tears in her sympathetic brown eyes. Tears! He felt rage. He felt as if he'd been slapped in the face. "Don't get all teary eyed over her being an orphan. She survived."

Diana felt a huge surge of anger slam into her and she winced. She saw the fury in Wes's eyes and stood openmouthed. Why had he taken such offense? Her mind whirled with questions about this unpredictable man.

"Horner was cared for by foster parents who approved her work for our government. Her education was excellent. She was tutored through high school and went on to get a degree in biochemistry." He deliberately looked at the papers instead of at Diana Wolf, whose compassionate expression only made him feel angrier. "She eventually became a supervisor at the lab and responsible for a lot of new psychic tools being employed in our country's defense." Wes glanced up. "I don't know exactly what she did psychically. But I was told she was very powerful. One of the best."

Swallowing her tears, Diana came and sat down on the edge of the bench. The anger had left Wes's face and voice, but she was still shaken by the suddenness with which he'd turned on her. Why couldn't he feel sympathy for Ruth Horner? What was the matter with him? Maybe he was so hard-bitten he hated tears, or at the very least, disdained them. Typical Neanderthal male, she thought, her own anger rising. How dare he. Her tears, her feelings, were genuine, and he had no right to deliver verbal assaults.

Diana had to remind herself she'd never been around a mercenary—had no idea what one might be like. Her ex-husband had been in the army, so she'd had a taste of the military, all right. A very bad taste that had left her bitter. Ruth's story haunted her, though, so she put her own feelings aside.

"Tell me more about Ruth."

"There's nothing more to tell—except this: she married at the age of thirty and divorced at thirty-seven. Recently, she went on a two-week vacation to Sedona, Arizona. The lab had her hotel room number in case they needed her for an emergency. When they had one and called her, she was gone."

"Gone?"

"Yes, disappeared."

"As in kidnapped?"

"We don't know." Wes heard himself say "we." It was a term he'd used often in Delta Force, where everything was approached as a team. Now he was automatically including this woman—who hadn't even agreed to accept the mission! Disgruntled at his slip, he muttered, "That's why they want you on this assignment. They need a psychometrist, someone who can pick up her whereabouts. The police have already checked the room and pursued the usual routes of investigation. They've found nothing. We were hoping you could give us something—anything—to go on."

She nodded. "I see. And *you* don't believe in this method of investigation?"

"What do you mean?"

"You don't believe people can have psychic gifts?"

"That's right."

Again, Diana felt herself up against that brutal interior wall of his. It was a defense, and she knew there were always reasons for that. Despite the anger and fear he aroused in her, she felt strangely drawn to understand the man behind the violent job. But instinctively, she realized he'd be the last person to open up and confide anything to her.

"What are your responsibilities in all of this?" she asked briskly.

"I'm basically a big guard dog, that's all. I'll interface with the local police and any other federal authorities, as necessary."

"Meaning this is dangerous?"

"No, it's a low-risk mission. The Psi-Lab suspects Ruth's been kidnapped. They used their own people to try and find her, but they had no success. They've already contacted other governmental agencies to start looking for her, through local as well as federal intervention. All they want from you is for you to pick up any vibrations—to try to get a *feel* for what might have happened."

She heard the derision, the disbelief in his voice that she might actually be capable of such a thing. She sighed. It would not be enjoyable working with this man.

"Perseus is offering you a large sum of money for your services," Wes admitted. He took a check from his briefcase and handed it to her.

Diana slowly held out her hand and took the crisp check. Ten thousand dollars! She gulped. To her, it was a tremendous amount of money—money that could be used to help her mother, who was always destitute because she gave everything away to those less fortunate than herself.

"This—this is a lot of money...."

Wes saw her wrestling with surprise and shock over the amount. "I guess they think you're pretty good." Damn! He'd insulted her again. Where was all this anger coming from? And why was he focusing it on her? Angry with himself, he glanced up to see how much damage he'd done with that comment.

"Look," he growled, getting up and stuffing the information file back into the briefcase, "this is probably going to be, at the most, a two-day mission." You won't have to work with me very long. Ten thousand bucks for two days' work isn't a bad trade-off for having to work with a bastard like me, is it?"

She glared at him. "I was going to do this for nothing, Mr. McDonald, because I felt sorry for Ruth Horner. You have nothing to do with it."

Wes nodded. Okay, he'd had that coming. He was surprised at how well she handled her own anger. Maybe he could learn a thing or two from her after all. "My boss is used to paying for what he gets, so keep the money and let me make the flight arrangements. All right?"

Diana hesitated. "I can't tell my mother where I'm going?"

"Sure, just don't tell her what you'll be doing."

She smiled a little. "You don't know my mother, Mr. McDonald."

"Oh?"

"Walk With Wolves is my mother's name. She is a very well known medicine woman here on the reservation, and very much loved by our people. She reads minds as easily as you and I communicate with our mouths. Even if I don't tell her, she'll know."

He snorted. "Come on!"

Diana's smile broadened, but the look in her eyes was one of challenge. "You don't believe me?" she taunted.

"No."

"Good. You make the travel arrangements, then meet me at four-thirty, when I get off work. I'll take you home to meet my mother, and you can see for yourself."

"What's to stop you from making a phone call to her in the meantime?"

Diana hated his snideness, his way of expecting the worst. "That does it! We're going home right now," she retorted angrily. "You're so negative! So distrustful!"

Wes grinned just a tad. She was beautiful when she got angry, he'd give her that. Her eyes gleamed with a golden light of challenge, her full lips pursed and her cheeks turned rosy. "Okay, let's go meet Mama," he said, his tone still cynical.

"Be sure to follow me back to my office—to make sure I don't try to call her," Diana jeered.

"I intend to do just that," he said silkily, falling into step at her side.

On the way home, Diana had Wes stop at the grocery and buy several bags of groceries.

"Why are we doing this?" he demanded at the checkout counter.

"Because it's bad etiquette to visit a medicine person's home without a gift."

"Groceries?"

Diana nodded and watched him slip several twenties from his billfold. "That's right. Mother gives the food away to those who need it."

"Oh..."

"You thought it was for her?"

"Sure."

"Just like a white man. You have no conception of true generosity of spirit."

He slanted a glance down at her. "You have spunk, I'll give you that."

"I don't care what you think of me," Diana said in a low, warning tone, "but you'd best not be rude to my mother, or I'll be in your face in a split second."

Wes grinned fully. He believed her. Picking up the grocery sacks, he said, "Let's go."

Diana felt shaky with anger, with the urge to slap his rugged face. Even his smile was twisted, as if he was in some kind of internal pain only he knew about. And that underlying pain was what stopped her from really wanting to slap him. Somehow, Wes McDonald was a beaten dog, and she'd never kick a hurt animal, no matter how many times it snapped or bit at her.

Wes was impressed with the beauty of the reservation as they drove deeper and deeper into the foothills crowned by the magnificent Smoky Mountains. The dirt road they drove paralleled another creek, and he wondered if there were some nice, fat brown trout in there just waiting to be someone's dinner. Soon the road narrowed, and they came into a hollow, a small meadow ringed on three sides by rounded hills aflame with autumn colors. At the far end of the yellow meadow stood a small log cabin surrounded by a white picket fence. A profusion of red geraniums graced its border.

Wes realized the log cabin was very old and in need of a vast amount of repair—beginning with its rusted tin roof. But the yard was neatly kept, the picket fence freshly painted and recently washed clothes hung on an outdoor clothesline. Obviously, this medicine woman didn't have a dryer.

"What does a medicine person do?" he asked as he slowed the car for a big rut in the dirt road.

"My mother is a healer. She has gifts that have been passed down through our family for six generations. People from the reservation come to her if they're ailing. She knows the ceremonies, the songs and herbs, so she's able to help most of them. The ones she can't, she sends to the hospital."

"Wise woman," Wes muttered. He felt Diana stiffen and glanced at her. "That wasn't an insult. I'm saying your mother knows her limits as a so-called healer, and wouldn't let a person die if she couldn't help them."

Biting back a retort, Diana said, "My mother is one of the most loving people you'll ever meet, Mr. Mc-Donald. But then, I have this feeling you don't know what love is, so it'll probably be lost on the likes of you."

His hands tightened on the steering wheel. "Are you always this solicitous or is it just me?"

"It's you," Diana agreed, her voice strained. "You work hard at making people dislike you, don't you?"

"I don't care what they think of me."

"No kidding."

"It's the job that counts, Ms. Wolf. I'm very good at doing a job and doing it right. That's where I get my satisfaction. I don't need pats on the head or a hug."

"Or love."

He glared at her.

She glared back, her face set, her lips tight with challenge.

"Shall we declare a truce while I meet your mother?"

"You'd better." Diana got out of the car and slammed the door. She didn't even wait for Mc-Donald, who was so utterly rude and hard that it sent her senses spinning. As she unlatched the white gate, her hands shook. Remember, she told herself, he's a beaten dog. In some way, he's been beaten until he believes himself to be ugly, hateful and bad. In her heart, Diana knew there was more to him than the defenses he presented to the world. Twice she'd seen his armor fall away for an instant—and twice she'd seen a vulnerable man beneath. But he was infuriating! Utterly in-furiating.

Before she reached the door, McDonald was at her side, grocery bags in his arms. Shooting him a dirty look, she opened the door and stepped inside.

"Mother, we're home," she called.

Wes followed her down the darkened hall and to the right, where he saw a large, overweight woman in a well-worn, dark blue cotton shift sitting at the kitchen table. Her gray hair hung in neat braids, and several polished-stone necklaces hung around her large neck. Wes had to admit he liked her face; it was plump and red-cheeked, with the most brilliant brown eyes he'd ever seen. The smile Walks With Wolves gave him went all the way to his soul.

"Hi, sweetheart, I was expecting you early," Walks With Wolves said, slowly, ponderously hefting herself upward. She hugged her daughter warmly, then de-voted her attention to Wes, who had just set the gro-cery bags on the kitchen counter.

"Golanoh, Raven, came to me late this morning," she told Diana, a twinkle in her chocolate-colored eyes as she made her way around the table toward Wes. "He came and sat on my windowsill and cawed at me. He told me a stranger, a warrior, was acoming our way."

Wes was riveted to the spot. Despite Walks With Wolves's immense weight—probably three hundred pounds on her five-foot-six-inch frame—she was the epitome of grace. She reminded him of those ample Hawaiian dancers, with their litheness and balletlike grace. Automatically, he held out his hand to the ap-proaching woman. His senses were confused and an incredible giddiness—something he'd never felt before—consumed him. Was it Walks With Wolves's dancing eyes? The warmth, the sincerity of welcome in them? Wes felt as if he were the only person on the face of the earth, and she was devoting a hundred percent of her considerable attention to him and him alone.

The feeling was irresistibly warm—and, for Wes, simultaneously uncomfortable. Walks With Wolves brushed aside his hand, grinning widely and threw her arms around him. Wes had never been given a bear hug in his life, but he was now. The strength of the woman was amazing as she trapped him against her, squeezing him hard enough to make the air rush from his lungs. At the same time, he felt a heat that started in his toes and shot upward, like jagged, hot lightning. Suddenly dizzy, he felt himself lifted off his feet! It was only for a second, but when his feet reconnected with the tile floor and Walks With Wolves released him, he staggered a little. He leaned against the counter, staring, stunned, down into her smiling face.

"Wes McDonald. That's who Golanoh told me was coming." She patted his arm in a motherly fashion. "Come over here, sit down. Sweetheart? Will you get Wes some coffee? I think he needs a good, strong cup." She poked him in the stomach. "You a little on the lean side for your height, eh? Been off your feed, have you?" She chuckled pleasantly, led him over to the table and pulled out a straight-backed chair. "Sit."

Diana curbed a smile while she made fresh black coffee for the three of them. Leave it to her mother to already know and fix whatever was wrong. All the anger left her, and it was replaced with an effusive joy.

The look on Wes's face was priceless. He hadn't expected Walks With Wolves to hug him. And when she had, Diana had seen a miraculous change come over his expression. She knew her mother, and the powerful healing that came from her heart. If Wes's own heart had been closed, it was open now, because no one could stand in her mother's presence and not feel love.

"So, you a warrior, eh?"

Wes rubbed his brow, still feeling dizzy. What had happened? He felt different. Something was still going on: explosions, fireworks, heat, light, all mixed deep within him on some internal, invisible level. He tried to tell himself he was crazy. That Walks With Wolves was crazy. That this whole damn situation was crazy. But it wasn't.

Walks With Wolves sat across from him, smiling at him, her hands folded on the table. Her eyes twinkled like a brilliant, starry night. She was the most beautiful woman he'd ever met, he realized, with the exception of her daughter. They both had sparkling eyes that spoke eloquently of what lay in their hearts and souls, full mouths that laughed and smiled easily.

"Yes, I'm a soldier," he admitted, his voice strained.

"You feelin' a little dizzy?"

He gave her a surprised look. "Well . . . yes, how did you know?"

She grinned and shrugged. "People who carry a lot of pain in their hearts get dizzy when their hearts fly open and the loads are taken away." She pointed toward his chest. "Feel a little warm around your heart, eh?"

A little? It felt as if a burning brand was searing into him. Wes nodded and absently touched his chest.

"It'll go away in a while, young man. You just sit there and thank the Great Spirit, have a cup of coffee and relax with us. It's been a long time since you've relaxed, hasn't it? Twelve years, eh?"

Completely shaken, Wes gaped at her. "How could you know?"

Diana giggled. She couldn't help herself. The coffee was ready and she brought over three white mugs. "See? I told you she could read minds."

Walks With Wolves lifted her head and raised her gray eyebrows. "I see you brought me food for the poor. That was kind of you, young man. The Great Spirit always rewards a person's generosity toward the people who need it. You're a good warrior, one with a heart."

Diana set the creamer and sugar bowl on the table, watching Wes closely. He looked shell-shocked. All the while, he was slowly rubbing the region of his heart. Good; her mother had given him a healing. There was no doubt in Diana's mind that Wes's heart had been closed up tighter than Fort Knox before she'd gotten hold of him.

"Good thing Mother healed your heart wound," Diana said as she sat down between them. "Otherwise, you'd have been headed for a heart attack down the road."

Chuckling, Walks With Wolves said, "That's right, young man. Give you another three years, and heart disease woulda set in. Yes, you are worthy of help in the Great Spirit's eyes, or you wouldn't have been brought to us."

Wes didn't know what to say. He felt uneasy, embarrassed, and at the same time completely welcomed into their small, humble home. "How do you know so much about me?"

"It's in your aura," Walks With Wolves said, making a general egg-shaped gesture around him with her index finger. "Your heart was closed up. You suffered early in life, maybe around age four."

Wes scowled and saw Walks With Wolves swallow whatever else she was going to say.

"Well, anyway," the medicine woman went on in a genial tone, "I know why you're here. Golanoh told me this morning on the windowsill. He said a warrior with a closed heart comes to us. He wants my daughter, Diana, to help him. There is a woman who is missing, eh?"

Wes was stunned. He stared at her with an open mouth. He knew Diana couldn't possibly have communicated with her mother. "Yes," he mumbled, "she's missing."

"And you want Diana to find her?"

"We want her to try to pick up on the woman's trail, to see if she can find us a lead."

Walks With Wolves looked at her daughter, then nailed Wes with a lethal look. "Now, you don't tell the whole truth. You know what it means to be a Cherokee warrior, young man? It means you never lie, you give away all you have to the old ones and the poor. You hunt for them. You protect all who are under your care. You give your life, if necessary. There aren't many warriors left in this world, but if you want to be one, you gotta walk their path, eh? Now, tell me the rest.''

Squirming, Wes glanced over at Diana's tranquil features. How beautiful she looked, how serene. He wished he could find that kind of peace, but he knew it could never be.

"If your daughter finds anything, we'll use it," Wes said abruptly. "I'll take whatever she gives us and pass it on to the authorities. I hadn't told her that before."

"That's better. You doubt my daughter's gifts, eh? Well, you'll change your tune." She wagged a finger at him. "You ought not make such assumptions so fast. A good warrior lets the truth be proven to him. He don't just make it up in his head before he sees all the facts." Chuckling, Walks With Wolves said, "It don't mean nothing, anyhow. You'll see."

He stared at the old woman. "Can you tell me anything about this missing woman?"

Chortling again, Walks With Wolves got up and went to the counter. She brought over the coffee and refilled their cups. "Now, young man, part of being a good medicine person is knowing when to say something and when not to."

Wes gave Diana a questioning look, but she merely shrugged her shoulders. "You know something, then?"

"Maybe. Maybe not." She set the coffeepot back in place on the counter and sat down again.

Diana added cream and sugar to her coffee, squelching a smile. Wes was obviously shaken—so shaken that he was talking about the "top-secret mission" to her mother! Of course, anyone who came to her mother realized very quickly that she was a woman of immense power and that she came from her heart. She admired her mother's ability to love—even someone as hard and hopeless as Wes McDonald. Maybe all Wes needed was a little love, a hug now and then. Who knew? Diana knew that she would find out.

"Your mother is something else," Wes admitted with a frown as they stood by his car an hour later. The sun was high in the sky, the warm autumn temperatures bringing the fragrance of decaying leaves like perfume wafting on the breeze.

"She's the soul of kindness," Diana agreed softly. "And believe me, Mr. McDonald, your secret is safe with her."

He nodded and stubbed his toe in the rich red dust of the road. "Might as well be on a first-name basis," he mumbled. "Call me Wes."

That was a large step for him, Diana realized. "Okay... you can call me Diana, if you want."

He lifted his head and nodded. "Yes, I'll call you Diana."

In that instant, Diana saw the man, Wes McDonald, not the warrior with his thick armor in place. Heat crawled up her neck and into her cheeks, and she avoided his dark, hooded stare. Something had changed. Drastically. Her mother had healed his terribly wounded heart, she realized. And that was good. Wes would probably never realize the full extent of her mother's gift to him, but it didn't matter. What mattered was that he was beginning to thaw—and that was a big step.

Running his fingers through his hair, he muttered, "I've got a lot to do. I'm staying at the hotel in town. How about if I pick you up tomorrow morning and we fly out to Sedona?"

She nodded. "That's fine... Wes. I'll call my boss. She'll give me the rest of the day off and I'll ask for a week of vacation. I know she'll give it to me."

A euphoria rose in him—completely unexpected, completely overwhelming. When Diana looked up at him, their eyes meeting, he felt a jagged bolt of happiness sweep through him. As Wes stood trying to assimilate what had happened, it occurred to him that for the first time in decades, he was *feeling* his emotions. Giving her a strange look, he opened the car door.

"Whatever your mother did is working."

"What do you mean?"

"Nothing." Abruptly, he got into the car. "I'll call you."

"You can't. We don't have a phone."

Wes looked up at her through the open window in disbelief. "You're joking."

With a laugh, Diana gestured to her home. "We've never had a phone, a television or a dryer. The only thing Mother has given in to is having a washer and electricity as a source of light. She likes living close to the earth, Wes. I don't think she'd even have a washer or electricity if she wasn't so busy as a medicine woman."

With a shake of his head, he said, "I've never met anyone like her." And then, wryly, he added, "Or you."

"I'm taking that as a compliment this time, not an insult. Should I?"

"Yes." He looked at the watch on his wrist. "When I've got everything in order, I'll drive back out and give you the details."

"Fine."

Suddenly, Wes didn't want to leave. This country hollow, with its cloak of reds, yellows and oranges, was enticing. It reminded him of a haven he'd looked for all his life and never found. Here, Wes realized, he felt safe. Stymied, not understanding all these new emotions and awarenesses, he gave Diana an odd look. "I'll see you later," he said gruffly.

Diana watched Wes back around and drive away. Pensive, she gazed at the cloud of red dust kicked up in the wake of the car. Finally turning, she went back to the gate and saw her mother standing on the porch near her favorite oak rocker.

She climbed the wooden porch steps slowly and took a seat in the other rocker.

"You knew he was coming?"

Walks With Wolves nodded, her hands in her lap. "For some time now."

Diana smiled a little. "You're a clever old raven, Mother."

"With reason," she counseled. Heaving a sigh, she said more softly, "You just be careful around that young man. He's a wounded cougar, you know. Got a deep wound in his heart. I don't know if it can be fixed completely."

"Or at all?" Diana guessed. She knew that when a person received a healing, if they didn't want to get well, they would throw away the healing energy they'd been given.

"That, too, sweetheart." Walks With Wolves chuckled. "My girls are strong, good women, though. You grew up here, in this cabin. You know about hardship, about work and sacrifice. If anyone can help that young man, it's you."

"Oh," Diana said, "I don't think so!"

"Sure. As badly damaged as his heart is, yours is that well and strong. You're a good match for each other, eh?"

The gleam in her mother's eyes unsettled Diana. "You're giving me that look again."

"Am I?" Walks With Wolves chuckled indulgently. "Well, Daughter, you've come to a fork in your path, too. I wonder which direction you'll choose? Will you walk alone or walk together?"

Diana was uncomfortable when her mother talked in symbolic terms. But she knew there was no use asking her to explain herself. No, it was typically a Native American way to learn through experience. Her mother would no more give her clues about what might or could happen on this two-day mission with Wes than tell her what her life would be like. Walks With Wolves had that power, she knew. There were times Diana had seen her gift a person with some knowing of the future—and her forecasts always came true.

But Walks With Wolves never told Diana or her sister anything about their futures. She'd always shied away from that. Still, right now, Diana felt like she could use all the help she could get. Wes McDonald was a breed apart from the men she had known. And in another way, she had to admit, he reminded her of the violent past, of a nightmare marriage she wanted to forget—forever.

CHAPTER THREE

Diana thought she should be excited about the flight, but she was curiously subdued, and felt on guard—against Wes. They sat in the first-class section of the airliner. Throughout the morning, Wes had been silent. He was no longer using his cutting, sarcastic tone, and she saw turmoil in his dark blue eyes. The set of his mouth was different—not as thin or hard looking as before. That was it: there was a new softness about him, however minor. Unsure of what to say, she found herself retreating behind a wall of silence, which wasn't her in the least.

The flight attendant, a smiling older woman, brought breakfast to them. Diana had never flown first-class and was impressed by the white china plates with gold trim and the extraordinary food set before her. The coffee was fresh, Colombia brewed, its fragrance wafting through the cabin.

Wes tinkered with his silverware and slid a quick glance at Diana. He wondered if she'd lived on the reservation all her life. Coming as she did from such a poor home with so little, he wondered if all of this was a bit overwhelming to her. Having slept very little the night before, and nakedly vulnerable from the gamut of feelings running through him, he played with the food on his plate. He wasn't hungry. What he was suddenly starved for was information about Diana. He knew she was divorced, but how recently? Was she involved with someone? Living with someone? For one of the few times in his life, he felt like a fish out of water. Where to start with such an intimate line of questioning?

Diana sensed a hesitancy coming from Wes, and it threw her off balance. She picked at her ham-and-cheese omelet, finally pushing it aside in favor of the fresh strawberries in thick cream.

"First-class makes you know what you miss when you aren't rich," Wes said experimentally.

Diana felt his attention, felt his nervousness. With a shrug, she said, "I've always been rich in other ways, so I never missed things like this. They're nice, but not necessary."

"Not like a hug?"

She smiled a little and met his shy glance. How terribly changed Wes was, in less than twelve hours. Diana knew the healing was responsible for it. She noted how red-rimmed and bloodshot his eyes were. He probably hadn't slept much last night. "Money can't buy a hug," she whispered in agreement, suddenly emotional.

"Your mother..." Wes struggled to find the right words. Lord knew, he wasn't good with words at any time, especially diplomatic ones. "She's...different."

"Maybe to you. White people aren't used to reservations or our way of life. I don't see it as different. I see it as normal."

"No, I meant her."

"The fact that when you came in, she hugged you like you were one of her children?"

He nodded and chewed on the food, not tasting it. "I felt . . . something. I've never felt it before. I don't know what to do about it."

With a gentle laugh, Diana put her utensils aside. She picked up the cup of fragrant coffee. "Don't do anything. Let it happen."

"What did happen?" He drilled her with an intense, probing look.

"You were given a healing, Wes. That's all."

His brows fell and his mouth compressed.

"It just happens," Diana said quietly. "Mother doesn't choose who is healed. She'll tell you herself that the healing energy comes through her, not from her. The Great Spirit chooses who will be helped. My mother is a very warm, loving woman, and she hugs everyone who comes into our house. Everyone is treated the same there."

With a slight, strained laugh, Wes said, "I felt like I'd been hit by a bolt of lightning, Diana." He pointed toward his loafers. "I felt this—this energy, this heat, come curling up out of my toes, shoot straight up both my legs into my torso and out the top of my head. When your mother was holding me, then lifted me off the ground, my head seemed to burst open like a ripe watermelon. It wasn't a painful sensation, just a different one. I felt this dazzling gold-and-white light throughout my head and body, and an incredible heat settle here." He touched his chest. "It burned for almost an hour afterward, but finally that sensation went away, too."

"Then what happened?" She saw the awe, the confusion and question in Wes's face. His expressive blue eyes were no longer as dark as before. She had no doubt that he had received a healing—and that it was working minor miracles for him.

Wes sat back and closed his eyes. "I went back to the hotel, back to my room, and I felt so damned dizzy I had to lie down. I guess I went to sleep." He opened his eyes and looked at her. Again he was struck by her serenity, that sense of wholeness that seemed to radiate from within her.

"When I woke up, six hours later, I felt pretty good. I got up, made the travel arrangements, checked in with my contact at Perseus and ate at a local restaurant." He shoved his fingers through his hair. "Last night was something else. . . ."

Diana felt him hesitate, as if to speak further would dredge up pain. Without thinking, she reached out, her fingers falling softly against the hard curve of his darkly tanned arm. She felt the instantaneous reaction of his muscles tightening beneath her fingertips. His eyes snapped upward to hers. Drowning in his narrowed blue gaze, she felt her breath being stolen from her. She felt his desire for her, felt it through every pore, every cell of her body. And in that magical instant out of time, she came in direct contact with her desire for him. It was physical, no question, but there was more. Much more. Shaken, Diana removed her hand from his arm.

Stunned, Wes continued to stare at Diana. How badly he wanted to reach out and touch her. He wanted to touch that soft lower lip, to find out just how wonderful she felt. Then he wanted to slide his hand behind her neck and gently draw her forward until their mouths met, melded. Heat unraveled wildly through him on the heels of those thoughts. How delicious she was—a ripe strawberry for the picking. Sweet yet tart in so many ways, offering succor on so many levels to his starving senses.

Struggling to curb the desires flaring white-hot through his body, Wes was silent for more than a minute. He'd never felt so much before—with such startling depth. There was just something so intrinsically simple and honest about Diana that he couldn't help but want her. He forced his raging inner needs under tight control.

"Last night I dreamed about the past. My past," he admitted roughly.

Diana nodded but said nothing, hearing the strain in his voice, seeing the terror mirrored in his eyes. She held her breath momentarily, knowing how important this moment was—to both of them.

Wes looked out the window, which revealed a sky filled with white strands of cloud against vivid blue. Wrestling with the words, he returned his attention to her. "I was given up for adoption when I was four years old. My mother..." He grimaced. "She was a drug addict. I remember her dropping me off at the welfare office, crying, and telling them she was a lousy mother and couldn't raise me right."

Diana expelled her breath. There was such torture in Wes's eyes that she overrode her mind's warning and reached out, touching his arm again. Unparalleled tension thrummed through him beneath her fingers.

"And last night, that old memory surfaced, didn't it?" she asked gently.

"Yes. Completely." Wes searched her face. "How do you know?"

"I'm not a mind reader. I've seen Mother heal hundreds of people over the years, Wes, while I was growing up, so I know the pattern of healing after they've been to see her."

"Old memories get dredged up?" he asked bitterly. Still, Diana's warm, dry hand on his arm was like a soothing balm to his tattered emotional state.

"Yes, but they're brought up for the person to see and feel, and then they're released once and for all. It's the way the body heals, Wes—the cells, tissue, bone and organs remember every trauma we've gone through. And until you work through it on the emotional level, that memory remains within you. Not just in your heart and mind, but in your body." She smiled a little and, without thinking, raised her hand and barely grazed his recently shaven jaw. "You're going through the releasing process, and that's a good sign."

The touch of her fingertips was evocative, stirring, arousing heat wherever it fleetingly lighted. Something good and solid was growing between them—he recognized that much. A slight, hesitant smile tugged at one corner of his mouth.

"It may be good, but it hurts like hell. When I close my eyes, all I can feel are those old emotions I stuffed away decades ago. I feel like I'm that four-year-old kid again, getting left at that office, with my mother crying and apologizing."

Her heart twinged with his pain. "It must have been terrible for you to be left standing there with a stranger, watching your mother leave."

Wes nodded. "I kept dreaming about it all night—waking up in a sweat." He didn't want to admit he'd cried. How many decades had it been since he'd cried? Muttering, he said, "I stopped crying a long time ago."

"And I'll bet you feel like crying all the time now, right?"

Somehow it was impossible to deny Diana's knowing. Finally, he rasped, "Yes."

Her hand tightened briefly on his forearm. Diana felt some of the tension draining from Wes as he talked. Well, that was what he needed—a friend to talk to, someone who would listen. She wanted to be that to him—and more. "What else?" she prompted gently.

Wes forgot where they were, because it no longer mattered. His world was about feelings and emotions he thought he'd buried forever. Diana was here, at his side, touching him, holding him in her own way, and he was grateful. "I was four years old and—isn't it funny?—I can remember it as clearly as I'm sitting here." With a shake of his head, he went on in a quiet tone. "My mother wasn't a bad person, Diana. She did the best she could. I realize that now. But then, as a kid, I thought she was abandoning me. Giving me away."

"You felt she didn't love you enough to keep you?"

"Yes. But I know different now. She just couldn't kick her drug habit. At least she saw what it was doing to me. She loved me enough to give me to a foster family, who eventually adopted me." He folded his scarred hands and stared down at them. "From the day she gave me up, I never saw her again. My foster mother finally told me that she had died of a drug overdose a couple of years later."

Diana closed her eyes. Her fingers automatically squeezed his arm in comfort. When she looked up at Wes again, she saw tears glimmering in his eyes and realized just how deeply he was affected. Then, just as quickly, she saw him force them back, swallowing hard against the flood of emotions.

"But you knew she loved you, didn't you?"

Wes shook his head and placed his hand across hers. It was an instinctive gesture, one born out of need, out of... He didn't know what label to put on his feelings for Diana. She was a safe haven in this passage through the painful past, someone who genuinely cared, listening with her heart as well as her ears. Maybe it was the shimmer of gold mixed with the tears in her velvet-brown eyes that triggered the depth of his feelings. Wes wasn't sure of anything anymore, except that he needed her.

"No, not at that time. After my mother died, my foster parents, who had managed to stay in touch with her, told me everything. From the time I went to live with the McDonalds, they reassured me that my mother loved me. What I didn't know was that they'd struggled to keep in contact with her as my mother moved from city to city, state to state. Sometimes they'd get phone calls from her in the middle of the night. She was calling to see how I was doing."

"Even though she was hurting, she loved you enough to stay in touch," Diana murmured.

"Yes." Wes lifted his head. "That wasn't all. The year after my mother gave me up, she hustled to save money. She had a bad drug habit, but I found out later that she'd been getting clean, because she went to a couple of halfway houses for help." He shook his head. "Imagine my shock when I was eighteen and my adopted parents told me my mother had saved ten thousand dollars before she died. My adopted father was a stockbroker, and he invested the money for me. By the time I was eighteen, there was enough for me to do whatever I wanted."

"What did you do?"

"I went to college for a degree in civil engineering. I could have had my pick of jobs, but I went into the army instead."

Diana gaped. "You were in the army?" Automatically, she lifted her hand from his arm, memories of her past overriding everything else.

"Yes." Wes's mouth quirked. "I wanted to build bridges for the army, but they said they wanted me in Delta Force, as one of the officers."

"Delta Force?" Her eyes widened. "That's the antiterrorist team that goes undercover anywhere in the world to help out in military situations."

"That's right." Wes saw the mixture of emotions in her eyes. "Remember the *Aquille Lauro* incident, where terrorists boarded the ship and started killing the passengers?"

"Yes."

"I was there." Wes sighed. "I was also on one of those helicopters President Carter sent across the desert. So many good men died on that mission. So many mistakes were made...."

Reeling, Diana sat amid her own conflicting feelings. "You were in the army," was all she could say. No wonder she had felt the warrior around him. The violence.

"I got out two years ago and went to work for Perseus last year. I spent a decade in the army and I was disillusioned. After losing so many of my friends on that botched mission, I had a bad taste in my mouth for the military."

Diana sat back, her arms folded tightly across her stomach. "I have a bad taste for the army, too, for different reasons," she whispered.

Wes saw anger in her eyes—and sadness. "Tell me about it?"

With a shrug, she said, "I'd just as soon forget."

"Healing comes with talking. Remember?" He smiled slightly for her benefit.

The warmth that came to Wes's eyes released Diana from her world of anger, grief and confusion. His entire face changed with that smile, and it stunned her. The hardness disappeared, if momentarily. Wes was reaching out to her. She was sure he didn't do that very often. His gesture touched her more deeply than she could ever have imagined.

"We share a common past," she said finally. "My ex-husband was in the army."

Wes nodded. He saw and felt her anxiety. Her fear. It was the first time in his life he'd been aware of anyone's emotions to this degree or intensity. No longer could he deny that something had truly opened up his scarred heart. Now it was his turn to comfort her. Reaching out, he closed his hand over hers, which lay clenched in her lap.

"Can I read between the lines? He was a real bastard to you?"

Needing Wes's touch, Diana nodded. She was surprised by his reaching out, but grateful. "Bob Parker was the consummate army officer," she began bitterly. "He was hard on his troops and he brought that same cruelty to our home."

"A hard-ass."

"Was he ever."

Wes searched her eyes, which were fraught with pain. "What happened?"

"Plenty." Diana looked up at the ceiling of the aircraft. "I was young, easily impressed, and I didn't listen to my mother. I should have. Bob was on leave when I met him. I was eighteen and had just graduated from high school. Living on a reservation all my life hadn't prepared me for the outside world. At least, not then. Now it's different. I fell head over heels in love with him. He was a warrior, and I was enamored with men like him. But I was idealistic. I didn't see all of Bob."

"So you married him?"

"Two weeks after I met him." Diana shook her head. "I was crazy to do that. But I was starry-eyed. I listened to no one. I knew my mother saw things in my future, but she didn't say anything. She just begged me to take my time, to think through Bob's proposal. I didn't. I thought I knew everything."

"Yeah, at eighteen I was pretty cocky and sure of myself, too," Wes said wryly.

"I think it's a teenage disease." Diana managed a laugh, but it was filled with the pain of memories.

"So you married him. What happened?"

"Too much to go into, except for the spectacular highlights." Diana met Wes's somber gaze. "Bob was a closet alcoholic. He spent more time at the Officers' Club than home with me. When he did come home, he beat me up."

Wes's hand automatically tightened over hers. "He hit you?" Rage filled him.

Diana shrugged. "I'm ashamed to admit it. I'm ashamed to tell anyone that I stayed in that miserable excuse for a marriage for seven years. But I was too ashamed to tell my mother and sister what kind of a hell I was going through. I knew I'd made a terrible mistake, and I didn't know how to correct it. I was raised to think that marriage was forever. My mother married my dad, who was a white man. They had a wonderful, happy marriage, and I thought that I'd automatically have the same thing. That's why I was eager to get married—to find that happiness I'd seen at home."

"It doesn't work that way. I wish it did, but it doesn't."

"No..." Diana cleared her throat and went on. "Bob made major, then lieutenant colonel. We moved more places around the world than I can remember. I was alone. I was like a cowering animal just waiting for him to come home every night, drunk and violent."

"What ended it for you?" Wes asked quietly.

A tremble went through Diana, and she opened her hands and tightly grasped his larger, stronger one. "I— it's so hard to talk about. I've only been able to tell my mother, not even my sister, Wes. I'm so ashamed...."

"Your secrets are safe with me," he whispered roughly, cupping her jaw and forcing her to meet his eyes. Her gaze was tortured, and he managed a poor semblance of a smile for her benefit. "Remember? *I'm* the one with the secrets? If I can trust you to hold mine, will you trust me to hold yours?"

It was so easy to whisper yes, to drown within the vivid blue of his clear, warm eyes that Diana felt tears sting her own. She was wildly aware of his hand gently cupping her face, his fingers calloused and rough. How much pain Wes had endured, and yet he was able— somehow—to reach out and help her heal. His depth amazed her, for she'd never encountered it in a man— though admittedly she'd been afraid to look since her failed and miserable marriage.

"Oh, Wes, it's so painful to talk about...."

"I know, I know," he soothed, "but a lady I like one hell of a lot told me that talking and sharing is part of the healing process."

Her lips parted and she felt the warmth of tears trickling down her cheeks. "I—I became pregnant, Wes. I know I was about three months along when I told Bob." Her lashes dropped and she took in a convulsive breath. Forcing herself to look at him, to see his reaction to her trauma, she whispered, "When I told him I was pregnant, he started hitting me. He beat me up so badly that I ended up miscarrying and almost dying."

Wes's mouth thinned. He turned in his seat and framed her face with his hands. He could see her abject misery, the way the guilt and torture over her lost baby was eating her up. "Listen to me," he rasped unsteadily, "it wasn't your fault. Get that? Men like him are sick. I saw guys like that in the military. They're little men with brittle egos and nothing inside themselves, so they hurt and humiliate women and children to try to feel strong and important." He stroked her cheek. "I'm sorry, Diana. I'm so damned sorry it happened to you." His mouth worked, and he couldn't repress the gamut of emotions he was experiencing. "I wish I could make your pain go away. Make the memory leave, too. But they won't. Just know that you did the best you could in a hellish circumstance. At least you got out. You have to give yourself credit for that."

In that moment, Diana felt her heart opening, in a way it hadn't for years. Wes had said her mother was a healer, but in his way, he was a healer, too. The discovery was poignant, beautiful. She raised her hands and placed them against his. "It's taken me the past two years to realize that, Wes." She shrugged. "I came back to the reservation and lived with my mother. I needed to be here, to be home, to heal my grief."

"I see it all now," Wes said, taking her hands and holding them across the armrest between their seats. "I understand your reaction to me. I'm the past. I'm ex-army. I bring back everything bad that happened to you." The corners of his mouth turned in with pain. "No wonder you didn't want to be around me."

"No!" Diana lowered her voice. "No...I—I felt the violence around you, Wes. I misinterpreted it. I thought you were the same kind of man that Bob was—an abuser. But you aren't. Wh—when I pick up feelings, I don't always filter them correctly." She touched her brow and gave him a weak smile. "Just because I'm psychic doesn't mean I'm always right. Just like anyone else, every feeling, thought or sensation is run through the filter of my life experiences. Because of Bob's abuse, if I sense violence around any person, I automatically and unconsciously react to it."

Reaching over, Wes took a strand of her hair and tamed it behind her delicately formed ear. The gesture was satisfying to him, and he wanted to touch her more, touch her intimately and with love. Love? Where had that feeling come from? Wes laughed at himself, but it was a laugh filled with pain and longing, not humor.

"I'm glad to know all this."

"About my past or my psychic gifts?"

"Both," Wes murmured, caressing her thick, black hair. Like yesterday, she wore her hair in braids, and on Diana they were beautiful—and natural. He met and held her tear-filled gaze. "You've had two years of healing. I don't know how long it takes to get over something like that. Or if you ever do."

"Mother says I will, with time." Diana closed her eyes, absorbing his trembling caress. How she ached to kiss Wes, to move into his arms and be held—and to hold him. They both needed to be held, she realized, for different reasons. But she also realized that somehow they fed each other in a positive sense, and were able to give something good and healing to each other.

"If we weren't here," he told her in a low, gritty tone, "I'd kiss you. I'd kiss you until you melted into me and I melted into you, Diana."

Her lashes lifted, and she felt his growling words vibrate through her, touching her wounded heart and thirsty soul. The flame in his blue eyes was inviting and made an ache begin low in her body, fanning out until she was consumed with the knowledge that she wanted more than just his kiss. Coming together with Wes felt more right than anything in her entire thirty years of life. And she was old enough, experienced enough, to know the difference now. Her lips parted into a shy smile.

"And I'd return your kiss."

Her words fell like molten heat across him. He saw the sincerity in her brown-and-gold eyes. He absorbed her honesty, her courage to reach out to him—her woman to his man. Gently, Wes brushed her lower lip with his thumb. "This world isn't for cowards," he told her unsteadily. "You have to have a lot of heart, a lot of belief in yourself, in order to survive. And you have, Diana. Maybe you're not whole, but nobody is." He stopped caressing her lip and forced himself to place his hands over hers.

"Damaged goods," Wes muttered. "That's what we all are. My adopted mother worked hard and long on me, to make me understand that my real mother loved me enough to give me up to a better life, where I'd have a chance."

"And because I'd had such a loving, secure childhood, it gave me the courage to finally leave Bob, to break free," Diana quietly admitted, soaking up his small ministrations.

Running his thumb across the back of her hand, Wes murmured, "In a way, we're both lucky. We got a lot of love when we were young, and it helped us survive." And right now, he wanted to love Diana. Already he saw obstacles to those possibilities. He was ex-army, a stark reminder of her tortured past and the loss of her baby. Could she look beyond those life-wrenching elements to see him for himself, not in relation to her nightmare? Wes didn't know how, and he wasn't going to force his attentions on Diana. The last thing she would respond to would be any sort of aggressive move.

He smiled wryly. "Your mother broke loose a lot of stuff with that healing, didn't she?"

"Then you believe that it happened?"

He shrugged. "Proof's in the pudding, isn't it?"

Internally, Diana sighed. "I'm so glad you accept the gift that was given to you, Wes."

His laugh was derisive. "I don't think I had much choice in the matter, do you?"

Her spirits lifted at the sound of his deep, husky laugh. How wonderfully the shape of Wes's face changed when he laughed. That hardness that usually kept his expression rigid and emotionless had dissolved. In its place was a radiating joy. Oh, how Diana wished they could be anywhere but here right now!

"I wish—I wish we were back on the reservation," Diana admitted softly, "so I could take you to my old childhood haunts, those favorite places where I was happy, where I dreamed dreams."

Wes nodded. "Maybe, when this mission is over, we can do that...together?" Did he dare to hope? Dare to dream? How many dreams had been torn away from him in his life? Reality was so harsh, so demanding, that he had learned to stop dreaming. Idealism never went hand in hand with realism. Ever. But as he held Diana's joyous gaze and saw the hope and desire burning in the depths of her eyes, Wes did dare to hope. To dream.

Diana smiled through her tears. "I'd love you to come home with me, Wes. To see where I come from. Who I am. I'd like nothing better."

Wes sat very still, enjoying the timbre of her husky voice. Had he heard correctly? His mind wanted to reject it as impossible, but his heart was pounding like a runaway steam engine. Grappling with his strewn emotions, he rasped, "Yeah, I'd like that, too, Diana. I'd like to see where you were raised. What's made you the wonderful way you are...."

Diana listened, believing but still stunned by his agreement. "You and I," she began unsteadily, "are a lot alike, I feel."

"Yes and no." He picked up her hand and placed a small, warm kiss on top of it. His gaze drifted to hers to see her reaction. He saw surprise, and on its heels, warmth and desire in her eyes. "You come from a world I've never known. It's a world of invisible things. Unproven things. I come from a prove-it-to-me world of reality. If I can't see it for myself or in some way prove it, I'm lost, Diana."

Sadness blanketed her joy. "I was raised to believe in the unseen, the invisible, Wes. I saw my mother perform healings all my life, with unseen energy. But I did see the results of those healings. I saw the goodness she gives to others without thought to herself. My sister and I were raised in a home where songs, chanting, rattles and ceremony were a natural part of our life. My mother's a pipe carrier, and I saw that if she prayed with the pipe, miracles could happen for others." She gave him a bleak look. "All of these are invisible things, Wes. I can't show you how it works—or even why it works—I just know that it does."

"In your world you live on your faith, your belief," he said.

"Yes, every moment I breathe is an act of faith. Faith in the unknown, knowing that it is there—even if I can't see it or prove its existence with human machines or methods."

"My world is on a different level."

Sadly, Diana nodded. It was vital to her that Wes accept her reality, although it was diametrically opposed to his own. If he could not, then she knew there would be no bridge built between them. And she saw that he understood that, too. Grief serrated her. Wes had given her life when she thought no man would ever touch her heart again. But Diana couldn't offer her heart to him unless he accepted her world; to do so would be living a lie. She had lived a lie once before, and she'd sworn never to make the same mistake twice.

"Bob always made fun of my beliefs, my gift for psychometry," she said softly, opening her hands. "He hated my mother and said she was a witch."

"He didn't respect either of you."

"That's true." Diana's voice became low and fervent. "Wes, you need to understand, I can't give any man anything unless he values what I bring to him. He doesn't have to embrace it, but he has to accept it."

"I know...." And he did. "All this talk about songs, rattles, ceremony and pipes is alien to me, Diana. It's like having someone from outer space drop in and talk to me."

Miserably, Diana nodded. "I realize that."

The utter grief in her eyes moved him deeply. "I know I'm not the most open-minded person in the world, but you have to understand where I come from. In Delta Force, everything was black and white. It was all about training, about men working as a team, getting reinforcement from satcoms, satellite communications—real things we could see and hear." Gripping her hand, which was now cool and damp, Wes probed her sad gaze. "We had no room for feelings, for intuitions or some psychic energy floating around us, Diana. Hell, if any of us had counted on those kinds of things, we'd be dead."

"Maybe not," Diana said quietly. "Maybe if someone had used his intuition, his gut hunch, he might have checked those helicopters before they took off and crashed in the desert, killing so many of your friends."

Bleakly, Wes held her gaze. "I don't know...."

"I do. My psychometric gifts aren't my imagination, Wes." She held out her hands to him. "Why isn't it possible that some people in this world have hands that can feel more than just the texture of something? Why isn't it possible to pick up the energy that surrounds that object? The whole universe is composed of nothing but sound vibration. Why isn't it possible that a human being could pick up on these subtle vibrations and be able to accurately interpret them?''

"I don't know," he said grimly.

Desperately, Diana searched for a parallel in Wes's world. "What if you're out in the desert and there are hidden enemies in front of you? What tells you there's danger ahead?"

Wes shrugged. "Experience."

"What do you base the experience on?"

"The fact that it's happened before."

Frustration thrummed through Diana. She sat up and gestured strongly. "You haven't seen them or heard them, yet you know where they are. How do you explain that, Wes?"

Stubbornly, he shook his head. "You don't understand, Diana." He jabbed his finger into the air. "If I have an enemy in front of me, I'll be looking and thinking about a lot of things based on my training and experience. First, there are better places for an enemy to hide than others. I'm trained to look at camouflage and terrain for a potential hiding place. Secondly, if I have radio contact with other squads, infrared info or satellite intelligence, I can narrow it down even further." Wes saw her disappointment. "Everything in my world can be explained."

"Mine can't be."

Wes shook his head. "No."

Grimly, Diana sat back. "Then I'll have to prove to you. Somehow, before this is over, you'll understand, Wes." Somehow...

CHAPTER FOUR

Diana took in the natural beauty of the red-rock country of Sedona, Arizona. They had landed at Phoenix International Airport an hour earlier, then hopped a single-engine Cessna aircraft that took them a hundred miles north to the smaller airport just outside the town of fifteen thousand people. The red sandstone rose around the tourist community like natural cathedrals against a dark blue sky. A white limestone cap on the sandstone made the geology even more spectacular. Wes, however, seemed immune to the staggering beauty of the region. He had said little since landing at the Phoenix airport.

They met a local police officer, Larry Thomas, at the gate, and Diana followed the men, locked into absorbing the sensations of the area. Her mother had told her that Sedona was a very sacred place to all Native People in North and South America. It was a female region, an area rich with energy and invisible vortices that whirled at incredible rates of speed. Indeed, Diana felt a bit dizzy from the powerful energy surrounding the airport, which was high atop a mesa overlooking the town.

The sun was shining brightly, and the temperature hovered in the nineties, but Diana felt comfortable in her short-sleeved, white cotton blouse and light blue

skirt. Glad she'd worn sandals, she continued behind
the men into the geodesic-looking airport building to
retrieve their luggage. Sedona was high desert country
at four thousand feet above sea level. The red earth was
thickly dotted with dark green junipers for as far as she
could see in any direction. Officer Thomas was speaking in low tones to Wes, who nodded occasionally. But
Diana was content to wait in the center of the airport
structure while they retrieved the luggage. If Wes
wanted her to know something, he'd tell her. She was
glad to be left alone just to *feel*. And feel she did. The
invisible force of the vortex was incredible, and her
body swayed subtly with the flow of the circular release of energy coming from deep within Mother
Earth.

She spotted many colorful flyers on a bulletin board.
Going over, she began to read some of them. They were
all New Age related. Smiling, Diana noted one flyer
showing a vortex right where the airport sat! She wondered what the vortex energy did to the flight instruments on planes. Walks With Wolves had taught her
much about vortices. They were a natural part of
Mother Earth, and they existed all over the world in
different sizes and degrees of energy output. The Sedona vortices were known to be among the most powerful in the world, mainly because there were four of
them in such a small, concentrated area. That was why
Native Americans held the region sacred. Too bad,
Diana thought, that the white man had seen fit to build
a tourist trap of a town on top of such sacred land, but
it was typical of their attitude toward anything outside
the context of their accepted reality.

Feeling a little sad about the situation, she turned when she heard Wes coming. It was more a sense of his approach than actually hearing him, because he walked soundlessly. Hefting one of their bags, Officer Thomas guided them out the door, and they left the airport in a Sedona police cruiser. In the back seat, Diana remained quiet, inwardly attuning herself to the area's vibrations. Occasionally, Wes gave her a strange look, a question in his eyes, but he said nothing.

Thomas drove them to Los Piños, a five-star hotel and resort near Oak Creek, on the west side of Sedona. Diana appreciated the Santa Fe-style architecture of Los Piños. Its walls were stucco and painted a pink shade to mirror the red of the sandstone buttes, hills and mountains that surrounded them. Nothing here was more than two stories tall, so that every visitor might enjoy the dramatic scenery. The resort itself was a series of over fifty casitas, or small stucco homes.

Wes leaned over and said, "People pay five hundred dollars a night to stay here."

"The Palm Springs of Arizona?" Diana ventured.

"Yeah, this is a popular watering hole for the rich and famous. Officer Thomas was telling me that the Hollywood jet set comes here to get away from the gawkers and autograph hounds in California."

"Somehow," Diana said, "I can't feel sorry for them. Can you?"

"No. They've made their bed, now they can lie in it."

"Can't we all?" She hadn't meant to sound derisive, but it came out that way. Giving Wes an apologetic look, she added, "It must be the vortex energy. I've been feeling out of sorts since we've landed."

"Vortex?"

"Yeah," Officer Thomas piped up with a laugh. "All the New Age hippie types come to Sedona swearing there are vortices here. A lot of them live in the area because of them. They're nuts."

Diana held on to her anger. She saw Wes's jaw tighten, because he realized she believed in vortices.

"I think," he said lightly, "that your opinions aren't shared by everyone in the cruiser, Officer Thomas."

"Oh...er, sorry, ma'am. I didn't mean to insult you. It's just that...well, you know, we get some crazy fringe factions out here. You know how it is."

Diana smiled, just barely. "Officer Thomas, I am the fringe faction."

"Oh, er..."

Wes laughed deeply. He saw the sparkle in Diana's eyes and knew she hadn't taken offense at his laughter, realizing it was directed at the embarrassed officer. "It's all right," he told Thomas, and sat back, grinning.

"You're enjoying this immensely," Diana accused him.

"Yeah, I am." He placed his hand on hers. "Tell me about these vortices. What are they?"

She could see that his question was sincere. His warm, strong hand over hers rattled her, but Diana realized Wes was truly trying to understand her, and a warm feeling unexpectedly flowed through her heart.

"Vortices are natural areas where energy is discharged from inside Mother Earth. The energy is invisible to the naked eye, but can be seen by someone who is clairvoyant or has what is known as the 'sight'."

"What kind of energy?"

"Depends. Vortices are outlets. Energy builds up in and around Mother Earth, and it has to be discharged. You can think of vortices and their energy as her invisible circulatory system. Just as we have blood that runs through our arteries and veins, Mother Earth relies on her own 'blood'—this unseen energy. Without it, she would die."

"Interesting analogy," Wes said, trying to grasp her concept.

Diana pointed to the west. "I can feel something over in that direction."

"That's Boynton Canyon." Officer Thomas spoke up, trying to make amends for his faux pas. "They say there's a vortex in that canyon, ma'am."

"Thank you, Officer." Diana smiled over at Wes.

"So you can feel them?" Wes was impressed at Diana's ability to sense the presence of another vortex.

"Yes, anyone who is sensitive can. Animals can. Insects and birds certainly do."

"Do you think Ruth Horner knew about the vortices? That she might have come here for that reason?"

"I don't know. If she was as psychic as you say she is, then I'm sure she felt them just as I now feel them."

"What do vortices do?"

"Most release energy, but some have other special functions."

"Yeah," the officer put in, eavesdropping on their conversation, "they say the one over on Bell Rock is a physical vortex that can heal you, and the one in Boynton Canyon brings back past-life memory recall.''

"Exactly," Diana said. She pointed to Wes. "In the Hindu religion, as well as many Far Eastern religions, they recognize that we humans also have an invisible energy 'circulatory system,' with major centers called chakras. They look like wheels with spokes in them, and they rotate. We have one on top of our head, one at our brow where the 'third eye' is located, one at our throat, our heart, our stomach, our abdomen and, finally, at the base of our tailbone. These chakras turn, like spinning propeller blades on an airplane, drawing in the invisible energy that surrounds us. The Hindus called it *prana* which is another word for life.''

Scowling, Wes nodded. "Okay, so far so good. I follow what you're saying.''

Diana smiled a little and gestured with her hands. "*Prana* is sucked up into our chakras by the spinning blades and then distributed throughout our aura, that electromagnetic eggshell that surrounds everything, including human beings. If the chakras are open and running, we are healthy. If they're closed or blocked, we can get very sick." She placed her fingertips against Wes's chest. "When my mother hugged you, healing energy flowed to your closed heart chakra, and it flew open. The blades started to spin, and that's why you can feel again. You aren't numb any longer.''

Wes gave her a strange look. "How did you know I felt emotionally numb?''

"My mother taught us that when the heart chakra closes down and stops spinning, you are cut off from your feelings, Wes. When it's open you can feel. Don't look at me like that. What I'm telling you is the science of metaphysics—those things that exist beyond the reach of our naked eyes."

Ruminating over her explanation, Wes pondered her impassioned plea. "So these vortices—how are they connected with our chakras?"

She smiled, pleased by his grasp of her information. "Vortices are Mother Earth's chakras." She held her hand about six inches away from Wes's heart. "You see, each chakra spins, and as it spins, it creates a flow and releases energy. You can actually feel it in the palm of your hand if you're sensitive enough."

Wes felt *something*. Although Diana's hand was well away from his chest, he could feel heat radiating from it. "I feel warmth."

She smiled. "Yes."

"What's going on?"

"My hand is making contact with the energy being sent out from your heart chakra, that's all. It's a nice feeling, isn't it?"

He nodded, more than a little impressed, but not willing to believe all of it quite yet. "Do you think Ruth Horner was out here to investigate these vortices?"

"I don't know. Sedona is certainly rich with metaphysical phenomena," Diana murmured. "But we need to get to her casita, and I need to touch something she owned before I'll know more."

Wes had Officer Thomas wait outside in the cruiser, then he opened the door to the casita Ruth Horner had vacationed in for two weeks. Placing his hand in the small of Diana's back, he guided her into the posh residence. The interior was painted a dusky mauve, the drapes pale pink and the carpet pale green—all colors in keeping with the Southwest tradition, he supposed.

Curious, he watched Diana after he removed his hand from her back and quietly closed the door. She moved to the center of the room and stood very still. Remaining silent, Wes realized she was picking up on something. He searched his own senses but felt nothing in the silence of this large casita filled with expensive, overstuffed furniture and art objects.

"I feel a lot of anger in here," Diana said in a low voice. Her eyes closed, she slowly turned, sensing, picking up information on the intuitive level. "There." Opening her eyes, she pointed in the direction of a large pink-and-white-striped satin sofa. "The anger is really strong here, around the sofa." She walked over and slowly moved her hand from side to side, allowing her ultrasensitive palms to pick up information.

Wes walked over and held out his hand in the same general area. His frown deepened. "I don't feel anything."

"That's okay."

He looked more closely at the sofa. "Officer Thomas said they found nothing in the casita. Ruth Horner and her luggage had literally vanished."

"I don't think so." Frowning, Diana closed her eyes and placed both hands on one of the sofa's plump seat cushions. She continued to feel, to receive impressions. "Fight. There was a terrific fight. I feel her anguish." Jerking her hands off the couch, Diana straightened and shivered. "A horrible fight."

Wes moved closer, hearing the tremor in her hushed tone. Without thinking, he placed a hand on her shoulder and felt the tension thrumming through her. It was difficult for him to think that she might be making all of this up. He already felt he knew and trusted Diana enough to realize she felt something.

"What kind of fight? Physical? Verbal?"

Releasing a sigh, she twisted her head to look up into Wes's grave features. She liked having his hand on her shoulder, and the feeling of stability it gave her. Even more, she liked what she saw mirrored in his eyes: concern. How could she ever have thought he was violent as Bob had been? The violence she felt around him had come from his experiences in Delta Force, one of the most lethal military teams in the world.

"I don't know. At least, not yet. Let me touch some more things...."

Wes looked around. "While you're doing that, I'm going to nose around. I don't trust the local cops to see everything. They must have missed something."

"Okay." Diana felt him move away, and she closed her eyes again. By closing them, she automatically switched to the right hemisphere of her brain, where her sensing equipment was located. She could feel more by moving her hands lightly across fabric, a desk or chair, than by looking at it. Information, sometimes pictures, would flow into her mind's eye, that screen where her third eye was located. When she opened her eyes, the pictures or symbols disappeared.

She moved slowly, sensing, feeling. The anger was worst around the sofa, although in the bedroom, she felt a confusing mix of emotions. Touching a pale pink satin comforter that covered the king-size bed, she felt tears, sadness. When she skimmed her left palm upward toward the pillow, the sensation became stronger. By the time Diana actually felt the pillow, the one she was sure Ruth Horner had slept on, she wanted to cry herself.

"Are you okay?" Wes stood in the entrance to the bedroom. He saw the grief-stricken expression on Diana's face as she held a pillow against her body.

"Y-yes." She put the pillow back down and wrapped her arms around herself. Wes came over and stood inches from her. When he placed his hands on her arms, she whispered, "Ruth Horner was a very sad woman. She cried so much. So much..."

Wes tightened his grip on Diana's arms. Her voice was shaken, and he felt her empathy for Ruth Horner. "Lean on me," he entreated softly near her ear. And she did. Wes stifled a groan deep within him as she leaned shyly against him and he took her weight. She felt good. Everything felt so right with her. She was warm and soft and rounded in all the right places, fitting perfectly against the hard, more angular planes of his body. Even her hair smelled fragrant—a scent he could swear was gardenia. Without thinking, he placed a kiss against her thick, black hair, shining in the light from the stained-glass windows behind them.

Diana felt his kiss, felt the pressure of his mouth against her hair and trembled. Not from fear, but from anticipation. If only... if only he was kissing her lips. Her fingers were firm on her arms, and he was stalwart, his body hard but at the same time comforting. She closed her eyes, surrendering to him in every way—

although she knew he didn't realize it. Wes wasn't much of an intuitive, not perceptive enough at reading body language to realize the gift of herself she'd just given to him. But it didn't matter, because he was opening up. With time, she knew he would be able to read even her most subtle body signals. Did they have that time?

Opening her eyes, Diana forced herself away from Wes, away from the strength and invitation of his body. Although she ached to turn and slide her arms around his neck, she fought the urge. She must concentrate on the job at hand.

"Earlier I picked up a very different feeling near the clothes closet," she said, hoping he didn't notice that she was blushing. Her cheeks felt hot, and she kept her back turned to him as she moved toward the closet.

Wes nodded and stood for a moment, absorbing the last sensations of Diana's body against him. The moment had been too short, and he felt denied. Did she? He turned, but she was moving away from him. If he didn't know better, he'd think she seemed a trifle nervous. Perhaps because of his boldness?

Wes didn't have much experience with Diana's kind of woman—a woman who'd been hurt by another man. He was terribly unsure about how to approach her. What was appropriate? What wasn't? Shaking his head, he followed her over to the light blue French doors. The closet was large, covering half the wall in front of them. When Diana turned, he felt instant elation. Her cheeks were bright pink, and her eyes ... He groaned to himself. Her eyes were a soft, velvety brown with gold flecks. Yes, she'd liked him holding her, kissing her hair. Wes wanted more. Much more. Suppressing his clamoring needs, he put them aside and focused on what she was saying.

"When I came into this room, I felt a lot of confused energy. I felt repugnance and disgust, along with a lot of grief." Lifting her hands, she added, "I don't know what to make of it, Wes."

"What did the bed area feel like?"

"Grief, sadness."

"Can you conjecture why?"

"She was sad. Crying over something."

Scratching his jaw, he said, "She was married once, you know."

"What caused the divorce?"

"I don't know. I asked the same question of the chief of the Psi-Lab, and he said only that her husband, Richard Horner, didn't like the long hours she spent at work."

Diana lightly ran her hand along one French door. "I see."

"What do you feel here?"

"Something...odd. Dangerous." She shook her head. "Wait, let me see if I can be more specific." She faced the closet, closed her eyes and placed both hands on the French doors. For a minute she was silent.

Wes waited patiently. He saw Diana's brow furrow and her mouth curve downward. "What is it?"

Jerking her hands away from the closet, she whispered, "Something *evil* is in there!" She shook her hands to fling off the energy they'd accumulated by having contact with the closet doors.

Frowning, Wes pulled her away. "Stay back," he warned, before carefully opening one of the doors. It was dark inside the closet, but he knew in a casita like this, where no expense was spared, there would be a light switch. Fumbling, he found it. Once the light was on, he hauled both giant doors outward and folded them back for a better view.

"Look!" Diana gasped, pointing up to the right-hand corner of the closet about the clothes rack.

Wes tensed momentarily, his hand automatically going for his revolver beneath his jacket. His gaze settled on the red object in the corner. "What the hell..."

"Wait! Don't touch it!"

He glanced at her as she came over to where he stood. "Why? What is it?"

"I think it's a rattle of some kind."

"So?" He itched to reach up and retrieve it.

Gulping, Diana stood on tiptoe to get a better look at it. "It is a rattle! A ceremonial one, from what I can tell. Wes, don't touch it, please. It could be dangerous."

"How?" There was disbelief in his voice. It looked like a gourd that had been sloppily painted a red color, with two black feathers attached to the wooden handle.

Gripping his arm, she kept her gaze fastened on the gourd. "Rattles are like loaded guns, Wes. You don't handle them unless you know exactly what they are and what you're doing."

"Explain." He was fully aware of her fingers digging into his arm, as if she was afraid he wouldn't listen to her warning.

"Rattles are like pipes—they're all different. Usually, they're made out of a gourd of some kind, or a turtle shell or deer hoof. People making rattles, if they know what they're doing, will fill them with stones. Those stones usually come from around an anthill."

"Do you mean it's dangerous if someone throws it at me?" he asked wryly, a grin crossing his mouth.

Diana's heart wouldn't stop pounding. She sensed real danger and wasn't in the mood for his teasing. "This isn't funny, Wes! I've seen people pick up a rattle and get thrown clear across a room, unconscious by the time they hit the other wall. Rattles are nothing to play around with. If the maker of a rattle is a good person, it can be beautiful, healing and powerful. But if a sorcerer—a person with evil intent—makes one, the rattle can kill. Please, you've got to believe me!"

"I didn't say I didn't," Wes muttered, desperately wanting to hold the object.

"That rattle has no markings, no symbols on it."

"So?"

"Usually the very powerful rattles have no markings."

"It has feathers."

"They look like buzzard feathers to me," Diana muttered, craning her neck. "It's a rattle of transformation."

"Meaning?"

She wiped her damp hands on the sides of her skirt. "That rattle was made to transform something."

"Give me an example."

Nervously, Diana backed away from the closet. She was grateful Wes came with her. Above all, she didn't want him picking up the rattle without a knowledge of what he was doing. She sat down on the edge of the bed.

"Healers usually possess a transformation rattle. If the rattle is shaken near a sick person, the vibration of the stones striking the gourd can help break or dissolve invisible blocks in the patient's aura and make them well."

"That's not evil," Wes said, sitting down beside her, folding his hands between his long thighs.

"No," Diana agreed, "it's not. But I've seen my mother come up against both male and female sorcerers from time to time, and they always use a gourd of transformation to try and get her."

"Get her?"

"Kill her."

Wes stared at her, dumbfounded.

Diana pointed to the gourd. "If that is a sorcerer's gourd and the wrong person picks it up, it could be fatal."

His eyes grew round.

"You don't believe me, do you?" Bitterly, Diana rose.

"I didn't say that."

"You didn't have to. It shows in your eyes, Wes." Frustrated, she whispered, "That rattle is *dangerous!* I don't want you picking it up! Do you understand?"

"If it's that dangerous, what is it doing here? Besides, it might have fingerprints on it that can give us a lead."

"I don't know. And it may or may not have fingerprints on it."

"Did Horner buy it? Was it placed here and she picked it up? What if she did pick up a gourd of that power? What would it do to her?"

Confused, Diana shook her head and opened her hands. "Wes, I don't have all the answers. I wish I did. The feeling around that rattle is evil, that's all I can tell you."

"I find it odd the police didn't find it," he muttered, rising to his full height and going over to the closet to stare at the red gourd. "Of course, knowing they're local cops, I'm not surprised. One of them probably opened the closet doors and looked in but didn't turn on the light. You'd never see that gourd unless the light was on."

Rubbing her brow, Diana felt a terrible sense of dread. "I'm going to have to hold it, whether I want to or not."

Wes glanced at her sharply.

"You just told me it was dangerous."

"It is—to you." And maybe to her, but Diana didn't say that. She saw the aggravation, the question and disbelief in Wes's eyes. A part of her was angry, because she knew what she sensed wasn't wrong. Diana couldn't give Wes the full answers he was seeking. Watching him place his hands defiantly on his hips, as if to dispute her right to touch the gourd, she said testily, "I'm in a position to know how to protect myself before I touch it."

"And I'm not?" Wes didn't quite *not* believe Diana about the gourd. He couldn't explain it, but he'd felt unsettled ever since they'd opened the closet to reveal the damn thing. There was no explanation for his feelings, but his gut was clenching, and that was all the red-flag warning he needed.

"No, you don't," she flung back heatedly, moving forward. Before he could step into her path to stop her, she stretched upward and grabbed the rattle. She couldn't risk his death, or his insanity, if he touched a sorcerer's gourd without proper training or protection. But did she have enough protection? Diana wasn't sure, but she said a swift prayer to the Great Spirit and wrapped her fingers around the object before Wes could stop her.

Wes cried out her name, but it was too late. He watched as Diana picked up the gourd. Almost instantly, he saw her go ashen. When she staggered backward, as if her hands had melted onto the rattle, he reached out for her.

"NO!" Diana gasped. "Don't touch me!" *Oh, no!* She was off balance. The power of the gourd was overwhelming. Shocking. She felt a violent, burning heat sting the palm of her hand and race up her arm. Breathing violently, she gasped again and again. The gourd was trying to shut off her ability to breathe! Invisible strands wound around her throat, and she gagged. Somehow, she had to get rid of the thing, but it clung to her like glue.

Falling to her knees, Diana rasped harshly. Her throat was closing. Her breath was failing. *No!* She didn't want to die this way! She heard Wes shout her name. Grayness replaced her vision, and she knew she was dying. At the last moment, as the heat raced for her throat, she called upon all her reserve strength. With a cry, she flung the gourd away from her. She felt herself falling, falling, in a downward spiral, a deadly whirlpool of energy. Shutting her eyes tightly, she became locked in an inner battle on an invisible dimension with the red gourd. It was a spider gourd, the most dangerous of all rattles a sorcerer could make.

Choking, her hands gripping her throat, Diana felt the invisible heat, like spider webs, that encircled her neck with lethal intent. Blackness closed in on her. She heard Wes's strident, off-key voice, felt his hands gripping her shoulders. She was floating. Floating. Little by little, the invisible cords wrapped around her neck began to ease. Slowly, her breathing became less harsh. Moments melded into one another, and all Diana was aware of was her heart thundering in her breast—and Wes holding her hard against him.

Gradually, the darkness began to ease and she saw grayness again. Her fingers loosened from around her throat, and she felt terribly weak. She sagged, her head lolling against the warmth of Wes's chest. She realized she must have fallen to the carpeted floor. He'd knelt over her, scooping her into his arms. Diana honed in on his ragged breath, his voice calling her, his hand touching her here and there to make sure she was going to be all right. The intensity of his care for her dissolved whatever terror remained.

"Diana! Talk to me!" He was wild with fear. He divided his attention between her and the deadly gourd that now lay on the floor no more than six feet away from them. Anxiously, he held her in his arms, her body still limp against his, although her skin was slowly beginning to regain its color. Touching her cheek, he felt warmth flowing back into her. Moments before, she'd been chilled, her flesh icy to his touch. Breathing hard, Wes caressed her hair, her cheek.

"Are you okay?" he demanded.

Weakly, Diana lifted her lashes. She saw the burning light in his eyes, the grim set of his mouth as his hand fluttered nervously across her. Trying to smile and not succeeding, she whispered, "I'll be okay...just give me a moment, please?" Her voice was off-key, faint.

Wes was torn between getting up, racing out to the police cruiser and ordering the officer to get an ambulance for Diana, and staying here at her side. But what the hell would he tell the man? Indeed, what could he say to a doctor at a local hospital emergency room? That Diana had touched a red gourd and had gone into an anaphylactic reaction where she'd stopped breathing and turned blue-gray? They'd look at him as if he were certifiably insane. No, he'd best stay with her. The color was coming back to her face and her eyes no longer looked as traumatized. He loosened his iron grip on her and held her more gently.

"You scared the hell out of me," he rasped against her ear. "Don't ever do that again, you hear me? I care too much for you, Diana. Too much...."

CHAPTER FIVE

Diana stared up at Wes, not quite believing what he'd said. The feelings coursing through her confirmed what she'd heard. To be in his arms, to feel his natural strength and be the recipient of his care overwhelmed her confused senses. Other pictures kept impinging upon her consciousness, and she struggled to sit up on her own.

"Wes . . . get a paper and pencil." She pressed the palms of her hands against her closed eyes and leaned forward, resting them against her drawn-up knees. "Hurry. I'm getting all kinds of impressions. . . ."

Muttering beneath his breath, Wes heaved to his feet and raced into the living room of the casita to retrieve his briefcase. Throwing it on the bed, he glanced anxiously at Diana, who remained motionless on the carpeted floor. His heart was pounding with fear as he found a legal pad and pen. Sitting down next to her, his back against the bed, he said, "Go ahead."

"I see her. I see Ruth. She's a small woman, built like a bird, very skinny. She looks so gaunt. So unhappy." Her voice broke with tears. "The gourd. She held the gourd. It stunned her. She threw it up into the closet." Diana tried to take the urgency out of her voice, but she felt so many serrated emotions. "I hear angry voices. She's arguing with someone . . . a man. It's a man." The pictures faded and she waited. Perhaps more would come.

Wes waited tensely, pen poised above the pad. He was holding it in a death grip. Glancing over at the dangerous gourd, he wondered how he possibly could have questioned Diana's knowledge. Angry at himself because she had deliberately put herself on the line for him, to protect him from his own ignorance, he compressed his lips.

"Wait..." Diana tried to relax. She knew that only if she was calm and serene within herself would the pictures come. Trying to settle her racing heart and concentrate fully on the sensations she retained from touching the gourd, she whispered, "I see something...."

A canyon materialized, a red-sandstone canyon. Diana began to describe it. "I see the entrance to this canyon, and what I see most prominently is a profile of a man's face on this huge rock. It looks Mayan, or Aztec, and he had his mouth open, as if he's singing...." The picture dissolved, and moments later Diana saw another scene. "I see a dusty, rocky path, and I'm walking along it. It's very steep and veers off to the right. Oh... I see, there's a cave up there. A huge cave carved out of red sandstone. There's an ancient Indian dwelling in it. I see a small tree at the back of the cave. It shouldn't be living there, but there's a small pool of water around it. Enough water seeps through the sandstone walls to keep the tree from dying, and sunlight reflects in off the walls."

The picture dissolved and Diana waited. Nothing more came. Shakily, she removed her hands from her eyes and looked at Wes. Nothing could have prepared her for the tortured expression on his face and the care burning in his eyes—for her alone. Her mouth suddenly dry, she reached out, her fingertips grazing his hard, tense forearm.

"I'm okay. Really."

Wes nodded. "Let me decide that," he said gruffly.

Her mouth lifted at the corners just enough to let him know that she honored his statement. "Those are all the impressions, Wes. I wish there were more, but there aren't."

"Who was she arguing with? Did you see him?"

"No... unfortunately. I heard a man's voice. It was a deep and angry voice."

"Did you hear what they said?"

She held out her hands, palms up. "I never hear exactly what is said, I only receive impressions."

"Could the man have been the sorcerer? The one who gave her that gourd?"

She shrugged. "It's possible. But I saw her pick up the gourd and I feel strongly Ruth knew the consequences of her action. I saw her throw it up into that closet."

"Damn...."

"There's more, Wes." Taking a deep breath, feeling better, Diana said, "I think I know where Ruth is."

His eyes narrowed. "Where?"

"In that canyon where the cave is located. She's close." Diana looked slowly around the room. "I can feel her presence still in the Sedona area."

"I wonder how many canyons have caves in them?" he asked, disgruntled.

"I have no idea. We can ask Officer Thomas to assist us. Besides, the canyon entrance had this Aztec-looking singer." She gestured with her hands. "The face of the rock profile was at least a thousand feet tall, Wes. How many canyon entrances have that?"

He brightened. "Not many. It should cut a lot of time off the search."

"Right."

He put the pad and pen aside. Getting to his feet, he took the large wastebasket and nudged the rattle into it with his foot.

"Stay put," he ordered. "I'm going to have that officer put the rattle away for safekeeping."

"Make sure no one touches it."

"Don't worry. I will."

Wes reappeared minutes later. He came and knelt down beside her. "You look tired."

"I feel it." She grimaced and looked at the red gourd. "It's a powerful and deadly rattle, Wes."

His hands tightened on her shoulders. "You shouldn't have done it, Diana. You shouldn't have picked it up."

She felt the warmth of his strong, dry hands on her and wanted more. The urge to reach out and kiss him was too much to resist. Diana knew he cared for her—deeply and without question. Guided by her knowing, she slowly rose from her position and knelt beside him. With her hands she framed his rugged, harsh face and with her eye held his dark, tortured gaze.

Without a word, she leaned over and placed her lips against the hard line of his mouth. She wasn't disappointed. Closing her eyes, she melted against his opening mouth, felt him groan, felt his arms wrapping around her, bringing her even closer. His mouth was strong, cherishing. Their ragged breathing mingled. The strength of his kiss, the barely controlled power behind it, washed across Diana. His hands ranged roughly across her shoulders, down her torso to her waist. He wanted her. All of her. Suddenly, nothing had ever seemed so right to Diana. She might have died from the power of the gourd, and she would never have known the tender, gentle side of Wes McDonald.

Breathing unevenly, she eased back from his hungry, searching mouth. If she continued to deepen the kiss, deepen their exploration, she knew she wouldn't be able to stop. With a hesitant smile, she stroked his thick, short hair.

"Can we go somewhere? Be alone?"

Wes nodded, internally shaking like a leaf in a thunderstorm. He ached to take Diana, here and now. To hell with the police. To hell with the mission. Gazing at her, the flushed quality of her cheeks, the vulnerability of her parted lips, he realized with a sureness that stunned him that he loved her. All of her. All of who she was.

"Yes, we can," he said, his voice rough with desire. Unwinding, he stood up and offered Diana his hand. She took it. As she came to his side, her arms sliding around his waist, her head resting on his chest, something old and hurting dissolved deep within his heart. An avalanche of euphoria swept through Wes, and he experienced a joy he'd never known existed.

* * *

The Oak Creek Hotel, situated five miles into a forested canyon above Sedona, had a wide, clear creek running alongside it. Wes liked the rustic atmosphere and privacy the place afforded. The cabin, built from pine, sat no more than fifty feet from the rushing, pristine water.

The fragrance of the pines was perfume to Diana. But she was distracted from the beauty by Wes, who had just finished telling Officer Thomas to pick them up tomorrow morning.

Coming up behind her, Wes placed his hands on her shoulders. "Beautiful, isn't it?" he asked near her ear, wanting her more than he'd ever wanted anything in his life.

She nodded and rested against his tall, hard frame, content. "Yes..."

"What I'm looking at, what I'm holding, is even more beautiful," he rasped, and gently turned her around so he could see her reaction to his admission. Diana's face was glowing with such loveliness that Wes leaned down and picked her up in his arms. He saw the surprise and then the happiness in her eyes as he carried her to the bedroom, to the old brass bed.

The sun was filtering through windows laced with old-fashioned curtains, creating light-and-dark patterns across the quilt on the bed. As Diana lay down, with Wes at her side, she recalled times when darkness had ruled her life. As he ran his hand down her arm, gently cupping her breast beneath the fabric of her blouse, she closed her eyes, absorbing his touch, filling herself with the essence of him as a man whose heart was open and receptive to renewed life. Wes symbolized sunlight to her, overtaking the darkness of her past. No longer was he a hard warrior without a heart, without a soul. No, he was a man in touch with his heart now, and she savored the fact deeply as he began slowly, one by one, to undo the buttons of her blouse.

Diana opened her eyes and smiled softly up at Wes. His eyes burned with hunger, like a wolf who has gone too long without a mate. His search for a mate was over as far as she was concerned, and she reached up and unbuttoned his shirt. She felt him tremble as she slid her hand across his darkly haired chest, his muscles tensing beneath her inspection.

"You are so beautiful," he whispered raggedly, pushing her blouse aside. He captured her lips with his as he removed the rest of her clothes, lost in the heat, the sweetness of her full, blossoming mouth. Wes had never believed there was much happiness in store for him; he'd seen very little of it in his lifetime. As he and Diana undressed each other and lay on the colorful quilt, he knew he had it now. Urgency thrummed through him, and he didn't want to wait, but he controlled himself. Loving was about giving and taking, not just taking. And Diana's body was so warm, so alive as she pressed against him, begging him to be one with her. He groaned. It was a groan of pleasure, the fire wreaking its special magic from the core of his body outward.

Sunlight and shadows fell across them, and as he moved above her—their eyes locked on each other, his hands capturing hers above her head—he knew. Wes knew without a doubt that this was the woman he'd waited for all his life. And as her eyelids drooped slightly, those gold-and-brown eyes alive with desire for him alone, he slid into her heated, welcoming depths. Tensing, frozen with pleasure, with reward, he gripped her long, unbound hair. And then she began to move, gently at first, rocking, cajoling, and his lips drew away from his clenched teeth as he tried to control himself for her sake. It was impossible, and he plunged deeply, repeatedly into her, taking her, giving to her, smothering her mouth with his own and tasting her—absorbing her into himself, into his pounding, thudding heart.

The shadows mixed, melted together. Light became dark, and dark light for Diana. The power, the consummation of his love for her was never questioned. He took her hard and fast, and she matched his fierce tide of love in return. Within moments, her world exploded into a bright, golden light deep within her body, and she cried out, gripping Wes hard, gasping for breath as she felt the absolute beauty and pleasure of what their love for each other produced. Moments later she heard him growl, felt him stiffen against her, his fingers tangled in her hair. Their hearts were thundering, their breath hot and moist. The moments melded, and Diana lost herself completely in Wes's arms, held tightly against him, her head buried beneath his jaw.

The moments flowed together, and gradually Wes became aware of outside sounds—the creek babbling across the stones, the slight breeze lifting the lace curtains and cooling his damp body. He was hotly aware of Diana's curved form against him, and he moved his

hand with a newfound tenderness across her damp
back, her rounded hip and thigh. She was like liquid
sunlight in his arms, he realized with awe. Her skin was
golden, her hair black as the night itself. More than
anything, he liked the lustrous look in her half-closed
eyes and the delicate curve of her lips that told him he'd
pleased her.

Leaning down, he kissed her forehead, then tucked
several strands of dark hair behind her ear. He liked it
when she touched him in return, liked the feel of her
slender hand caressing his chest, his shoulder and, finally, cupping his jaw. He could see such courage in her
eyes, and a special knowing. He smiled a little.

"I dreamed. But not like this."

"Me either." Diana sighed, contentment thrumming through her. "I don't want this moment ever to
end, Wes. Not ever."

He gave her a heated look and continued to stroke
her long, thick hair, flowing like an ebony river across
his arm. "It doesn't have to." He held her widening
eyes. "I'm not into one-night stands, Diana. Never
was."

Did she dare hope? She tried not to kid herself. Wes
was a mercenary, someone who traveled the world
over. She knew her ex-husband had had a woman in
every port of call. Drinking in Wes's newly softened
features, she wondered if Wes would really be so different from Bob.

"You looked worried," he said, his voice thick.

"It's nothing...."

With a short laugh, he shook his head. "Honey,
'nothing' is never nothing. What's bothering you?" He

held his breath. Did Diana not want a long-term relationship working toward the possibility of marriage? Wes did. He'd never been more sure of anything than he was of his feelings for her.

Sitting up, Diana remained in his arms as he settled his back against the brass headboard. "My ex-husband had a lot of affairs, Wes...."

He nodded. "A woman in every port. Yeah, I know the type."

She frowned and searched for the right words. She felt his fingers tunneling through her hair and looked up at him.

"You want to know if I'm the same, don't you?"

Marveling at his brutal honesty, Diana admitted, "I—yes. I know it's not fair—"

He laughed derisively. "Nothing in life is fair. You have every right to wonder about me. I'm ex-army, like he was. I'm an itinerant wanderer who can be sent anywhere in the world." Gently, he cupped her jaw and saw the worry, the apology, in her eyes. She could hide nothing from him, and it amazed him that he could intuitively sense her questions and worries. "Diana, I've never played around. When I'm in a relationship with a woman, she's mine and I'm hers. I won't cheat on you."

With a sigh, Wes framed her face and stared deeply into her tear-filled eyes. "Honey, what I have in mind for us isn't some throwaway relationship. I never was an eighties kind of man. I have my own rules of operation regarding relationships, and I live by them." He knew his voice sounded harsh, and he felt frustrated because he only wanted to convey to Diana how much he loved her. "Look," he began, a new desperation in his voice, "I love you. I've never said that to a woman before, Diana. In Delta Force, I never knew if I'd be coming back from a mission. I didn't want some woman, a family, waiting to hear I didn't make it."

He held her more tightly. "I never wanted to put someone through that, Diana. So I kept things on a light level. If I did get involved with a woman, she knew going in what the score was. I never lied and I never will." He tightened his arms around her when he felt her tremble. He closed his eyes, and his voice grew hoarse. "Something happened when I met you. I felt all these walls falling away from me, leaving me exposed, vulnerable. It's you," he whispered, pressing a kiss to her hair. "I can't fight this, Diana. I don't want to." Easing her away from him so he could see her expression, he said, "What I have in mind is marriage, honey. Nothing short of that. I know we haven't had enough time, and I'm willing to wait, but my hope, my dream . . . is marriage—to you."

Stunned, Diana sat very still. She not only heard Wes's strained words, his sincerity moving her as nothing ever had before, but she felt each word in her heart. His honesty was refreshing, because she'd met so many men ready to lie to her or give her a line—men who were afraid of a real commitment. But Diana couldn't doubt Wes's words; she could see the fierce, burning light of honesty in his eyes. Reaching out, she touched his clenched jaw.

"I feel the same way," she quavered. "When this mission is over, I want you to come home with me, Wes. Come home and find out who I am."

He grinned a little. "Morgan isn't going to be happy about that, but I'm allowed thirty days off between missions. I've got about a hundred twenty days coming to me at this point and I'm going to take them all." He touched her warm, flushed cheek. "I'd like nothing better, Diana."

Looking around the room, she smiled gently. "I wish, in some ways, this mission was already over."

"So do I," he murmured, taking her into his arms and lying down with her. "But tomorrow morning isn't here yet, honey, and I want to love you again. This time slowly and thoroughly."

A ribbon of heat uncoiled within Diana, and she sighed. "Tomorrow is tomorrow," she agreed. Reaching up, she slid her arms around Wes's broad shoulders and drew him down upon her.

The cool morning air seemed in direct contrast to their heated night of loving. Diana stood with Wes at the entrance to Boynton Canyon. Her body still tingled, and she was vibrantly aware of him standing at her side, map in hand. It was nearly 6:00 a.m., the sky a cloudless blue, early sunlight striking the thousand-foot red-and-white cliffs before them. Boynton was a box canyon, they'd discovered. Although it was long and rectangular, a high rock wall prevented exit at the other end.

"This path seems familiar," she told Wes, pointing to a well-trodden trail of red dirt littered with red, white and black stones.

He frowned and looked at the entrance. "I don't see any singer in the rock face."

"I know, but can we hike down the trail a little bit? Officer Thomas said the actual entrance to the canyon is a mile and a half away."

With a nod, Wes refolded the map and tucked it away in his knapsack. Today they both wore jeans and loose cotton shirts. Wes had given Diana a baseball cap to protect her head from the sun that would soon be blistering down on them from overhead. In the knapsack he carried a knife, several bottles of water and some trail mix. His revolver was hidden beneath the lightweight cotton jacket he wore.

Motioning to the left, he growled, "I see some enterprising businessman put a fancy resort at the entrance of this canyon. What made him do something like that? It ruins the atmosphere of the place."

Answering anger sizzled through Diana. "As I understand it, this entire canyon is sacred to the Apache and Yavapai people. It was Forest Service land until they sold it to a rich white man. Now, with this resort, the canyon's sacredness has been desecrated."

The monstrosity looked painfully out of place in the natural beauty that surrounded it. Wes put an arm around Diana's shoulder momentarily. "I wish they could have left something this special alone and untouched."

She shook her head. "Greedy businessmen see this beauty and want to put something man-made right in the middle, Wes." She took in a ragged breath. "They see only dollar signs and growth potential, not the deeper, more sacred needs of others. This path was made by Native Americans who would not be turned away from coming here to pray, to perform the ceremonies of their people deep in the canyon, beyond the resort.''

"Then let's get going. We'll hike to the canyon mouth,'' Wes murmured, giving her a quick hug and releasing her. He felt guilty. After all, he was a white man, too. But he quickly separated himself from that stereotype as they hiked the rugged path. The beauty of the canyon was stunning—he could certainly see why some astute businessman would want to place a resort at Boynton. Dark green juniper lined the path, and century plants with their long, thin spiked leaves grew everywhere. The red-barked manzanita bushes were swollen with dark brown berries that had hardened beneath the hot sun. Prickly pear cactus also proliferated in the area, its purple ''pears'' ripe for the picking. Dozens of birds flew and rested and sang in the natural cover the terrain presented.

The trail paralleled the edge of the resort property, where huge, glaring signs read Keep Out, Private Property. Violators Will Be Prosecuted. That alone, Wes mused, was enough to make everyone feel unwelcome.

Diana kept looking up at the stone walls that rose at least a thousand feet straight up on either side of the canyon. Just hiking with Wes was a pleasure, making the morning even more special. She walked ahead of him, her hiking stick in hand, careful to watch where she placed her feet on the rocky, dusty trail. They'd walked for another twenty minutes when she heard the caw of a raven.

Halting, Diana snapped her head upward toward the sound. Her mother's chief spirit guide was a raven! Her jaw dropped and she called excitedly, "Wes! Look! Look!" as she pointed up toward the large black bird circling along the canyon wall.

Wes came to her side and looked in the direction she indicated. "I'll be damned," he breathed. There was the Aztec "singer," just as Diana had described it. In awe, he marveled at the thousand-foot profile, carved out of the cliff face by rain, sun and wind, not by the hand of man. He grinned at her. "You're pretty good." And he meant it.

She smiled broadly. "The raven is our guide, Wes. She's shown us where the cliff face is, now she'll guide us to that cave." Gripping his hand, she laughed. "Isn't this synchronicity wonderful? The way it all works?"

Wes nodded, humbled. Clasping her hand in turn, he lifted it and kissed the back of it. "You're wonderful. What you do is something else, too. I can't explain it."

"At least you believe me now." It was so important that Wes believe in her abilities. Her ex-husband never had.

Becoming somber, Wes said, "Honey, I've come to the conclusion that just because I don't know how your gifts work doesn't mean they don't exist. Fair enough?"

Glowing, Diana nodded. "Come on, let's find that cave! I feel it's very near!"

Wes followed her, staying hyperalert. He didn't know who might be with Ruth Horner. A kidnapper? If so, there might be trouble. Or a sorcerer? Wes wasn't going to take chances with either Diana's life or his own. For the first time in his miserable life, he had something to live for, and he wasn't about to have it torn from him.

The cawing of the raven grew muted, more distant as it flew around another bend in the canyon. Yet Wes could still hear the bird's insistent call, as if it said "Follow me! Hurry up!"

Diana gave a shout of discovery as they rounded the next curve of the trail. She grinned and pointed upward, toward a cave carved out of the red sandstone high above the trail.

"Bingo," Wes said. He took off his knapsack and pulled out a pair of powerful binoculars. "Let's see if we can see anything," he murmured. He quickly scanned the area. About half the cave wasn't visible due to its elevation and the thick carpet of juniper trees blocking the way. "I see an ancient Indian dwelling up there," he murmured, "but no people."

Diana nodded. "Ruth is up there. I can feel her, Wes."

"Is anyone with her?" he asked, handing her the binoculars.

Grimly, she nodded. "Yes."

"What else do you pick up?"

"Nothing," Diana said unhappily. "I wish I did, but I don't."

Wes no longer questioned Diana's knowing. Taking the binoculars when she'd finished with them, he repacked them and shrugged into the knapsack. Pulling the bill of his baseball cap a little lower on his brow, he moved ahead of Diana. "From here on, you follow me. If I tell you to hit the deck, you hit it, no questions asked. All right?"

Her heart was pounding from the elevation and the climb. She nodded. "I wish I was more like my mother," she complained under her breath.

Wes smiled and turned toward her. "I love you just the way you are."

The words melted into her heart, her soul. How much she loved Wes for his courage to tell her. Without a word, she followed him up the steep, rocky trail, which twisted and wound like a mountain goat's narrow, dangerous path. Sharp pebbles bit into her soft palms as she scrambled and sometimes fell. But Wes was always there to lend a hand and help her back to her feet. Finally, after nearly half an hour's climb, they stood at the foot of the cliff-dwelling area.

The huge slope directly below the dwelling was powdery with light brown dust scattered with chunks of black lava. Here and there Diana could see potsherds sticking up out of the earth. At the top of the slope, they could see three rooms fashioned from long, thin pieces of red sandstone. The back of Diana's neck prickled. It was a warning. She gripped Wes's arm to get his attention. He'd told her to communicate by hand signals in order not to give their presence away.

He leaned down, placing his ear near her mouth, and Diana whispered, "I sense two people up there. They're in the dwelling."

With a nod, he straightened. Sliding his hand into the fold of his jacket, he unhooked his Berretta 9 mm pistol from its holster. Snapping off the safety, he put a round in the chamber. Wes saw the terror in Diana's eyes, and he was sorry she had to see this side of him—the mercenary, the soldier. But above all, he didn't want her harmed. Gripping her arm, he pressed her back against the smooth sandstone cliff, a huge alligator juniper providing them some cover.

"Stay here," he rasped in a low tone. "Whatever happens, you stay here until I call for you to come up."

Diana nodded. She reached out, gripping Wes's arm. "Be careful. Please..."

"You can bet on it, honey." Leaning over, he captured her lips, kissing her deeply.

Then he was gone, silently climbing the slope toward the cave dwelling. Diana touched her tingling lips where he'd branded them with his molten kiss. She knelt down, allowing the juniper to keep her hidden from view. She was seeing Wes in action, and he was like a lithe, dangerous cougar moving silently toward the cave. Her heart was thundering in her chest. Diana could taste the fear in her mouth as he quickly moved into the cave, his pistol drawn and ready to fire, and disappeared from view.

Swallows sailed effortlessly around the opening to the large-mouthed cave. The raven, perched high atop the canyon wall, was cawing nonstop. Diana froze with anxiety. What had Wes found? She tried to brace herself for the sound of gunshots. Terror paralyzed her. What if Wes was shot? Killed? Tears blinded her, but she anxiously wiped them away.

Wes reappeared. He had holstered his gun and was waving for her to come up. Releasing her breath, Diana quickly scrambled from her hiding place. What had he found? As she carefully made her way up the sucking, sliding sand of the slope, she wondered if he'd found anything at all.

CHAPTER SIX

Diana joined Wes just outside the three-room Indian dwelling, gasping for breath, and he quickly guided her to the second room of the complex. Ruth Horner was sitting on the ground, next to a large, heavy set Native American dressed in a white cotton shirt and jeans. He held a blue-painted rattle in one hand and a brown-and-white eagle feather in the other. Ruth wore a pale pink tank top, a pair of jeans and sensible hiking boots. Both stared up at Diana and Wes accusingly, their privacy obviously disturbed. Diana felt heat rush to her face.

"I'm so sorry," she stammered, opening her hands. "We didn't mean to intrude upon your ceremony." She looked to Ruth, who had piercing green eyes. The woman's gray-and-brown hair had been fashioned into short braids, and without a doubt, she looked different and better than the picture of her in the lab coat that Wes had shown Diana days ago. Happier, perhaps.

Wes placed his hand on his hips. "Psi-Lab sent us after you."

Ruth's face crumpled. "I didn't think you'd find me," she said in a low voice. She glanced at her companion. "I thought the red gourd would throw you off my trail."

Wes sat down on a flat rock, keeping his eyes on the scowling Indian. He introduced Diana. Ruth Horner's face was taut with distrust and unhappiness.

Diana hesitantly took a seat on a nearby rock. She could feel such sadness around Ruth. When the tears glimmered in the woman's eyes, she wanted to weep in empathy. "Could you tell me why you put that dangerous gourd in your room?"

Ruth rubbed her eyes and shrugged. "I knew Psi-Lab would send out guard dogs to find me. I bought the rattle from a Navajo sorcerer in Gallup, New Mexico. I was hoping that it would throw them off my trail." She gave Diana a strange look. "But neither of you are from Psi-Lab."

"No," Wes said quietly, "we were hired by them to find you. They thought you'd been kidnapped when you didn't return from your vacation."

With a brittle laugh, Ruth looked at her Indian companion. "I'm sure they were very worried—for their own sakes." She gestured toward the Indian. "This is Elmer Running Antelope. He's a Yavapai medicine man, my friend and teacher of ten years."

Elmer nodded briefly to them, his mouth set, his coal black eyes snapping with anger at the intrusion. Ruth laid a hand on his thick, heavy shoulder.

"What you don't know is I've been walking the Red Road for that time. I met Elmer a decade ago in Gallup at a powwow, and we struck up a friendship. Over the years he's been teaching me."

Wes frowned. "Red Road?"

"Yes," Diana said, "it's a term that means a person has embraced a Native American way of believing and living."

Ruth smiled a little, got to her feet and dusted off her Levis. "That's putting it mildly. Elmer and I had very long, involved talks when we first met. I began to see the world through another filter of reality. A Native American one." She lifted her hands to encompass the huge, dry cave. "The more I heard, the more I realized just how far I'd gone."

"Gone?" Wes asked, confused.

"Gone in a negative sense, Mr. McDonald. Psi-Lab isn't a very friendly place, you know. No, you probably don't. It takes a Q-Clearance even to get in the door, which means only a very few people at the top levels of federal government even know of our existence." Ruth pinned Diana with a worried look. "Whatever you do, don't get tangled up with them. Do you understand?"

Diana nodded briefly, taking the warning at face value.

Ruth picked up from the earth a wand of dried sage ceremonially wrapped with red yarn. It had been lit earlier; almost half the wand was burned away. The faint smoke wafted upward on a slight breeze. She lifted the sage close enough to inhale the fragrance. "Psi-Lab hires green, idealistic psychics and trains them to be sneaks, thieves and killers in the other dimensions—in the name of our 'enemies,' whoever and wherever they might be. Patriotism, motherhood and apple pie—all the watchwords they pound into you during the brainwashing phase." She stared at Wes.

"You don't believe me. That's okay, because I know the truth." Looking fondly at Elmer, she added, "He taught me a long time ago that the truth needs no defense, Mr. McDonald, so I'm not going to try to prove anything to you."

"There is a great danger in the other dimensions," Diana said quietly. "I know people can die if they aren't properly protected or trained."

"Your mother is a medicine woman. You know exactly what I'm talking about."

"Yes." Diana felt a mild alarm that Ruth Horner was so psychic as to know that her mother was a medicine woman. It was one thing that her mother should have such faculties in place, quite another that this woman should. Her mother was a known quantity, responsible with her gifts. But then Diana told herself to relax, that Ruth wasn't a threat to her.

"Your mother should be proud of you, you know?" Ruth smiled sourly. "I figured I could disappear, this time for good, and no one would ever find me. I didn't feel Psi-Lab had anyone in its unit good enough to track me after the red herring I left behind in the guise of that gourd. It would stop them from finding me. The power from that gourd was enough to confuse and throw anyone off my trail. What I didn't count on was them hiring a Native American from the outside to hunt me down. They're smarter than I gave them credit for."

"Why did you want to leave?" Diana asked. "Couldn't you go to your boss and tell him you wanted to quit?"

Laughing harshly, Ruth moved the wand of sage in a gentle semicircle from right to left, dispersing more of the thick, pungent smoke. "Quit? My dear young woman, there is no such thing as 'quitting' Psi-Lab. I've been their virtual prisoner since I was ten years old." Her face hardened, emphasizing the lines at the corners of her mouth and eyes. "I was a slave of sorts, to do their psychic bidding. I had no life of my own. I lost my marriage...."

Diana looked at Wes. What would he do? Would he make Ruth come back with them? Back to Psi-Lab? The woman was terribly unhappy about the prospect.

"What was the argument in the casita all about?" Wes asked.

Ruth gave him a pained look and sat back down, the sage carefully cradled between her thin fingers. "Elmer came to pick me up after I'd put the gourd in place. We had a horrendous argument because I was feeling guilty about leaving Psi-Lab, and he jumped all over me about it, about what they were doing to me— messing with my head, messing with my life.... They were, you know. I felt as though I had to stay at Psi-Lab. If I didn't, many of my friends, people I literally grew up with, would be left in danger." She shrugged.

"In danger?" Diana asked.

"Yes. You see, in our own metaphysical way, we're in the business of discovering the enemy's strengths and weaknesses. Usually, during sleep lab, we'd travel astrally via what you call an OOB—an out-of-body experience—to a prearranged overseas mission, as a team. Everyone relied on me. I did most of the traveling, most of the defending when we were on an astral journey somewhere to eavesdrop on a conversation or ferret out a piece of information deep inside some high-security-clearance place." She gently set the sage back onto the rich, red earth between her legs. "I was afraid if I left, I'd be leaving my friends wide open and defenseless. That's not true, but it was the fear they'd programmed into me. Elmer made me see the reality. That was the crux of the argument."

Diana felt the power around the medicine man. He was no one to be trifled with. "You left because there was no other choice?"

"None," Ruth answered flatly. She looked at Wes. "You're military. You know how the government functions. Once a marine, always a marine—that's the saying. Well, it applies in top-secret areas, too, especially one like Psi-Lab. We're a very hush-hush, super-specialized unit with a small family of coworkers. We can't talk to anyone about what we do, the stresses, the strains." She grimaced. "That's why I lost my marriage. I had horrible responsibilities and stresses on me, but I couldn't even talk to my husband about them. I couldn't talk to anyone. Psi-Lab officials didn't care about me as a human being they just wanted to squeeze me dry of my psychic abilities. I'm sure they would have wadded me up and thrown me away once I burned out. I think that's what scared me into planning to run away and cover my trail after me. I've seen them do it before, and some of those poor souls who wanted to quit or retire ended up in insane asylums, locked away, prisoners forever." Ruth grimaced. "So much for government pension and all that. No, with my kind, the superpsychics, once we've burned out, we conveniently disappear and our families are told that we're undercover. Maybe six months later, the family receives a visit from a government chaplin telling them we've died in the line of duty. Of course, it's not true. We've just been put away—permanently. There was no way I was going out like that. No way."

Horrified, Diana stared openmouthed at Ruth. "Are you serious? They'd lock you up in an asylum?"

She chuckled, but it was a deadly sound. "That's right."

"But...why?" Diana insisted. "You served your country. Why would they reward you like that?"

"Because," Ruth said in an undertone, "we're the elite. We have Q-Clearance. Psi-Lab officials are afraid that if any of us filter back into the general population, we might talk. They're deathly afraid of us spilling the beans on what we do there for them. In order to minimize that risk, the older members of our team conveniently 'disappear.'"

"Can you prove this?" Wes demanded, scowling.

"What's there to prove?" Ruth shrugged. "One of my dear old friends, Tony Lodge, visited me astrally one night. He woke me from a deep sleep. Clearly terrified, he begged me to follow him, to let him show me where they'd taken him." She gave Wes a guarded look. "You see, Tony had just retired after thirty years of service to Psi-Lab. He was looking forward to moving to a cabin in Montana, where he planned to fish for the rest of his life. They had a retirement party for him. And of course, we all had sugarplums dancing in our heads about Tony getting to leave Psi-Lab and fish happily in Montana. We were wrong." Ruth crouched down and sifted some red soil through her fingers, watching the particles fall back to earth. "I followed Tony astrally to where his physical body was lying. He was at an insane asylum in upper Vermont, near the Canadian border." Her mouth thinned as she looked up at them. "He told me they'd escorted him to the airport as planned, but on the way there, they'd shot him full of drugs that knocked him out. When he regained consciousness some time later, he was in a padded cell."

Standing, Ruth dusted off her hands. "That was just the beginning of my reality check with Psi-Lab and how it cares for its patriotic employees, Mr. McDonald. I could tell you other stories, but I won't. I was able to prove, at least to myself, that the government had Tony's sisters and brothers convinced that he'd gone undercover and been killed. The funeral was closed casket, so who knew if poor Tony was in there or not?" She smiled grimly. "Neat and tidy, aren't they?"

Wes nodded. "If it's true, yes, they are. So instead of trying to retire, you've just disappeared on them?"

"That's right. I'm not going to end up like Tony. If I thought I could get him out of that padded cell, I'd do it. But I'm only one person, and he's heavily guarded by two feds posing as doctors at that facility. You see, I found the place isn't really for the insane, it's for government spies and the like who know too much, who the federal government can't trust to go back into mainstream America. Instead, they tidily put them away—forever."

Wes gave a slow nod. As a member of the elite Delta Force team, he'd heard rumors along this line, but had never talked to someone close to the situation—or the truth. He had seen other highly secret government departments make decisions that might have been more in their best interests than in those of the person or people involved.

Ruth rubbed her hands down the sides of her Levi's. "Well, you have a choice to make. Are you going to take me back against my will or let me walk free?"

Wes compressed his lips. He glanced sideways at Diana's very readable features and saw she was silently begging him to let Ruth Horner walk away. "Can you give me a good reason why I shouldn't take you back?" he asked quietly.

"I have a God-given right to live my own life the way I see fit," Ruth answered in a low voice. "Psi-Lab owned me, Mr. McDonald, just as Delta Force owned you for the time you were with them. Maybe you enjoyed what you did with them, but I don't like what I do. I work on the dark underside of metaphysics. I fight battles in the unseen dimensions. I'm sick of the power struggles, the death...."

Uncomfortably, Wes nodded. He realized that Ruth was reading his mind to know he had been in Delta Force. "A reluctant warrior?"

"You could say that, among other things." She pointed to her lined face. "I'm fifty years old. I want what's left of my life for me. I don't want to be owned by the company store anymore, Mr. McDonald. That's what Elmer and I were doing: performing a cutting-away ceremony to free me of Psi-Lab forever. And right in the middle of the ceremony, you walked in. How ironic." She shook her head and sat down next to her teacher again.

Diana bit her lower lip. If she had her way, she'd let Ruth go. It was obvious the woman was tired, embittered and needing rest. But unfortunately, it wasn't Diana's decision to make. It was up to Wes. Silently, she pleaded with him to make the right choice.

Slowly unwinding, Wes stood up. He looked down at Diana and saw her eyes filled with anguish and hope. Without a doubt, he could feel her, could sense what she wanted him to do. The Yavapai medicine man was staring at him, too, his eyes as unblinking as those of a deadly rattlesnake. When Wes looked into Ruth Horner's eyes, he saw a tired, jaded human being who had been asked to do too much for too long. He was all too familiar with that feeling himself, after serving with Delta Force. His responsibilities had been many; the lives lost beneath his command would be on his conscience until the day he died.

"Okay," he told Ruth quietly, "we'll leave. I'll make out a report tonight for Psi-Lab and fax it to their office tomorrow, saying that we came to a dead end in our search for you."

Ruth nodded, tears springing to her eyes.

Filled with joy, Diana gasped. How badly she wanted to hug Wes, but now was not the time or place.

"Thank you for your heart, your understanding, Mr. McDonald," the older woman said.

Elmer spoke up. "He's an honorable warrior. He knows what you have walked through. He honors the courage of your convictions."

Wes nodded. "Warriors get tired, too," he agreed. "You're not stealing government secrets, and you're not in trouble or danger at all, so it's an easy decision for us to make." Looking around the cave, he noticed the small tree at the rear of the cave that Diana had described earlier. Pride moved through him as she rose and joined him, her arm sliding about his waist.

Ruth stood up and walked over to Wes, her hand extended. "May you walk in peace, too, Mr. Mc-Donald."

Diana smiled through the tears.

"I'm trying to, Ms. Horner." He released her cool, slender hand.

"I'm going to miss my friends and colleagues at Psi-Lab," she told them, her voice trembling with emotion. "I wish—I wish you could tell them that I'm all right, that I'm safe, but I know you can't. I wish I could warn them about their fate, but I can't even do that. I don't even dare astral travel to any of them for fear they trace me back to where I'm living."

"Maybe a letter written in some city you're passing through might do the job. You could tell them you're safe, happy," Wes suggested gently, realizing the trauma that Ruth Horner was going through. How would he feel, cut off from his buddies still in Delta Force? He didn't have many friends, but the ones he had, he cherished. His respect for Ruth's courage increased.

"That's a thought," Ruth mumbled, wiping her eyes self-consciously with the back of her hand.

"Just be sure to mail the letter without fingerprints, so the FBI can't trace it to you."

She laughed a little. "Well, where I'm going to live, no one would find me, believe me."

"Good." Wes wasn't about to ask where that was. If he was asked by Psi-Lab officials, he wanted to be able to answer honestly that he didn't know. He put his hand up in a sign of farewell to them. "We'd better get going. I've got a Sedona police officer at the bottom of the trailhead, waiting to hear if we've found you."

Diana disengaged her arm from Wes and impulsively reached out, throwing both arms around Ruth. How thin and strong she was! "May there be rainbows in your life, Ruth. Walk in peace with the Great Spirit," she whispered before she broke the embrace.

Ruth smiled and sniffed. "Thank you, Diana." She touched her shoulder momentarily. Lowering her voice to a bare whisper, she said, "And take care of this man of yours. His heart's open now, and you're so special to him...."

Smiling softly, Diana nodded. "I will, and thanks."

"One more thing, before you leave," Ruth said with a frown. Pinning most of her attention on Diana, she asked, "Have you ever heard of a half-blood medicine man by the name of Rogan Horsekiller?"

"No," Diana said.

"He's trouble," Ruth warned darkly. "Ask your mother if she knows of him." She glanced back at Elmer. "I swore I was done with psychic work, but Elmer was telling me of this métis medicine man who is a power stalker. He's causing a lot of problems within the Native American community. Elmer's worried that Horsekiller has big plans. Bad ones."

"I've never heard of him," Diana said lamely.

"Well, you will. Sooner or later. Just inform your mother so she's prepared for the bastard."

"I will. Thanks."

Wes took Diana's hand. "Come on, let's go talk to that policeman."

"Are you hungry?" Wes asked casually. They sat in a small vegetarian restaurant on the outskirts of Sedona. At 3:00 p.m. the place was relatively empty of customers, and the booth they sat in was at the rear, where there was less chance of being overheard.

Diana took a drink of a thick carob milkshake. She blotted off the mustache left by the shake with her paper napkin. "Would it be unseemly to admit I'm hungry for you, not food?"

Wes had the good grace to blush. "You're a pretty brazen lady."

"Wait until you get to know the rest of me."

His grin broadened and he reached across the Formica table to grasp her hand. "I like a bold woman."

"Being around you takes every ounce of my courage," Diana admitted, nudging the milkshake in Wes's direction. He'd been eyeing it ever since its arrival at the table.

"Thanks." He took a few sips and sat back, watching her. "I hope Ruth is going to be happy."

"Do you believe what she said about Psi-Lab? Putting their burned-out or retired psychics into a special government-run mental ward?" Shivering, Diana added, "It sounds horrible."

Wes nodded. "I don't think she's lying. But I don't know the whole truth of it, either. Who knows? Maybe

Tony *was* mentally deranged by what he did for Psi-Lab. Maybe he wasn't to be trusted out in the world again." With a shrug, he added, "I get the sense that, because of the high paranoia of their work, being spies in a psychic or metaphysical sense could breed that kind of suspicion. I've met some pretty crazy spies who were undercover too long, too stressed-out or broken to really function normally. Maybe what Ruth saw was the government's way of helping someone who'd been shattered by his work the best they knew how. Maybe Tony wasn't really a prisoner."

"But why would they have told his family he was dead?"

Wes shook his head. "I don't know. I don't think Ruth has all the answers, and I know we don't. Like I said, the government operates in gray areas, not black-and-white ones."

"It's all so macabre, Wes. Frightening. Our own government!"

"Honey," he said, putting the glass aside, "being in Delta Force taught me a lot about the quirks and foibles of our government. Things aren't always as they seem."

"Yes, but to imprison people for the rest of their lives just because they had burned out..."

"I know, I know."

"Do you think the report you make out to Psi-Lab will be sufficient? Do you think they'll send someone else to hunt Ruth down?"

"I don't know." Wes squeezed her fingers, longing to lean over and kiss her ripe, soft lips. "You can help me write the report. You're the psychic. You'll know what to say to throw those goons from Psi-Lab off her track.''

The warmth of his fingers, the way he caressed her hand, filled Diana with an undeniable need. Need for him. "I had so many questions to ask Ruth. How do they recruit their clairvoyant people? And what's this about killing? Mother said that she's been in some psychic battles where, if she lost, she would not have been able to go back to her physical body, and over time, she would have died.''

"That possibility right there would stop me from wanting to be a psychic,'' Wes said wryly.

"Believe me, when you grow up in a psychic household like I did, you see all sides of the gift. I guess that's why I've resisted becoming a medicine woman in training with my mother. My sister went her own way, and she's a shaman, but that's dangerous work, too. No,'' Diana murmured, turning over her hands and looking at her palms, "I like being something simple, like a psychometrist.''

"Simple?'' Wes teased. "There's nothing 'simple' about you, honey. You're complex and you have a lot of facets.'' He kissed her fingers. "Like a diamond.''

She flushed. "Is that how you see me?''

He eased out of the booth, drew a couple of dollars from his billfold and placed them on the table. He smiled down at her. "If I told you the truth, I wonder what you'd say or do?''

Rising, Diana slid her hand into his as they exited the restaurant. "No matter what you told me, Wes, it wouldn't scare me into leaving you, if that's what you're worried about.'' She thought about his childhood, the fact that the one person he loved most in the world, his mother, had left him and later died. Did Wes think, because she was woman, she was capable of abandoning him, too?

The heat of the day hit them as they stepped out of the restaurant. Wes led Diana to the rental car and opened the door. He leaned down and kissed her quickly on the mouth.

"I'm glad you can't read my mind."

Her lips tingled, and she reached up and grazed his cheek. "Why?"

"Because," he said lightly, holding the door for her while she got into the car, "I feel like some wretched, impoverished gold miner with you. You're the biggest, most beautiful gold nugget I've ever seen, and now I'm feeling greedy—like I want to keep you to myself forever. I'm afraid if I let you out of my sight, you'll disappear like a dream I've been dreaming all my life."

Touched, Diana waited until Wes got into the car. As she strapped on the seat belt, she turned to him. The heat in the car was stifling until he turned on the air conditioner. "What have you been dreaming, Wes?"

He sat for a moment, his hands resting on the steering wheel. "After college I entered the army, and I saw a lot of marriages go on the rocks. I saw friends who loved each other get torn apart by the long duty hours, the overseas time apart. The duty put incredible strains on a marriage. I decided I wasn't going that way."

He turned to her. "My foster parents had a good marriage, Diana. Growing up with them gave me a whole perspective on life. They loved each other deeply. They could never have children, and they were happy to have me. When I left for college, I was determined to have a marriage like theirs.''

"Not all marriages in the military break up, do they?''

"No, not all, but a high percentage do,'' he said wearily. "What I wasn't counting on was getting drafted by Delta Force right off the bat. It's too high-powered an organization, Diana. The time you spend in training alone is enough to shatter any except the strongest marriage. I saw my fellow officers struggling to hold it together, and I knew I didn't want that.'' He picked up her hand and held it gently in his. "I wanted one marriage. I wanted forever. I didn't want to lose the woman I fell in love with.''

Diana's hand tingled. "You were afraid of love?''

"No. I wanted it. I'm human. I wanted to be able to settle down, go home at night, kiss the wife, hug the kids—all that stuff.'' Wes gazed down at her work-worn hand—a hand that made his heart sing, made him want her all over again. He looked up at her. "I made a decision,'' he told her heavily. "I knew then that love and marriage couldn't work for me because of the demands and stresses of my job in Delta Force. The other thing I worried about was what if I got killed and left behind a wife and children?''

Diana nodded, seeing the roots of his logic. "Your mother gave you up and died,'' she whispered, a catch in her voice. "You didn't want to leave anyone behind, didn't want them abandoned as you were abandoned.''

"That's right," Wes admitted softly. "I knew what it felt like to be alone. For so many years, Diana, I lived off an anger that fueled me. That's partly why I agreed to join Delta Force—I was a living time bomb of rage. I had to work it off, work it out somehow." His eyes grew sad. "I didn't want my own children ever to have to suffer the kind of rage and hatred I felt for so many years toward my real mother and my situation."

"You aren't angry with her any longer, are you?"

He gave a sharp laugh and released Diana's hand, leaning back against the seat. Staring out the window at the blue, cloudless sky, he said, "Not anymore. Ten years of aggression is enough to wring out any amount of bitterness and rage."

"And that's why you left the army? Delta Force?"

Wes rolled his head to the right and held her gaze. "When the anger had finally worked through me, I felt hollow. Empty. I woke up one morning in the B.O.Q. and wondered what the hell I was living for. I realized a lot that morning, Diana. I realized my mother had done the best she could for me under the circumstances. To this day, I wonder how she managed to give me up for adoption, because there is plenty of evidence that she did love me." His mouth quirked. "When I was eighteen, my parents gave me a small box of letters my real mother had written to them. I still have them."

Diana felt pain in her heart for him. She reached over and gently caressed his arm. She could feel the tension Wes still held over his painful childhood. "The fact she loved you enough to give you up tells me she had an incredible kind of courage."

"Yeah," he sighed, "she loved me more than she did herself. Figure that one out. She thought so little of herself that she let drugs run her life and kill her."

"But she wanted a better, more positive life for you."

"Yes." Wes's lips thinned. "So, once I realized all of this, I quit Delta Force. I had a lot of leave accrued, and I just wandered for about a year, all over the face of the earth. But everywhere I went, I felt empty. I drank a lot. I partied a lot. I tried to find out why I couldn't *feel* anymore." He tapped his gut. "I didn't find an answer, so I came back stateside. That's when one of my friends told me Morgan Trayhern of Perseus was hiring qualified mercenaries." His mouth curved slightly. "I was hired within two weeks, after a lot of testing and snooping into my background. Trayhern doesn't hire just anybody. He's got to know his staff is trustworthy."

"And you've been working for Perseus for how long?"

"A year."

"Do you like the work?"

The corners of his mouth curved a little more. "It's been okay. At least with Perseus there's satisfaction in getting a mission accomplished. That was a new one for me. At Delta Force, we had a lot of scrubbed missions. We would train for months, even years, then go out on a possible mission only to have it scrubbed. It was frustrating. With Morgan's company, I'm able to go in, do the job on my own terms, complete it and walk away from it."

"But you didn't want this mission, did you?"

Wes laughed as he picked up her hand and squeezed it. "No. But I'm awfully damn glad now that I took it."

Her heart beat a little harder. "Do you understand the psychic gift I have now?"

He held Diana's uncertain gaze, seeing the fear in her eyes. "Are you asking if I believe in your gift?"

She shrugged. "I guess I am. It's important that you accept me for who and what I am, Wes. I know at the beginning, you thought I was a fake."

"Not a fake," he remonstrated gently. "Never that. I just hadn't run into the kind of world you lived in. It was foreign."

"You used the word *alien*."

"Yes, I did. That's how I felt—at first." Wes held her hand more tightly, aware how much it meant to Diana to have him accept her abilities. "Try to put yourself in my place for a moment. Try to understand that I had no education whatsoever in metaphysics. To you, it's like breathing air. To me, it's something strange that I can't prove."

"But you've seen it work, Wes. I was accurate on all counts about what I felt in that casita. What I saw after holding that gourd."

"Yes," he said, "I realize that now. I still can't prove how it works, Diana, but I do recognize your gift. I believe in you, in your abilities, whatever they are. Okay?"

Relief splintered through her and her eyes grew as she stared at Wes. He wasn't kidding her at all; he was serious. "Oh...good."

He grinned. "What do you say we go back to the hotel?"

A feeling of satisfaction soared through Wes as he left the hotel office. The night was alive with a swath of stars that blanketed the wide sky above Sedona. He whistled softly, happier than he could ever recall being. The fax detailing his report on Ruth Horner had been sent to Morgan at Perseus, and he was very sure the Psi-Lab officials would stop looking for her after receiving it. Shrugging his shoulders, feeling many loads he'd been carrying slip free, he smiled to himself.

Could anyone have predicted that in three days' time he would feel like a new man? Feel real hope for the first time in his life? He thought not. Diana's compassionate face filled his vision, filled his heart. She was soft in so many ways—ways in which he was still hard and unyielding. Diana would teach him about dissolving those barriers he'd lived behind for so many years. She'd teach him about living fully, with all his senses and emotions engaged.

He found Diana out on the deck of their cabin overlooking Oak Creek. The starlight gave a mute radiance to the darkened deck and emphasized the knee-length white cotton nightgown she wore. She turned, as if sensing his presence, because he knew he'd made no noise in approaching. The nightgown was simple but revealed her lovely curves, the lace at her throat emphasizing her femininity. A hair brush was in her hands, and Wes smiled as he drew near.

"Come here, I want to brush that beautiful hair of yours." He pulled up two lounge chairs and placed them one in front of the other. Wes liked the way her eyes smiled, the way her lips parted at his unexpected request. Taking the brush, he guided her to the chair. She sat with her back to him.

"This is something I've been wanting to do ever since we met," he told her in a low voice as he began to unbraid her thick hair.

With a moan of pleasure, Diana closed her eyes. "You are spoiling me absolutely rotten, Wes Mc-Donald."

He allowed the glistening strands to fall between his fingers. "I'm spoiling both of us. I've always wondered what it would be like to brush a woman's hair." Picking up the brush, he whispered near her ear, "Now I'm going to find out."

A shiver of pleasure raced up Diana's ear and neck as he placed several small, moist kisses beneath her earlobe. "You talk of dreams," she said as he began to gently move the brush through her hair. "You're one to me."

"I don't see how," Wes said with a grimace, being very careful not to pull her hair and hurt her. "I was a hard son of a bitch when you met me."

"Still," she said, "there was something about you that drew me, Wes." Her eyes remaining closed, she absorbed his touch as her hair cascaded about her shoulders. "I could tell you were hurting. I could sense it."

"But I was taking it out on you."

"I know." Her lips parted and the corners turned upward as he tunneled his fingers through her hair. He began to gently massage her scalp, and she lost all thought and simply felt his gentle assault upon her. For a warrior, Wes was incredibly tender. In her mind, Diana replayed their earlier conversation in the car, about him wanting a home, a wife and a family.

Easing away just enough to turn around, she faced him. The satisfaction burning in his eyes made her respond effortlessly as she framed his face with her hands. She could feel the prickle of his beard beneath her palms, feel the warmth of him as a man. His shadowy eyes burned with desire for her.

"When we go home to Cherokee, I'll take you to a small cabin on a stream that by mom owns. I'd like to stay there for a week just hiking, fishing and sharing with you."

"Sounds good," Wes rasped as he slid his hands around her waist and drew her onto his lap. Diana settled against him, her arms going around his neck. As she rested her head against his jaw, he sighed. "I'm still afraid this is a dream," he admitted slowly. "That you're a figment of my desperate imagination. I've dreamed so long of being able to fall in love, Diana. To dare to think that someone might love me as much as I loved her. To marry and—" he ran his hand gently across her curved abdomen "—to watch a baby grow inside the woman I love, knowing it belongs to both of us. Knowing that the child would have two loving parents who would never give her or him up—ever."

Diana caressed his hair with her fingers and felt his pain and his dream. There was such fragility in Wes, so much hope linked to so much desperation from his past. "Among the Cherokee people, children are sacred," she whispered near his ear. "Sacred and greatly loved and protected. An outsider might say we spoil them, but we spoil them with love."

Wes closed his eyes, his hand resting gently against her belly. She was warm and soft against him, and the light scent of gardenias filled his nostrils. "Morgan's going to be awfully disappointed that I'm taking all this time off, but he'll understand. He loves his family with a fierceness I've rarely seen in a man. But then, he lost a lot, too, so he knows...."

With a gentle smile, Diana raised her head just enough to connect with his shadowed gaze. "And you will, too. People who lose that much very often cherish what is given back to them. I don't think you'll be an exception, darling."

Burying his face in her thick, silky hair, Wes held Diana with a fierceness that spoke of his love, his commitment to her—to their future—forever.

* * * * *

Dear Reader,

The warrior breed stands apart from all other types of men. Nothing is more dangerous than a mercenary. Nothing is more mysterious than one. Wes Montgomery, once an officer in Delta Force, has a dark past that plagues him. Trained for years in the army as one of the most lethal warriors in the world, he turns to Morgan's Mercenaries after he leaves the service. He is a man in pain, who believes in nothing and no one but himself. Meeting a woman with psychic gifts couldn't be more far afield from his view of reality. I found Wes fascinating. I hope you do, too!

Lindsay McKenna

STORM-TOSSED

Lee Karr

PROLOGUE

With the roar of a monstrous beast, raging winds uprooted huge oak trees on a knoll behind the clinic. The rain-soaked earth gave way with thunderous cracks. Gnarled roots rose like tentacles from the earth, stabbing the air as they broke free from the ground. Leaves, sand and rain spewed upward. Debris whipped across the ground, greedily sucked into a churning cauldron as dark waters crept closer.

The cries of children called to him. Love stronger than the manacles of eternity summoned his anguished spirit from its torment. With a shrieking cry that rose above the demonic holocaust, he broke free.

CHAPTER ONE

Standing behind her desk, Elizabeth Preston sent an anxious glance out her office window. The catch on one of the metal shutters had broken loose and a large expanse of glass was exposed as the shutter banged against the outside wall. She knew she was at risk but the need to find transportation kept her at her desk, making frantic calls.

"This is Elizabeth Preston of the Charleston Psychiatric Clinic. I have three patients waiting for transport inland, plus three personnel," Elizabeth explained to a man in the State Emergency Preparedness Office. "We're one vehicle short. It was supposed to be here but hasn't shown up. Can you help us out?"

"Charleston Psychiatric Clinic?" he repeated wearily. "Where are you located?"

"East on Highway 17, just beyond the tidal creek bridge on Pirate Island."

She heard the man suck in his breath. "All the island roads are clogged with vehicles trying to get inland," he replied in a frazzled tone. "The whole coastline is on emergency alert. We've got every available cruiser out warning people that they must leave without delay. I don't have any vehicles that haven't already been assigned."

"We have three children patients who *must* be transported inland to another clinic in Columbia." She tried to keep a rising panic from her voice. Once the hurricane touched land, the chance for evacuation would be gone. "You have to find something!"

"Believe me, I would if I could. We just don't have the resources to meet all the demands," he answered defensively. Hurricane Andrea churned and spun off the South Carolina coast with winds up to one hundred and ten miles per hour.

"We can't stay here." Evacuation of the clinic had been nearly completed by midafternoon. Everything had moved smoothly until the last medical van failed to show.

"I'm sorry, ma'am. I really am. We've tapped all the public resources available. The trip to Columbia is taking eight hours. The roads are clogged. Only one-way traffic out. If you leave now, you'll be en route when the full force of the hurricane hits. My advice is to take as many precautions as you can—and pray. In the meantime, I'll do the best I can."

Her lower lip trembled as she hung up. The storm was a crazed monster angrily tearing at the building, screeching, hammering against the walls with diabolical frenzy as if the legions of hell had been set loose upon the earth. She'd never been so terrified in her life.

A shroud of black clouds covered the sun, putting the landscaped grounds in deep shadows. Rain came down in slanted sheets. Leaves whirled upward as trees arched in the fierce wind, and debris flew against the stucco building. A cacophony of noises rose over the roaring of the wind and rain. The whole building vibrated as if it might be lifted off its foundation at any moment—and the real force of the storm was still offshore! According to weather predictions, the brunt of the hurricane would hit after dark.

Frantically she glanced over her list of emergency numbers again. She'd already called them all, some of them twice. There had to be—

That thought was cut off by a cracking boom. Her eyes jerked to the window just as a branch of a large oak tree began to splinter.

"Down!" someone shouted from the hall doorway behind her.

The crash of glass came at the same instant that two strong arms threw her to the floor and rolled her under the desk. As the branch flew into the room, shards of glass scattered in every direction. The wind tore pictures off the wall, crashed objects to the floor and swirled papers out a gaping hole in the ceiling. A scream caught at the back of her throat. The earth was exploding.

Cold fear ran through her as she cowered under the desk. She shivered and the strong arms around her tightened. She couldn't see her rescuer's face. His breathing rose and fell in measured rhythm, a mockery to her thumping heart and quickened breath. Her gaze fell on the hands holding her. They were broad, suntanned, and a tarnished gold ring set with a cat's-eye stone circled one finger. As she stared at the amber stone, it glowed with hypnotic dazzle. Her breath suddenly short, she shut her eyes against the glow, feeling a rise of emotion she didn't understand.

He was a stranger—she knew that. Yet as impossible as it seemed, she recognized this man on some deep level that went beyond words and senses. A compelling force that radiated from him was in some indefinable way a part of the storm. She felt a bewildering sense of familiarity and an emotional connection with him that had no basis in reality.

She pushed against the man, trying to free herself. "I have to go. See to the others."

The weakened wall of the office could come crashing in on them any minute. And what about the rest of the main building? The two resident wings? She couldn't stay cowering under her desk. The nurse, her aide and the three young children were waiting in the dayroom to be transported out of this hell. Everybody else had been evacuated with Dr. Radison, the clinic's medical executive. Those who were left were her responsibility. Her stomach churned. She cared about the children more than anything in the world and she was filled with a terrifying helplessness. Dear God, how was she going to keep them safe?

"The children . . ."

"Listen to me."

She gasped at the sound of his voice and lifted her head enough to glimpse a cleft chin, bronze skin and dark hair.

He tightened his grip and pressed his mouth against her ear to be heard above the bedlam. "The hall door may be hard to open. We'll go together."

They backed out from under the desk and bent forward against the wind's fury and pelting rain. Pressure against the door was as fierce as he had predicted.

He opened it enough for them to squeeze through into the hall before it slammed shut again.

She leaned against the wall, gasping for breath. Her head was reeling and every nerve in her body was raw edged.

"Are you all right?" he asked, standing close enough to steady her if she wavered. His damp red Windbreaker clung to a magnificent torso and his black shirt was open at his tanned neck. Black pants hugged his flat stomach and outlined long, muscular legs. Longish black hair drifted forward on his well-molded cheeks. An ugly scar pulled one black eyebrow upward and spoiled the symmetry of his rugged features.

A piercing shaft of light in his eyes held her gaze much beyond her willingness to be drowned in their murky blue-black depths. His presence disturbed her in some way she couldn't define. A rise of panic was at odds with the knowledge that his presence was a blessing she should grab with both hands. She needed all the help she could get. No time for melodramatic impressions, she told herself, giving a firm lift to her chin.

As his gaze passed over her face and traveled down the length of her nearly six-foot slender frame, she was suddenly conscious of her bedraggled appearance. Her short white skirt had twisted to one side and her soft peach blouse was pulled out at the waist. Under his scrutiny she made an effort to smooth back damp blond hair plastered on her cheeks.

"I'm fine," she finally said. "Thanks for your help." Then her eyes suddenly rounded with a spark of hope. "You aren't, by any chance, the driver of the van we requested?"

"I'm afraid not, Elizabeth."

She was taken aback by the use of her first name—even though it was plainly printed on her office door. The intensity of his mesmerizing gaze softened as he reached out and removed two leaves stuck to the top of her head. "If you are going to ride out the storm, it's foolish not to have all the doors and windows boarded up."

His criticism broke through the haze of unreality. Her temper flared. She'd never been very gracious about accepting unwarranted criticism under the best of circumstances, and the tension she was presently under made her temper even shorter. It was Dr. Radison who should be here. He was the medical director, after all, but he'd left with the first evacuation vehicle. She didn't need this stranger dumping the blame for the ugly situation on her. "Thank you for the advice, Mr. . . . ?"

His eyelids flickered in a thoughtful way. Then a hint of a self-mocking smile touched his lips as if he were enjoying a private joke. "Davin Delmar."

Davin Delmar. She couldn't remember seeing the name on any of the records. "You have someone here at the clinic?"

Before he could answer, a deafening roar like a giant buzz saw ripped through the building. Elizabeth stifled a scream and instinctively grabbed his arm as her eyes flew upward to the acoustic ceiling. Fright pounded in her ears. She was used to Chicago blizzards. Anybody with any sense stayed indoors while one was raging. In the warmth and protection of a solid roof and firm walls, a winter storm could even bring a feeling of security and peace. But there was nothing but raw terror and vulnerability in a storm like this. Roofs and walls could be instruments of death if the building couldn't withstand the fiendish destruction reaped upon it. Another jetlike boom roared down the hall.

"Who's left in the building?" he demanded.

"Three patients . . . children. A nurse, and an aide." Elizabeth swallowed back a lump of terror. *Damn Dr. Radison. Damn his yellow hide.* Fury sent adrenaline flowing through her. The medical director should have stayed in the clinic until the last person was evacuated. Her responsibilities were in the business office, ensconced behind a computer and poring over printout sheets. She wasn't prepared for a life-and-death situation involving five other human beings. *Prepared or not, start coping,* said an unsympathetic inner voice.

At that moment, Mrs. Tompkin, a stocky woman in a white nurse's uniform hurried down the hall toward them. Perspiration glistened on her middle-aged face. "You'd better come, Miss Preston . . . right away."

"What's wrong?" Elizabeth's heart stopped. She had left the three children in the dayroom with Mrs. Tompkin and the aide while they waited for the evacuation vehicle to show up.

"It's the aide, Marietta. She's frightening the children. I had everything under control until I sent the woman to the linen room to get some extra blankets. . . . I thought we'd better take some extra with us . . . you know, in case we might get stuck on the road longer than planned. According to the radio, the roads are jammed. . . . Anyway, Marietta came back shrieking hysterically about roots of falling trees tearing up the ground behind the clinic where the pirate cemetery is supposed to be. She's spouting that nonsense about the spirits of the murdered captain and his men leaving their graves during storms like this." The nurse snorted in disgust. "She's wailing as if she expects to be ravished at any moment."

Damn, swore Elizabeth silently. She didn't have time to waste on some ridiculous local superstition. The area directly behind the clinic was supposedly an old graveyard where the victims of a massacre were buried when early English settlers murdered the crew of a pirate ship that had been cast ashore. And according to the superstition, any deaths or tragedies that occurred during violent storms were caused by the evil spirits of the murdered seamen seeking revenge. It was all nonsense. Very often Elizabeth had eaten her lunch in the shade of those trees and her dreamlike fantasies had been anything but fearful. In fact, some of her musings filled her lonely life with a strange, comforting spirituality. "I'll talk to her," Elizabeth told the nurse briskly.

"I've got my hands full, Miss Preston. Marietta's no help. She's going on hysterically about ghosts and evil spirits when she should be tending to the children." The older woman scowled. "How much longer are we going to have to wait for transportation? When are we getting out of here?"

Elizabeth attempted to give the nurse a reassuring smile without answering her question but the older woman wasn't fooled. "God help us all." She turned and headed back down the hall.

"Damn, that's all I need," swore Elizabeth. "Some idiotic old wives' tale sending Marietta into hysterics."

She looked up into the stranger's eyes and saw that their color had darkened. His body was close enough to brush against hers and she was aware of the same dangerous sexual response she'd felt when his body shielded hers under the desk. As the hurricane's uproar vibrated in her ears, a bizarre need to feel his protective arms around her again overtook her. His expression was unreadable. She'd always had her emotions well under control when it came to romantic impulses. She was chilled and frightened by her response to this stranger. "I have to go, Mr. Delmar," she said briskly. She took a step away but he stopped her with a firm hold on her arm. The warmth of his fingers on her flesh was startling. Piercing. Burning. *It was as if the enraged storm flowed through him.* She jerked her arm away.

"There's no time to waste. I'm sorry if I frightened you but I can't help unless I know what the situation is," he said in a reasonable tone that mocked her rising hysteria. "You do want me to help, don't you, Elizabeth?" His midnight blue eyes searched hers.

She gave him a shaky nod even as a disturbing thought flickered through her mind. *Was there a price to pay for his help?*

"What precautions have been made to make the building secure?"

She gave herself a mental shake and tried to think. "I know that the building has weathered several tropical storms in the past. Most of the windows have metal shutters. I don't know about emergency supplies. When Andrea became a hurricane, Dr. Radison decided on evacuation."

"And he left three of his patients and staff?"

"He was certain that he had arranged for enough evacuation vehicles. Only...only he left before the last one arrived."

"He should have seen to the children." His voice was harsh. A deep torment in his eyes shocked her. His expression took on a frightening intensity.

He must be a parent of one of the children. That would explain his presence in the clinic. "I'm sure Dr. Radison would have remained if he'd known there was going to be a problem." Why she covered for her boss she didn't know. She put as much conviction into her voice as she could. "The last vehicle will probably be here momentarily."

"And if it isn't?"

"Then we'll have to cope." The strength of her voice surprised her since she was quivering inside like a vibrating leaf. *Cope.* How did one cope with a world suddenly devastated by an uncontrollable force?

"Has anyone determined which part of the building might be the safest?" he asked. She could feel his breath touching her cheeks as he leaned toward her.

"No, I...I..." she stammered.

"I'll check it out. We don't have much time. Get the children ready to move."

He didn't wait for her response. Before she could move, he was gone, out of sight in a nearby corridor. *Don't leave me!* The silent cry came from an unreasonable fear that he would disappear as suddenly as he had appeared in her office.

She hurried down the main hall to the children's dayroom, which was in the west wing of the building. Elizabeth could feel the force of the storm stronger in the annex hall. *Not a safe place.* She should have moved the three children to a different part of the building earlier. *But I thought we would be gone by now.*

She opened the door and glanced quickly at the three children she had come to know so well. Buddy Benson was a seven-year-old autistic boy who lived in his own world with a complacent, unruffled detachment. Elizabeth saw that he was sitting in his usual corner mesmerized by something in his lap that no one else could see. He constantly moved his head back and forth as if his straight chair was a rocker.

A little blond girl spun around and around in erratic circles, humming in a high-pitched tone. Her name was Debbie and she, too, was going on seven. The youngest child, Patty, only five years old, sat at a small round table tearing pages from a book as fast as her hands could move. She laughed merrily as she threw the sheets of paper up in the air with wild abandonment.

Nurse Tompkin caught Debbie in the middle of a spin. "Quiet," she ordered firmly as she eased the child down on a rug. "Quiet, Debbie. Quiet." The little girl's response was a blank stare but she stayed on the floor and continued her high-pitched humming.

"Good," the nurse told her, then hurried over to the girl who was destroying the book. "That's enough,

Patty." The nurse stilled the child's hands with her own. "Leave the book alone."

Elizabeth gave Mrs. Tompkin a grateful smile and then turned to Marietta who was standing at the nurses' station. An eighteen-year-old native of Barbados, the dark-haired young woman spoke English well, had a quiet manner that was good with children, but her serene composure had been shattered and her dark eyes betrayed an inner hysteria. She hugged herself as shivers attacked her slender body.

Elizabeth put an arm around the girl's waist. "It's all right, Marietta. Everything's under control," she lied. "We're going to move to a safer place."

"There's no safe place," she wailed.

"Marietta, you have to get a hold of yourself," Elizabeth said sharply. "We have to think of the children."

Tears ran down Marietta's cheeks and beads of sweat glistened on her forehead. Her lips trembled as she sobbed. "The graves are open, Miss Preston. I saw the trees fall. The earth flew up into the air. The evil spirits came out."

"Nonsense!"

"I saw them. They're coming after us."

"What you saw were leaves and branches whipped upward by the storm. There are no evil spirits. No open graves. All of that is just an old wives' tale."

Marietta set her chin and her eyes widened. "Captain Hawksley is going to find a woman and take her back to his grave."

Elizabeth's tone was sharper than she had intended but she didn't have time for such drivel. "There are no pirates preying on young women. No avenging sea captain. You've got to pull yourself together. We need your help with the children."

"Please, we can't stay here," she pleaded. "We have to get away." She seemed ready to bolt from the room.

Elizabeth grabbed her arm. "It's suicide to go out in a wind that's blowing a hundred and ten miles an hour and getting stronger every minute."

"Can't we get away from here? It's not safe," she wailed.

"There's no place guaranteed to be safe," Elizabeth said, turning up the volume on the small portable radio sitting on the nurses' desk. Thank heavens that Mrs. Tompkin had foresight enough to find one, she thought. Maybe relief was on the way. Surely, some kind of a rescue unit would come and take them to a shelter on the mainland.

"All coastal areas have been evacuated as Andrea moves inland. Hospitals and storm shelters are stockpiling food, water, fuel and medicine," reported the newscaster. "Sandbags have been issued to Charleston residents preparing to wait out the storm. Public buildings have been turned into shelters. A late bulletin—a hurricane just touched down on Myrtle Beach!"

Marietta screamed, and at first Elizabeth thought that Marietta's shriek was in response to the news on the radio. Then she saw that the young woman was pointing to the door.

Elizabeth swung around.

Davin Delmar stood there framed in the doorway, a dramatic figure in his red-and-black attire, and dark hair framing his bronze face.

"It's him," Marietta croaked with terrified eyes. "Captain Hawksley. He's come." A shudder racked her small body and she slumped to the floor.

her roll." Was the grinned after her had kept ivery
Captain Hawksley was behind [...] a double
[...] look and she turned it to the chief.

CHAPTER TWO

Before Elizabeth could react, Davin had brushed her aside and swept Marietta up into his arms. For a bewildering moment, Elizabeth was convinced that he was going to flee from the room with the limp girl clutched to his breast. Such a dramatic fantasy seemed ridiculous when he spun on his heels and laid Marietta gently on a nearby sofa. He moved back as Mrs. Tompkin bent over Marietta.

His dark eyes were hooded as he turned to Elizabeth. The black eyebrow that touched his scar raised. "What did she call me?"

"Hawksley."

His absorbing gaze held hers for a long moment. "Someone who frightens young women, I presume?"

"Local superstition has it that a murdered pirate, Captain Hawksley, and his men rise from their graves during a storm. Marietta saw the roots of a tree tear up the earth where the bodies of pirates are said to be buried and she swears she saw spirits escaping from the graves."

"So she believes that Captain Hawksley is wandering about looking for a young woman to carry back to the grave with him?"

"Exactly."

"And what do you think?"

"The dark tale gives Pirate Island a bit of local color, that's all. It's all nonsense, including the bit about that small knoll being a graveyard for dead pirates." Elizabeth gave a dismissing laugh. "I've spent some lovely moments sitting under those very trees. If there are any spirits there, they have only made me feel less lonely."

He reached out to touch a wisp of hair dangling on her forehead. "Aren't you afraid that the avaricious sea captain may choose you? He could be enchanted by the sea green flecks in your eyes. And the shimmer of your golden hair."

The poetic compliment took Elizabeth by surprise. She felt color sweeping up into her face even as she dismissed his remarks as out of line. This wasn't the time or the place for flirtatious foolishness.

His fingertip slipped down her cheek and cupped her chin. "There is danger, you know," he said solemnly as his eyes narrowed.

She pulled away from his touch. "Yes, I know. We have to make some decisions," she said in a brisk tone that she hoped hid the sudden warmth sluicing through her. "What's the situation in the rest of the building?"

All softness in his eyes disappeared. His expression hardened and his voice was laced with anger. "Bad. The outside walls are crumbling under the pressure of the winds. No one should have been left in this building!" Fury blazed in his eyes. "Especially the children."

"I told you. Arrangements had been made for another vehicle but it didn't show."

"All the children should have been evacuated first! The annexes are taking a beating. This wing is especially vulnerable."

"I...I didn't know," stammered Elizabeth. "It seemed the best place for the children to wait." Two wings of the bracket-shaped clinic bordered a center courtyard, the children's ward on one side and adult patients on the other. All of the other facilities were located in the main section.

"The center of the building would provide more protection. There's a room off the hall—"

At that moment a blast like a charging locomotive accompanied the sound of shattering glass and splintering timbers. It sounded as if that end of the clinic was being swept away.

Elizabeth stifled a scream. Davin headed for the door. She ran after him. "Where are you going?"

"To see what's left."

Her irrational impulse was to bolt from the room and run out of the building as fast as she could. She was convinced that the roof and walls were about to fall in. They would all be buried. The panic must have shown in her eyes for he quickly put his hands on her shoulders. "Easy...easy."

The contact was like a live current, snapping every sensory cell in her body. The wild clamor of the hurricane faded and a silence descended upon her. "I want to stay with you," she heard herself saying.

His startling blue eyes lost their shine. "It's not possible," he said.

"You can't leave me!"

A flash of pain crossed his face, his eyes dark and tormented. "I came for the children. I mustn't fail them again."

What was he talking about? His haunted expression frightened her. What horrible demons made his voice so tortured? She wanted to retreat from the darkness that seemed to engulf him. Why was she drawn by an indefinable psychic force and yet repelled by it?

His hands moved down her arms, holding her steady as he looked down into her face. "I'll come back for you."

She moistened her dry lips. "And if you don't?"

A muscle in his bronze cheek flickered. "I won't leave you until you're safe."

Her bewildered gaze searched his face, unspoken questions in her eyes.

"I came because you needed me," he said simply.

"But how did you know? We've never seen each other before today."

His mouth softened in a rueful smile. "That's only half true." A blast of air came in the room as he slipped into the hall and slammed the door behind him.

Elizabeth took a deep breath. The three children were still sitting passively where the nurse had left them and Marietta was beginning to stir on the sofa.

"She's coming round," Mrs. Tompkin said, not bothering to hide her irritation. "Just what we need in this situation. Someone blabbing about dead pirates and evil spirits."

Marietta's eyelids began to lift. A frightened cry broke from her throat. She cowered back against the cushions. "I saw him." She pointed to the door. "Standing there."

"You saw Davin Delmar," Elizabeth told her firmly. "He's no sea captain's ghost but someone who is going to help us cope with this emergency."

"It was Hawksley!" Marietta insisted with a hysterical sob.

"Stop this nonsense!" snapped Mrs. Tompkin. "Marietta, I need help with these children. We've got to be ready when transportation gets here." Her eyes met Elizabeth's. "We *are* going to evacuate, aren't we?"

"I don't know," Elizabeth confessed. "I've called every emergency number several times. Asked for help from all available services. I was told that requests for help have exceeded the State Emergency Preparedness Office's resources. Their representative said he'd try but he made no promises."

"If we're not going to evacuate we'll have to make sure we've got water, food and medicine within reach," Mrs. Tompkin said practically. "I've been in storms before and if the building stays dry, we'll be all right."

As if to mock her words, a gush of water came under the crack in the door and formed a growing puddle on the brown carpet.

Mrs. Tompkin's ruddy complexion turned a sickly color. "If the building floods we'll have no place to go. A tidal wave could wash the whole thing away—and us with it!"

Elizabeth's stomach made a sickening plunge. They could hear the wind shrieking like a monster as it battered the building. The full force of the storm was

hours away and the clinic had already begun to col-
lapse. *Was there any room in the building that would
stay dry?*

The older woman's eyes fixed on Elizabeth as if to
say *You're in charge. What do we do now?*

Elizabeth returned her steady stare, trying to look
calm and firmly in control while an inner voice
shrieked, *I don't know what to do.* She walked quickly
across the room to the nurses' desk and tried the
phone. No tone. The telephone was out. How long
would the electricity stay on? The radio was already
reporting blackouts in some areas. A decision borne of
desperation made her announce in a general's crisp
tone. "We'll have to transport ourselves."

"What?" gasped Mrs. Tompkin.

"If no vehicle is coming for us, we'll have to provide our own," she told her. Her small coupé could
take three people squeezed in the front. "What kind of
a car do you drive, Mrs. Tompkin? How many people
could you take?"

The nurse shook her head. "I don't drive to work. I
ride with one of the waitresses who works at the Sea-
haven Hotel. She called me an hour after I got here this
morning and told me she was heading back home as
fast as possible. She wanted me to leave. I told her that
I had to stay with the children."

Marietta said that she lived on the island and walked
to work.

Six people plus Davin. *He must have a car. Where
was he?* Why was he chasing off when the building was
crumbling around them? They had to leave now! The

clinic wasn't going to survive the brunt of the storm. They had to get off the island to the mainland.

Marietta was obviously relieved to hear they were leaving but the nurse shook her head. "We'd better stay put. You're new to this part of the country, Miss Preston. You don't have storms like this up north."

"No, thank God," breathed Elizabeth.

"A snow storm is nothing like a tropical hurricane," Mrs. Tompkin told her needlessly.

Elizabeth nodded. "I never expected to experience something like this when I left the clinic in Chicago and took this job. I pictured serene summer days and warm tropical nights."

"And romance?" Mrs. Tompkin eyed her with a knowing look. "Lots of young gals come south in search of true love."

"I came because my mother died and I didn't want to go on living in our house all alone," replied Elizabeth with a sudden sadness in her eyes. "I thought new places, new people and a new job would give me a new lease on life."

"And has it?"

"No. I'm afraid I brought my loneliness with me. But I'm glad I made the move. The children help me feel needed."

"You're good with them," Mrs. Tompkin admitted. "Maybe you should have trained to be something else instead of a bookkeeper."

"I didn't have much choice. The fact was that I had to start earning money as quickly as I could out of high school. My mother was working two jobs to support me and my little brother. A business course took only

a year. There were expenses—'' She broke off. No use
going in to all that now. She had no one left in Chicago so she'd come to Charleston, and rented a small
apartment on the north side. If the old building with-
stood the hurricane she'd be surprised, Elizabeth
thought as she listened to the havoc being wreaked
upon every section of the city. She had little in the way
of material possessions to lose if her tiny two rooms
were part of the destruction. Anyway, she couldn't
worry about that now. ''There has to be a way to take
care of ourselves,'' she told the nurse with a stubborn
jut of her chin.

''Listen,'' Mrs. Tompkin ordered as she bent her
gray head toward the radio.

''Surging tidal waves have swept ashore on all the
islands,'' the announcer reported. ''Boats have been
torn loose from docks and moorings. Dwellings along
the beach have been leveled by flooding waters and
roads have been washed away. All bridges connecting
the islands to the mainland are down,'' he continued.

All bridges down. Cold sweat beaded on Elizabeth's forehead. No help was coming. No chance of
leaving.

The island was isolated.

CHAPTER THREE

Darkness closed in around Davin and rain beat against him with frenzied fury. The boards beneath his feet rose and fell as the gale drove him backward. He reeled, fought for balance. Crashing beams fell with a force that sent spumes of water shooting into the air. Blinding objects sailed out of the murky blackness, striking him. A thousand cymbals crashed in his ears. Above the tumult he heard the terrified cry of a child.

I'm coming. I'm coming. He lunged forward, struggling to find purchase beneath his feet. *Where are you? Where are you?*

Out of the darkness a piece of jagged metal came flying through the battering rain. He cried out as it struck his forehead. Warm blood flowed down the side of his face, blinding him in one eye. He swiped at his face. His hands were covered with blood as he tried to staunch the flow.

The child's cries were fading.

Dizzy, reeling, he grabbed a post, lurched forward, spun and fell. Rising water washed over him as his fingernails clawed the floor. His screams broke in his ears as he was sucked into a watery darkness.

He groaned. Pressed his hands against the floor. Wavered to his feet. Unsteadily he leaned up against the wall. He pushed back shocks of wet hair clinging to his cheeks. His fingers touched the old scar on his forehead. He looked at his hand and felt his face. Clean. No sign of blood. The murky shadows in his mind slowly lifted. Where was he? Then he remembered.

The west wing of the clinic had given way.

Elizabeth cried out as he came in. He no longer wore his red Windbreaker. His black shirt and pants were drenched. Wet strands of black hair stuck to his cheek. He looked as if he'd been in a fight.

"Good heavens," breathed Mrs. Tompkin, taking a step backward.

Marietta whimpered and cowered away from him.

Alarm caught in Elizabeth's throat. Davin's expression was dark, intense, and his eyes held the haunted look that had frightened her before. "What is it? What happened to you?"

His eyes betrayed a split second of confusion before they focused on her. Then his gaze traveled over her face as if searching for an answer to her question.

"Davin, are you all right?"

He brushed a hand over his forehead. "I...I..." he stammered and then drew in a deep breath. "I had trouble getting back." His forehead creased. "I was sucked out into the storm...."

"Oh, my God." Elizabeth closed her eyes and pictured him lying unconscious, buried under a rubble of glass, wood and mortar. Lifeless. His head twisted at a gruesome angle. The vision was so real that an anguished cry broke from her lips. "You could have been hurt. Killed—" Her voice broke in a jagged sob.

He touched her arm. "I'm all right. I made it back. That's all that matters. Everything's all right now." She gave a slightly hysterical laugh.

"Everything's all right." Hot tears were ready to spill from her eyes, and she didn't know whether to reach out to this stranger or run from him. "The bridges to the island are all washed-out. We couldn't leave if we wanted to."

"You should have been out of here hours ago." Once more she sensed anger building in him. His eyes settled on the children and a pained expression crossed his face. He clenched his fists as if he longed to squeeze the life out of someone.

A shudder went through her. There was something savage in his dark glare. "I thought we might evacuate on our own ... in private cars...."

"Trying to outrun the storm at this stage isn't a good idea."

"Good or not, we don't have a choice," she told him. "We'll have to stay now."

He nodded. "But not here. The windows and walls in this wing are already giving way. There's a gymlike room in the main section of the building. If we can move everyone quickly enough, we can get settled before any more of the building collapses."

Elizabeth nodded. Protected by inside halls and other rooms, the adult recreation room might be the safest place in the building. She should have thought of it earlier but all her energies had been focused on getting away from the clinic—not staying. She turned to Mrs. Tompkin and told her what Davin suggested.

Mrs. Tompkin nodded. "Good idea. Most of the building could fall away and we'd still be safe there." The nurse started giving Marietta orders. Fortunately, medicine and blankets and such had been assembled for the evacuation. Mrs. Tompkin quickly loaded up Marietta's arms. "Take these down to the adult rec room and then come back for another load."

The young woman fled the room, giving Davin a wide berth as she scooted past him.

"What about food? Water? Emergency supplies?" Davin demanded. "Has there been any preparation for a storm like this?"

Mrs. Tompkin scowled. "Since Dr. Radison decided on evacuation I have my doubts."

The nightmare increased every minute, thought Elizabeth. No food, bottled water, nor emergency supplies. *And three mentally disturbed children in a building that was being blown apart.* She swallowed back a churning nausea and kept her voice firm. "We can solve those problems later. First we need to get the children settled."

Davin smiled, and her leaden spirits were lightened by the tender way he looked at her. She was buoyed by the knowledge that Davin Delmar would not leave them until the crisis passed. A spurt of exhilaration took her by surprise. *I must be compensating for being damned scared,* she told herself. She couldn't think what else could explain a spurt of happiness that went beyond all rationality.

Mrs. Tompkin spoke to the children. "We are going for a walk. Won't that be nice?"

Elizabeth took Buddy's hand. He knew her. She had spent a lot of her free time with the little boy, often staying after work and coming in on holidays to be with him. Much to Elizabeth's anger, Buddy's family had abandoned him. They paid the bills and that was about all. Very quickly the seven-year-old found a place in Elizabeth's heart—the place her little brother had left. She still missed sweet little Teddy who had been born with a birth defect that had made his life span only five years. Their father abandoned them soon after it became evident that his son was physically and emotionally deficient, making it necessary for their mother to work two jobs. Elizabeth had given herself to the little boy every day of his precious numbered days and when Teddy died when she was sixteen years old, a part of herself died with him. Her experience with Teddy was responsible for her decision to take a position in a clinic where she could be with children who needed her. Buddy had been the one who most captured her heart. She often walked around the grounds with him, sat under the large oak trees behind the clinic for a picnic and talked and sang songs to him just the way she had entertained her brother. Buddy loved to hear her simple songs over and over again and sometimes the child was ready to join in when she sang to him. Being with the little boy helped stay her own loneliness. His hand rested confidently in hers as she pulled him to his feet.

Davin bent down in front of five-year-old Patty, and a mixture of emotions swept across his face as he smiled at the little girl. Elizabeth was startled by a change in his whole bearing. He was no longer the brooding, tormented and angry stranger who made her cautious about trusting him. The love that flowed from him was so strong it brought a tightness in Elizabeth's heart. She watched as he lifted the tiny girl into his arms, then leaned his dark head against her fair hair. He closed his eyes for a long moment before he placed a tender kiss on her forehead. Elizabeth was almost positive that a glint of moisture filled the corners of his eyes.

Was Patty the reason he had come? He'd never been to the clinic before, as far as she knew. Elizabeth had met the little girl's parents and knew Patty's background. To her knowledge there had never been a hint of a Davin Delmar in connection with the child.

Davin led the way with Patty cradled in his arms. His deeply tanned hands were a startling contrast to the child's pale skin. There was a rhythmic grace in his movements and once again Elizabeth gave a prayer of thanks for his presence.

Little blond Debbie walked with her head turned to one side, not looking ahead where she was going but responding to the guiding touch of Mrs. Tompkin's hand in hers. Marietta, who had returned from her errand, had her arms full with a second load of pillows and blankets.

The roar of the thrashing wind and rain was like the rising crescendo of an orchestra in the center corridor. Elizabeth was relieved to see that the tongue of water had not reached that far. All of the doors had been shut along the inner hall and as they hurried past them, the corridor seemed like a confining tunnel that might close in on them at any moment.

Elizabeth was afraid that Buddy Benson would throw his head back and charge forward in a crazed fashion—the way he usually reacted to stress. Even though he was small for a seven-year-old, he was a handful when he became belligerent. Fortunately the storm didn't seem to intrude upon the boy's private world.

Watching Davin stride ahead, she was conscious of the way his damp clothes molded the muscles of his back and legs. The hard sinews of his back flickered with each step and she remembered how his body had felt curved around hers. Even before she had looked into his face, a bewildering sensual attraction arched between them. She had been shaken by her reaction to his protective embrace under the desk . . . and frightened by it.

It was the storm, she rationalized. Only the hurricane made her long to bury her head against this stranger's chest and close out the world. She jerked her eyes away from his imposing figure and denied the warm desire uncurling within her.

Her relationships with men had always been the feet-on-the-ground kind. No wild thumping of the heart, no breathless anticipation. Before any commitment, she'd been careful to calculate the pluses and minuses of any affair. Not that she hadn't made mistakes. A case in point was the charming doctor whom she'd met recently at the clinic. He was a credit to his polite Southern upbringing—only he turned out to already have a wife of fifteen years. He apologized profusely for the deception. Elizabeth's pride had been hurt, but the pain had not gone much deeper than that. She'd always been guarded in her romantic relationships, but now she was experiencing wanton desires that defied her true sensible nature, and it dismayed her. She couldn't keep her eyes off the stranger's commanding stature, and his rugged handsomeness made her want to touch the lines and planes of his face.

As if he felt her eyes upon him, Davin glanced over his shoulder and gave her a smile that made her feel vulnerable in a way she didn't understand. On some level she welcomed the inexplicable magnetism that was drawing them together, yet a warning flickered deep within her.

They passed the closed doors of the business offices, dispensary, record room and staff lounge. Muffled sounds of destruction outside the building warned of the storm's increased velocity. Elizabeth uttered a prayer of thanks when they reached the recreation room without incident.

Davin quickly surveyed the room, which was filled with exercise equipment, mats, game tables, chairs and a variety of other casual furniture. There was a small kitchenette in one corner. Two doors led to adjoining rest rooms and another into a small storage room lined with shelves of recreation equipment. He set Patty down in a chair and then dragged a huge exercise mat out in the center of the large room.

"We can bed the children down on this." He picked Patty up again and gently set her down on the padded mat. "Nice bed . . . a nice bed," he said in a soft reassuring voice. He motioned to Marietta to give him a pillow and blanket, which she did in haste, backing quickly away from him.

"Good boy, Buddy," Elizabeth cooed as she eased him down on the mat. The little boy began rocking back and forth on his knees, singing frantically, "Row, row, your boat...row, row, row your boat...row, row your boat." Over and over and over again he repeated the same refrain. His voice got louder and louder. Elizabeth was familiar with this outward sign of stress. Her chest tightened. What would they do if things got worse and they had three uncontrollable children on their hands?

The nurse laid Debbie down with another pillow and blanket. A loud whimpering came deep from her chest and Mrs. Tompkin sent Elizabeth a worried look.

"Where's the storage room?" demanded Davin. "I'll check and see if I can find anything that looks like emergency supplies."

Elizabeth told him and with a sinking heart watched him stride out of the room. *What if he didn't come back?* Last time he had returned disheveled and shaken. Maybe a second time he wouldn't be so lucky. *Please...please come back safely.*

Mrs. Tompkin began to organize the things they'd brought with them. Elizabeth checked the kitchenette where drinks and simple snacks were usually prepared. The small refrigerator held cheese, peanut butter, a package of lunch meat, milk and juice. "We'd better fix them something now," she told Mrs. Tompkin. Supper was going to be a lean affair.

The nurse nodded. "Marietta, you help."

Elizabeth did the best she could to encourage the children but none of them ate very much. Her own tense stomach muscles mocked the idea of food.

When Davin came back, she felt a spurt of relief. "Did you find anything?"

He set down one box marked Emergency. It contained one Coleman lantern and four flashlights. His expression was grim. "There might have been more but that part of the building is taking in water. Big chunks of the ceiling have already fallen in."

"Well, one box is better than none," she said with an optimism she didn't feel.

"We have the medications that the children usually need," Mrs. Tompkin assured him. "All three of them are on mild tranquilizers but I'm wondering if we shouldn't give them an additional mild sedative to keep them under control."

"Do what you think best," Elizabeth told her, worried about Buddy's growing agitation. She had to trust the nurse to know what medications to give. It would be better for everyone if the children slept through the brunt of the storm.

"I sure could use a cup of coffee, though," the nurse said regretfully as Davin opened cupboards and closets and made a pile of towels, ropes, canvas and extra gym clothes in the middle of the floor.

"I'll slip down to the staff lounge and bring back the coffeemaker from there," Elizabeth said. "We ought to brew a pot while we can. No telling how long we'll have power," she said as a shiver of apprehension made her breath short. *The lights could go any minute.*

"I don't think you should leave this room," countered the nurse.

"It'll just take a minute. The lounge isn't that far away."

"I'll go with you," said Davin, coming up behind her.

"No—"

"We might find some other things we need." He took her elbow as if the matter were settled.

She knew she should show him that she was an independent woman who could take care of herself, but to be honest she wasn't keen on flying any women's lib banners at the moment. She was grateful for his arm around her waist as they hurried down the hall to the staff lounge.

"Here we are." She held her breath as they opened the door and then let it out when she saw that the room was still intact. The lounge was usually a haven of quiet, a place to escape from the emotionally draining demands of patients. There was no peace and quiet in the lounge now as the storm wreaked its havoc upon the building. Metal shutters on a high narrow window vibrated as if ready to give way at any moment and demolishing blows against the outside wall sounded like a giant wrecker's ball.

The furnishings included a daybed, various chairs and a sectional sofa in front of a television set that had gone dead. A microwave oven, refrigerator and a three-burner stove provided the staff with the comforts of a private kitchen.

"I'll get the coffee." Elizabeth said, reaching into a cupboard for a can of coffee and boxes of packaged sugar and creamer. "We have several nurses with a sweet tooth. There's probably a hoard of cookies and crackers in the cupboard," she told Davin.

"You're right," Davin said as he retrieved cookies, three large Hershey bars and a box of chocolate covered cherries. "Have one?" he offered, holding out the opened box of chocolates.

"No, thanks . . . we have to hurry."

He took one of the chocolates out of the box and popped it into his mouth. A look of utter enjoyment crossed his face as he savored the candy. A wet strand of hair dangled on his forehead and for the first time she saw a boyish glint in his eyes. She was surprised by the surge of tenderness that swept over her. He had lost his formidable brooding air. She found herself smiling at him as his tongue swept over his lips to savor the last speck of chocolate. Her gaze fastened on his moist mouth, soft and inviting. She wondered what it would be like to share the sweet warm taste of his lips. "Are you sure you don't want one?"

"There isn't time."

"There's always time," he corrected, and then added ruefully, "but not always enough of the right kind."

She found herself smiling at him as his tongue swept over his lips to savor the chocolate. "You missed some." She lifted a drop of chocolate from the corner of his mouth with her finger and held it in front of him.

With a knowing smile he took her hand and licked the sweetness, nibbling and kissing her finger. The brush of his tongue stimulated a spiral of startling warmth.

"We have to go," she protested as he pressed a kiss in the soft curve of her palm. She quickly took her hand away but his face remained breathtakingly close to hers. "We have to go," she said again, but the protest was hollow. She closed her eyes as his mouth found hers. His kiss claimed her with a fierce passion that was bewildering.

"My precious love," he whispered as she clung to him. "Mine...mine..."

She was aware of a timeless, boundless tie to this man that went beyond rational thought. His kiss deepened, his hands shaped the curve of her back and waist, and an explosive force like the storm arched between them. At that second a deafening crack like the strike of lightning exploded close by.

The lights went out.

CHAPTER FOUR

Elizabeth cried out as darkness enveloped her like a shroud thrown over her head. Her heart hammered loudly in her ears. She fought against the sensation of being sucked into the swirling nothingness. She couldn't see him. She couldn't see anything. The crashing yowl of the storm filled the darkness, rising in tempo and pitch. A hysterical sob broke from her lips. She pushed against the arms holding her. "Let me go."

For a moment, he tightened his grip on her. Then he set her back on her feet.

"I can't see...I can't see." The monstrous storm was like a swarm of demented creatures trying to get to her. She couldn't see them but they were there. She flayed her arms trying to defend herself.

"Easy, love," he soothed. "The darkness won't hurt you." He caught her hands and held them tightly.

She gasped for breath that seemed to evade her. Her eyes rounded and very faintly she was able to see his shape in the fractured light coming through minute cracks in the shutters. Her ragged breathing became less shallow and some of the stiffness went out of her body. She let herself lean against him, an anchor in her sudden blindness.

He swore softly. "We left the flashlight behind. We weren't thinking ahead, were we? Are there any in the lounge?"

"I don't know."

He started to pull away from her but she tightened her grip on his arm. The terror of being alone was too great. She couldn't control an unreasonable fear that the darkness would swallow him up if he moved away from her.

"No use for both of us to stumble around," he reasoned quietly, gently loosening her grip.

She swallowed back a plea for him not to leave her. *Get ahold of yourself.* They were in no more danger in the dark than they had been when the lights were on. It was just her imagination that had brought a rise of hysteria. A childhood fear of the dark had overtaken her.

"I thought I saw a cigarette lighter on the table," he said. His deep resonant voice steadied her.

Elizabeth forced some moisture into her mouth. "One of the nurses is a closet smoker," she answered, trying to match his tone. "She's always leaving a Bic lying around." She drew in a steadying breath. "Let me get it. I know the room better than you do."

He hesitated a moment. "All right. I'll wait here."

Her mouth was dry as she stepped away from him but anything was better than standing still, frozen with fear. She felt her way along the counter until she reached the end of it. Slowly she walked ahead with arms outstretched, fighting the terror of falling into a dark abyss with each step.

Where was the sofa? She stopped after a few steps, searching the wavering black shadows. I must have walked past it. Suddenly she was completely disoriented. She'd lost all points of reference. The fiendish storm battered her ears with crazed howling. The darkness was alive with demons and shapeless ogres. She wanted to cry out to him to come and rescue her.

"Don't be afraid," his voice cautioned.

A stubborn pride kept the plea lodged in her throat. Slowly she turned around, holding out her arms. Her breath caught in relief when her fingers touched the back of the sofa. The rough texture of the floral slipcover was reassuring. Sliding her hands along the cushions, she circled the couch.

"What's happening?"

"I'm circling the couch." A moment later her knees touched the low coffee table. She let out a breath of relief and bent over. "Now I'm looking for the lighter."

She blindly explored the top of the low coffee table. Her fingers brushed over a couple of magazines and then inadvertently knocked over a small vase of flowers, spilling water all over the tabletop. "I can't find it."

"Maybe I was mistaken," he replied evenly.

"No, here it is," she called triumphantly.

"Good girl." His voice was closer than she had expected. In the next instant he was beside her.

She clicked the lighter. Brief specks showered away from the flint. She clicked it. Again. And again. "Damn, it's out of fluid." The nurse probably tossed it on the table instead of in the trash.

"Here, let me try." He took the lighter from her hand.

"I don't think—" Her next word was cut off as a red spark exploded in a flash. She threw up her hands in front of her face as the bright light blinded her. As suddenly as it had been pitched into darkness, the room was flooded with electric light.

She lowered her hands and stared at him in disbelief. He stood before her, a black figure in his damp open-neck shirt and narrow trousers. Tufts of dark hair on his chest matched the flowing ebony strands around his bronze face. Nothing about him was ordinary. Not his stature, his mesmerizing blue eyes, nor the powerful magnetism radiating from him. There was an arrogant lift to his handsome head. *As if the electricity were under his command.*

A cold chill brought a prickling to her skin. Who was he? She had surrendered to his kisses and caresses with an urgency that dismayed her. She had wanted him beyond reason.

He reached out for her but she stopped him. "No. don't touch me."

She was afraid of him. He had drawn her into a frightening intimacy that was beyond rationality. She'd been unable to deny a startling sexual awareness his touch had created even before she'd glimpsed his blue eyes and handsome face. Even now, she wanted to shut out everything but the surge of desire that flared between them. "What's the matter? Didn't you want the lights back on?" he asked with an arched eyebrow.

"Yes, but—"

"A backup generator must have kicked in."

She stared at him. Was it just a coincidence that the backup power kicked in when he had the lighter? "Is that what happened?"

"What else?" He lightly stroked her arm. "I guess the clinic had a backup after all."

Common sense told her that the electricity could have come on a moment earlier when she was clicking the lighter. But it hadn't. The timing had been exact! To the same second! A sixth sense quivered. Nothing about him was commonplace. Not the dark intensity of eyes, nor a hint of fierce nature beneath the carefully controlled exterior. He was like someone fighting an inner demon.

Stop it! she told herself. It was the storm. How could anyone think rationally in the horrible cracking, booming, snapping barrage of rain and wind? Her desire for this man was edged with insanity. She knew nothing about him. And yet she wanted him with a hunger that mocked every romantic liaison she had ever had.

"Don't be afraid of me," he said with a gentle sadness in his eyes. He reached out and pulled her against him.

She wanted to bury her head against his firm chest and at the same time she wanted to get away from him. "We have to get back to the others," she protested. She was filled with an irrational fear she didn't understand. It had nothing to do with the hurricane. The danger lay within herself. "Please let me go."

He held her firmly for a long moment and then he released her. He murmured under his breath, "Yes, I'll let you go when the time comes. I promise."

He wanted to say more but the time wasn't right. He handed her the packages of cookies and candy, then picked up the can of coffee and the coffeemaker. "We'd better get back before..."

The lights flickered in warning.

When he opened the door, he looked in both directions before he let her step out. The inner hall seemed to be intact but there was a strong draft whipping around the corner that led to the front entrance. Above the howling wind and rain, he could hear a shattering of glass.

The front windows had blown out, he thought. That meant that destruction of the front lobby had begun. Both of the side wings had already been damaged. They couldn't return to the children's wing now even if they wanted to. The main section of the building was divided by several halls and the adult recreation room was the most protected because the corridor that ran past it was at the center of the main building. They had moved the children just in time. The wrathful storm would eat away at the building, biting away each wall and room until the structure was leveled.

"What's happening?" Elizabeth's voice was tight.

"I don't know," he lied.

They couldn't see the damage taking place at the front of building and he was grateful for that. No use building any more anxiety than was already filling her eyes with fear. "This part of the building is holding. Let's get back to the rec room."

He slipped a free arm around her waist. She stiffened for a brief moment and then seemed to give in to the protective strength of his arm. She looked up at him, her eyes asking him desperate questions that he could only ignore. He knew she was fighting to understand what was taking place between them. He had no answers. None that he could tell her.

The compulsion that had driven him to come to the clinic that morning was beyond any simple explanation. He only knew that she was in peril and he had to be with her. The first time he had seen her moving across the clinic grounds she had been wearing a yellow dress. The soft fabric had gracefully swung around her legs, and her corn-silk hair had bobbed gently on her shoulders. When she disappeared into the clinic, he had felt a deep sense of loss.

Unseen he lingered close to her. Watched her arrive in the mornings and leave late in the evenings. He had been nearby when she and the little boy sat in the shade of the old oak trees. He had listened to her sweet voice singing to the child, and something sharp like a grappling hook had sunk into him.

It was the same every time he saw her. When she was in the company of a tall professional-looking man, he especially had to hold back, resisting a mounting need to take her for his own. And when she began to come and go by herself again, he experienced a deep sense of relief. He never understood his compulsion but waited for the right moment to make himself known to her.

Now he was here with her and the children. His torment was easing. He was almost at peace.

CHAPTER FIVE

They found everything in chaos when they returned to the recreation room. Mrs. Tompkin had been ready to give the children their medication when the lights went out. The plunge into darkness had sent Marietta into a frenzy and she had dropped the bottle of tranquilizers all over the floor. She was on her knees, frantically picking up the pills.

"Thank God you're back," cried Mrs. Tompkin.

Patty wailed at the top of her lungs, lurching around on the mat like an off-balance top. Mrs. Tompkin had her arms around Debbie who was screaming and striking out with her arms.

"Pop goes the weasel . . . pop goes the weasel . . . pop goes the weasel!" Buddy bounced on his knees. His eyes were rounded, a grotesque tightness ringed his mouth and his head drooped to one side as if too heavy to hold upright.

Elizabeth threw down the things they had brought from the lounge. She hurried over to Buddy. Davin ignored Marietta's frightened scramble to get away from him and he knelt down beside Patty.

Elizabeth managed to stop the little boy's erratic bouncing and to hold him firmly against her chest. The boy kept on singing like a broken record but his voice grew softer and softer until he finally stopped. She murmured reassurances into his ear and stroked his dark head. Her brother, Teddy, had cuddled in her arms the same way when he was disturbed, and as she pressed her cheek against Buddy's, her eyes filled with tears of remembrance.

Davin picked up Patty and began walking around the room with her. He moved his strong arms in a cradling motion and from the movement of his lips, Elizabeth could tell that he was singing to the little girl. His tenderness stirred Elizabeth. This sharing of love and compassion for the children strengthened a growing bond between them. Thank God, he'd come. She didn't understand how he had known her desperation.

The clamor of the storm rose every minute. The whole building shuddered. The wind howled. The sound of ripping metal exploded like a series of gunshots fired overhead. It took several minutes to get the three children under control and lying quietly on the mat again.

Davin looked up at the ceiling. "We have to get them some protection in case the roof falls in."

She shivered in raw panic. *If the roof fell in, nothing would protect them.* They'd be helpless. The wails of screeching winds battering the building were like a thousand tormented souls. Their screams rose in pitch, swelling and swelling until their tortured cries threatened to burst the eardrums. There was no escape. She covered her ears with her hands. How were they going to protect the children if the building fell apart around them? Her lips trembled and she knew that hot tears were spilling into the corner of her eyes.

He gently pulled down her hands from her ears. He stroked her head the way he had little Patty's. "It's going to be all right, love." An unwavering strength radiated from the depths of his midnight eyes as his gaze bathed her face. "I won't leave until you're safe."

Leave! She clutched his arm. "You can't leave me."

His eyes were as dark as cavern pools. "When the time comes, I must go."

"I don't understand...?"

"There isn't time now to explain."

She wanted to protest but explanations would have to wait. Like a satanical force the hurricane was upon them, howling with glee as if mocking their feeble efforts to avoid complete disaster.

"We have to move quickly," he said. "Help me move the Ping-Pong tables."

She didn't question his order but did as he directed. She'd always prided herself on taking charge when a situation required it, yet she was grateful to relinquish the reins to someone else. There was nothing in her experience that she could draw on at a time like this.

Hurriedly they moved the large game tables across the room and placed them over the mat where the children, Mrs. Tompkin and Marietta were huddled. The tables made a roof over their heads.

"Stay in a safe place," the announcer on the portable radio repeated over and over again. *But what if your safe place wasn't safe any longer?* What if this room flooded? What then? Climb up on the furniture to keep from drowning? They'd have to forgo the protection of the table above them. Then they would be vulnerable to falling boards and mortar. *The children could be buried in the falling debris.*

Elizabeth couldn't see the faces of Mrs. Tompkin and Marietta but their fear radiated toward her as they huddled with the children under the Ping-Pong tables. Tears of fear swelled behind Elizabeth's eyes as the fury of the storm rose with deafening crescendo.

"We'll move that other table out into the center of the room," Davin said pointing to a long table with sturdy legs that held a variety of sports equipment. "And you can get under it."

"What about you?"

"I want to secure the room as best I can. The full force of the storm is only minutes away. If the room starts taking in water, we'll have to be prepared to get off the floor."

Elizabeth watched him with a chill that was bone-deep as he started piling up exercise equipment, chairs and tables. She realized he was attempting to make a kind of platform that was several feet off the ground. With horror she pictured all of them huddled together on the small precarious structure while rushing waters swirled below and sent the whole platform crashing down.

Marietta scurried out from under the table to get things that Mrs. Tompkin wanted. She gave Davin a wide berth, keeping a fearful eye on him as she gathered some objects from the kitchen counter. When he came close to her she cowered away from him like a frightened child.

Davin looked grim as he said something to her. Elizabeth couldn't hear the words but whatever he said didn't lessen the fear coating her face. She dived back under the table as if fleeing from the devil himself.

"We better take the children to the bathroom," said Mrs. Tompkin as she climbed out from under the Ping-Pong table. She disappeared into the adjoining rest room with the two little girls while Marietta waited with Buddy.

When Mrs. Tompkin came back, she said, "I was ready to give them a sedative when the lights went out," the nurse said. "We'd better get them settled for the long night. God help us all," she breathed as the sound of breaking glass rose above the clamor of the wind.

Davin put his arm around Elizabeth's shoulders. She allowed herself to relax against his protective strength. *It was going to be all right,* she told herself. She looked at the makeshift platform Davin had built and prayed they'd never have to use it.

"The generator could go out at any minute," he warned. She nodded. No telling when they would be plunged into darkness again.

"Time is running out," he said with an emphasis that seemed to put a double meaning to his words.

Her heartbeat quickened. Was he warning her that he was about to leave? "No," she protested, clutching him.

"We'd better get everyone settled in...including you, love."

"Please don't—"

At that instant the covering on an air duct burst free from the wall. As the mesh frame sailed across the room, a wave of sea gulls poured into the room.

"Oh, my God," gasped Mrs. Tompkin.

Elizabeth threw her hands up over her face as the birds dived with open beaks and curled claws.

Marietta shrieked hysterically. "Evil spirits...evil spirits." She crossed herself and fell to her knees.

Wings thrashed the air. Live birds crashed into the walls. Their screeching cries filled the room. Dead gulls fell heavily to the floor.

The birds, like evil harbingers, were everywhere.

CHAPTER SIX

Marietta's shrieks could be heard above the whirling birds and crackling wind. "Possessed! Possessed!" She pointed hysterically at the sea gulls. "Evil spirits . . . they've come. They've come!"

Elizabeth grabbed the young woman's trembling shoulders. "Stop it, Marietta! Stop it."

Buddy lurched to his feet and raced around the room as if a sea gull was riding on his shoulders, whipping him into a frenzied gallop.

"Stop him!" Mrs. Tompkin cried as the boy jerked open the hall door and ran out. Frantic sea gulls swooping around the room flew out into the hall through the open doorway. They disappeared as quickly as they had come, leaving only the dead carcasses of a half-dozen gulls behind.

Davin ran after the boy. After a long suspenseful moment, he brought Buddy back into the room.

Elizabeth breathed a sigh of relief as she put her arms around the little boy. The incident had left Elizabeth's nerves threadbare. She wanted to draw upon Davin's presence for reassurance but the invasion of the sea gulls had left him a disquieting stranger. His mouth was set in a hard line and the veins in his forehead bulged as he clenched his jaw. There was a harshness about him that dissolved any intimacy that had been between them only minutes before.

Elizabeth talked reassuringly to Buddy as she settled him on the mat again. "It's all right, Buddy. It's all right."

"Spirits . . . spirits . . . spirits," he said in a singsong chant, echoing Marietta's cries.

Mrs. Tompkin turned on Marietta and gave her a tongue-lashing. "I've had it with you, girl! One more peep out of you and I'll give you a slap that will knock some sense into you! Understand?"

Marietta whimpered and nodded. Elizabeth knew what it was like to be filled with terror and as soon as she could she put her arm around Marietta's trembling shoulders. "It's going to be all right."

"Watch the children, Marietta," Mrs. Tompkin ordered as she disappeared into the adjoining bathroom.

Marietta's hysterics had lessened now that the flying birds had gone and their evil spirits had failed to carry her off. Her wide dark eyes pleaded with Elizabeth for understanding. "I . . . I'm sorry," she stammered. "I'm afraid."

"We're all afraid," Elizabeth answered. "The storm—"

"Not the storm." Marietta's gaze fixed on Davin as he went around the room, picking up the dead birds and putting them into a sack. Her lips quivered. "It's him. He's not real."

Not real! The charge was so ridiculous that Elizabeth suppressed an involuntary laugh. Davin's hot-blooded kisses had been real enough to send her heart pounding as no man had ever done before. The warmth of his embrace, the protective strength of his body pressed against hers and the surge of desire that snapped between them were anything but an illusion. He was every inch a virile male and she had never felt so in tune with her own femininity. She didn't even have to look at him to feel his nearness. His presence was as real as anything she'd ever experienced.

"It's your imagination, Marietta. You've let some stupid superstition affect your good sense."

"Sea gulls carry the spirits of the dead," she answered flatly.

"That's rubbish. The birds got caught in the duct and were blown into the room. All kinds of crazy things can happen in a storm like this."

"There's danger...much danger," Marietta sobbed as she clutched Elizabeth's arm. "You have to protect yourself...from Captain Hawksley."

Elizabeth's temper flared. "Marietta, stop acting like some spooked child who's been listening to ghost stories. Your fears are not only ridiculous but are adding to the real danger of keeping everyone safe through the storm. You ought to be thanking Davin for being here. His presence is a godsend. If we make it safely through this hurricane, it will be because of him! I don't know how we would have coped without him."

"He's after a woman," Marietta insisted with rounded eyes.

"You're talking utter nonsense." Elizabeth took a deep breath. True, Davin Delmar's commanding strength and imposing physique were not ordinary. She could see why he had triggered Marietta's weird accusation. He certainly wasn't like any man she'd ever met and she knew nothing about him. Under the circumstances there had been little time for casual conversation. They had bypassed all the ordinary steps of two people getting acquainted. The passion that had ignited between them defied any need for conventions. She knew she wanted this man, wholly and completely, on every level of her being.

"He's the Captain. I know he is! He's come back." Marietta hastily crossed herself, murmuring a prayer with a choked voice. "He's put a spell on you."

"He hasn't put any spell on me!" Elizabeth countered, but in spite of her terse reply, there was an edge of uncertainty in the denial. She had experienced a sexual attraction that went beyond anything she had believed possible. When he took her in his arms, all rational thought vanished. Not even the monstrous storm could lessen the growing hunger to be in his embrace. She was mesmerized by the way his dark, brooding countenance could give way to tender, loving softness. There were depths to this man that mocked the little that she knew about him, but it was the drama of the storm, she told herself, that made him the focus of Marietta's hysterics.

"Please, Miss Preston, don't let him—"

"That's enough," Elizabeth told her sharply. "Keep your eye on the children while I fill every container we have with water." She was standing with her back to the hall door when Davin opened it and disappeared with the bag of dead birds.

After a couple of minutes, Mrs. Tompkin came back into the room. "Buddy—where's Buddy?" Marietta looked blank and then peered anxiously under the

Ping-Pong table. Only the two little girls huddled on the mat.

"He was here a moment ago," Marietta wailed.

"Maybe he went back to the bathroom." A clutching of raw fear grabbed Elizabeth's stomach. She remembered that Buddy and Marietta had just come from the lavatory when the birds invaded the room. Buddy had raced toward the door and Davin had brought him back. After that, Elizabeth's attention had been shifted to Marietta.

No sign of the little boy in the lavatory. Elizabeth opened the door to the small storage room to see if he'd ducked in there. It was empty. They searched the large room. Cold sweat beaded on Elizabeth's forehead. "He's not here."

"But where—?"

"He must have followed Davin out the door," Elizabeth said in a tense voice.

"Why didn't he bring him back?"

"Maybe he didn't see him."

The building vibrated from the onslaught of the quickening hurricane. Pounding rain and howling wind rose in a deafening crescendo. They could hear the crashing boom of windows and walls.

"What are we going to do?" Mrs. Tompkin's face was the color of chalk.

Elizabeth had her hand on the doorknob when Davin pushed the door open.

"Buddy? Did you see Buddy?" she cried as he came in.

His startled expression was her answer.

"Buddy...he's gone. He must have slipped out somehow."

He swore. "I was checking to see how much of the building is already flooded."

"We have to find him." Elizabeth bolted forward but Davin grabbed her shoulders. She winced from the pressure of his fingers. "He'll be killed," she protested. "We have to go after him."

"The whole place is falling apart. Don't leave this room—for any reason. Understand?"

"But—"

Davin swung on his heels and was out the door again before she had a chance to protest.

Mrs. Tompkin took her arm and pulled her toward the mat. "He's right. You can't help by getting yourself lost."

Buddy! Buddy! Elizabeth choked back the hard wedge of fear in her throat. Why hadn't she kept her eye on him every minute? She felt the same kind of guilt she'd felt when her little brother died. She'd gone to business school while her mother worked and they had left Teddy with a neighbor. The doctor said his heart gave out but Elizabeth had always mourned that she wasn't there to hold him close when he drew his last breath. Now it was Buddy who could die alone without her arms around him.

"Let's see what the radio is saying," said Mrs. Tompkin, turning up the volume as they huddled together under the Ping-Pong table.

With mounting apprehension, they listened to an announcer warning that the full force of the storm would hit the area in less than three hours. Power had already been cut off for miles around Charleston. High-voltage wires lay on the ground, sparking and jumping. Trees were breaking off like matchsticks and the air was filled with flying debris. Huge oak trees like the ones behind the clinic were being uprooted.

"A twenty-foot tidal wave along the coast is carrying boats inland," the announcer reported. "And piling them up like broken toys."

Elizabeth closed her eyes and let hot tears ease down her cheeks. Time passed with excruciating slowness. *Davin! Buddy! Where were they?*

Davin fought his way through fallen timbers, hurling rain and wind. A mounting crescendo burst in his head. Clanging bells pealed frantically above screams and cries for help in the black abyss of wind and water.

The child? Where was the child?

He couldn't see. An inner blindness blocked his vision. Remembered torment lashed at him. Anguish. Helplessness. Pain. All of the despair was there, like serpents striking him again and again.

The violence around him increased to a horrific pitch. Cracking boards and ripping canvas mocked his helplessness, assaulted his ears, and the violent roll of the ship sent him to his knees. His lungs filled with air and then he shrieked—a cry that rose jagged above the clamor of the storm.

Would the torturing memory ever be over? Would he ever be free? Must he live it again...and again... throughout eternity?

The ship was overloaded. Women screamed in terror. Men cursed or prayed to God to save them. Death was everywhere. Huge masts crashed down upon the floundering vessel with a deafening roar. Blood flowed down his face. He crawled and scratched his way to the deck.

He screamed her name and heard the child's cry, sharp and clear above the deafening din. He plunged forward in the raging tempest. Then he saw her. His beloved golden-haired Alicia. She was at the railing, pushed and shoved by a crazed crowd trying to flee the sinking ship.

He almost reached her when the boat rose up out of the water and fell into a deep trough. He was thrown backward. He nearly lost consciousness as his head struck the side of the hull but he fought his way to his feet again, screaming her name.

He brushed aside the shock of drenched hair hanging on his face. *Where was she?* He couldn't see her anymore. He staggered to the railing. His heart leapt. Looking below he saw her. Someone had put her into the tiny lifeboat being lowered into the raging sea.

"Alicia!" he called.

She looked up. "Papa...Papa!" She held out her arms just as the small boat hit the water. In the next instant a monster wave engulfed the boat.

His agonizing scream filled the air as the boat's timbers broke apart. His child's fair hair bobbed in the water and then disappeared into the murky depths of the Atlantic.

What if he didn't come back. What if he couldn't find the child? A band of fear brought a sharp pain into her chest. Both of them might already lay buried under collapsing walls and ceilings. "Please, please keep them safe," she prayed. She buried her face in her hands and pressed her fingers against her temples. "It's going to be all right...it's going to be all right." Davin would find the little boy and bring him back safely. They both would escape death. They had to! She couldn't bear to lose either one of them. In some strange way they had become linked in her affections. And with sickening certainty she knew that if she lost one she would lose them both.

She didn't understand what had happened to her. It must be the intensity of the storm's devastation and the immediate threat of disaster, she rationalized. In times of war, people gave in to feelings that bypassed the trivial and ordinary. Time had no meaning when every moment had to be treasured. And maybe there was no time left.

Mrs. Tompkin was visibly shaken. "It's my fault. I should have kept my hands on him. What if Buddy runs outside? What'll we do? Dear God in heaven, it's my fault—"

"No, it isn't. It's...it's all of our faults," Elizabeth said with dry lips.

Marietta wailed. "The evil spirits took him away."

"Stop it! I won't listen to this! Davin will bring him back."

The young woman's dark eyes were mournful. "Your captain will not be back. His avenging spirit is appeased. He is at peace. He has claimed the child."

CHAPTER SEVEN

He sought total oblivion, but grief denied him peace. Like a dagger thrust into his heart, he heard the child's scream. Was there no escape? Was he doomed to wander through all eternity haunted by the failure to save his own child from a watery death?

Driven by helpless desperation, he shoved aside fallen timbers and waded through rising waters swirling knee-high around his legs. He crawled on hands and knees over mounds of canvas and wood. His inner blindness kept him on the rolling deck of the sinking ship until at last it gave way to images of halls and rooms filled with jagged glass.

The cries of his child echoed in his memory.

"Row, row your boat...row, row your boat...row...row." A cracked little voice filled his ears.

Layers of confusion slowly lifted. Then he remembered. Buddy! The swirling darkness of his eternal purgatory dissipated. Buddy! The little boy was one of the children who had drawn him to the clinic. In the depths of his own woe, he had felt their need...theirs and Elizabeth's. His vision cleared. "Buddy! Where are you?"

The lyrics rose into a wail. "Row your boat...row your boat..."

The plaintive song drew him to the doorway of a large room . . . a lunchroom. Shutters on the windows rattled like screeching banshees trying to get in. Davin's frantic gaze went around the room. He could still hear the haunting little voice but he couldn't see the child anywhere.

The moment was like his never-ending nightmare. He was caught again in that anguish of trying to save his child, and watching helplessly as she had been taken from him. Now another child was calling to him. He mustn't fail again. This chance for redemption might not come again. He had been drawn back into the living and given a chance to put his soul to rest. If he could save the children and Elizabeth he might find peace for his restless spirit. But if he failed again—

"Buddy! Buddy!" Where was the child?

Davin splashed through the mounting debris, calling and searching. Water was spilling into the large room with a force that was beginning to float chairs off the floor. He threw aside chairs, serving carts and shoved tables out of his path. Fear and frustration was fused into a burning fury. He clenched his fist and swore in anger. He wouldn't fail again. His body rippled with a dynamic power that matched the crazed forces of the hurricane.

Then he saw him.

The little boy was sitting on the floor in a puddle of water, clinging to the leg of a lunchroom table. Buddy's head was thrown back at an awkward angle, his eyes closed, the strangled singing coming from his little throat.

Davin called out to the child, "Hold on. Hold on." He battled his way over piles of overturned chairs and fallen shelves. "I'm coming!"

Rain and wind assaulted the room like an enraged monster. Acoustic tiles in the lunchroom ceiling began to fall. Before Davin could reach him, the little boy let go of the table leg. Instantly the uneven pressure sucked the child across the room toward the shattered windows.

Davin lunged forward, a cry of anguish and despair bursting from his lips.

Elizabeth hunched under the Ping-Pong table, staring at the hall door as if a force of will could make Davin and Buddy appear. She had lost track of time. It was an eternity since Davin had left to find Buddy. What if the generator gave out and the building was plunged into darkness again? What chance would there be that either of them would get back safe?

When the door did open, she thought she was hallucinating. It took her several seconds before she reacted, weak with relief. *They were safe.* She bounded out from under the table, joyful tears spilling out from the corners of her eyes.

Davin carried Buddy into the room and quickly shut the hall door. Water ran down Davin's face, dark hair was plastered to his cheeks and a sleeve on his black shirt had been torn off. His arms were bruised and the hands that held Buddy close against his chest were scratched and cut. But a glow radiated in his eyes. "He's all right. He was almost swept away but I got to him in time. He's all right."

Elizabeth was so overcome with emotion she couldn't say anything as Davin set the boy down. She just hugged the child and let the tears run down her cheeks.

Mrs. Tompkin rushed forward. "Thank God! Thank God. Where'd you find him?"

"He'd made his way to the lunchroom."

"The lunchroom! Heaven help us. That's got a wall of windows overlooking the courtyard."

"If I'd gotten there a couple of minutes later..." His voice trailed off.

"But you didn't," the older woman said briskly. "Some things are meant to be. I'm a firm believer in fate." She took Buddy in hand and they disappeared under the shelter of the table again.

"Fate?" Davin gave Elizabeth a rueful smile. "Yes, fate." His deep blue eyes were filled with warmth and concern. "You okay?"

"I'm... fine," she lied. Her heart was pumping madly. Her skin was moist with cold sweat. She'd never been so terrified in her whole life. What if he'd gone away as quickly as he had appeared? Her lips quivered and she couldn't find the words to tell him how empty she'd felt without him. She recognized a mystical bond between them that extended far beyond the few hours they had spent together. None of it made sense. She knew that the communion she felt with this man went beyond the bounds of reality, as if a spiritual connection existed between them, stronger than any physical ties. How could it be? She felt destructive forces in him as strong as the raging hurricane.

"It's going to be all right. Trust me," he said, smoothing the furrows of her brow.

Trust. A simple word but one that had never proved of any value to her. She had trusted her father and he'd run out on her. The men in her life who she had thought loved her had betrayed her. Why should she trust this stranger?

As if answering her silent question, he touched her cheek with a trailing finger. "I'll keep you safe. I promise." Until the storm was over, he would give himself to her and the children. Then it must end. Somehow he must find the strength to turn away from Elizabeth and her love now that he had found it.

She searched his eyes. An unwavering strength radiated from eyes as dark as a cavern pool. The indigo depths were lost in shadows. She didn't understand her readiness to put herself in his hands. His lips, poised so dangerously close to hers, sent all rational thought from her mind. She wanted to put her head in the curve of his shoulder and feel the length of his virile body against hers. Marietta must be right. He *had* cast a spell on her. She'd never felt this way about a man before, never experienced this sexual awareness at every touch. Bewildering desires and responses that were at odds with her nature took her completely by surprise.

The lights flickered at the same moment the deafening roar exploded. *Andrea had arrived.* Davin grabbed Elizabeth's hand just as the lights went out. He guided her across the room, led her into the small storage room and quickly shut the door behind him. When he drew her down beside him on the floor, she went into his arms with a whimpered cry. Once more she was sheltered in the protective curve of his body. The golden eye of his ring shone brightly in the pitch-black darkness.

She touched the dazzling stone and said with surprise, "It's warm."

"A Chinese friend of mine who was dying gave the ring to me and told me to wear it always. He said it would remind me that life is a precious gem that can be shaped in many different ways, but its center beauty remains pure and unchanged."

Davin held her close, their bodies pressed together, arms and legs intertwined as if defying the strongest force of nature to tear them apart. His spirit began to find peace as he touched her soft lips with his kiss. The never-ending loneliness that kept him restless and tormented, the struggle that tore him apart, the guilt and the failure to keep his loved ones safe, all began to ease in the warmth of her embrace. From the first moment he'd seen her, he had known that she could heal him. Everything about her offered a new beginning. Even though he knew his need was a selfish one, all that mattered was that in a moment of desperation, he had found her. He would have to give her up. He knew that. He prayed he would not give in to a selfish anguish to keep her with him.

His hands molded her yielding softness and the sweet scent of her damp hair and skin filled his nostrils. He tightened his embrace with a possessive grip. A jagged groan came from the depths of his chest.

"What is it?" Her fingers traced his face in the darkness as if trying to understand the overflow of his emotions.

Even if he shared the painful memories, she wouldn't understand. She was life. Wonderful and precious. Like a shaft of brilliant sunshine piercing a dark abyss. "It's nothing," he lied.

"You can tell me," she insisted.

"No, I—"

"You must!" she said firmly.

"You wouldn't understand," he said sadly.

She said simply, "I have to know."

She pressed closer to him, and her warmth eased away the chill in his heart. A quiver of hope overtook him. Was it possible she could know the truth and still accept him?

"Please, I must know. From the way you looked at Patty. The tender way you held her. And the sadness in your eyes. You have a child?" she asked softly.

"How did you know?" he asked. His voice was threaded with anguish. "I lost her. I failed to keep her safe. And the others, too." Bitter memories, guilt and heartbreak swelled within him. She would recoil when she heard the truth but he knew that he couldn't hold back any longer.

She pressed her lips against the wildly beating pulse in his neck. "I want to know everything."

His chest moved in a deep sigh. The moment of truth had come too soon. He wasn't ready to face the horror in her eyes. "You must promise to hear me to the very end."

"I promise," she said.

He pressed his cheek against hers. The raging storm receded into the background. The present faded away into the past.

"I am Captain Davin Hawksley."

Elizabeth's breath caught but she remained motionless in his arms.

"I was the captain of a merchant schooner sailing down the Atlantic coast to the Bahamian islands when I met the beautiful daughter of an English plantation owner. Roseanne Halstead. She captured my heart the moment I saw her and I lived in agony that each time I returned to the islands I would find that she had married someone else. I couldn't believe that she wanted me, a brash young sea captain, who had nothing to offer her but long periods of loneliness while I was away on the high seas. But marry me, she did, and a year later Alicia was born. My wife and baby stayed in her father's house when I was gone on my trips. When I was in port, they came aboard my ship and shared my quarters with me."

His voice faltered. "One night when they were on the schooner with me, a renegade Spanish ship drew alongside. The pirates attacked my crew, beat and whipped me to an inch of my life and killed my wife in front of my eyes."

Elizabeth gasped.

"By some miracle they overlooked the baby." Raw emotion swelled in his chest as he described the carnage the Spanish pirates had left on his ship. "I swore to avenge the brutal pillage. I left Alicia with her grandparents and wreaked devastation on every Spanish pirate vessel that came within sight of my ship."

Elizabeth nodded to show she understood. He tightened his embrace. "When Alicia was five, her grandparents died and I was taking her back to England to be raised by an aunt when a hurricane like this one assaulted the Atlantic coast. I was certain we could keep ahead of the storm but another schooner filled with settlers was in distress and we took on her crew and passengers, which overloaded my ship. It became impossible to outrun the storm.''

Anguish made his voice thick. ''Alicia was put in a lifeboat that broke apart. She was reaching out to me when she went under.''

''I'm so sorry,'' whispered Elizabeth.

''The ship hit a rocky coast and only a handful of my men made it to safety. When dead settlers washed ashore it was believed that they had been aboard my ship as prisoners. No one would believe that the rescue of the settlers' schooner had doomed my ship.''

''So the story is true,'' Elizabeth said in a strangled voice. She lifted her head from his shoulders. ''You are the ghost of the murdered Captain Hawksley.''

He sighed patiently. ''No ghost. I am the living spirit of myself.''

''But I don't understand.''

''Nor do I. But I am here, drawn to loving you with every sense and fiber of the man I was...and am.'' He held her closer. ''My restless spirit has been hovering close to you, watching and loving you. When you sat under the tall oak trees and gazed into the heavens, I was there with you. When you sang to Buddy and hugged him to your breast, I was drawn into the circle of your love. Sometimes I thought you felt my presence there because you would smile softly and seem content.''

"Yes," she murmured. "I didn't feel lonely anymore. Somehow my life became fuller and rewarding after I had spent time in that spot. The loss of my brother Teddy seemed easier, as if I were sharing it with someone. But I don't understand, if you were an unseen presence, then how—?"

"How did I become a living man? I felt the terror in your heart and knew the children's helplessness. It's my redemption . . . to keep you and the children safe. I am here because your love has brought me life."

She raised her lips to his. "And you have given me courage."

"Enough for what lies ahead?" he asked. As his mouth claimed hers, she answered with a tightening of her arms around his neck. Her lips parted and her fingers threaded the thick strands of his moist hair. His mouth found the warm hollow of her neck. Her buttons fell away as he buried his lips in the soft crevice of her breasts. All darkness within fled as the fiery heat of passion ignited between them.

Flying debris bombarded the building as if it were artillery. Howling and roaring like a demented beast, the hurricane wind raged destruction around them but the lovers heard nothing but the wild beating of their own hearts. The brunt of the storm hit with a vengeance. And in the explosive tumult they came together in a wild frenzy that defied even the force of imminent death to part them.

And then there was peace. Quiet. Serenity. She raised her head from his shoulder. The moment was suspended in time. Unreal. She cried in alarm.

"The eye of the storm," he said softly.

CHAPTER EIGHT

"It's over," she breathed.

"Only for a few minutes," he warned. "The back of the hurricane will be upon us just as fiercely as before once the eye has passed."

The eye of the storm. The center of chaos. She shivered. The eerie stillness was in its own way as nerve-racking as the deafening uproar of lashing wind and rain. All around them the air was heavy and charged, as if waiting for a spark to ignite it. It seemed impossible that the hurricane winds were revolving furiously around them, while in the center of destruction there was this false reassurance that the storm was over—the misleading promise that tragedy had been averted.

"We'd better make use of the time we have."

"No." She caught his arm as he started to leave her. "Don't go."

"It'll be ten to fifteen minutes before the back of the hurricane hits," he assured her.

I'm not frightened of the storm! she screamed silently. She couldn't put her fear into words. She didn't want to be alone in the eerie momentary hush. He had come to her in the dangerous fierceness of the storm. *He was a part of that tumult.* She had given herself to him, experiencing a sexual fulfillment she had never known before. Even as the world had been destroyed around them, she had been content, accepting him as an anchor in a bewildering reality she no longer understood. But now she was frightened. The unreal silence and the air of suspended waiting threatened what had been between them. On some level beyond rational thought, she knew that in the eye of the storm, she could lose him. "Stay here," she pleaded.

His hand stroked her hair in a soothing fashion and his lips brushed her forehead with a kiss. "Have to see what the damage is. If the building is flooded, we'll have to move everyone off the floor. I need to see how much of the roof is gone. It's all right, love. Trust me. You'll not come to any harm." He reached for a nearby flashlight and turned it on.

"I'll go with you—"

"No, it's better that you stay with the children in case..."

"In case you don't come back?" she finished in a leaden voice that failed to disguise her misery.

As the yellow light of the flashlight touched his face, she saw his dark eyes narrow with a sudden sadness that was akin to pain. "When the time comes, there will be no choice."

"I want to be with you."

"I know." He groaned. "I never should have come."

"Did you have a choice?"

He didn't answer but lowered his lips to hers. There was an edge of defiance in the kiss, as if he challenged some malicious fate to keep them apart even for a minute...an hour...a lifetime.

"I love you." Her arms closed around his neck as if to hold him always. She recognized a love for him that had been with her forever... never ending and without a beginning. Only when she had lost herself in his warm protective embrace had she begun to know herself. "You can't ever leave me," she begged.

He set her away from him. "I have to go." Before she could protest again, he had turned on his flashlight and was gone.

She touched her mouth, feeling the warmth that his lips had left on hers. Her thoughts were muddled, confused. Her logical mind warred with the acceptance of a reincarnated lover. She'd always been a skeptic about psychic happenings. Nothing akin to the paranormal had ever touched her life before. Even now, some mocking voice challenged her to believe the story Davin had told her. But why would he claim to be a resurrected sea captain if it wasn't true? Nothing made sense. She had never felt so utterly alive and happy in her whole life. She had to hold on to the exquisite joy she'd found with this man.

She located another flashlight just as Mrs. Tompkin turned on a small lantern and crawled out from under the Ping-Pong table. The nurse groaned as she straightened up and rubbed her back with her free hand.

Marietta followed after her. The aide looked around anxiously as she got to her feet. Her expression was one of relief when she saw that Davin was nowhere in sight.

"Well, we're in good shape so far," said Mrs. Tompkin as the three women stood in the radius of the lantern light. "But we'd better get some additional things we need while we have a chance. Debbie's breathing is getting tight. She needs her asthma medicine . . . Proventil." She looked at Elizabeth. "There's some in the pharmacy if the room is still intact."

"I'll check," said Elizabeth, relieved to have something to do.

"Stay safe," the nurse ordered. "And get back before the storm hits again." She turned to Marietta. "Marietta, go to the supply room and . . ."

Elizabeth was out the door while Mrs. Tompkin was still giving Marietta instructions.

The inner hall was still dry and intact but when Elizabeth turned a corner leading to the entrance of the building, she could see in the moving circle of her flashlight where walls had been blown in and rubble lay everywhere.

"Oh, my God." She froze, staring ahead.

The foyer was gone and the whole front of the building was ripped open. Water ran in rivulets through gaping holes in the roof and swirled around her legs. She couldn't believe her eyes. If the adult recreation room hadn't been in the center of the building, they would have been at the mercy of falling walls and rising water. Thank God Davin had moved them. She couldn't bear to think what would have happened if they had remained in the children's wing.

Where was he? She stilled a rise of panic. He had said he was going to check the roof. With a catch in her voice, she called out his name. "Davin . . . Davin . . ."

In answer, his voice came out of the blackness somewhere ahead of her. "Elizabeth! Go back."

"No! Where are you? Keep talking so I can find you." She edged her way through a gaping hole that had once been a front window.

"Damn it," he swore. "I told you not to come. I'm here, outside."

She climbed over a mound of debris at the front entrance and once outside, she became completely disoriented in a world of utter chaos. She reeled in shock. No familiar points in the hushed landscape remained. The trees were gone. Water was everywhere. Landscaped lawns and gardens around the building were covered with heaps of twisted metal, splintered boards and jagged glass. Fallen trees lay all over the ground, snapped in pieces like matchsticks.

Muted moonlight fell upon mangled boats, bits of houses and unidentifiable debris that covered the parking lot. An eerie calmness permeated the night sky.

Her eyes widened with horror. Most of the clinic's roof had been peeled off like the skin of a banana. If they had been anywhere except in the center of the building, they couldn't have escaped the storm's fury. "I can't believe it...I can't believe it," she murmured, unable to accept what her eyes were showing her. Exterior walls had been blown in. Exposed rooms had been laid stark, stripped of all their contents. How much more punishment could the roof take? They'd been lucky that an updraft hadn't taken off the whole thing.

"Davin?"

His figure was silhouetted in a gray mist rising from the ground. Was he real or a phantom? Had she already lost him to another dimension? Her breath came rapidly as she waded through the murky water to reach him. Then he disappeared before her eyes.

"Davin!" She lurched forward. Sobs caught in her throat but the next moment, he touched her.

"I'm right here."

She was weak with relief. "I thought you'd..." She pressed her face against his chest. The regular thumping of his heart was reassuring. He was flesh and blood.

"What are you doing wandering around out here?" he chided. "I told you to stay in the room."

"Mrs. Tompkin needs some medicine from the pharmacy."

"That's only two doors from the staff lounge."

"I know, but—" She swallowed hard.

"But what?"

"I had to make sure that you...that you...didn't need help," she finished lamely.

"I want you to stay..." His voice faltered. *Away from me.* "It's not safe, my love. Not safe at all."

"I feel safe," she countered, somehow knowing that his unspoken words weren't referring to the renewing of the storm but to her insistence on being near him.

He gave an exasperated sigh, pulled her close, pressing his cheek against hers for a long moment.

"I can't survive this nightmare without you," she whispered as she clung to him.

"Yes, you can, dear heart. It was your courage and selflessness that brought me to you. You deserve life in the fullest—and I'll not take one tiny moment away from you." Then he set her roughly away from him. "Go back to the room and stay there."

"But I—"

"Sweet Elizabeth. It's no good! Don't you understand? It's no good! I gave in to the driving need to be with you. I thought I could control my emotions, deny the longing to make you mine, but...'' His voice thickened. ''The temptation to fill my empty spirit with your love was too great. Too powerful to deny.'' She thought she heard a catch in his voice. ''Beloved, I should have kept an emotional distance from you. I didn't mean to cause you pain....''

''But I love you,'' she protested. ''Finding you has been the most wonderful thing that has happened to me. I don't want to lose you—ever!''

''You mustn't love me,'' he said sharply. ''It's too dangerous. There are forces that I can't control.'' Anger stiffened the muscles in his arms. He clenched his fists. ''I never should have allowed this to happen.''

''But it did happen!'' she protested. Her body was still caught in the lingering ecstasy of their lovemaking. She wanted to be close to him, feel his protective arms around her. She wanted to bury her head against his chest, and feel the strong rhythm of his heartbeat. ''Surely you can't deny what is between us?''

''Only because I must,'' he answered huskily. ''You and the children have given me more than you can imagine. Come on. I'll take you back inside.'' His tone was harsh, his manner abrupt.

She was bewildered by the barrier he silently raised between them as they made their way through the shattered building to a small pharmacy that somehow had remained almost untouched by the desecration on every side.

''Be quick,'' he ordered. ''Find what you need and then get back to the rec room.''

"You'll meet me there?" she asked with lips that were suddenly dry. "Davin?" His name was a desperate cry. "You can't leave me!" She grabbed his arm. *Why was he putting this distance between them?*

"I'm afraid for you, love." With an anguished groan his arms went around her. He held her in a fierce embrace, and then pulled away. In the next instant, his figure had melted away into the darkness of the beleaguered building.

She choked back hot tears, struggling to get control of her shattered emotions. What did he mean? *He was afraid for her?*

The sound of the rising wind was a warning. The eye of the hurricane had almost passed. She gave herself a mental shake. She had to think of the others who were depending on her. Biting her trembling lip, she let the flashlight play over the small pharmacy, and then began to search white cupboards for the medicine Mrs. Tompkin had needed. By the time she found it, a loud rumbling vibrated overhead.

The force of the storm was back. The velocity of wind and rain increased with every second and after the hushed stillness, the rising crescendo seemed diabolically unreal.

She quickly left the room and had taken a few steps down the hall when she heard screaming. The cries were coming from the direction of the supply room. Marietta!

"I'm coming! I'm coming," Elizabeth cried. The screams grew louder as she turned a corner and the beam of her flashlight shot ahead. The radius of light caught Davin's black figure at one end of a small hall-way.

Elizabeth froze in shock. Her legs refused to take another step.

Davin carried a struggling Marietta in his arms. She flailed her arms wildly against his iron grip. "Help me! Help me. Don't let him take me!"

"Stay back," Davin shouted, tightening his grip on the struggling girl. His brazen blue eyes flashed angrily. The dark tan of his face had deepened. The scar on his forehead slashed through his eyebrow in an ugly line. Nothing about him invited the tender emotions that had sent her pulse racing in his embrace.

The young woman writhed in his arms, trying to fight him off, and Marietta's superstitious warning burst full-blown in Elizabeth's head.

It's him! Captain Hawksley. Fresh from the grave . . . looking for a woman to take back with him.

CHAPTER NINE

"No!" A wrenching scream tore from Elizabeth's chest. "Let her go!"

"Get back!" he shouted again, tightening his grip on Marietta's struggling body.

At that instant the end of the building behind Elizabeth disintegrated. There was no time to react. The roof was gone in a splintering roar. Walls crumbled outward. Rumbling wind and rain created a lashing maelstrom, blinding her with its fury. In a split second she was a helpless victim, mauled by the savage hurricane. A vicious suction like giant hands grabbed her. Breathless screams were driven back down her throat as she was lifted from her feet and sucked outside.

She was tumbled over and over with other flying debris as angry rain blew horizontally across the ground. The earth and sky churned. She cried out as hard objects struck her and bruised her skin. As water rose over her, she fought against being swept away and flailed her arms in every direction trying to grab on to something.

I'm going to die.

An instinct for survival kept her battling against the deadly forces. Scratched and bleeding, her fingers miraculously closed around an exposed pipe sticking out of the ground. Her fingers curled around the wet metal in a desperate grip as water beat against her, twisting her body this way and that.

Water poured over her. Her hands began to slip. Pain shot up her arm and she lost hold of the pipe. She floundered in the water and then was lifted up in the air.

Carried by a swift current? By the wind? Her senses delivered contradictory sensations. She no longer had the strength to battle. With a sob of resignation, she gave up and let her body go slack.

The hold on her tightened. Through a straggly mask of drenched hair, she glimpsed a face. Burnished skin, black hair and depthless blue eyes.

Davin.

She whimpered with relief. She was in the cradle of his strong arms. Waterlogged clothes hung heavily on her even as a strange warmth sluiced through her. There was no thought beyond the joy that she was safe in his arms. Her bruised and tired body relaxed against him. The nightmare faded into a kind of dream. In the midst of the warring tumult, she felt strangely content.

The yowling storm buffeted them as he bent forward against the gale. Every muscle in his strong body strained as if in mortal combat. Flying missiles struck him like the spears of a thousand savage barbarians. Surging water threatened to sweep his legs out from under him.

Elizabeth's ears filled with a roaring that vibrated through her whole body. For a terrifying moment, the storm threatened to strip her out of his arms. He gave a jagged cry as he pinned her to him with steel-like arms. She circled his neck, locked her hands tightly together and sobbed against his chest.

After an agonizing eternity, they were back inside the building again. Elizabeth whimpered when he abruptly set her on her feet. Disoriented, she wavered for a moment before she saw Marietta standing against a wall, holding a flashlight in her hand. There was blood on the young woman's face and she was gasping for breath. Elizabeth realized that they were still in the service area just beyond the place where the end of the hall had given way.

A spurt of joy shot through Elizabeth. Davin must have carried Marietta to safety and then gone back to rescue her. *He had saved them both.* What idiots they had been—jumping to the wrong conclusion when Davin had tried to get Marietta out of danger before the wall gave way. With a cry of relief she turned to Davin, but his expression was fierce and frightening.

"Go! Now!" He gave Elizabeth a rough shove forward. "Get out of here!" he shouted at Marietta and pushed her after Elizabeth.

A splintering roar overhead echoed his shout. Elizabeth grabbed the flashlight from Marietta's trembling hand and pulled her forward. When they reached a corner in the corridor, Elizabeth flung a frantic glance over her shoulder. "Davin—?"

She was never sure whether or not he heard her. He stood motionless in the shadows. She stopped, turned the flashlight back in his direction and called to him again.

At that instant the section above his head gave way. Before her horrified eyes, he disappeared, buried under a mountain of debris.

CHAPTER TEN

Elizabeth ran back screaming. She threw down the flashlight, pulled at splintered wood, lifted twisted pipes and tried to shift chunks of heavy mortar and plaster. *"Davin...Davin..."* She cried his name over and over. Tears ran down her cheeks. Sobs caught in her throat. Her fingers were raw and bloody as she frantically dug for him. When she discovered his hand a burst of hope went through her.

She'd found him!

Despite her desperate efforts she could not move the heavy beam that lay across the mound of wood, steel and plaster that buried him. His hand was the only part of him that she could uncover.

She screamed at Marietta to help her. The aide came running to her side. The two women tried to move the heavy weight but their strength was lacking for the impossible task.

He's still alive...he's still alive. Elizabeth clung to the impossible hope. She grabbed the wrist of his exposed hand and felt for a pulse. *Please...please...*she pleaded.

There was no sign of a heartbeat, no warmth, no response in the hand. The amber stone in his ring was dark and without color. The glowing dazzle that had been shining with vibrant life was gone.

Marietta pulled at her. "We have to go! We have to go! The rest of the roof...it's going to fall!"

Elizabeth pressed her cheek against his hand. She couldn't leave him. She couldn't. *Come back. Come back.*

A warning rumble came from the one wall still standing in the service area. Above the deafening din, she heard his voice, clear and commanding. "See to the children."

Slowly she straightened up. Her heart was beating with a quickened pulse. "See to the children." *His spirit was speaking to her.*

With tearful lips, she placed a kiss in the palm of his hand and in a choked voice whispered, "I'll always love you."

Marietta pulled at her. "Hurry." Elizabeth nodded. He was gone and a part of her had gone with him. In her heart she would never let him go...never. She took Marietta's hand and they hurried back to the center of the clinic.

"I'm sorry...sorry," Marietta whimpered. "I saw him coming toward me. I was scared and ran away. He shouted for me to come back but I didn't. He ran after me and grabbed me. I...I...didn't know he was just trying to carry me to safety. And then you came and—" She broke off weeping. "When you were swept out of the building, I thought I'd never see you again. He left me where it was safe. Went after you." Her lips quivered. "He saved us both. I'm sorry that I said bad things about him. Foolish things. I know now he wasn't Captain Hawksley."

But he was! Elizabeth choked back the cry. Davin Hawksley had broken free of a dark eternity to become flesh and blood. And now he was gone again...forever. He was kind, wonderful and self-sacrificing. No one would understand. No one would believe her. She wanted to scream her anger, rile against the malicious fate that had brought him to her and then snatched him away. She was devastated. Heartsick. Now that she had lost him, she cared little about her own safety but she wouldn't let him and the others down.

Save the children.

When they returned to the rec room, she had little time to think about anything but immediate survival.

"Thank God, you're back," Mrs. Tompkin anxiously greeted them as she climbed out from under the Ping-Pong table with a lantern in her hand. "Good Lord—" Her eyes widened as she stared at Elizabeth whose clothes were torn and covered with filth. Her face and limbs were scratched and bruised.

"What happened?" asked the nurse. Marietta sobbed as she crawled on her knees under the table and covered her face. Elizabeth followed. The children were asleep. The three women huddled together.

"The service area in the building gave way," Elizabeth said in a neutral voice that surprised her. "Davin was carrying Marietta to safety when I saw them. I thought..." Her voice faltered. She was ashamed. How quickly she had been ready to believe the horrid superstition that the evil pirate had come back from death to wreak harm on a young woman. For an absurd moment she had thought that her beloved Captain

Hawksley was taking Marietta away with him. Elizabeth took a deep breath. "I was sucked out of the building when a wall gave way...and...and Davin saved me. He fought the storm and brought me back inside."

"Where is he now?"

"He's..." She swallowed hard. "He's gone."

"Gone? Gone where?"

Elizabeth stared into the darkness without answering. *Back to his grave.* She put her head down on her pulled-up knees and closed her eyes. *Davin...Davin.*

Marietta told the nurse how he had been buried when part of the service area gave way.

"If you hadn't believed all that superstitious nonsense, none of this would have happened."

"I know...I'm sorry...sorry. But there was something about him..."

"Don't start that nonsense again," snapped Mrs. Tompkin. "Patty's breathing is getting tighter every minute. Did you find the Proventil?" she asked Elizabeth.

A pang of guilt swept over Elizabeth. "Yes, but I lost it. I was coming back with it when...when I heard Marietta screaming."

Should she go back to the pharmacy for another one? She could hear more of the building falling away with every blast of wind and rain. Maybe the pharmacy was gone by now. There was no question that the destruction was coming closer and closer to the center of the building.

What should she do? Precious lives were in her hands. It wasn't fair. She wanted to shriek and curse at the malicious fate that had brought Davin into her life only to snatch him away again. *I need you... I need you.* The silent cry was a mixture of anger and anguish. She wanted his arms around her, to feel his hands caressing her and delight in his warm mouth upon her lips. He had made her feel alive and fulfilled for the first time. She had loved him with a passion that defied time and reality. But he was gone. The last sight she'd had of him was of Davin standing there in the shadows, waiting—as if he had known his time had ended.

See to the children. He had come, seeking peace from the torment of losing his own child. If they survived it would be because of him. Elizabeth felt a swish of cold water on her feet just as Mrs. Tompkin cried, "The room's flooding."

Raw terror grabbed Elizabeth. The impulse to run, to flee from the surging water was overpowering. But where would they go? The whole building must be taking in water now. She could picture them floundering amid collapsing walls and falling ceilings.

Stay here.

Davin's voice was as clear as if he'd been speaking into her ear. Her mind suddenly cleared. He had anticipated flooding. The structure he had built of exercise equipment stood in the middle of the room. There was a small covered section at the top of the weird scaffold. Would it hold all of them?

"We have to get the children off the floor. Hurry."

"Where are we going?" asked Mrs. Tompkin anxiously. She had already told Elizabeth that if the building flooded there would be no place to stay safe.

Elizabeth took the lantern and placed it at the bottom of the bizarre structure. Davin had made a covered platform at the top about five feet off the floor. Not very high if the water continued to rise but at the moment it would keep them all dry.

By lantern light, they drew the children out from under the table and carried them across the room. Water had already risen almost to their knees and water-soaked partitions in the ceiling began falling from the added weight. Streams of water created waterfalls all over the room as it flowed through holes in the ceiling and splashed onto the floor below.

Elizabeth feared that the jerry-built tower might be swept out from under them at any moment but it was the only refuge in the room of rapidly filling water.

"You go first, Mrs. Tompkin, and then we'll hand the children up to you."

The nurse eyed the scaffold with open distrust. She gingerly climbed up the collection of bars and machines. When she reached the small space at the top, she lay down on her stomach and reached down for the first child, which Marietta and Elizabeth held up to her. Debbie next, and finally a groggy Buddy.

"Now you, Marietta," Elizabeth said.

The young woman needed no urging and quickly joined the others on their precarious perch.

"Come on, Miss Preston. Hurry," Mrs. Tompkin called down.

She had just put a foot on the first bar when the hall door tore away the brass hinges. A bank of water swished greedily through the room like a rising surf. The pressure almost pulled Elizabeth's legs out from under her. She held on tightly, and gingerly found leverage for her feet as she climbed upward. At the top she eased into a small space beside the others. Pressed closely together, each woman held a child in her arms.

She was instantly beset by worries. Would the metal structure hold? Would the covering Davin had stretched over the top of them withstand the falling ceiling tiles? She closed her eyes and buried her face in Buddy's hair. She remembered the way Teddy had felt in her arms and caught herself believing that it was his warm body she held close to her. The love she'd felt for her brother mingled with the love she felt for the child in her arms and in some strange way her grief for the loss of her brother was finally eased.

The night dragged on. In the throes of utter mental and physical fatigue, a strange kind of peace settled on her. She no longer felt the biting loneliness that had kept an ache within her heart. A wounded part of her had been healed. She relived the moments in Davin's embrace and a wellspring of happiness flowed free within her. She closed her mind to the hurricane roaring like a demented creature in search of prey, gave in to an invading weariness and slept.

Hours later, she lifted her head with a start.

Sunlight slanted through jagged openings in the roof. Tatters of blue sky shone above. A haunting stillness was carried on a soft whispering breeze.

Hurricane Andrea was over.

CHAPTER ELEVEN

Elizabeth eased away from Buddy. Everyone else was still sound asleep. Mrs. Tompkin was snoring slightly with her mouth open. Marietta's long and tousled dark hair covered most of her quiet face and the two little girls were curled up in fetal positions.

Elizabeth looked down from the jerry-built structure. She was startled to see that there was little visible in the room except the structure on which they perched. Dirty water covered the floor, obliterating everything except piles of tumbled objects that made islands of trash everywhere. The walls of the room had stayed intact but not the corridor outside. Elizabeth could glimpse scraps of daylight where the inner hall had been. How much of the building was left?

Her heart quickened in her chest. It was a miracle that they had survived. Without the platform that Davin had built, they would have been helpless against the invading water. *"Thank you, my love,"* she murmured. He had kept them safe. A sudden fullness in her eyes spilled tears down her cheeks.

At that moment the utter desolation was broken by the faint sound of an engine. A boat? A plane? It was a long moment before a distinct sound triggered Elizabeth's recognition. A helicopter! *Looking for survivors?*

She scrambled down the piled-up gym equipment and hit the water with a splash. As she made her way out of the rec room into the hall, she could see the outside through jagged openings, but everywhere she turned her path was blocked. Wading through muck, water and sand, she climbed over obstacles of every shape and size. She unwittingly dislodged boards that gave way with a roar. A nearby wall crumbled like bent cards, sending a spray of water and plaster dust up into the air.

She scrambled away in a different direction. All thought was lost in a panic to reach the outside. Everything looked as if a giant foot had crushed furniture, equipment and even bent steel beams into pretzels.

"We're here. We're here," she cried in desperation as precious minutes were lost.

She finally broke free of the demolished clinic and she shaded her eyes against a bright sun. Frantically she searched the sky.

No sign of a helicopter overhead.

A sob caught in her throat. *Come back. Please, come back...now!* The children needed food and warm clothing. Patty needed her medicine. Even a few hours without the care they needed could be disastrous for these special children.

The melancholy cry of a waterlogged sea gull was her only answer. Everything was quiet and peaceful. No clouds scudded across the wide expanse of blue sky. A benign soft breeze touched her moist skin. Only the utter destruction in every direction verified the reality of a killer storm a few hours past.

Her vision blurred with the onslaught of bright light. She climbed up a mound of sand and rocks and searched for some sign of life. She couldn't believe her eyes. Parts of houses and boats were piled in heaps like gigantic junkyards. Branches stripped bare of leaves hung lifeless on trees that had been uprooted or broken into splintered pieces. She could see the irregular line of the coastline. Water and sky melted into a gray wash. As her eyes focused on the distant horizon, a tiny speck grew bigger and bigger.

Was she hallucinating? She held her breath as the moving object grew bigger. Then joy leapt into her tight chest. Her eyes and ears were not deceiving her. An aircraft's engine broke the suspended stillness.

The helicopter was coming back!

She waved her arms furiously. Would they see her? For a long, torturing moment she thought that the helicopter was going to pass right over her and never stop, but it made a wide circle and came back. Like a bird searching for a place to nest, the craft hovered lower and lower and finally set down upon a windswept area that might have been the parking lot of some building that had blown away.

The rescue team quickly brought the children and the two women safely out of the building.

"Glory be," breathed Mrs. Tompkin, her eyes filled with thankful tears. Her gray hair hung limp around her face, her white uniform was wet and black with grime, but her round face was creased with a broad smile. "I never have been so happy in my whole life." She was like a mother hen with all her chicks safe and sound.

One of the young men offered Marietta a helping hand with the children and she gave him a smile so warm that it brought color into his cheeks.

There wasn't room for all of them in the small craft because the men had already rescued a family of three from a capsized boat.

"I'll wait," Elizabeth said readily, relieved that there wasn't any question about her remaining behind. She was determined not to leave until Davin's body could go with her. He was the one who had kept them safe. They owed their life to him. She couldn't leave him behind. Her lips quivered with emotion as she watched the helicopter fade into the distance.

She hugged herself against a sudden chill as she walked around the edges of the devastated building. She waded through pools of water, circled the piles of fallen walls, jagged glass and splintered wood and laboriously made her away around to the back where the service entrance had once been.

Tears of frustration flooded the corners of her eyes as she searched in the rubble for some sign of the place where Davin had been buried. More destruction had taken place and his hand must have been covered up with more falling debris.

Sobs racked her body. "Davin . . . Davin."

Her only answer was a warning rumble that some more of the weakened building was giving way. Soon there would be nothing left standing. It was hopeless.

She turned around and froze. All breath left her lungs. Her heart stopped. Through a wash of sudden tears, she saw him!

The phantom was standing a few feet away on a mountain of rubble, like the one that had buried him. Captain Davin Hawksley smiled and held out his arms.

She couldn't move. She was overwhelmed with the fear that if she rushed forward and tried to embrace him, her arms would only touch empty air. She was afraid to blink, apprehensive that he would disappear in a flicker of her eyelids. She just stared at him and after a moment he lowered his arms and a deep sadness passed over his face.

"Don't go," she pleaded in a hoarse voice. "The children are safe," she added quickly, afraid that he would fade away and disappear. "They've gone. A rescue helicopter took them away."

"And you stayed?"

She nodded, her eyes etching in her mind every line and plane of his beloved face. She sought to build a memory that would last a lifetime.

"Why didn't you go?"

"I couldn't."

"Couldn't? Or wouldn't?" he prodded.

"There wasn't room for me in the helicopter and . . . and I had to stay . . . with you." Her lips quivered. He was going to disappear from her life as mysteriously as he had first appeared. "But I didn't know where you were. I couldn't find the place. I wanted to...to..." She faltered.

"To keep a vigil over my dead body?"

She nodded. "I had to be with you."

"Even in death?" He came slowly toward her.

"Yes," she said.

He stood in front of her. His black clothes were covered with dirt, his face was scratched and bruised. She was startled to see that his old scar was fresh and bleeding. His eyes met hers. "You would stay with me...forever?"

"Yes...yes. Oh, Davin...I can't let you go."

A gentle smile curved his lips. "Sweet love, don't you understand?" His warm breath bathed her face as he drew her close. "I'm not dead...not anymore. Don't ask me how or why. I'm alive...alive."

"But you can't be," she protested, even as her breathing quickened with hope. Her heart raced as she dared to reach out and touch him. She let her fingers trace the strong curves of his cheek and chin and face. Then she looked at the warm blood coating her fingertips.

"Dead men don't bleed." A joyful laugh came deep from within his chest. "No more darkness, no more endless torment. I'm free to live...and to love again." She saw then that the ring on his finger glowed with a brilliant dazzle. The stone's promise was true—life was a multifaceted jewel with happiness forever at its center. She cried with joy. A miracle of resurrection had given him back to her.

In the midst of the destruction they clung to each other and a bright sun beamed down upon them with a new promise. The storm had passed. Emptiness and sorrow had given way to a miracle. They had found a love so strong that it could encompass a whole lifetime... and a new eternity.

* * * * *

Dear Reader,

I have to confess that there have been many dark and dangerous lovers in my life. I fell in love with the first one when my eighth-grade teacher read aloud *The Highwayman* by Alfred Noyes. How my young heart quickened at that romantic, rhythmic verse: "the highwayman came riding, riding, riding up to the old Inn door." The Frenchman in Daphne Du Maurier's *Frenchman's Creek* stole my heart, and I was fascinated by the dark hero of *The Devil on Lammas Night* by Susan Howatch. I read Gothics by the hundreds, and when I decided to write, I discovered that my passion for dark and dangerous heroes had followed me into my work. I am delighted to share my latest mysterious lover with you in "Storm-Tossed."

Please enjoy!

grandparents died and I was taking her back to En-

THE
ANCIENT ONE

Rachel Lee

CHAPTER ONE

Moonlight betrayed the ancient secret. Pouring into the isolated canyon like molten silver, it found its way beneath an overhang and revealed in luminous detail the shapes of an ancient dwelling. Not Anasazi. Here were no keyhole doorways and rectangular windows. Here were triangular openings unlike any seen before. Here the stones were so old that the wind had scoured them smooth. Here the shadows whispered of even older dreams, older ways, older powers.

As the moonlight slipped silently across the buildings, it highlighted etchings carved into the stone. Here a bird, there a buffalo, now a waterfall. A man. A woman. A child.

And then it fell upon strange symbols etched inside a triangle, something like an Egyptian cartouche, an oblong outline filled with hieroglyphics, but resembling nothing Egyptian. Resembling nothing known.

Something in the shadows sighed, disturbed by the light, as if summoned by the touch of a moonbeam on the triangle filled with strange symbols. From dark corners came whispers, as if the night came alive where the moon did not reach. Something stirred and then settled again, as if not quite waking.

The Ancient One slumbered on, and the night remained silent.

* * *

Lynn Carstairs saw the pueblo first in the moon-light. She was camped across the canyon, watching the play of silver illumination on the canyon wall facing her when the moon betrayed the secret of the hidden dwelling. Her breath locked instantly in her throat, for the triangular shadows of windows and doors alerted her to the discovery of something alien. *Not Anasazi.* The thought floated into her head with deceptive quiet. And then, surging suddenly, excitement hammered in her veins.

Oh, my God, she thought, and reached for the bin-ocular case. No, she told herself. No. It had to be an illusion of moonlight and shadow. It had to be just another Anasazi cliff dwelling. Even a canyon as iso-lated as this must have been thoroughly explored in the years since the first cliff dwellings were discovered. Surely no one would have missed this....

But she had been in this canyon for a week now, cataloguing other sites for future excavation, and it was only an accident of moonlight that had revealed that dwelling to her. For seven previous nights she had sat here and watched the waxing moon spread its silver light across the canyon, and never before had she seen that alcove. Even in broad daylight, nothing had been visible there.

Grabbing the binoculars, she held them to her eyes and focused. Her hands trembled, and she drew a deep breath to steady them.

There, shaking in the lenses, was indeed a cliff dwelling unlike any other. Unlike any hitherto cata-logued. Unlike any the Anasazi had ever built anywhere in the hundreds and hundreds of square miles they had occupied. Those triangular doors and windows were not mere accidents of shadow.

As she watched, the moon moved slowly in its course, and gradually, but still too quickly, it left the high alcove once again in shadow. The dwelling vanished, and even the alcove seemed to disappear, as if she had imagined it.

Afraid she might lose track of the location if she didn't immediately fix it firmly in her mind, Lynn headed away from her campfire and farther out into the shadows of the canyon, memorizing landmarks on the canyon wall ahead of her. She was thinking that she might be able to approach it from below just as a sudden, eerie cry from behind her made her spin around and seek its source.

There, high atop the canyon wall that faced the cliff dwelling, stood the silhouette of a man. A man such as she had never seen, apparently nude except for a loincloth that flapped visibly in the breeze, and feathers that hung from his long, dark hair. In one powerful arm he held a long stick from which hung a cluster of large feathers, and he raised it high above his head.

He chanted something in a deep voice, in words she didn't know and a language she didn't recognize. His voice echoed eerily in the canyon, bouncing off the cliff faces and making it sound as if dozens of other warriors answered him.

And then, as she blinked, he vanished. Gone. As if he had never been.

Later, huddled in her sleeping bag with her back to a rock wall and her eyes scouring the dark at the edges of the firelight, she wondered just what she had seen. The Ute reservation wasn't too far away, she recalled, and the Four Corners area also held the Apache reservation and the Navajo reservation.

Someone had just come out here to perform some kind of ceremony at the full moon, that was all. No big deal. Certainly nothing to frighten her. Whoever the man had been, he must have seen her fire long before he opened his mouth in that strangely beautiful and haunting chant.

It was so dark out here! For that reason alone, she didn't want to let the fire die down. Unlike most places in the country, the Colorado plateau wasn't covered with large metropolitan areas, with the result that out here in the canyons there was no artificial light to create a hazy glow in the dust and clouds. Here the night was absolute, punctuated only by the moon and stars, and now that clouds had moved in to cover the sky, there was no light at all except for her fire.

And no sound. The silence was deafening to ears accustomed to civilization. Not even the whine of a car engine or the sound of a human voice broke the absolute silence. So quiet! Even the soft breeze was silent.

A sound overhead—an owl, perhaps, or a bat. Some flying inhabitant of the night. A distant clatter as a pebble rattled down a cliff side. Normal, ordinary sounds.

Nothing to justify her feeling that the night had grown threatening.

Nothing to explain why she knew with absolute certainty that she was being watched.

* * *

Dawn announced itself with a lightening of the sky from indigo to royal blue. The clouds of the night before had vanished. No streamers of pink-and-gold glory in this arid sky, just that lightening of night into the blue of day.

The air was chilly, surprisingly so, though at this altitude the air was thin and didn't hold the day's heat well. Shivering a little within her sleeping bag, reluctant to even poke an arm out, though she finally did, Lynn threw more wood on the fire and then shoved the coffeepot closer so it would begin to perk. She had learned to drink coffee as a child while camping with her father, and she never tasted it on a cold morning without remembering her very first cup of the bitter brew.

The memory always brought a smile to her lips, and she was smiling as the clatter of pebbles alerted her to someone's approach. At once she forgot the cold and stood, letting her sleeping bag fall to her feet.

A tall, powerfully built man seemed to coalesce out of the half twilight. He strode purposefully toward her, and her heart lurched uneasily in the instant before she recognized the silhouette of his hat.

A park ranger! Relieved, she hunkered down again and pulled the sleeping bag up around her shoulders, watching as he strode closer.

"Morning!" he called, his voice deep. It echoed off the canyon walls, a crazy cascade of cheerful sound as the sky grew steadily lighter.

"Good morning," she called back.

"Do I smell coffee?"

''Pull up a rock and join me.''

He was close enough by then for her to make out the details of his brown and green uniform, the light jacket, the Park Service insignia.

''I'm Cody Walker,'' he said as he stepped up by the fire. Squatting, he offered his hand.

''Lynn Carstairs.''

''I saw your fire from farther up the canyon, and I thought I'd drop in and say hello.''

He was an exotic-looking man, she thought, surreptitiously glancing at him as she dug out a second tin cup from her supplies and handed it to him. Hair that was truly black and was caught back at the nape of his neck with some kind of leather string. Dark eyes, eyes almost as black as his hair. Coppery skin that proclaimed him to be Native American. High cheekbones, a narrow nose. Angular. Lean. Hard.

''Almost nobody comes into this canyon,'' he remarked as he settled cross-legged in the dirt. Holding out the cup she had given him, he let her fill it. ''Thanks. Smells really good.''

''I'm doing an archaeological site survey,'' Lynn told him. ''I have permission to be here.'' The ruins of the park were protected, and careless scavenging was seriously frowned upon.

''I know. I heard about you. Les Chandler is really excited that somebody's finally surveying this canyon. He's been trying to get funding for it for years.''

Chandler was the park's archaeologist and a good guy. ''He told me. I'm really thrilled to be the first, but I have to admit, I'm astonished that no one has done it before.''

He turned his head a little and looked at her from dark, expressionless eyes. "Some say the canyon is haunted."

For an instant, just an instant, Lynn thought he was joking. A polite laugh was already bubbling up in her when she realized that he was deadly serious.

And suddenly the chilly dawn air and the lightening sky no longer seemed to hold the promise of day. The shiver that rippled through her now was not from the cold. "Um...haunted?"

He sipped from his cup and tilted his head back a little, looking up toward the facing canyon wall. The wall where she had seen the strange buildings the night before. It was on the tip of her tongue to mention them, but she bit back the words. Some secrets were better kept.

"Haunted," he said after a moment. "Of course, you know the Navajo have great respect for the spirits of the dead, and they never occupied any of the old Anasazi dwellings, because they were believed to be haunted by the spirits of the ancient ones."

Lynn nodded; she had learned that in her own studies. The name Anasazi was a Navajo word and referred to the culture that had existed on the Colorado plateau until the late 1300s, when they suddenly seemed to disappear. The Navajos had come into the area later, and had been faced with the mystery of all the abandoned cliff dwellings. The strange structures she had seen last night were not Anasazi, though. Again excitement niggled at her, and she hoped Cody Walker would move on soon, so she could investigate her discovery.

"It may be," he said slowly, "that the idea that the canyon is haunted simply comes from that. From all the abandoned cliff dwellings in here. I don't really buy that, though, because there are plenty of other canyons with as many dwellings. I don't think this canyon is any eerier than any other."

"Me either," Lynn said quickly, trying not to think of the Indian she had seen last night, or the sense of being watched that had kept her up most of the night.

Cody Walker shrugged. "They say that a shaman's ghost haunts the canyon, protecting an old burial ground from desecration."

Was that what she had seen last night? she wondered as unease trickled through her, freshened by what he was saying. Had she seen a shaman's ghost on the cliff top? But she didn't believe in ghosts. No. It had to have been some local Indian performing a ritual of some kind.

"Well," she said after a moment, when it was apparent the ranger had nothing more to say, "I should be safe, then, because I don't want to desecrate anything."

He turned to look straight at her. "Really? You don't think anyone will come out here to excavate once you've mapped all the ruins?"

For an instant she thought he was serious; then she picked up the faint tone of sarcasm threaded through his words. "I think," she said quietly, "that archaeology does a great deal to preserve things that would otherwise be destroyed by the elements and by curiosity seekers."

"I get upset when I think of all the medicine bundles that lie exposed in museums. I get really disturbed when I consider that the bodies of my ancestors have been dug out of the ground and put on display in glass cases for the entertainment of those same curiosity seekers."

Lynn felt herself flushing. "The museums are arranging for reburial."

"Only because we've made such a stink about it, Ms. Carstairs. Some Native American cultures believe that a spirit wanders eternally if the body isn't buried. What a horrible, horrible fate."

Lynn felt the early prickle of anger and knew her mouth was thinning. "Is there a point to this?"

"If you mean am I trying to discourage you, no. I straddle two worlds, Ms. Carstairs. I don't mind you mapping here. But the old shaman might. I guess what I'm saying is, be careful. You're all alone out here, and if something happens, you might need help. I'll be around and about making sure curiosity seekers don't get into this canyon and the neighboring ones and tear things up, but I can't keep a constant eye on you."

That might almost be taken as a threat, Lynn thought, feeling her scalp prickle uneasily. Except why should a ranger be threatening her? She was here with Park Service approval to perform a simple site survey. That couldn't possibly threaten anyone, could it?

She watched as Cody Walker reached out with a long arm to poke a stick at the fire and stir it up. The sky overhead now held the brightness of early morning, while the canyon floor remained in shadow.

He might, she found herself thinking, have a hidden agenda that had nothing to do with his job as a park ranger. Where would his first loyalties lie? And yet the people who had built these cliff dwellings, the ancient Anasazi, had no living descendants who felt compelled to protect these canyons as shrines.

So there was no reason anyone at all should object to her mapping this canyon, not even Cody Walker.

Therefore, he hadn't been threatening her.

Satisfied with her conclusion, she reached for the pot and poured them both some more coffee.

"How long have you been a ranger here?" she asked him.

"A long time. Almost my entire career." He glanced at her but didn't smile. "Sixteen years."

"That's unusual, isn't it?"

He gave a shrug. "Every rule has an exception. This is where I'm most useful, so this is where I stay."

Another enigmatic statement that could be interpreted in many ways.

"And you spend most of your time policing the canyons?"

He nodded. "Someone has to. I like it out here. It's quiet. Very quiet."

"Do you see many people?"

"Some." Again a long look from dark eyes that revealed nothing. "People go everywhere these days. In the course of a week during the height of the season, I'll run into dozens of backpackers and hikers."

"Even this far out?" The thought made her distinctly uneasy. She'd driven most of the way in, then had packed her supplies into the canyon in three trips.

The difficulty of it had left her feeling safe in her isolation.

"Even this far out," he replied. "It's not something you need to worry about, but don't be surprised if you come across other people. And let me know if you catch any of them pot hunting. We can't have that."

"No, that wouldn't be good." In spite of herself, she looked around, half expecting to see backpackers emerge from the shadows beneath the cliffs.

"Don't try to interfere if you *do* see any pot hunters," he told her. "Just make note of what they look like and anything else that may help to identify them, but don't attempt to stop them. Most of them wouldn't give you any trouble, but there's no point in taking a chance."

Certainly not, she thought, and suddenly remembered that these days park rangers wore bulletproof vests. Maybe it wasn't as bad as a city street, but it could be dangerous out here. Unconsciously, she sighed.

"I'm sorry," he said abruptly. "I didn't mean to disturb you."

She looked straight at him then and felt a shiver trickle through her, a shiver compounded of a sudden, forceful sexual attraction to this man, mixed with fear of him. A subtle fear she couldn't quite put her finger on. A fear born of the conviction that he *had* meant to disturb her.

A conviction that Cody Walker wanted to scare her right out of this canyon.

CHAPTER TWO

The noon sun baked the canyon floor and glared blindingly off the sandstone of the canyon walls. Lynn's left leg, lame since an auto accident years before, ached with a constant throbbing that matched her pounding headache. Even a broad-brimmed straw hat offered little protection from the glare, and none from the heat that baked the rocks.

And despite the brightness of the day, despite the sounds of insects and birds, she was uneasily aware of the terrible emptiness of this canyon. She had been ever since Cody Walker had strode away this morning, leaving her alone with her thoughts and a new crop of fears.

The belief that he had deliberately fed her fears had worn off as the day grew hotter. In retrospect, she was able to convince herself that she'd been imagining implied threats simply because she hadn't slept last night. In the bright light of day, it was impossible to believe such things. Impossible to believe that a park ranger had gone out of his way to warn her off a task that the Park Service itself had approved.

But what was really bugging her was that the alcove had disappeared. There wasn't a sign of it anywhere. The landmarks she had been so sure would guide her seemed to have vanished, too. In utter frustration, she

perched on a boulder and stared up at the cliff wall. It
was hard at the best of times to pick out the dwellings.
Made of native stone, they blended in perfectly with
the cliffs. The cliffs themselves were craggy and full of
deceptive shadows, and even when you knew there was
a dwelling there, you could stare into an alcove and
never see the buildings.

The talus slope, covered with sage and yucca, rose
steeply before her to the cliff face, which itself rose in
apparent uninterrupted splendor.

But it had been *here,* last night, that she had seen the
strange cliff dwelling, the place of triangular doorways. There was no way, absolutely *no way,* that she
had seen an illusion created by moonlight. Up there
now, concealed in the confusing camouflage of light
and shadow and the black streaks of so-called desert
varnish, there was an alcove, and under the natural
arch and on the floor of the alcove were the buildings
she had seen last night. Beautiful buildings of an ar-
chitectural style unlike anything else in the Anasazi
world. And she was, damn it, going to find them.

But the light was defeating her now, so she reconciled herself to waiting a couple of hours, until the
shadows lengthened and changed, and the passage of
the sun from the zenith put this cliff wall back into
shade.

It was an opportunity to make notes on all that she
had seen this morning. An opportunity to check her
position on the Global Positioning System receiver she
carried and record it. A chance to lie back under the
shadow of her hat brim, drink a little water and study
the cliff face casually.

A chance to think about Cody Walker and wonder about the tale he had told her. Wonder about *him*.

The momentary attraction she had felt this morning, the memory of his tight bottom in his green uniform slacks as he walked away—these she dismissed. She had long, long ago reconciled herself to a celibate existence and had learned to ignore her occasional responses to the opposite sex. She had never been especially pretty, but since the accident had left her with a horrendous scar on her left leg and a noticeable limp, she'd found that men tended not to notice her at all. Not that they had noticed her much before. The kindest thing she'd ever been able to say about herself was that she was mousy. Plain and mousy.

So she had concentrated on her assets—a good mind and a lively curiosity about the past—and become an archaeologist with a growing professional reputation. She loved her work and told herself that she needed nothing more. Nothing more at all.

With a sigh, she poured a little water from her canteen onto her bandanna and wiped her dusty face and throat with it. It got so *hot* at the bottom of these canyons at the height of the day. Right now the air was motionless, and only the dryness kept it from being oppressive. It felt like being on the inside of an oven.

Leaning back against a boulder, she stared up at the cliffs and thought about the people who had lived up there so long ago. They had farmed the mesa tops and climbed down to their dwellings using painstakingly carved handholds and toeholds in the sheer rock faces. In some places it appeared they had built reservoirs to collect water on the mesa tops right over the cliff dwellings. Then the water would seep down through the sandstone and provide a spring in the village in the alcove below; in other places the sites had clearly been chosen because there were natural springs.

Life had been short and harsh; most of the Anasazi had lived only into their early twenties. Broken bones had been common, as had malnutrition and one particularly painful genetic disease. But short and hard as their lives had been, they had persevered, building their beautiful dwellings in the alcoves that gave them shade from the heat of the day, a glorious view along the canyon and protection from their enemies...if they had any. No one was really certain why the Anasazi had chosen to build in such difficult places. There was no evidence of war.

What there was was an abundance of beauty that said no matter how hard their lives had been, they had still taken the time to beautify them with their pottery and their weaving.

That always touched Lynn somehow, that those short, hard lives had yielded such grace and loveliness. It touched her to think that these people had cared enough about themselves and their environment to take the time to beautify their world. Such a triumph of the human spirit, she thought.

But somewhere up there were the remains of a different culture. Perhaps one that had preceded the Anasazi. Or one that had come later. But different. Incredibly different, to judge by the patterns she had seen last night in the moonlight. Perhaps somewhere up there were the real answers to why the Anasazi had built in alcoves that were so difficult to reach. Perhaps there was an ultimate answer to why they had vanished so abruptly from these canyons. Yes, the drought theory sounded good, but it was only a theory. Other things might have caused their departure. Things that had to do with the strange dwellings she had seen last night.

Feeling impatient, she took her binoculars from the case and started to scan the cliff face again. She would have to rappel down into the site once she located it, but she *would* locate it, and she *would* investigate it. If her eyes hadn't totally deceived her, it would be one of the most exciting archaeological discoveries in North America in decades.

She got butterflies in her stomach just thinking about what it could mean. There might be answers to mysteries up there, answers to why the cliff dwellings were built in the first place, why they were so abruptly abandoned. So many answers... Or just so many questions?

In the heat of the day, she dozed.

She was shocked awake by a splash of ice water on her face. Gasping, she sat bolt upright and found herself face-to-face with a squatting Cody Walker.

"I figure," he said calmly, while she gasped in outrage and wiped water from her face, "that you're going to look like a boiled lobster in a couple of hours. Lady, you don't fall asleep in the noonday sun—especially at *this* altitude. You can fry faster than an egg on a griddle."

She glanced past him and saw that the shadows had deepened a little. An hour, maybe a little more, since she had fallen asleep. He was right; she would have burned, except that she was wearing a strong sunscreen.

"I hope you're wearing sun block," he remarked as he straightened and screwed the cap back on his canteen.

"Of course." She was glad to be able to prove she wasn't a total idiot. Good grief, this man was... different. Strange. Irritating. "I didn't expect to see you again so soon."

"Lucky for you you did. Four or five hours in this sun would really test that sunscreen of yours."

"SPF 45." She wasn't a *complete* fool.

He grunted. "You haven't seen anyone, have you?"

"Not a soul. Why?" She reached for her canteen and opened it, watching as Cody scanned the canyon.

"Some evidence of recent pot hunting I came across. The dirt hadn't been turned up long enough to completely dry out, so I'd guess it had to have been dug within the last several days."

Lynn definitely didn't like the sound of that. "Whereabouts?"

He pointed. "About three-quarters of a mile up the canyon. There's a tower ruin in an alcove with a chimney that runs right up to the mesa top."

"I know the one you mean. But I haven't seen anyone other than you—" She broke off as she remembered the Indian last night.

"What?" Cody squatted, looking intently at her. "You did see someone."

Lynn looked at him and nodded reluctantly. "Last night, just as the moon rose over the eastern wall, there was an Indian on the mesa.'' She turned and pointed. "Right about there, between those junipers. He chanted something and disappeared.'' She looked at Cody. "But he wouldn't be pot hunting, would he?''

He shrugged. "Indians have to eat, too, and they can make just as much money off Anasazi pottery as anyone else.''

There was certainly no arguing with that.

He fixed her with hard, dark eyes. "You really shouldn't be out here alone.''

"Well, I am. And I'm safer here than on a city street.''

"That's debatable. If you fall down on a city street and crack your head open, you can be reasonably certain someone will call for help. Out here, you could die and be eaten by buzzards before anyone noticed.''

At that she smiled faintly. "You trying to scare me off, Walker? I'm careful. I have a radio. If I don't check in each evening, *you'll* hear about it and be told to come looking.''

At that, finally, he cracked a smile, an attractive expression that revealed even teeth. "Yeah, I reckon that's exactly what'll happen. Doesn't mean I approve of people hiking into the wilderness all by themselves.''

"What about you? You're alone.''

"That's different.'' His smile widened. "I've been doing this all my life. Have you?''

"Often enough,'' she hedged. Really, all you had to do was be careful and not take ridiculous chances. "Once I've located all the sites I can, I'll need to rappel into them and actually survey them. I'll have help then—when I need it."

He held up his hands, as if to say okay. "Have it your way. But don't fall asleep in the sun again, Ms. Carstairs." Turning a little, he indicated the cliff face with a jut of his chin. "There's nothing up there. This part of the canyon is pretty well empty of dwellings from what I've been able to see."

She almost—*almost*—told him what she had seen in the moonlight. But until she could confirm it, she felt that keeping silent was the safest thing to do. At the very least it would keep her from looking like a fool.

"I was just waiting for the sun to pass over," she said, by way of explanation. "It's hard to see anything at midday."

He nodded briefly. "Next time, do it in the shade."

Before she could respond with an irritated remark, he rose and turned slowly, looking as if he were actually tasting the breeze. Somehow Lynn didn't doubt that if there was another person nearby, Cody Walker would have sensed it. A few more seconds ticked by, and then he looked down at her. "Are you mapping the entire canyon?"

She shook her head. "I'm an archaeologist, not a geologist. I just want to locate all the sites and then begin a survey of them, to get an idea what's here." She stood up, absently brushing the seat of her pants and stretching her lame leg. "See that alcove over there?" She pointed northeast, to an alcove that contained an astonishingly well-preserved cluster of buildings amid the rocky debris of six centuries. "I'll sketch the cliff face into a grid and use the Global Positioning System to accurately identify the ends of the grid so the alcove can be located again easily. So it never gets lost again. When I finish this survey and have identified which sites, if any, are worthy of further investigation, I'll come back with a team. For now, I just want to locate everything and identify any especially interesting sites. It's basic, boring work, but it gets me out of the office." Boring except for whatever she had seen last night. Boring except for the man who stood beside her.

Cody looked down at her. "So you'll have to go up on the mesas to complete the work?"

Lynn nodded. "From down here I get one perspective. From up there I'll get an entirely different one, and I'll probably find sites I missed from below." They were standing with their backs to the cliff where she had seen the strange architecture last night, and that was the way she wanted it. As the shadows lengthened, the possibility that the alcove would become visible was increasing, and if Cody saw what she had seen, he, too would want to investigate. She didn't want anyone in her way until she knew what she had found.

That was when the back of her neck began to prickle with the uncomfortable sensation that somebody was watching them from behind. That eyes were intent upon her back. She forgot about the alcove she had pointed out to Cody and tried to ignore the absolute conviction that someone was right behind her. No way. There was nobody else in the canyon. . . .

Unable to stop herself, she whirled around and saw nothing. Nothing. No one was there. A shuddering sigh of relief escaped her.

"Lynn? Lynn, what's wrong?"

"I ... thought I heard something," she said finally, unable to look at him. She had never been able to lie with any skill.

"Yeah?" He took a couple of steps in the direction she was staring. "Maybe a mouse knocked a pebble. Sorry, I didn't hear anything."

But the feeling hadn't gone away, she realized. As her initial relief at not seeing anyone passed, she realized that she still felt *watched*.

But she didn't want to say that to Cody Walker. Life had taught her that men tended to dismiss women's feelings as hysterical, and he would probably just pat her shoulder and tell her that it was the emptiness of the canyon spooking her.

And maybe that was all it was, she told herself as she looked up and around, trying to find any sign that there was another human being within sight. Maybe that was all it was, because there certainly wasn't another person visible. Not anywhere.

Unable to find anything at all unusual out there, her eyes gradually returned to Cody—and found him looking down at her, his expression an enigma.

"I'll stick around," he said abruptly.

Contradictory feelings flooded her. On the one hand, she wanted to be utterly alone to look for the strange cliff dwelling; on the other, she didn't want to be alone with the feeling that she was being watched by something sinister. "There's no reason," she heard herself begin to protest uncertainly.

"Sure there is," he said flatly. "You're as spooked as a horse who's seen a rattlesnake. What exactly did you hear?"

Uncomfortably aware that she hadn't heard anything at all, she merely shrugged. "I'm . . . not sure."

His eyes, she thought, were as deep and dark as the night . . . and as forbidding. He knew she wasn't telling the truth, she realized. He knew it and was wondering what to make of it.

After a long, intense moment, he looked away. "Come on," he said. "There's nothing around here. I'll walk you back to your campsite."

She opened her mouth to argue, then bit the words back. No. No, she couldn't argue. If she argued, she would have to explain what she had seen last night, and she wasn't ready to do that.

But the real reason she didn't argue was the sudden, frightening feeling that Cody Walker was deliberately trying to get her away from here.

Why would he want to do that unless he knew about the strange dwelling? And if he knew about the dwelling, why would he want to keep it secret?

None of the possibilities that occurred to her did anything to ease her mind.

CHAPTER THREE

A coyote howled somewhere in the night, and the lonesome sound echoed through the canyon. The moon was rising over the rim of the eastern mesa, the first silvery beams touching the top of the western cliffs.

Lynn sat huddled within her sleeping bag, knees drawn to her chin, eyes intent upon the canyon wall where she had seen the strange dwelling last night. If it *had* been an illusion created out of shadows and moonbeams, she wouldn't, in all likelihood, see it tonight. The moon would be in a different position, and the shadows would not be the same.

The coyote howled again, such a lonely, forlorn sound. A few hours ago she had been relieved when Cody Walker made it apparent that he didn't expect to put his sleeping bag next to hers; by sticking around, he merely meant that he wouldn't be too far away and would check on her frequently.

But now, now that it was dark and the coyote was howling and things were moving out there beyond her firelight, she wished he *had* wanted to share her fire. And that made her mad, because she wasn't a chicken, because she had camped out many, many times by herself, and she was, by far, safer here than on the streets of Den— *What was that?*

A soft sound . . . a sound other than the slither of a lizard or the quiet scamper of mice. Something was out there. Something that was trying to be quiet.

Shivering, she began to think wildly. She hadn't come prepared to deal with anything like this. She had no way of defending herself if someone really were out there beyond her firelight, someone who meant her harm.

But why should anyone be there? She must have heard something else. Maybe a coyote. Heavens, there must be hundreds of larger animals out there that she might have heard. There was no reason to think it was anything sinister at all. . . .

Except that it was dark and she was alone.

She sat with her campfire behind her so that it wouldn't blind her as she watched the moon's rays slowly inch down the face of the cliff. As moments passed and nothing seemed to move in the gradually brightening canyon, she began to relax.

It was night, and her nerves had just magnified the sound, that was all. Some little thing had sounded huge because it was dark. Nothing to worry about. Nobody was in this canyon except her and the ranger.

And the Indian she had seen last night. But if he'd been a threat, surely he would have concealed himself from her last night. He must have known she was there; in a night as unbroken as those here in the canyon, her fire had to stand out for miles.

So he was no threat, either.

Behind her the fire popped and crackled, flaring briefly before settling down to a dull, red glow that barely touched the nearby sage. And the moonlight crept down the canyon wall.

Imagine—a legend that some ancient shaman protected a burial site in this canyon. How would such a legend have come down, anyway? These dwellings had been abandoned three hundred years before the Navajo rediscovered them and named the lost people the Anasazi. Could Navajo beliefs that the ghosts of the dead remained in the dwellings where they died have given rise to the legend?

Or had something happened that had caused it to be born? Damn, she wished she had thought to ask Cody about the origins of the tale. They could be as informative as the tale itself. If he even knew.

All of a sudden she heard the sound again. The back of her neck prickled, and a chill trickled down her spine. *Something was out there.*

And now she desperately wished Cody were here. The dark was suddenly populated by demons and bears and all the things that went bump in the night, and she didn't feel a whole lot different than she had as a small child when she had been convinced there was a monster in her closet.

A soft whisper of sound overhead caused her to jerk her head upward to look, and for an instant she glimpsed the passage of a shadow across the stars. Some bird of prey, of course. But the logical explanation didn't quiet the hammering of her heart or stop the crawling fear that crept along her nerves.

She wasn't alone.

The night was alive with threat. The darkness, filled by the whisper of the wind, grew ominous. The coyote had stopped howling. The sage hissed almost inaudibly as the breeze stirred it with chilly breath. Skeletal fingers of cold moonlight crept lower on the facing cliff, illuminating some surfaces, failing to penetrate the dark in others.

No insects, she thought suddenly. There were none of the night sounds of insects. No sound at all except the wind. An unnatural quiet.

Something was out there.

Little by little she was inching backward toward her fire, torn by the need to be perfectly still, so as not to attract the attention of whatever was out there, and the need to escape somehow. There was no escape, though. None. She could run wildly into the night and not escape whatever was out there. The fire offered no protection at all, a small heap of glowing coals that gave warmth and little light, but she somehow felt slightly safer with the heat of it at her back.

Despite her fears, her eyes kept straying back to the cliff. Damn, the professional opportunity of a lifetime, and she might miss it because of the crawling sense that there was something out there in the dark watching her.

And that was all there was, she told herself. Just the *suspicion* that something was out there. Pure imagination. Pure childish—

"Leave."

He was there suddenly, conjured out of the darkness, a shadowy figure in feathers and paint. A huge, looming shadow at the very edge of the firelight, almost invisible.

"Leave."

They say the ghost of an old shaman protects a sacred burial ground....

Shock held Lynn perfectly still as she stared up at the mythical figure towering over her. A ghost? Was she seeing a ghost?

He might have been. He seemed to hover in the darkness, little more than a glimmer of paleness against the pitch of night. But then he moved a little, and suddenly his head was silhouetted against the brightening cliff face behind. A strong, powerful head, long hair decorated with feathers that dimly reflected the pale moonlight.

Real. No ghost. She should have been able to see the canyon wall right through a ghost. Shouldn't she?

"Who...who are you?" she managed to croak. Her heart galloped like a stampeding horse, and she gasped for air in a universe gone insane. Not a ghost. Couldn't be. No such thing...

"You trespass."

It took a moment for that to penetrate her fear-clogged brain. And into the haze of fright came a flame of anger. "I am *not*," she said. "I have permission to be here from the Park Service. Who the hell are you to tell me to get out of here?" Oh, God, Lynn! Arguing with a ghost? Or worse, arguing with a man who could do her serious harm?

Shadowy though the figure was, she could see an almost impatient movement of his head.

"You trespass," he said again. "There are older things than your Park Service. Older taboos you might break. Dangerous grounds you might tread upon. Leave before you get hurt."

"Are you... Are you threatening me?"

He moved. If he made any sound, the wind swallowed it. Feathers bobbed and tossed, shadows among shadows, giving off little glimmers as the rising moon began to brighten the night. Behind him, silver light poured slowly down the cliffs.

"No," he said. "This is a warning. There are dangerous things in this canyon. Spirits older than time have left their powers here. Ghosts lurk in the dark places. Leave them alone."

But Lynn had waited too long for this opportunity and wanted too badly to see the strange village she had glimpsed in the moonlight last night. Nor was she a physical coward. Oh, she was afraid of rejection; it was the primary reason she avoided men. But physically, any fear she'd had of pain or risk had vanished long ago during the torturous sessions of physical therapy that had made it possible for her to walk again. No, she was not a coward, and she understood that to accomplish anything important, a risk had to be taken.

So she gathered her courage, pushed the sleeping bag off her shoulders and stood. The man never moved, as if nothing she could do might threaten him.

"I don't intend to disturb any ghosts," she said as politely as she could. He's one of the local Indians, she told herself. Respect his beliefs, but remain firm. He doesn't want trouble any more than I do. "I'm simply doing a site survey. Do you know what that is?"

"And after you come the diggers. I know. This is sacred ground. You can't dig here."

"I'm *not* digging here. I'm merely mapping sites. I don't threaten any sacred ground. There's no reason anyone would *want* to dig here in the foreseeable future since we feel we've learned about all we can at our present level of technology—unless something really new turns up. The pot hunters are more dangerous." She hesitated, trying to find a way to reach this man...if he *was* a man. "Um, who are you? Why is this place so important to you?"

For a moment, it seemed the shadowy figure wouldn't answer. But then his deep voice rolled forth in an almost ritual cadence. "I am called Starwalker. I am the Guardian. Leave this place."

Lynn's mouth opened on another question, but before she could speak, he vanished. As if he had never been there. As if... As if he were made of nothing but the shadows from which he had emerged.

As if he were a ghost.

She collapsed near the fire, her legs feeling like rubber, and started shivering. Rationally she didn't believe in ghosts, couldn't logically accept the idea of spirits that remained earthbound. Wasn't even sure she believed anything survived death.

Now this. Had she been talking to a man? Or to the ghost of the ancient shaman? Oh, heavens, was she losing her mind?

And just how much of a threat was that warning? He'd told her to leave, warned her that she was trespassing, but he hadn't said the equivalent of "Go, or you'll get hurt."

Not in so many words, but the implication had been there. The warning could have no other meaning. No other meaning at all.

Oh, where was that damn park ranger when she needed him? But as soon as she had the thought, she chided herself for cowardice. In the first place, Starwalker had disappeared. If he intended her any harm tonight, he certainly wouldn't have done that, would he? So what did she need Cody Walker for?

Companionship in the dark. A childish desire, she told herself. Purely childish. But childish or not, it would have been a relief to hear another voice, a reasonably friendly voice. It would have been a relief not to be alone in the night.

Shivering in reaction, she drew the sleeping bag up around her shoulders again and scanned the cliff face. Another hour had passed and, unless she was mistaken, the moon had nearly reached the place where it had illuminated that strange alcove last night. At any moment now she might see it again.

"Evenin'."

Now. Now, of all times, the ranger stepped out of the shadows and into the dim red glow from the coals of the fire. Now, when she didn't dare take her eyes from the cliff for fear of missing the moment of transformation, when the secret dwelling would emerge from the shadows.

"Hi," she said, but beyond one swift glance, she didn't look at him. "This place is as popular as Grand Central Station."

"What do you mean?" She sensed rather than saw that he squatted beside her, looking out across the valley as if he was trying to ascertain what held her attention. For a long moment she was torn, wondering if she dared to chance missing the moment when the light would be just right. But tomorrow night the moon would have moved even more, and there was always a chance that it wouldn't illuminate the alcove at the angle that would reveal the dwelling.

Besides, if she acted distant enough, maybe Cody would leave her alone. Not that she really wanted to be alone with the night and the threat Starwalker might represent. She shivered again, and wished Cody would go away—but not too far away.

"Lynn? What do you mean? Was someone else here tonight?"

In spite of herself, she looked at Cody...and caught her breath. Lord, he was beautiful, ruggedly beautiful even in the dim light of moonrise and the fire's glow. Her heart pounded harder, refusing to let her ignore her reaction to him. "Somebody called Starwalker," she said, forcing her attention back to the cliff. Struck like a silly teenager, she thought, mooning over the way a man looked. Disgusting.

"Starwalker? What was he doing?"

"Warning me away." She battled the urge to look at him again. He needed to know about this guy, but she didn't want to miss her moment in order to drool while she told him. "He said I was trespassing and should leave. When I told him I had Park Service permission to be here, he said there were older taboos and dangers, and that I should be careful not to disturb any ghosts. Said he wasn't threatening me, just warning me."

"Maybe you ought to consider clearing out until we can find out what this guy is up to."

"Damn it, no!" The force of her own conviction startled her a little, coming as it did hard on the heels of her fright.

For a moment Cody didn't reply. There was a scraping sound as he moved, and Lynn dared to glance at him. He was lowering himself to the ground, sitting cross-legged beside her.

"Did you feel threatened?" he asked finally.

"A little. Good grief, Cody, he came out of the dark. Out of nowhere. And he was dressed in feathers and paint.... Yes, I felt a little threatened by him." She dragged her attention back to the cliff and tried not to think how good it felt to have this man beside her, a bulwark against the things that lurked in the dark. She hated to admit even that much weakness.

"Maybe we ought to get you out of here until we're sure you're safe."

In that instant anger surged in her, driving out the fear, at least temporarily. Leave? *Leave?* Run away with her tail between her legs because of some mumbo jumbo about old taboos and ghosts? No way! "I don't think so. I have a job to do."

The fire crackled behind them, and moonlight dripped a little lower on the cliff face. Soon, Lynn thought. Soon. Her heart accelerated a little, and wind caught at her bound hair, snatching some loose strands and whipping them across her face. The night was growing steadily chillier.

Cody stirred. "The mapping will still be here in a few days or weeks, Lynn. It's not as if it's going to go away."

But there was a stubborn streak in her that kept her going long after others quit. Back in high school they had told her that she would never walk again, so she'd made up her mind to prove them all wrong. In fact, if there was one thing guaranteed to get her going, it was someone telling her that she couldn't, or shouldn't do something.

"I'm sorry, Cody," she said flatly, without looking at him. "I don't turn tail. I don't quit."

"I'm not asking you to quit. I'm suggesting you wait until we can be sure this guy isn't a threat to you."

"How can you possibly determine that? Find him and question him? If you do, he'll only tell you that he was warning me about taboos and ghosts. No answer at all. If you can ever find him." She gave a nervous laugh. "I'm not at all sure he wasn't a ghost, or some kind of bad dream, actually."

As soon as the words were out of her mouth, she was horrified for admitting such possibilities. Good God, what would he think of her? A crazy archaeologist who thought she saw ghosts!

"Well, you wouldn't be the first one who saw weird things in the moonlight around here," Cody said after a moment, sounding as if he wasn't at all disturbed by her admission. "Usually, though, things like that don't talk. You didn't imagine it or see a ghost. And that's what worries me. Somebody—a human somebody—wants you out of here, and I don't trust humans much more than I trust an ornery rattler."

Lynn was a little surprised to realize she felt pretty much the same way. She glanced at Cody, then returned her attention to the cliff. She could swear that moonlight was about to touch the place where she had seen the strange dwellings last night. Her heart took another leap, and she resisted the urge to look at Cody. It was hard to keep her gaze on the cliff when he was right beside her, and she resented that.

"Look, Lynn," he said when she didn't answer him, "you can always come back later this summer."

She shook her head, feeling her chin set mulishly. Long ago she had learned that giving in to fear only made you a prisoner of it. If she gave in now, she would lose everything she had worked so hard for. "No. I came to do this now and, by God, I'm going to do it! That character is going to have to do a little more than mumble about taboos and ghosts to get me out of here."

All of a sudden every hair on the back of her neck stood up, and chills trickled slowly down her spine. *There it was.*

The dwelling.

CHAPTER FOUR

It didn't look quite as it had last night. Last night, when the moon had struck it, the dwellings had seemed to leap out of nowhere, as if they had been brilliantly conjured from moonbeams. Tonight she never would have noticed it if she hadn't already known where to look. If she hadn't already had a template stamped in her mind so that those patterns of light and dark made sense.

It was there, and she drew a soft, sharp breath of exhilaration. It was there.

"Lynn? Lynn, what is it?"

She didn't answer him; she was too busy taking inventory of the cliffs, trying to pinpoint the position of the alcove by noting landmarks on the mesa above. And as soon as there was light enough at the bottom of the cliff, maybe she could locate some landmarks on the talus slope.

But for now she simply stared in quiet wonder, trying to memorize every detail so that she could remember them all come morning.

The wind picked up suddenly, its icy breath snaking into the neck of her jacket, whistling forlornly in her ear. And in the instant before a cloud from out of nowhere scudded across the moon and concealed the cliff dwelling, the feeling of being watched returned.

Someone was out there. Someone was watching. Someone was stalking her.

She turned to look at Cody, suddenly needing human contact and closeness, even with this stranger. She nearly reached out to him, but in the dark, his face highlighted on one side by the redly glowing fire behind them, he suddenly looked . . . frightening.

"What is it?" he asked again.

She looked past him, into the dark, and wondered if Starwalker were out there watching them. If there was something else or someone else, or if she were just losing her mind.

The moon slipped out from behind the cloud, and she turned swiftly to look at the cliff. The dwelling was once again invisible, hidden within the shadows and the camouflaging patterns of light and dark.

Say nothing. The whispered warning snaked through her brain, a cold sensation of distrust she didn't like. Say nothing about the dwelling. Nothing. How did she know she could trust Cody Walker simply because he wore the uniform of the Park Service?

"Nothing," she said finally, her voice rusty. "Nothing. I thought I heard something. Guess I'm spooked."

"That's understandable." He shook his head, hardly more than a shadow among shadows. "I'll stretch out here with you tonight. In the morning we'll talk more about this."

"Fine."

Fine. She spread her sleeping bag out beside the fire and lay on her back, staring up at the incredible carpet of stars dimmed slightly by the brilliance of the moon.

Something out there was watching her, she thought again. And somehow she didn't think it was anything as ordinary as a man named Starwalker . . . and he was already far from ordinary. It was all too easy, suddenly, to believe in ghosts and curses. All too easy to believe that the night posed a threat.

At dawn the sky was streaked with pearly streamers of pink clouds. The lightest of dews had settled, making everything damp. Lynn's eyes opened slowly, and she found herself staring at a spiky yucca plant. Amazing, she thought sleepily, how many uses that plant had. Its spines became needles, its fibers strong thread, and its fruit was an edible delicacy. . . .

A snuffling, scraping sound behind her alerted her, and she sat bolt upright. For an instant, just an instant, she stared into huge yellow eyes, and then the animal bolted in terror.

"Coyote," Cody said.

She turned and saw him walking toward her from around a large boulder. He had probably gone to answer nature's call, she thought, then blushed, quickly looking away.

"*Coyotl,*" he said, squatting beside the fire and beginning to carefully layer small twigs and grass on the coals. "It's straight from Nahuatl, the language the Aztecs spoke. *Tomato* is another word from there. *Tomatl.*" He ended each word with a sound very similar to a short burst of static.

"Do you speak Nahuatl?" she asked, making no attempt to imitate that final sound.

He shook his head. "Just a few words. I speak English, because it's an English-speaking world. The same as you."

Feeling chastised in some inexplicable way, she turned her attention to wiggling out of her sleeping bag and into her jacket. The morning air was chilly, clear and very, very quiet. Only soft crackles from the growing fire disturbed it.

Moving with easy efficiency, Cody filled her coffeepot with water from one of the water bags she'd carried in. "How many scoops?" he asked as he opened the can of ground coffee.

"Four."

He glanced at her, a faint smile creasing the corners of his eyes. "You like it strong."

"And thick."

With an effort, she resisted the temptation to watch him finish making the coffee and instead made herself survey the canyon and the long shadows of early morning.

"I'll take you up the canyon today," Cody said abruptly. "Closer to the cliff dwellings. Away from here. Maybe this Star guy will forget about you if he sees you're gone from here."

No! The resistance was almost a thunderclap in her mind, so strong was it, but she managed not to voice the word aloud. Somehow, some way, she had to stay here, had to find the time and privacy to locate the cliff dwelling that was visible only by moonlight. She couldn't let anyone or anything stand in her way.

Some corner of her mind noted that she was behaving a little strangely, as if obsessed by the dwelling to the exclusion of everything else, even her own safety. That corner of her mind tried to remind her of Starwalker and his vague threats, tried to argue that she could always return in a few weeks when the threat was reduced or removed. That the village she had glimpsed wasn't going to vanish if she waited until it was safer to investigate.

That she was behaving as if she were possessed.

The thought was like a chilly little trickle of ice down her spine, impossible to ignore. It was a wild thought, a thought so alien as to seem as if it had come from somewhere else. Uneasiness niggled at her, an awareness that she was not behaving like herself, that her determination to stay was foolhardy, and she was *never* foolhardy. Courageous, willing to take calculated risks for which she had fully prepared, yes. But she was *not* foolhardy.

She didn't want to think about such things. Her mind shied away from the very idea that she might be reacting to external forces in some way. That something else might be influencing her on an unconscious level. It was incomprehensible to her that she should feel this way, yet she did.

But she refused to accept it. Didn't dare admit to herself that anything other than her own wishes and desires might be motivating her. She had to dismiss it because there was no alternative. She might well be on the verge of making the discovery of a lifetime. She couldn't afford to turn tail because she felt frightened and uneasy.

She wouldn't be able to look at herself in the mirror every morning if she fled because of an inchoate feeling that some unseen presence was lurking at the corners of her mind.

Ghosts and ghoulies. Stuff and nonsense. Suppressing a shudder, she stiffened her spine.

She looked at Cody. "I have to finish mapping this section before I move on."

He tilted his head back and looked at her along the length of his nose, making her feel like some kind of specimen under observation. "You can continue the mapping of this section anytime. Besides, there's nothing here of archaeological significance, anyway."

"Then that needs to be accurately established, not guessed at. And to do that, I need to complete the survey."

"Which you can do at a better time. This canyon won't go away, Lynn."

"Neither will I. I'm not going to be run off by hints about taboos and curses. I've invested too much time and effort in this project to be scared off by a bogeyman."

"But you have to consider—"

"No." Almost at once, she wished she could call the word back. She wasn't usually so blunt, preferring to be diplomatic when disagreeing rather than creating hard feelings. But this time she wasn't being diplomatic at all, and it was apparent that Cody Walker wasn't pleased.

But he didn't threaten to have her forcibly removed, which surprised her in retrospect. Later, after he'd downed his coffee, grunted something about people too stupid to be on their own and vanished up the canyon, it struck her as surprising that he hadn't pursued the argument. He could have threatened to have her removed. And he probably could even have forced her removal on the grounds that her safety was in doubt.

But he hadn't. Which meant that he didn't think the threat was all that serious. Or, at least, that was what she wanted to believe. Unfortunately, remembering the dark shadow of the Indian who had warned her away last night, she wasn't at all sure about that.

But she was going to stay anyway, and for the moment she quit wondering at her own uncustomary foolhardiness. The compelling need to explore her discovery outweighed her fear of Starwalker. That was enough.

Someone was watching her.

The chilling awareness struck her right in the middle of her back when she was halfway up the talus slope. She froze, trying to hold her breath so she could hear. Her back ached, her gimpy leg was throbbing, and sweat had soaked the back of her cotton safari shirt. A trickle of perspiration ran down her nose and hung there, itching.

But she didn't move, not a muscle. Someone was watching her. It might well be Cody, worried about her safety. Or it could be the man who called himself Starwalker. Or it could be someone—or some*thing*—else.

A coyote, she suggested to herself. Even one of the wildcats that still occupied the high altitudes in diminishing numbers. Lynx? Mountain lion? Whatever it was in these parts. She'd seen them before, felt the pressure of their steady stares as they considered whether she was friend or foe. They were no threat to her, unless she disturbed their young.

And that was a thought that sent more ice trickling along her spine. Good Lord, could she be approaching some cat's den? How would she know? She knew nothing about the habits of mountain cats...except that they liked to sun on rocky ledges in the heat of the day.

And maybe that was what one of them was doing right now, from one of the many ledges above her.

Slowly, taking care not to move suddenly and startlingly, she eased herself down on the steep slope and turned around so that she could sit more easily, with her knees up and her feet resting at a lower level.

Listening to her own breathing, just about the only sound in the canyon, she looked up and down the length of the gorge. If Starwalker or Cody were out there, perhaps she could pick him out. But only if he moved, she realized. The brush on the canyon floor was dense, here and there punctuated by an elderly juniper.

The chances were equally slim that she could pick out a cat on one of the ledges above. Its coat would blend perfectly with this kind of terrain, and it wouldn't be moving, either.

That left her with the creepy feeling of being observed by someone or something unknown. The back of her neck prickled uneasily, but there wasn't a thing she could do to ease it.

Except continue her climb and remain alert. She *had* to reach that dwelling.

The obsessiveness of the urge troubled her a little, but she reassured herself that it was good old-fashioned scientific curiosity. The desire to discover something hitherto unknown. Not foolhardiness. Not some dark, alien impulse.

The air stirred, carrying a welcome breeze, and for a few moments she forgot about the lurker. When the sun climbed, these canyons seemed to capture the heat and hold it, and when the air was still it became suffocating. The breath of relative coolness was welcome, and she tilted her head back a little in pleasure.

But the desire to reach the dwelling goaded her, making it impossible to sit still for long. Hardly aware that she sighed, she turned and began climbing again. There was loose talus, and the slope was steep enough that she stayed in a crouch, using her hands as often as not. Gloves and long pants protected her from minor scrapes, but they couldn't prevent bruising.

And nothing was going to stop her this time. Last night she had marked the distinctive outline of a juniper on the mesa directly above the dwelling. This morning the juniper didn't look quite the same, but she was pretty certain it was the same one. She had simply crossed the canyon, heading directly for the juniper, and when she had reached the foot of the talus slope beneath the tree, she had noted distinctive landmarks in the cliff face that would guide her when the tree was no longer visible from below.

Simple, straightforward navigation by sight, and a dozen things could have screwed it up. Even now, she might be climbing toward the wrong landmark, because as shadows shifted with the passage of the sun, things no longer looked quite the same. And as she drew closer to her landmarks, she saw them more clearly, and they didn't look quite the same, either.

It was the best she could do, though—that and check her compass to be sure she was staying on the heading she had given herself. If she got within a reasonable distance of the dwelling, she ought to at least be able to see it and get to it.

It was odd, though, how it was so invisible in the light of day. Yes, other cliff dwellings were deceptive, but none were quite as invisible as this one. If you stared long enough into an alcove, eventually you saw the straight line of a window, door or wall that betrayed the presence of an Anasazi ruin. Mostly you needed patience and a knowledge of what you were looking for.

But patient looking didn't reveal this site at all, and that intrigued her as much as anything. Certainly when the morning sun shone into the alcove it ought to create shadows that would betray the presence of a structure—just the way the moon had done the last two nights. But that didn't happen, and she was dying to know why.

Excitement kept her going long after her leg had begun to shriek in protest, long after her hands became swollen and bruised. Her back ached, and perspiration plastered her shirt to her skin in places, but she hardly cared. She was on the brink of a discovery that might well change the way the past was viewed.

Perhaps there had been a civilization here before the Anasazi. Or a very different one concurrent with the Anasazi. What if the widely accepted theory that the

Anasazi had vanished from this area because of a severe drought proved to be wrong? What if they really had built their dwellings so inaccessibly in the alcoves in order to defend themselves against attack, a theory that had come into disrepute?

All of a sudden the chill that had touched the base of her skull was all around her. A huge dark shadow swept over her. Just a cloud passing over, she thought...except that the temperature dropped so startlingly. Too much to be explained by a cloud.

She froze, her mind rebelling against what her senses were telling her. It was so cold and so dark within the shadow that it was as if she sat within a patch of night, while just beyond the edge of the shadow the day glimmered with blinding brilliance.

Turn over and look up, she told herself. Turn over and look up at the cloud. But some part of her didn't believe it was a cloud. Her mind insisted on connecting it somehow with the sense of being watched...and she was afraid of what she might see.

And then, in an instant, the shadow and the cold were gone, though not the feeling of being watched. The hot sun was again hammering on her back and blinding her with its brilliance. All was again normal.

But it didn't feel normal. Somehow she felt as if she had just returned from another place, as if what had once been familiar had somehow become unfamiliar—the way home felt when she'd been away on a long trip. And hovering around the edges of her mind was the memory of the touch of something *other.*

CHAPTER FIVE

Somehow, impossibly, she had reached the wrong alcove. After an arduous climb nearly straight up the side of the cliff, she had arrived at a spacious but empty alcove in the cliff face. Lying exhausted on the dusty floor, looking up at the overhang that protected it, then beyond to the crystalline blue sky, she wondered how she had managed it.

Her leg ached fiercely, a sharp throbbing that she couldn't ignore, spearing her from her hip almost to her ankle. No way was she climbing any farther today, either up or down.

Beside her lay her knapsack, which held some food, a couple of Mylar survival blankets and a water flask. She could stay here overnight without any problem at all, and that, she decided, was exactly what she was going to do.

And maybe she could figure out where she'd gone wrong in her navigation. Oh, it was easy enough to drift even when using a compass, but she'd thought she had lined up her visual cues sufficiently to keep on course. Apparently she hadn't, because this alcove sure appeared to be empty.

Not that it was. There were probably the remnants of Anasazi occupation here somewhere, and she needed only to look. Most of the major alcoves displayed some sign of habitation. But she was here to map the more spectacular sites that might need work to preserve them from further deterioration so that nothing priceless would be lost. The collapsed remnants of a kiva—the traditional round underground ceremonial chamber—or a tumbled-down masonry wall were not the kinds of things she was here to uncover.

She *would* look, though, because she was here.

But first she had to get past the pain in her leg. It was something she was used to, something she lived with and didn't think too much about, except when it became really sharp. When that happened, there was nothing she could do except try to think about something else until it passed.

The wind whistled around the corners of the alcove, a soft, mournful moan. If she had to live in these canyons, she would want to live in the alcoves as the Anasazi had…provided she could find an easier, safer means of access than hand-over-hand climbing. The alcove provided shelter from the sun, rain and snow, along with security from intruders. There was a lot to be said for it.

The breeze cooled her off, and gradually the pain in her leg eased, allowing her to sit up and survey a truly spectacular view of the canyon. The other benefit of living in these alcoves, she thought. The panorama was breathtaking, and from here she could see some of the dwellings farther up the canyon. They were small and distant, but knowing they were there, she could make out the sharp lines of shadows that were too square to be accidental. Often, even when dwellings were known to be in a particular area, they could be almost impossible to locate.

How different it must have been when a couple of hundred people were living in one of those alcoves. It must have seemed busy and active and noisy. Colorful. Now it simply seemed . . . sad. Only the wind occupied the cliff dwellings of the Anasazi now.

Turning, she looked deeper into the alcove, which was shadowed now as the sun sank behind the mesa. Facing east, it would catch the glory of the sunrise but by noon would be in shadow. And in the early evening, as now, it was almost dark in here.

All of a sudden she stopped breathing and froze. Something was back there in the shadows, deep in the alcove. Someone or something. Instinct held her still, keeping her motionless in a way that would reduce her visibility. Hoping against hope that whatever was there wasn't intelligent enough to recognize that she wasn't just a piece of upthrusting stone.

Endless seconds ticked by as she waited for any sign, any sound, that would betray whatever was in the shadows, but nothing moved. Finally she decided that she must have heard the wind stirring some sagebrush. Or a small animal moving across some loose rock.

Gradually her pulse returned to normal and she relaxed again. It was getting too dusky in the alcove to do any serious site evaluation, but she decided she could still wander around and get a feel for the place.

No photograph could truly capture the size of some of these alcoves, or the feeling of standing beneath a rock sky. This one was huge, which made it all the more surprising that it didn't contain visible ruins. As she wandered, she picked up scraps of wood and dead vegetation that would permit her to make a small fire.

Deeper in the alcove, near where the overhang arched downward to create a back wall that met the floor, uneasiness began to grow in her. Unsure what was niggling at her, she turned to look out toward the canyon and saw that the blue sky was still bright. It was early evening yet, too soon to worry about loss of light.

After a moment's hesitation, she continued her exploration, sweeping her gaze expertly over the ground, seeking any betraying signs of demolished structures or digging of any kind.

There was a large round depression, like a shallow bowl, at the southern edge of the alcove, and she paused to squat and look across it. A filled-in kiva? Or the partially collapsed roof of one? It appeared to be about twelve feet across, and perfectly round. Reaching into her back pocket, she pulled out a notebook and scribbled quick impressions. This was a site worth recording on her survey.

By the time she had finished writing her notes, evening had settled over the land, casting the alcove into a dim twilight. Conscious suddenly that she would soon be able to see nothing at all, she tucked the notebook away and made her way cautiously back toward her knapsack, taking care to circle the kiva.

Just as she came around to the far side, a chill settled over her that had nothing to do with the darkening night. It was as if she had stepped into a sharply defined pocket of frigid air—*clammy* frigid air. A shudder ran through her, and a darkness seemed to settle over her mind, a feeling of black hatred.

The emotion was so intense, so out of context, so unlike anything she had ever felt, that she cried out and instinctively recoiled. Some smidgen of awareness reached past her shock, however, catching her in the instant before she set her foot backward into the depression of the buried kiva.

Again she froze, balanced on her bad leg, not sure what to do or where to go. The hate that swamped her came from without; there wasn't a doubt in her mind. Something external was generating that terrible emotion, and it terrified her to be able to feel it. Terrified her that something unseen could project a feeling into the very air.

She needed to get away from it, needed desperately to be free of that horrible black well of feeling. Unable to do anything else, she swung her leg and stepped forward.

The feeling intensified, becoming an intangible pressure that seemed to weigh her down as if she were walking through molasses. Feeling a cold sweat break out on her forehead from the effort, wondering if she were having some kind of stroke that was causing this nightmare inability to move...

As suddenly as she had become swamped in the black emotion, she was free of it. The air again became crisp and clean, and she could even hear faint birdsong as twilight purpled the sky. It was as if someone had thrown a switch.

With the greatest reluctance, she forced herself to turn around and look behind her. She expected to see something—anything—to explain or somehow validate what had just happened. There should have been a rippling of the air, or a dark shadow wavering there at the edge of the sunken kiva. Something.

There was nothing at all. The air looked perfectly normal, the ground exactly as it had been before she stepped into... into what? A miasma of hatred that seemed to have penetrated to her very soul?

Shivering, wondering if she were losing her mind, she turned swiftly and hurried to her backpack. She would light her fire before it became totally dark, and drive back the night.

A small, very small, beacon against whatever dark thing had touched her.

She wished, crazily, that she hadn't come up here alone. That she'd confided in Cody about the strange village she had seen. His presence right now would be a genuine comfort. Surely, if she had told him about the village, he would have been as eager as she to climb up and investigate.

In retrospect, her reluctance to tell him about what she had seen seemed strange. It wasn't like her to be so compulsively secretive. Not like her to strike out like this without telling someone what she intended. Good Lord, it was foolhardy not to have told someone her plans. If she injured herself, they might never find her, because they wouldn't know where to look.

Whatever had she been thinking of? Or more to the point, why hadn't she been thinking?

She could scarcely believe she had been this foolish.

The fire she built was small, designed to give her something to warm her hands over until she went to sleep. Designed to give her psychological comfort as much as anything. It would hold back the shadows, and some primitive part of her felt that it would hold back the evil things that somehow seemed to lurk in the dark.

Tonight that sense of something evil was stronger than she had ever felt it. It kept her sitting up long past the time she would have liked to curl into her Mylar blankets and sleep in comfortable warmth on the hard ground. She couldn't bring herself to close her eyes, couldn't bring herself to allow anything to approach unseen.

Which was ridiculous, she told herself. Utterly and completely ridiculous. There was nothing at all up here that she needed to fear. Mice, maybe a coyote, birds... only small animals could reach these alcoves. Logically, she knew there wasn't a damn thing she had to fear.

But logic didn't banish the dark shadows that seemed to move and sway beyond the firelight, taking on substance and then trickling away into the deeper recesses of the night. Nor did logic banish the overwhelming sense that she was not alone, even though she knew for a fact that she had to be. If there had been anyone else up here, she would have seen them, and no one could approach silently up that talus slope. She knew that, but it didn't help one bit to remind herself of it.

The thin air of the high altitude relinquished the day's heat rapidly. Long before weariness overtook her, she was pulling a Mylar blanket around her shoulders and huddling closer to the fire. It was going to be a long, miserable night.

"Leave..."

The whispered command wove into her dreams,

rousing her from her doze. She was still sitting before the fire, the blanket drawn around her shoulders, her neck stiff from the way her head had drooped. Flames leapt high as the fire burned brilliantly, a beacon against the night.

"Leave..."

Eyes glimmered at her from the far side of the fire. Human eyes. Dark, intense, reflecting the flames. The rest of him blended with the shadows beyond the fire, shadows that concealed his face in dimness.

Seconds passed as she stared, not awake enough to react, half-convinced she was still dreaming. Then understanding penetrated and ice filled her veins. Starwalker was here. On the ledge with her.

"Leave." This was no whisper, but a firm command.

He wasn't real, she thought wildly. He couldn't possibly be real. As nervous as she was tonight, she would have heard his approach long before he got up here. She never would have slept through any unnatural sound, not tonight, when she was so uneasy. She knew from experience that she wouldn't do that.

"You must go. You trespass."

She was trapped on a ledge from which there was no escape, caught in the dark in isolation with...with what? A ghost? He must be a ghost...but she didn't believe in ghosts.

Whether she believed it or not, fear trickling along her spine insisted he was a ghost, because he couldn't have materialized beside her fire any other way. And if he were a ghost...

If he were a ghost, he couldn't hurt her.

Could he?

But the appalling fact, the one that kept her glued to the spot and defiant despite fear, was that if he wanted to hurt her, there wasn't a damn thing she could do to prevent it.

"I'm not trespassing," she whispered finally, and then wished she had remained silent. She sounded so frightened and small when what she needed was to sound firm and in charge.

"You tread on sacred ground. You disturb ancient spirits. You break taboo."

"What taboo am I breaking?"

He shifted, a shadow moving among shadows, ghostlike in the way he seemed to have no substance. Another chill ran down her spine like icy water. "None shall walk where the Ancient One sleeps, except the Guardian."

"And you're the Guardian?" No answer was forthcoming. But then, why should there be? He had identified himself to her as the Guardian the first time he had warned her off. The Guardian and the Ancient One. "You, um, guard the Ancient One's sleep?"

"Yes."

"Where does he sleep?" Again she received no answer, but she hadn't really expected to. That was the kind of information she would expect Starwalker to keep secret whether he was a ghost or a man. Her heart was still beating rapidly, but no longer the swift tattoo that left her nearly breathless. And as she calmed a little, her curiosity began to grow swiftly. "Um . . . what happens if his sleep is disturbed?"

There was a long silence in answer, but this time Lynn didn't get the feeling he was refusing to answer. Instead, she felt he was pondering what to tell her. Did ghosts ponder? Considering that she knew nothing about the subject, she guessed it was possible. He certainly wasn't one of those ghosts who threw things like a mischievous child, or one who haunted the hallways of an old house. If Starwalker was a ghost, he was unique.

She wanted very much to believe he was real, but she couldn't quite make herself. A real man couldn't have climbed to this alcove without making noise that would have alerted her. He just couldn't have. But every intellectual bone in her body rejected the notion that he was some kind of spirit…until she looked into his dark eyes and saw the flames of the fire reflected there. She shuddered.

"The Ancient One's slumber must not be disturbed," he said slowly but forcefully. "His awakening will unleash a blight across the lands, and the people will die."

"What kind of a blight?" This sounded like some curse out of a role-playing game. Surely no modern person could take such a thing seriously? But Starwalker seemed to, and the gravity of his voice, his insistence on the taboo, could not be treated lightly or dismissed out of hand. At the very least, his beliefs deserved to be treated with respect.

Nor did she want to anger him. His role as the Guardian, whatever that was, might include murdering trespassers. The back of her neck prickled with the uneasy awareness that there was no escape. She was utterly and completely at the mercy of this man—if he *was* a mortal man. Oh, how she wished she had asked Cody to accompany her.

She looked toward the mouth of the alcove, into the unremitting black of night, and let the wish wing forth. There was a whisper of sound, the fire flared . . . and when she looked back, Starwalker was gone.

Suddenly terrified, she looked around wildly, trying to see him in the shadows, but he had completely vanished.

"Oh God," she whispered on the merest breath as her heart kicked into overdrive. He must have been a ghost or spirit of some kind. No mortal man could have vanished so quickly and soundlessly.

Or perhaps, equally unnerving, he was lurking in the deeper shadows, waiting . . . waiting for what? For her to fall asleep? Surely he didn't need her to fall asleep in order to kill her. He was a large, powerful man, perfectly capable of disposing of her without any difficulty. Hell, all he had to do was pick her up and throw her over the edge. The world would think she had slipped and fallen—if they ever found her.

Shivering almost wildly, she let the Mylar blanket fall from her shoulders. It made her too visible, its silvery surface catching and reflecting whatever light there was. Her denim jacket and jeans would be much harder to see.

Now to get away from the fire, to slip back into the shadows herself and hide from Starwalker if she could. But moving around on the ledge in the dark would be dangerous. She had located signs of one buried kiva;

there could be other deep ones, and it was conceivable that she could fall into one and break her neck.

But the alternative, to sit here beside the fire and make a perfect target of herself, was even more terrifying after Starwalker's visitation. She had to hide, and she had to do so while she had an opportunity. At any moment he might spring out of the shadows and attack her.

But which way to go? Should she just walk away from the fire into the dark and hope he would lose track of her among the shadows? Could she be quiet enough not to give herself away?

The bottom line was that she couldn't sit here beside the fire like a lamb awaiting slaughter. She had to move, had to take a hand in protecting herself. The way Starwalker had left, without answering her question, without warning her of his departure, made her supremely uneasy. He could only intend some kind of harm, she thought. Something awful.

Rising slowly, so as not to startle Starwalker if he was nearby, she turned and walked casually away into the shadows at the back of the cavern. It seemed wisest to get away from the cliff edge, where she would be easy to push over and kill.

The skin between her shoulder blades prickled as she walked away from the fire, as if she could actually feel eyes upon her. Step by step she eased into the shadows, farther and farther from the illusory protection of the fire. Her inclination was to head toward the buried kiva, because she knew the ground better there, but she couldn't forget her horrible experience there earlier, when it had been as if she had stepped into a pool of icy, distilled hatred.

When she reached the back of the alcove, she stopped and turned around, gratefully pressing her back to cold stone. It was such an absolute relief not to feel that something could walk up behind her and attack her. Whatever came after her would have to come head-on. She would at least stand a chance.

But nothing moved in the alcove, as far as she could tell. Nothing at all. Her fire, looking so small and alone in the darkness, danced and burned, but nothing else moved. The shadows had grown still, and not even the wind whispered now. She shivered from both cold and fear, and yearned for the night to end.

Long, long minutes passed. Still nothing moved. No sound pierced the quiet night air. Starwalker was gone.

And then she heard the clatter of falling rock.

CHAPTER SIX

It was as if all the air had been siphoned from the universe. She couldn't breathe, and her heart hammered so loudly that it deafened her to any other sounds.

Oh, God! Was Starwalker stalking her through the dark alcove? Or was someone else climbing up from below? She had no way to know, no way to judge the threat. All she could do was press her back to the rock wall and hunker down low, making herself as small and invisible as she possibly could in the shadows.

And wait.

Time stretched, nerve-racking, endless minutes as she strained her ears trying to pick out another sound. Any sound that might give her warning as to what was coming. Any sound that might guide her away from danger.

But, other than the drumbeat of her heart, the world seemed to have grown silent. Anything could have loosened that rock, she told herself. The cooling night air could have caused the rock to contract and complete a split begun ages ago. Oh, there were natural explanations... but she didn't believe them. Something was out there.

Again the sharp clatter of a falling rock. Her heart slammed forcefully as she tried to determine where it came from.

"Lynn? Lynn, it's Cody. Are you okay?"

The shadow of a man appeared at the mouth of the alcove, a silhouette she definitely recognized.

"Lynn? Are you there?"

Relief was so strong that for a moment she was paralyzed and couldn't even reply. But then she was free of it and stumbling out of her dark corner toward Cody. "Oh, Cody...Cody..."

And somehow she was in his arms, held snugly to his chest, her face pressed to his shoulder. "Lynn...Lynn, what's wrong? I didn't mean to scare you."

"It was him. Starwalker. He was here, telling me I have to leave because I was breaking a taboo.... Oh, Cody, who is he? Is he real? I didn't even hear him climb up here! And then he just vanished! I was so frightened...."

He didn't say anything for a long time, just held her and murmured soothing sounds until her heartbeat slowed to near normal. Until the threat of the shadows receded and she was calm enough to become aware of other things. Of the man who held her. Of how badly she wanted him to hold her even closer. Finally a little murmur escaped her, and she leaned into him, softening as everything inside her turned weak with a woman's needs.

He must have sensed it, because his embrace changed. When he slipped his fingers beneath her chin and tilted her face up, she gave a little sigh and closed her eyes, eager to savor any touch he wanted to give her.

He surprised her. Instead of kissing her immediately on the mouth, he held her face still and brushed the lightest of kisses on her eyelids, on her cheeks, on the tip of her nose. The softness that had weakened her grew, until she felt as if she were melting inside.

Tiny, gentle kisses were tenderly laid along the column of her throat, causing her to draw a little gasp of pleasure. As easily as that, he had her throbbing and aching and ready to surrender.

"Come over by the fire."

She opened eyelids that felt as heavy as lead and tried to understand what he wanted. Go over by the fire? Oh, yes. . . .

Walking back to the campfire woke her from the drowsy softness his touches had evoked, and she was a little unnerved to realize how quickly and easily she had succumbed. He hadn't even kissed her mouth!

But maybe he hadn't wanted to. The thought was humiliating, and her cheeks burned. Maybe he had only kissed her as he had because she had invited it and he didn't want to embarrass her. Maybe he had no desire whatever to kiss her any more deeply. Maybe she had made an absolute fool of herself.

When they got back to the fire, he shook out the Mylar blanket and wrapped it around her shoulders. Then he sat cross-legged beside her, draping his arm around her shoulders as they watched the flames dance.

"Starwalker was here?" Cody asked.

Lynn nodded. "Right there, facing me across the fire. Except that he stayed back in the shadows so I couldn't see him very well. And he told me to leave."

"Told you? Just like that?"

"In so many words."

Cody looked at her, his dark eyes enigmatic in the dim light, then returned his gaze to the fire. "He could be dangerous, Lynn. We really need to get you out of here until we get to the bottom of this."

There it was again, she thought, anger warring with the remnants of fright. *Get out of here.* Everyone wanted her to get out of here it seemed. Starwalker tried to frighten her with talk of taboos and death, and then Cody aided him by insisting she had to leave until they could ensure her safety. But leaving wouldn't get her job done, and if she didn't do what she had come here to do, she was going to have to return all of the grant money, a large sum of which had already been spent to get her here to perform the survey. And then there was the problem of needing to do the research so that she could write the necessary paper this academic year. There were, in fact, a whole host of reasons why she couldn't afford to leave before her task was complete.

But apart from that, there was the strange village she had seen. No way was she going to waltz out of here without nailing that down and writing a sufficiently detailed description of it to make waves throughout the academic world, whose inhabitants believed only the Anasazi had dwelt here.

"No," she told him.

He glanced at her again and shook his head. "Look, I've got a lot of things to do besides play bodyguard for you. I can't hover over you every minute to make sure nothing is wrong."

"Did I ask you to?" Her tone was more belligerent than she would have liked, but the truth was that she was angry. Angry that he was trying to get her to leave, angry at the way he had kissed her and left her wanting, angry at the implication that she was expecting him to baby-sit her. "Did I ask you to come up here with me? What are you doing here, anyway?"

He snorted. "Damn good thing I showed up, considering you were hiding in the shadows, scared out of your mind! Damn it, I saw your fire and figured it had to be you up here, and I was worried about you. And I figured if it wasn't you, it was pot hunters. Either way, I had to check, and it's a good thing I did! How can you be so pigheaded? Everything in this canyon will still be here in a week, or in a month...or however long it takes to get to the bottom of this. You can come back as soon as it's safe. Is a site survey worth risking your neck for?"

"Quit shouting at me!"

"I'm not shouting!"

But of course he was, and he appeared to realize it as soon as he shouted the denial. He looked away for a moment, then shook his head. "I'm sorry. I'm worried about you. I'm worried you might get seriously hurt."

She softened again, sensing that his concern was real, not a perfunctory expression stemming from his job. "I won't get hurt."

"How can you *know* that?" he demanded angrily. "This Starwalker has told you that you're breaking a taboo! How do you know what he might do? This is serious business, Lynn, not some kind of joke."

"I didn't think it was a joke. But he's never threatened me directly. He's always been vague about it. If he starts telling me he's going to cut my throat—"

She broke off abruptly, unable to believe she was saying these things. The argument was ridiculous. She *was* being warned. Maybe the threats weren't being spelled out in so many words, but she was being warned. The implication of harm was undoubtedly there.

"I'm sorry," she said to Cody. "I'm sorry. But I'm not going to back down. I'm not going to be driven off with vague references to some obscure taboo! Good grief, the occupants of this canyon have been gone for nearly seven hundred years. What possible taboo could there be? And how would anyone know about it if there was? It doesn't add up, Cody. It doesn't add up at all. And unless I get more to go on than that it's dangerous to disturb the sleep of some ancient shaman . . . well, I'm not going to worry about it."

"He told you it was dangerous to disturb the ancient shaman's sleep?"

"That's what he said. Something about people dying if the shaman's sleep is disturbed."

"That's a common form of legend, I gather. I suppose you don't believe it, and there's no reason you should. But damn it, Lynn, don't you respect the beliefs of other cultures?" The question held an unmistakable note of challenge.

"Of course I do! But what culture? What belief? All we have here is some guy in feathers claiming to be a guardian and mumbling something about some ancient shaman who's buried here, and people dying if his sleep is disturbed. How can I be sure he's not just some nut who ought to be locked up at the first opportunity? If this ground is so sacred in some way, why isn't that common knowledge? Why isn't it talked about in broad daylight? Why are the only persons who seem to know about it a park ranger and some guy who only shows up in the dead of night? And if there really *is* some taboo, how come when I question him I don't get any answers? This is crazy, Cody! Crazy!''

Cody poked at the fire and threw on another branch. "I *have* heard some stuff about this canyon," he said slowly. "I told you. Bits and pieces of an old story about an evil medicine man."

"But nobody *else* seems to know anything!" She sighed. "Could that be what Starwalker is talking about?"

"Might be."

Lynn pulled the blanket tighter around her shoulders and tried not to look into the shadows beyond the fire. "Tell me about it?"

"Well . . ." He paused, seeming to gather his words. "There's something about two powerful medicine men who got into a fight. The bad guy eventually got killed, and the good shaman imprisoned his spirit forever so he couldn't do any more harm."

"And you think that's what Starwalker is talking about?"

"I'm not sure, but that would be my best guess. Especially since what I've always heard about it is that if anybody breaks the spell, it'll be the end of the world. Everyone will die."

Lynn found herself nodding her head. "That's sort of what Starwalker said. That thing about people dying if the shaman's sleep was disturbed."

"Then it's probably the same legend."

Lynn bit her lower lip and considered. "What about the taboo? Is there really one? Would you know?"

"There generally *is* a prohibition when it's a matter of life and death, Lynn. It's not necessarily promulgated like canon law. If something is likely to cause death and destruction, one isn't supposed to do it. It's just that simple."

She genuinely didn't want to violate any taboos or seriously offend anyone's beliefs, but she also didn't want to have to leave this canyon without finishing her survey. And she most especially didn't want to give up without seeing the strange cliff dwelling the moonlight had revealed. But the back of her neck prickled with an uneasy awareness that Starwalker might consider her a sufficient threat to be willing to do anything necessary to remove her.

But even that threat wasn't enough to shake her loose. Her mind kept throwing up reasons to stay, reasons to ignore the warnings, the threats, along with her own fears. A warning sounded deep within her, cautioning her that she was behaving irrationally, that even all her reasons together didn't justify risking her neck.

For a fleeting instant she once again sensed that she was being compelled by some external force. But that was insane.

She looked at Cody. "I'll think about it. I *will* think about it." But somewhere deep within, she knew she wouldn't. Not really. She was in the grip of something strong. Perhaps something stronger than her instinct for self-preservation. It was a scary thought, but fleeting, as the compulsion resumed control.

He nodded, satisfied for the moment. "Good." Then, calm as anything, he wrapped her in both his arms and reclined so that she lay on his chest. Before she could ask what he was doing, he turned her face up and covered her mouth with his.

This time it was a real kiss, deep, gentle and wet. Soft explosions detonated deep inside her, unlike anything she had ever felt, as she softened and opened to his kiss. Oh, how she had wanted this! Lying in his arms now, his mouth nibbling at hers, his tongue stroking her lips, she could admit how very much she had wanted him to do this.

Everything else seemed to fade away, unimportant compared to the caresses of Cody Walker. Starwalker vanished into the deep recesses of her mind, just as he had vanished into the shadows a little while ago. Her fears and worries and anger just seeped away into the night, leaving her an elemental woman who was yearning for her man.

Such sweet, sweet touches. She felt as if she were floating, her entire world consisting of nothing but this kiss, a kiss that permeated her whole being. It was so unexpected, so unthought-of, yet so very, very welcome. For the first time in her life she was wholly and completely glad she was a woman.

She sank into his embrace as if it were a warm feather bed, everything inside her seeming to let go, as if in a deep, heartfelt sigh. Every fiber of her being responded to his touch, like a cat being stroked. Good. So very, very good. And she wanted it never to end.

His tongue slipped past her lips, dipping within to tease hers gently. She liked the way he seemed confident of what he was doing yet didn't push her in any way. Never for a moment did she wonder if he would stop if she asked him to. He would. She had no doubt.

And that made her feel so wonderfully safe that she forgot for this blessed little space of time that she had anything to fear, anything to worry about. Instead she knew only that this man was evoking feelings in her that she had believed belonged only in fairy tales. That he was making her feel soft, so very soft, and open and welcoming, and supremely feminine.

His hands stroked her back with a kind of tender roughness, making her exquisitely aware of his strength and power, making her feel small and slight beneath his large, strong palms. The sensation was surprisingly erotic. And his tongue...his tongue just kept teaching her new games to play with gentle touches, teasing withdrawal, sudden inward thrusts.

One of his hands slipped around toward her breast, pausing as if waiting for her permission. She couldn't have murmured a sound to save her life, for her breath caught and locked in her throat, trapped by anticipation so sharp and exquisite that she was virtually paralyzed.

Evidently interpreting her stillness correctly, he slipped his hand around the rest of the way and gently cupped her breast through the layers of her jacket and shirt. Her reaction was instantaneous, sharp, delightful. Somehow his touch seemed to reach all the way to her womb, filling her with a wonderful heavy aching that made her move gently against him, encouraging him.

But then, in a searing moment of stunning awareness, she remembered where she was, remembered Starwalker's vague threat. But mostly she remembered the ugly scar on her leg.

Twisting, she wrenched away and curled up on her side with her back to Cody.

The wind moaned softly as it whipped around the corners of the alcove, a quiet note of despair that drowned out her own rapid breathing. She expected Cody to be upset with her, to call her a tease, but he said nothing for what seemed like ages. Just about the time she decided he was never going to speak to her again, she was astonished to feel a gentle touch on her shoulder.

"I'm sorry," he said. "I didn't mean to upset you. I had no business doing that."

Startled, she couldn't think of a thing to say in response. On the few occasions when she had pulled away from a man, she had been reviled. On the other two, when she had let things go further, they had been repulsed by her scar. Either way, it wasn't something she was eager to try again.

She waited, seeking the inner calm that had carried her through so many crises in her life, and presently she was able to roll onto her back and look over at Cody. His rugged face was a concerned mask in the ruddy glow from the fire. He had his cheek propped on his hand, and his gaze never wavered from her.

"I'm the one who's sorry," she said finally, forcing the difficult admission past her lips because she felt she owed it to him. "I'm sorry. I'm...skittish. It wasn't you at all."

After a moment he nodded. "Skittish is okay. You're entitled to be skittish, and you don't need to apologize for it."

Relief released the icy fingers gripping her heart. "Thank you. I'm...uh, my leg is...pretty ugly." The words burst out of her, emerging from some painful well deep in her soul, utterly unexpected because she hadn't intended to say anything so revealing, had never ever wanted to admit just how self-conscious she was about her scar, or to let anyone know that the scar on her leg was reflected by an equally large and ugly scar on her soul.

"I'm sorry," he said quietly. "I noticed your limp, even though you do a pretty good job of hiding it. I was wondering if it was just recent."

It wasn't exactly a question, but now that she'd revealed her concern about the scar, she didn't feel she could stop. In fact, she felt as if she owed him an explanation of some kind. "I was in an auto accident when I was fourteen. My leg got pretty badly smashed up, and my hip was injured. They didn't think I'd ever be able to walk again."

"But you can. You must have worked awfully hard at it."

She was surprised that he realized that. Most people assumed that her walking was just the result of good medical care, a miracle at a good surgeon's hands. Most never dreamed how many endless, agonizing months of physical therapy she had endured to get back on her feet. "I had therapy for eleven months."

He nodded slowly. "You're pretty remarkable, Lynn. An awful lot of people would have settled for the wheelchair."

She shook her head swiftly. "There were lots of people in therapy. Everybody was brave about it, Cody. There wasn't any alternative."

"Sure there was. You could have given up and made the doctors' prediction come true. You could never have walked again."

She looked away, knowing he was right and embarrassed by his praise. The truth was, she'd gone to physical therapy only because she had insisted on it. Her doctor never would have prescribed it, because he was firmly convinced that she couldn't possibly walk on that leg again. Only Lynn's stubbornness had made him write the order for therapy.

And it was because of her own determination that she was walking today. But she didn't feel that deserved any kind of praise. Her reward for fighting that battle was her ability to walk, and that was what she told Cody now.

He shook his head slightly and smiled, an expression that creased his face attractively. "Gutsy lady. Nothing stops you, does it?"

The words were spoken casually, with an almost teasing intent, but they fell into the air like heavy stones into a pool, laden with significance. *Nothing stops you, does it?* The memory of Starwalker's warnings danced along her spine. Nothing stopped her...except murder? She shuddered.

Cody sat up abruptly and stirred the fire, as if he had been jarred by his own words in precisely the same way. "I think you're to be commended," he said after a moment. "You have a lot of determination. But you need to exercise caution, too, Lynn. Sometimes it's best to back off."

Lynn sat up and looked around at the lurking shadows in the alcove. She felt cold and very alone. "I told you, Cody. I'm thinking about it. I will give it very serious thought."

He nodded and seemed somehow to relax. "I'd hate it if anything happened to you, Lynn. I'd seriously hate it."

Why, she wondered, did that sound like a threat?

CHAPTER SEVEN

The pearly pink glow of dawn washed the canyon and slipped into the alcove, illuminating the depression where the old kiva was buried. Lynn watched the delicate fingers of light inch across the cavern floor and wished she were an artist who could capture such things with oils or watercolors.

And then, between one breath and the next, memories of last night crashed in on her. *Starwalker.* He had been right across the fire from her and had hinted at impossible things. Things that, were they possible, would be terrifying.

What if the old shamans had really had the powers their people believed they possessed? What if they could send plagues and blights? What if she was toying with something inherently dangerous? Playing like a child who didn't understand?

She shivered and drew the survival blanket more snugly around her, trying to seal in her body heat. The morning air was cold, and her breath created a small cloud that caught the pink rays of light.

Her scientific training rebelled at the notion of things paranormal, but remembering how Starwalker had suddenly appeared across the fire from her last night, and the way he had just as suddenly disappeared, she began to wonder if she weren't deluding herself.

In childhood she had experienced a few things that had made her a believer in ESP, especially telepathy. Later she had squashed that belief, accepting the standard scientific position that such paranormal events were unproven and most likely coincidences. That was the rational view, of course.

But now, shivering here on an isolated mesa in southwestern Colorado, watching pink sunlight weave its beauty among the remnants of a civilization long dead and buried, she wondered about all the things that so-called rationality precluded without hesitation simply because the experience of it rested on someone's word.

The time she had known that a friend who lived several miles away was on the way over... a friend who rarely visited and never dropped in without calling first.

The time she had known...

She stopped herself, not needing to recall incidents from long ago to remember how convinced she had once been that people *did* have extrasensory capabilities that were just buried under layers of disbelief. Perhaps she had been right when she had followed her instinct on the subject. Perhaps the rational dismissal of such things as coincidence was mistaken.

That feeling she had experienced yesterday beside the buried kiva. That skin-crawling sense of cold evil, of complete, chilling hatred. She could blame that on some misfire in her brain... or she could go back and investigate it. See if it happened again in the same spot.

And if it did...

She shivered again, cold despite the sheltering blanket. Rationally, scientifically, she should go back there and see if she was struck by that feeling again.

And if she was . . . maybe she should give consideration to what Starwalker was saying. Perhaps there was a genuine threat in a dead and buried shaman.

More chills ran down her spine, and she couldn't hold still any longer. She had to find out *now,* if she had imagined the feeling beside the kiva. Throwing the blanket back, she sat up and reached for her hiking boots.

"Going somewhere?"

She glanced over and saw Cody sitting up on the other side of the fire. The last thing she wanted to do was tell him what she had felt near the kiva. It sounded . . . crazy. She shrugged and shook her head. "I'm just cold and stiff. I need to move around."

He nodded. "It's a beautiful morning."

"Yeah. I think I'll watch the rest of the sunrise." Which was a dumb thing to say, she thought, when she was planning to head away from the alcove opening. He would surely wonder what she was up to.

But it was too late now to take back her words. She would just have to wander around a bit and then appear to be drawn to the depression where there was probably a buried kiva. And, truth to tell, she was glad Cody was here. The whole thought of facing that terrible anger and hatred alone was unnerving. It wasn't external when she felt it herself. It wasn't the same as someone ranting at her. She had experienced the emotion from the *inside.* Not as if it were her own, but as she would have experienced it if it *had* been her own.

Oh, it was so hard to explain it, even to herself. The feeling had washed over her, as icy and chilly as being immersed in a frigid pond. The reality of the feeling was not in question; its source was. She *knew* it hadn't been her own emotion, even though it had been as intense as if it were. And there was just no way you could explain something like that without sounding totally crazy.

She looked at Cody again as she finished tying her bootlaces and wished she could confide in him. Maybe not about the experience by the kiva, but about the rest of it. She *wanted* to trust him, but she wasn't sure she could. He kept trying to persuade her to leave, after all, and was that really so different from what Starwalker was trying to do?

So she forced herself to look away from him and rise casually. Turning, she strolled toward the edge of the cliff as if she only wanted to watch the sun rise over the canyon. She felt his dark eyes on her back as she walked.

The pink glow was already beginning to turn into the buttery yellow light of early morning. Overnight the dust had somehow been cleared from the air, probably by dew, and Lynn caught her breath in awe when she saw how crisp and clear even the most distant parts of the canyon were this morning. She didn't think she'd ever seen so far with so much clarity.

But her purpose drew her, and after a couple of minutes she began to wander in the direction of the kiva. She didn't really want to feel that sensation again, that skin-crawling, chilling sense of hatred. Paradoxically, the closer she drew to the kiva, the more compelled she felt to investigate, and the more reluctant she grew. It was as if she was of two minds, each pulling in opposite directions. Never had she felt so torn.

And it was that torn feeling that caused her to stop suddenly. She felt as if she was being compelled by something outside herself, and she didn't like that feeling at all. All her life she'd had an inclination toward balkiness when she felt she was being pushed.

And she felt pushed right now—which was ridiculous. It had been her own decision to investigate the strange experience she had had beside the kiva. Why should she now feel as if she was being pushed into something she didn't want to do? Ridiculous.

But she stood frozen, anyway, troubled by feelings that felt subtly... alien. As if her desire to investigate had risen from without after all. As if she was being manipulated in some way she couldn't quite put her finger on.

And that really disturbed her. What if... What if her determination to keep the village she'd seen by moonlight a secret, even from Cody, had arisen from something or someone else? From outside of her? What if that shaman Starwalker kept talking about were not dead, but trapped?

She cut off the thought, horrified by the turn her mind had taken. This was insane. She was losing her marbles. All of Starwalker's crazy hints and the isolation of the canyon had combined to make her start imagining things she would be embarrassed to even hint at out loud.

She was going to investigate the experience she had had at the kiva, but that was *her* determination and decision, not some kind of impulse from without. She was a scientist by training, and scientists empirically investigated occurrences such as the one she had had to see if they could determine the cause.

That was *all* she was doing—not playing puppet for some unseen force.

That settled in her mind, she stepped toward the kiva, toward the place where she had had the strange feelings last night. She didn't want to feel them again, and dread tightened the back of her neck.

She had been standing there, just to one side of the depression, when the feeling hit. She told herself that she would not only see if it happened again but would see if it was confined to a clearly delineated area, or if it could happen anywhere around the kiva...or anywhere around the alcove. She was going to be methodical about it and prove to herself that *she* was in charge, not some vaguely imagined *other*.

And Cody was watching her. She could feel the steadiness of his attention as if his gaze were touching her physically. He was probably wondering what she was doing, but he didn't ask.

By the time she was almost at the spot where she had felt the strangeness yesterday, every muscle in her body was knotted with tension. At this rate, she warned herself, she was apt to imagine almost anything.

Then she took another step, and the chilling fury drenched her as if she had stepped into an invisible waterfall. In an instant she was gripped by the rage, by the hatred, that had swamped her yesterday. Even though she was prepared for it, it hit her with the same horrifying impact, threatening to overwhelm her with the sheer massive power of the feeling.

Her heart was hammering, her chest was heaving as she tried to drag in air, and every instinct shrieked for her to flee. She forced herself to remain, forced herself to absorb the buffeting of enraged hatred.

And dimly, behind the overwhelming feeling, she sensed something more. Whatever had left this consuming emotion imprinted on this place had left something more. A whisper of thought. A memory of . . . a man.

Leave.

The demand exploded like a thunderclap in her head.

Leave!

She felt as if the word were battering her with hurricane force, trying to drive her back from the kiva. No, farther yet. It wanted her out of the alcove, out of the canyon. As far away as it could drive her.

And as much as it terrified her to think of being the focus of that hatred, she knew she wouldn't leave. No spook was going to scare her away. Not Starwalker or Cody or whatever this feeling was could make her give up her task. She was as foolishly stubborn as a mule, and even as she felt that knowledge rise within her, even as her mind acknowledged her foolhardiness, she knew her course was set. No one and nothing had ever deterred her once she had made up her mind. And common sense had never stood a chance when she felt someone or something was opposing her. Stubborn. If it was something she wasn't supposed to do or someone didn't want her to do, it would become the very thing she *must* do.

Even knowing this about herself, there was no way she could change her own nature. Even the niggling feeling that some external force was using her own stubbornness to manipulate her couldn't stop her. She was, by God, going to get to the bottom of this, and get to the bottom of the village she had seen. Terror notwithstanding, she would not be budged.

With every stubborn bone in her body stiffening, she forced herself to move a little to one side, then a little more, testing whether this emotion that was battering her was confined to a measurable area. Another step. Another... and she was out of the field of hatred, as surely as if she had just crossed a line of demarcation.

Strange. Deliberately, she stepped back... and the hatred swamped her again. It was definitely localized, definitely repeatable... and, as such, not a figment of her imagination.

Moving slowly, stepping back and forth, she found that the hatred seemed to surround the buried kiva, and that she had stepped into a wider band of it last night, a band that protruded more than a yard from the edge of the depression. She paused to scuff the dirt each time she passed out of the hatred, and by the time she had circled the kiva, she had described an oval, something like an egg.

"What are you doing?"

She had forgotten Cody, she realized with a start. She had completely forgotten that he had been watching her odd behavior and by now was probably wondering if she were totally crazy. She had to tell him something, but what?

Feeling almost embarrassed, she tilted her head back and looked up at him. Far from scorn or wariness, what she saw reflected in his dark eyes was a gentle curiosity. In that moment, she realized she trusted him.

"There's, um, a buried kiva here, I think," she said.

He nodded and glanced toward the depression. "It sure looks like it."

"I was, um, just kind of marking its dimensions."

"Oh."

"Kind of odd how it's all buried. Most of the alcoves sheltered the ruins enough that there's something left aboveground, but not here. I wonder if it was deliberately destroyed at some point." She thought he stiffened for a moment, but when he looked at her again he seemed completely relaxed. She must have imagined it.

"Maybe," he said, "it was just poorly constructed. Water, freezing temperatures...it wouldn't take many winters to tumble it all down."

He was right, of course, and she couldn't know without excavating, but she still didn't think it looked right. But there was something concerning her more at the moment. She bit her lip, then looked up at Cody again, hoping she wasn't wrong about him. "Um... would you mind stepping inside the circle I drew?"

She could have sworn that he blanched, actually blanched, and hesitated perceptively. Then he shrugged. "Sure. Why?"

"Just...to test something."

Again there was that sense of hesitation, then he stepped forward into the circle she had described with her scuff marks. Lynn held her breath, waiting impatiently for some reaction. Any reaction.

Did he stiffen? She couldn't really be certain. He didn't move for the longest time, keeping his back to her, not even cocking his head or looking around. And that, more than anything, convinced her that he sensed something.

He turned abruptly and stepped out of the circle. "Okay," he said levelly. "What's going on?"

"Did you feel it? Did you feel anything at all?" She held her breath again, afraid he was going to say that he'd felt nothing.

His mouth tightened, but finally he nodded. "Yeah. I felt something."

"Was it kind of like . . . like cold hatred?"

Again a tight-lipped nod. "What's that circle you marked out?"

"It marks the area where I can sense that feeling."

He turned around and looked at it. "All the way around the depression."

"That's right. I wouldn't be surprised if it can be sensed all the way across."

"Well, don't try it. The debris that filled it in might not be stable, and there's no telling how deep the kiva may be."

Lynn nodded in agreement. "I wish I knew what caused that sensation. Whether it's something that's being generated right now, or whether it's an old emotion imprinted on the kiva like a tape recording."

"What could possibly be generating it now?"

She shook her head. "I don't know. This isn't my area of expertise. A ghost? Maybe the shaman Starwalker keeps talking about?" Cody didn't answer, but she didn't really expect him to. This was all speculation, and she wasn't comfortable even as she made the suggestion, even though the connection was neat enough.

She squatted down and looked across the depression, her eyes following the oval she had scuffed out. "It would sure explain why Starwalker is so convinced this is sacred ground around here. That something is going on."

Just thinking about the possibilities both excited and unnerved her. She didn't want to believe in ghosts, didn't want to think that someone or something long dead could influence events in the present.

But whether she wanted to believe it or not, she had to consider it, because something sure as hell was going on here.

"I saw a strange village in the moonlight," she said abruptly. She didn't look at him, but she could feel the sudden intensity of his gaze. "It wasn't just the usual cliff dwelling—at least, not from what I could see. The angles of the shadows indicated triangular doorways and windows."

He drew a sharp breath, and Lynn straightened so she could look straight at him. "What is it? Have you seen it?"

"Is that what you came up here looking for? I wondered why you climbed all the way up to an empty alcove."

"You've seen it!" She was sure of it. He was simply evading her question for some reason. "You've seen it. Cody, why haven't you told someone! It could be the archaeological discovery of the century!"

He shook his head. "It doesn't exist, Lynn. It's a figment of moonlight and shadow. Others have seen it and hunted for it, but they don't find it, because it simply doesn't exist."

She wished there was something to sit on, because right then her disappointment was so strong that her legs turned to rubber. Not until that very instant had she realized just how much she was counting on finding that strange village.

It didn't exist! Like the fabled city of El Dorado, it was a chimera others had chased. Giving up, she sat abruptly on the dusty ground, raising her knees and propping her cheek on her hand. "Others have looked for it?"

Cody dropped to sit cross-legged beside her. "A few. Evidently there are a couple of times a year when the moonlight is just right to create the illusion. I've seen it a couple of times because I'm out here so much, but I've never been able to track down anything remotely resembling the buildings. I'd love to be able to figure out what causes the illusion, though."

She nodded glumly, telling herself all sorts of encouraging things about how a discovery couldn't be lost if it didn't exist, and how it would at least be interesting if she could figure out what created the illusion. Somehow none of it helped. She had wanted to discover a totally new culture and had thought herself on the brink of it.

Instead she had been chasing a chimera and found some strange anomaly surrounding this buried kiva. Some kind of anomaly that might be a genuine paranormal experience. The discovery of a village would have launched her career to the stratosphere. On the other hand, if she even dared to mention this emotional miasma—for lack of a better description of the sensation the kiva gave her—she could reasonably expect to be laughed right out of the university.

But it was there, and it was real. Wondering what would happen, she slowly reached out with her hand and passed it beyond the edge of the circle. At once she felt again the chilling hatred. Only this time it seemed to zip up her arm like an icy electrical shock.

It was definitely localized around the kiva, seeming to be surrounded by an invisible wall. Contained, perhaps? She snatched her hand back and wondered if something that could generate so much emotion could also affect other things. Could perhaps cause harm.

The chill remained in her hand for a long time, as if some of the hatred had clung to her. If it could do that...

She shuddered inwardly as the dark chill that had touched her hand seemed to infect the morning light. She ought to get up and walk away, ought to go back to the task that had originally brought her here and forget what she had discovered in this alcove.

But she knew she wouldn't. Whatever had compelled her to search for the illusory village was now prodding her to get to the bottom of what was happening around this buried kiva.

To face the evil buried here.

CHAPTER EIGHT

"Come on. I'll walk you back to your campsite."

Lynn looked up at Cody, feeling like a dreamer awakening. Then she looked past him to the mouth of the alcove, where morning was brightening with promise. The dark feeling receded slowly. Go back to her campsite?

"Um…no," she said. "No. I need to map this site." Not that that would be difficult, or even take very long, as the only visible sign of habitation was the depression that presumably was a collapsed and buried kiva.

But now that she was here, despite her experience with the evil feeling surrounding the kiva, despite Starwalker's warnings, she wanted to remain. She even wished Cody would just go and let her do what she needed to.

And it was that wish that caused a tremor deep inside her, that made her aware she was not behaving normally. She couldn't possibly want to stay up here alone. Not really. The instant Cody was gone, she would become acutely aware of her isolation and vulnerability, acutely aware that something caused that feeling of icy rage and hatred she felt whenever she stepped close to the kiva. Something had touched her hand in a way that left it tingling even now.

What else might that something be capable of?

"You didn't bring enough stuff to stay another night," Cody argued quietly. "You need food and water."

"I have some dried food and half a canteen of water. I won't be comfortable, but I can manage."

He swore softly. "Look, Lynn, don't be foolish. At this altitude you need to drink a lot of water. The few ounces left in your canteen aren't going to cut it."

She knew he was right, but she shook her head, anyway. "I need to do this, and I don't want to climb all the way down just to climb back up again." Her bad leg twinged at the mere thought of making that climb again with a heavier pack. She would, of course, if there was no way to avoid it, but it was not the kind of thing she was going to volunteer for unnecessarily.

Cody made a quiet sound of exasperation and looked away. "I don't want to leave you up here alone. Something could happen. But somebody *has* to go down to get water and food. Especially water. I don't want you getting altitude sickness."

"I won't. Cody, it isn't as if I've come from sea level." But he was right about needing more water than what she had in her canteen. Why was she arguing with him? He was making sense and she was not.

She turned her gaze back to the buried kiva and knew she could not leave. For some reason, she had to remain. The compulsion was both clear and overwhelming . . . as well as terrifying. More and more she was beginning to feel like a puppet in the hands of some invisible force. Not even her growing fear could overcome the compulsion.

"Okay," Cody said after a moment. "I'll go down and get water. And some extra food. But damn it, Lynn, don't take any foolish chances. I'll be gone for several hours, and if you get seriously hurt you might die before I get back up here."

She watched his departure with a sense of commingled dread and triumph. She'd won the time alone she wanted up here ... and she wished she hadn't.

Finally the last clatter of his departure faded, and there was no sound, save the soft whisper of the ceaseless wind as it curled around the corners of the alcove and rustled the junipers and sage on the talus slope below.

She was alone, and a flash of awareness reminded her just *how* alone she was in this canyon. For miles around, there was probably no more than a handful of people, none of whom could come to her aid quickly if she needed it.

None who would hear her screams if she were hurt. Except for Cody, and he would soon be beyond range, too.

That was what she had wanted, wasn't it? To be free to explore this alcove unimpeded? This alcove that had apparently held a moon-created illusion of a strange cliff dwelling.

Turning, she stared into the shadowy alcove. It had looked far too real and too solid to her, and when she summoned its image to mind, she found it difficult to believe that it had been nothing more than a creation of light and shadow.

Squatting, she absently began to draw in the dust, trying to reconstruct the dwellings she had seen by moonlight. There was no reason to think Cody was lying to her when he said it was an illusion others had seen and pursued. No reason at all. And she had to admit that she'd been pretty astonished to find this alcove empty when she arrived, because her navigation skills weren't *that* bad.

Perhaps she *had* seen an illusion. An incredible, mind-boggling illusion. But then again...

Then again, perhaps she had seen the visual equivalent of whatever it was she felt when she stepped too near the kiva. Perhaps she felt a memory of a violent emotion that had once been experienced there. And perhaps the view of the dwellings she had seen by moonlight was a *memory* of what had once existed there.

The wildness of the thought didn't even occur to her. Instead she drew intently in the red dust, illustrating as best she could the structures she had seen with such clarity by moonlight. The compulsion was as strong as the one that had drawn her up here to begin with. The sun crept higher, but she lost all sense of time as she tried to capture her vision.

At some point she realized she was no longer trying to describe the frontal view she'd had from across the canyon. Somehow she had begun to draw what looked like a floor plan for a village that might have fit within this alcove. Rooms, not too large, three, four and five deep as they marched back into the alcove. A terrace along the cliff edge, a street or corridor running lengthwise between two rows of buildings. Here and there fire pits for cooking. Room for ladders to reach up to other levels. Kivas. Nearly twenty kivas, mostly of the small-kin variety, but some larger communal ones, as well, distinguished by their differing size. The main kiva there, where the depression was in the floor of the alcove.

It was past noon when she grew suddenly aware of what she was doing. Of what she had done. Despite the growing heat of the afternoon, she felt as if a chill had touched her.

What had she drawn? She didn't do things like this, didn't spend hours drawing in the dust like a child. She should have been exploring the alcove, mapping the location of the kiva, looking for other depressions or ridges that might signify other buildings.

Instead she had sat here for several hours drawing a floor plan in the dust. Could it have welled up from her subconscious somehow? If so, why? What a waste of time! It wouldn't help at all in any serious exploration of this alcove, wouldn't answer any questions or solve any mysteries. Just a waste of time.

She reached out to wipe her folly away, but something stopped her. Not just the normal hesitation of reconsidering before committing an irrevocable act. No, it felt as if something were physically preventing her from erasing her drawing, and the sensation was every bit as powerful and vivid as the emotion that had assailed her beside the kiva.

But it had a different tenor entirely. There was nothing evil about what stalled her hand. Nothing chilling or hateful in it. Instead it was more like...more like a plea. A request. As if someone had gently stayed her hand.

But no one was there. She was all alone on this cliff. Or, if not alone, then whatever was here with her was invisible.

She shivered despite the day's heat and pulled her hand back from her drawing. Again she peered into the shadows in the alcove, as if she really thought she might see something that would answer the questions she hardly dared speak. She saw nothing at all, and heard nothing but the whisper of the wind as it rounded the corner of the ledge and swept through the alcove.

She was all alone, but she was developing the distinct feeling that she was somehow being used.

And that was more terrifying by far than anything she had ever experienced in her life.

The afternoon baked. Even here, beneath the overhang of rock, sheltered from the sun, the air grew uncomfortably warm. Lynn opened the throat of her blouse and fanned herself with the hat she had forgotten she'd tucked into her pack. Surely Cody would be back soon with the water. She was feeling so parched from the hot, dry heat that it was hard not to give in to impulse and finish the water in her canteen. Instead she forced herself to be content with a single swallow when she began to feel she couldn't bear her thirst any longer.

She needed to get up and explore the cave, but something kept her sitting near the ledge, away from the darker and probably cooler interior. Something was keeping her from doing what she had come here to do. And it was not the same thing that had kept her from erasing the drawing, which was still clearly visible on the ledge a few feet away. For some reason she had needed to back away from it, but now that she had, she just sat there staring at nothing and watching the slow shifting of shadows in the canyon below.

The feeling that something external was working on her was growing rather than diminishing. In an almost clinical fashion she wondered if she was losing her mind—becoming schizophrenic—and then she recalled that schizophrenia tended to make its appearance in the early twenties, and she was well past that.

Besides, she wasn't hearing things or hallucinating. But she did have this horrifyingly unsettled feeling that something or someone was attempting to get her to do something. That someone or something was nudging her just below the level of conscious thought, urging her to...

To what? She'd been sitting here asking herself that question ever since something had prevented her from erasing the drawing, and she was darned if she could come up with an answer. And once Cody returned, it would only grow more difficult to get to the bottom of this, since he would provide a continual distraction.

She *had* to know what was going on, and if that meant risking being manipulated by whatever was trying to control her, she would have to face that possibility. She just couldn't bring herself to walk away without getting to the bottom of this; she'd never been the kind who could.

But how to start getting there? What to do first? What could she do that wouldn't make her feel like an absolute fool, anyhow?

Heck, she thought with sudden, wry humor, she should have brought a dowsing rod. It was probably the only thing that could improve matters. At least it might give her some indication of what direction to go.

But sitting here like this was ridiculous, even if she did feel an urge to do precisely that. Interesting, she told herself, the way it seemed to be able to cause her to battle internally, as if she held two opposing wishes.

But the truth was, feeling manipulated this way was scaring her half to death, and she needed to do something—anything—to reestablish her self-control. To prove to herself that she was in charge.

That was what made her stand up. Realizing that sitting there was not what she would have been doing if left to her own free choice. No, for herself she would choose to explore the alcove and seek other areas of energy like the one right around the big kiva.

So that was exactly what she *would* do. Right now. Without wasting another minute wondering what was going on and how something invisible could possibly be trying to get her to do something.

Pulling her notebook out with a burst of fresh determination, she made up her mind to section the entire alcove and methodically walk a crisscross search pattern. That way, if there was anything to be seen or sensed anywhere in the vicinity, she would be extremely unlikely to miss it.

And that was what she was there to do, after all.

But she hesitated again. Stepping into the cooler shadows at the back of the alcove ought to be easy, but something held her back. Something made her reluctant. It was as if something was lurking back there, something she couldn't see.

Biting her lip, she squinted, as if it would help her see into the shadows. It wouldn't, of course. The only way to know for sure that there was nothing back there was to *go* back there. It wasn't really that dark, she told herself. Not that dark at all. It was just the contrast with the bright sunlight outside the alcove.

She took a tentative step, then another, gaining courage with each one. It was silly, she told herself, to be afraid of something that had no substance. How could an invisible phantom possibly harm her? She tried not to think about Starwalker.

But now that she'd taken the first couple of steps toward the rear, it was possible to justify turning to the left to go to the very end of the alcove before she moved any deeper. She had, after all, promised herself that she was going to be methodical about this and section the entire cliff.

Of course, she would really need to stake out the entire area to do a flawless job, but she hadn't come prepared for that kind of work. No, she'd only come to identify sites and locate them on a map according to their GPS coordinates. Not to actually lay out a site as she would preparatory to digging.

When she reached the end of the alcove, the depth was only a half-dozen feet and she could see all there was to see, but she walked back, anyway, meticulously noting impressions in her little notebook. Then she moved a couple of feet to the right and walked back to the ledge, scanning with great care...and finding nothing remarkable.

Section after section, as the afternoon grew hotter, the air grew heavier and the shadows at the back of the alcove seemed to grow deeper, more... oppressive.

Here and there she noted minor shifts in the level of the ground that might have been the remnants of foundations for buildings, but it was hard to be sure. Given the kiva at the other end, there must have been other buildings here, she thought. The absence of even a scattered, tumbled pile of stones like those that marked all the other sites she'd seen could only mean one of two things.

The Basket Maker culture might have occupied this ledge and built their pit houses here. The tops of those were built with wood and thatch, and had frequently caught fire, leaving nothing behind to mark the dwelling except the pit.

Or—and this possibility made her breath catch in her throat—this village could have been deliberately and completely destroyed. The vengeance such an act would suggest boggled the mind. The hatred would be something like... what she felt surrounding the kiva.

Could two shamans really have warred here once and left such an indelible mark in the very stone? She shivered again as the air seemed to cool abruptly.

Was she tapping into long-ago events? she wondered uneasily. Was the village she had seen by moonlight a memory from long ago? The hate she had felt and the floor plan she had drawn—were these flashes from the past, etched somehow on the stone like a tape recording?

It sounded farfetched, but as she continued to crisscross the alcove she found what appeared to be the leveled foundations of structures—foundations so leveled they could not have gotten that way except through human agency—and suddenly it began to seem less farfetched. Events had occurred here seven or eight hundred years ago, and those events had been laden with a crushing weight of emotion. Why was it difficult to believe that those emotions might somehow have warped the very stones?

Not too difficult to believe at all, as the back of her scalp prickled with the sense that something cold had just touched her.

And once again she was warring internally, part of her longing to leave the dark places in the alcove and go sit on the ledge to wait for Cody...who was late, wasn't he? He'd said he would only be gone a couple of hours, but it had been more than twice that long already. What if he had gotten hurt?

The shadows seemed to be thickening somehow, growing darker, though it was high afternoon and there wasn't a cloud in the sky that was visible beyond the overhang. It was, she thought, the same kind of darkening that seemed to accompany the approach of a storm, only there was no storm.

At least, not a natural one.

"Well, damn it!" Talking to herself wasn't her usual behavior, nor was swearing at nothing in particular, but she did it now. Why was she toughing this out like some kind of macho idiot? There was something weird going on, something weird about this alcove, and there was no reason why she should feel foolish for being reluctant to explore it alone. Why should she feel she was failing some test if she didn't push ahead?

Because that was how she had lived her entire life. But maybe this time that was a silly attitude. This time she didn't know what she was up against or what to do about it. She didn't have a clue. And there was the uneasy awareness that the hatred she had felt was so powerful that whatever generated it might well be capable of doing something else.

The shadows seemed to be steadily thickening, and almost despite herself she began to inch toward the lip of the ledge. A deep instinct, far deeper than thought, was dragging her toward the light, overruling her desire to be strong and rational. She needed the sunlight. She needed the *protection* of the sunlight.

The thought jarred her, even as her body insisted on obeying it. Step by step, almost surreptitiously, she eased toward the daylight...as if she was being watched. As if she needed to sneak away.

And with each step toward the ledge, toward the light, something else seemed to tug her back, to demand that she turn and face the shadows, as if there was some answer there. Something she needed to see.

But she was scared to look back there. It was the same kind of fear that keeps a child pinned to her bed in the dark for fear of things lurking in the closet or *under* the bed. There was nothing there. Logically, intellectually, she knew there was nothing there. There couldn't be. If anyone had come to the alcove, she would have seen them. Anything else would have to be nonphysical, and something that wasn't physical couldn't hurt her. Could it?

Suddenly every hair on the back of her neck stood on end. Something was behind her. With a certainty that was soul-deep and terrifying, she knew she was not alone.

The urge to turn warred with the urge to run, and part of her still kept insisting that if she didn't look there couldn't be anything there. As if looking would give substance to whatever she sensed behind her.

It was foolish, she told herself, but her heart jammed up into her throat and began to pound at a furious pace. All the air vanished from the universe as adrenaline shoved her into high gear.

"You should have left."

She whirled around, crying out softly. There, little more than a shadow among shadows, was Starwalker.

And she was suddenly more terrified than she had ever been in her life.

CHAPTER NINE

"W-where did you come from?" The words escaped her on a breathless gasp. Instinctively, she stepped backward. He could not be human. No way! If anyone had entered the alcove during the past few hours, she would have seen or heard them. This was impossible.

"Leave now. Leave before someone gets hurt."

She backed up another step, then another. "Why are you threatening me? I'm not hurting you or anything else!"

"You're tampering with things you don't understand. Leave. Quickly. Before someone gets hurt!"

He turned a little, and with the shifting of the shadows she glimpsed an expanse of smooth, bronzed skin that surely could not have belonged to a ghost. There was a sudden noise behind her, a crashing as if a heavy rock had fallen. Instinctively she turned to look and saw that, indeed, a heavy chunk of rock had fallen from the overhang and crashed to the ledge not far from her sleeping bag.

She whirled back to look at Starwalker...and he was gone. Vanished. The shadows were empty now, merely areas of muted light rather than congealing threat.

Fear froze her to the spot, making it impossible for her to turn away from where Starwalker had been. He might at any moment reappear, coalescing from the shadows he had vanished into. But she needed to look behind her, to where the rock had fallen from the roof as if torn loose by a giant's hand. She needed to be sure there was no threat back there that she should be worrying about.

The shadows remained empty. Starwalker was gone. Slowly, almost jerkily, as her entire body resisted movement, Lynn turned to look at where the rock had fallen. Coincidence? Or threat?.

She was no longer willing to dismiss any of this. She was being consistently threatened by someone who had the ability to appear and disappear as quickly and inexplicably as a ghost . . . and something had made that rock fall. Yes, it could have been a coincidence, but she didn't believe it.

The question was, what was she going to do about it?

Sitting at the edge of the ledge, where the afternoon light was bright, she stared back into the alcove, at the deep shadows in the rear. *Leave before someone gets hurt* constituted a definite threat, though not one specifically directed at her.

Stupid, she told herself angrily. She was being stupid. This wasn't some academic argument, but a real and potentially deadly warning. Who *else* was likely to get hurt if she didn't leave? No one. There was no mistaking what Starwalker meant.

But what was she going to do about it? Put her tail between her legs and meekly disappear from this canyon? No. No. Somehow, someway, she had to get to the bottom of this. There was too much at risk—not least, her career, if she failed to perform the task for which she had received the grant. If she gave the money back ... well, that would be the end of any hope of future grants. She *had* to accomplish her task.

But to do that, she had to find a way to deal with this threat. To deal with Starwalker. And the only way she could see of doing that would be to get to the bottom of what was going on here. Find out who—or what— Starwalker was, and what he was protecting. And then she could figure out how to deal with it.

But first she had to know what Starwalker was. The way he disappeared ... Well, if he was human, there had to be a way to come and go swiftly and silently from this alcove. And the logical place for that to be was at the rear.

But she didn't want to go back there. Stubborn didn't count for much against true fear, and she was truly afraid. Afraid with a fear unlike any she had ever felt before. Always, in the past, she had felt there was something she could do. This time she felt helpless against forces she could hardly begin to imagine, and that fed her fear. What was that feeling beside the old kiva? How did Starwalker come and go in such swift silence?

Without any answers, she could only speculate, and her imagination was beginning to run riot with visions of ghosts and evil curses. Unfortunately, dealing with such things wasn't part of the average Ph.D. curriculum, and she had no idea where to begin.

But she couldn't begin at all without a starting place, and so far she had the kiva and the fact that Starwalker seemed to appear and disappear instantaneously among the shadows.

A secret passageway in the rear of the alcove? Such things were not unheard of. If she could find one, it would ease her mind considerably as to whether Starwalker was merely human. And if he was human... well, she could probably deal with that better than a homicidal ghost. At least, she *thought* she could.

But it would be better to wait for Cody's return, wouldn't it? Easy to convince herself that she would be foolhardy to try anything alone. And thinking of Cody filled her with such an ache, such a yearning. Was it possible to fall in love so quickly? She hardly knew a thing about him, yet she ached for him as if he were the very center of her universe.

But he was always trying to get her to leave, too, as if he were a friendlier version of Starwalker.... And when she thought of that, she made up her mind not to wait. Whatever courage it took to walk back into those shadows and hunt for a passageway, she would find it, because she couldn't trust anyone. Not even Cody.

The light was fading a little as the sun sank lower in the Western sky. A glance at her watch told her that she still had hours of daylight left, but as the sun declined in the sky, the shadows in the alcove were growing deeper. Thicker. More threatening.

Drawing her knees up to her chin, she wrapped her arms tightly around them and stared into the back of the alcove. Starwalker might still be there, hiding somehow. There could be a little crevice or a cranny of some kind that he was slipping into. Maybe she should wait until morning to explore back there.

But anything could happen between now and morning. Anything. Could she really spend another night here wondering? And if she waited for Cody to return, it might be too dark to accomplish anything at all.

Somehow she found herself on her feet, moving toward the back of the alcove. She felt oddly like a sleepwalker, as if something besides her own will compelled her to go back there. The oddest thing, though, was the way she didn't feel frightened by the sense that someone or something was silently urging her toward the shadows.

She moved slowly, determined and reluctant all at once. The shadows seemed to be thickening, taking on substance, growing denser with each step she took. She should wait for Cody. Oh, yes, she definitely should wait. But she kept moving, anyway.

The deeper she moved into the alcove, the more it seemed as if something was holding the light at bay. Not as if the light was weaker and thinner here, but as if something was actually preventing it from penetrating these dark places.

When she reached the spot where she had been standing when she saw Starwalker, it was as if an electric jolt zapped down her spine. She froze on the spot, her shoulders stiffening and the skin on the back of her neck crawling with an uneasy awareness that she couldn't see behind her. With a sense of impending horror, as if an ax was about to fall on her.

All of a sudden the air became dank, tomblike. And in that instant the last doubt in her mind died. Something was afoot here that was not human. Something that smelled of an open grave.

She wanted to stop right there. Instincts deeper than rational thought were urging her to flee right this instant, to get to safety. But there was another urge, a pressure at the back of her, almost like a hand that was telling her to move forward, to step into the shadows and discover the secrets hidden there.

And even her rational mind acknowledged that she could never complete her task in this canyon if she didn't solve the problem of this alcove.

But oh, how she wanted to be somewhere else!

Another step took her even deeper into the shadows. She could almost feel their touch on her skin, a cold clamminess like a rainy February day. Even the wind changed its tenor now, sounding less like a soft, lost wailing and more like whispers of dry, ancient voices. From time to time she could almost have sworn she heard words.

Another step. She felt as if she were sinking into something, as if the shadows were thickening the air, too. She wished she had some idea of what she needed to find. What it was she was looking for, other than a way that Starwalker could come and go with such startling suddenness. A cleft in the rocks, a chimney leading to the surface. A hiding place or a passageway.

Something chilly slipped across the back of her neck, something damp and cold. A shiver ripped through her, and she spun around, expecting to see almost anything.

She stopped breathing. Between her and the cliff edge the shadows had thickened, holding the afternoon light at bay. And in those shadows something made a wavery appearance, like a mirage over hot pavement. It was as if some kind of dull light blossomed and died within the shadows, first here and then there, trying to emerge through openings that kept closing up and reappearing somewhere else. Dimly, beyond the shadows, she could see the sky, the cliff wall on the other side of the canyon. The normal day, but faded, as if viewed through a dark curtain.

On that dark curtain shapes and shadows moved, appearing and disappearing as if something could not quite be born. Behind her, like an arctic breath on her back, the clammy chill deepened, seeming to try to drive her toward the curtain...or through it to the other side, back out into the untainted daylight.

She was tempted to give in to the urging, tempted to run. This cold pressure at her back was frightening, unlike the pressure that had urged her deeper into the alcove to begin with. Two warring forces. The two old shamans who had fought here so long ago?

She was past wondering at the sanity of her impressions, carried along on an inward tide of recognition that superseded rationality. She knew what she was experiencing. Two opposing forces were tugging on her, trying to get her to do different things. She couldn't imagine what they wanted from her, and she didn't want to imagine what they might do if she didn't give it to them.

The shadowy curtain separating her from the day seemed to darken even more, the shifting patterns of light within it growing more intense. Something was trying to coalesce, and her heart nearly stopped with dread. She didn't know if she could stand it if she saw a person in those shadows. A ghost.

But no, it was something else, something that spread from the central point to the far ends of the alcove, like a growing mural reaching outward to fill the entire chamber. Light, filtered through darkness, shifted and settled, then shifted some more.

It was trying to show her something, she thought. Trying to communicate something of great importance, but she couldn't make any sense at all out of the patterns of light and dark.

The cold behind her grew, becoming harder, sharper, more insistent. Run! Run!

But she didn't run. It was as if some invisible force nailed her feet to the ground, preventing escape, making her watch the play of patterns in the shadows, demanding that she try to decipher their meaning.

This time, when her heart stilled, it was not from fright. Awe caused her breath to catch in her throat as right before her very eyes the village she had seen in the moonlight appeared in the curtain of shadows, stretching from end to end of the alcove, filling it with images as it once must have been filled in reality.

This was indeed the alcove where she had seen the strange structures with their triangular doorways and windows. In the moonlight the illusion had filled the alcove with the beauty of its structures, and now it did so again, in the shadows somehow created despite the afternoon light.

She could see the masonry, so close was she now, could see the cut yellowish stones, so carefully dressed and laid together in neat patterns. Could see plasterwork on interior walls that were painted with lovely geometric designs in red and blue. Could turn her head and look down the length of a narrow street between rows of two- and three-story buildings with railless balconies. Could see the soot marks rising up the sides of some of the buildings above fire pits that must once have served for communal cooking.

And at the end of the street she could see the kiva rising now above the hollow that was all that was left of it. Round, carefully constructed, a low building above the pit that would have held the large vaults for foot drums, the banquette for seating or storage. High triangular windows to let in the light. A holy place where once a shaman would have held forth.

The similarities with the rest of the cliff dwellings were obvious, yet it was equally apparent that whoever had dwelt here had come from a different culture than the Anasazi. An older one, perhaps. One from which the Anasazi, who had once lived high on the mesas, might have learned to build the cliff dwellings that they had spread over hundreds of square miles. Or perhaps these people had been latecomers who had learned from the Anasazi and then built their own variations with triangular doorways and windows.

She would never know. Someone had gone to the trouble of destroying every vestige of the occupants who had once lived here. She had nothing but the illusion wavering in the shadows before her to tell the tale, and no one would believe what she was seeing without some concrete proof.

But she believed it. Fear was forgotten as she stared in wonder at a secret she could never share. Some part of her ached agonizingly for what was lost and could never be recovered. Such hatred and vengeance had gone into the destruction of these dwellings. Such extreme hatred—undoubtedly what she felt at the kiva.

What she was feeling like a threat at the back of her neck right now.

The cold was growing, strengthening, becoming a nearly physical pressure that was shoving her forward, trying to force her to walk through the image in the shadows.

The image would be gone if she did. How she knew that she couldn't say, but it would definitely be gone. And the cold feeling at her back was opposed to what she was seeing, had probably helped destroy the people who had once inhabited this place. It was the feeling that surrounded the kiva, desecrating it.

It was useless at this late date to think in terms of good and evil. She was an archaeologist, committed to discovering the truth of the past, not to judging it. But right now she felt with all her heart and soul that whatever had destroyed this village was evil. And that evil survived even now.

The images before her shifted and wavered, and she found herself looking at the village from a different perspective. She was staring at the back of the alcove in the image now, even though her back was actually turned to it. She recognized the lowering ceiling of rock, admired the buildings that wedged themselves into the small space, wasting nothing.

And past them, into more confined places where nothing was built. Children had played there, she realized. The children had loved to run in those smaller places and play in the dirt there with toys made of clay and twigs. There they had been safe from falling over the cliff, and out of the way of working adults.

And there was something back there she was supposed to see. Something that called to her. Something that the evil chill behind her wanted to drive her away from.

Could she turn and go back there? Could she make herself defy the cold hatred that was shoving her away with an almost physical force?

Just the thought of attempting it made her shudder, made a cold sweat of fear bead her forehead. If she turned—if she defied that thing—what might happen to her? The strength of it was so real against her back that she had little difficulty believing it could actually harm her.

Like that rock that had fallen from the overhang earlier—a warning? A coincidence? Yet if the cold hatred were capable of that, why hadn't it simply collapsed the entire alcove and made it impossible for anyone to find whatever it was concealing?

She had to turn. She had to go back there and look for whatever it was. Something had to be found. Only if this thing were found would the forces lingering here be set free.

She couldn't have said how she knew that. It was as if thoughts were flowing into her mind, as if they were part of her, but not part of her.

Could she turn? She had to turn, had to face whatever it was. But she couldn't quite make herself do it. Couldn't quite overcome a fear that seemed to be rooted in her very soul. Couldn't understand why she felt she *had* to. There was no rhyme or reason to what was happening here, no reason why she should even care about it. Certainly no reason why she should take any kind of a risk over it. She could just walk away from here now and never think about it again.

And leave something forever imprisoned here.

Tugged in two directions, she stared into the image of the village, at the place where children had played, and thought she could almost see the small brown bodies and dark heads. Little children whose lives had been destroyed by a rivalry they had no control over, by a lust for power that had known no limits.

She shuddered again and knew that the lust that had destroyed this place had left the cold chill that wanted to turn her away from finding the thing at the back of the alcove.

And that understanding awoke the mulish stubbornness that was at her core. No hateful feeling was going to stop her from getting to the bottom of this. No frigid, clammy patch of air was going to deter her. She might never be able to tell anyone about this place, but she would know herself, and she had to find out what had happened here. What was still happening here. She had to, because she would never rest unless she knew.

But more than that, something was trapped here, and it shouldn't be trapped. Nothing should be trapped this way, for eons.

But even as the thought crossed her mind, an icy prickle at the base of her skull reminded her that she didn't actually know what was trapped here. Her impressions could be wrong. The old legend that Cody had shared with her, the tale about an evil shaman having been imprisoned by a good shaman, might be the truth. What she was feeling right now, this almost overwhelming impulse to free the trapped being, might be a delusion. The evil spirit might very well be tricking her into believing that the good spirit, *not* the evil one, was trapped.

How could she possibly sort it out? How could she be so sure that it wasn't the *good* force that was trying to scare her away, rather than the evil one?

There was only one way to find out.

Gathering her courage, she turned sharply and faced the shadows at the back of the cave, feeling the blast of chilly hatred right on her face. And behind her she felt a warmer sensation, an almost gentle flow of encouragement.

It might be a deception, she told herself. Whatever these two forces here were, both might be equally evil. But it didn't really matter. She was going to get to the bottom of it.

Now.

CHAPTER TEN

Lynn wanted Cody. She wanted him so fiercely that the yearning actually hurt. Standing there, looking into the dark at the back of the alcove, knowing she had to step into that icy hatred, she knew a moment of amazement at how her feelings for Cody seemed to have become the center of her life. It was scary, as scary as whatever she was facing here. She had no idea whether he returned her feelings, and she knew so little about him. . . .

She shivered and forced herself to take a step into the shadows, into the frigid sea of rage and hate. What she had felt beside the kiva paled beside the strength of what she felt now.

She took another step, telling herself to concentrate on finding whatever it was she needed to find. An artifact of some kind, she was sure. Something she would probably recognize the instant she set eyes on it.

The temperature dropped sharply, and the air became bitterly cold. She wrapped her arms snugly around herself as the cold penetrated her clothes and seemed to bore into her skin. In moments her teeth were chattering. Maybe she should go back and dig her jacket out of her backpack.

"Lynn, what are you doing?"

As if someone had flipped a switch, the shadows vanished and the day regained its warmth. Lynn whirled around and saw Cody silhouetted against the blue sky beyond the mouth of the alcove. The shadows, where only moments before she had seen the strange village, had dissipated. The alcove had returned to normal—completely barren, empty of anything save herself and Cody.

"Lynn? What's wrong? Why are you shivering?"

She was shivering because the cold of the shadows had sunk into her bones, and though the air was once again warm from the afternoon sun, she couldn't feel it internally. Internally she felt the icy rage.

And suddenly, looking at Cody in silhouette, his figure merged with another and she knew: Cody and Starwalker were related.

"Who's Starwalker?" she blurted abruptly. "Your brother? Are you trying to get me to leave, too? What the hell are you two hiding here?"

"Lynn . . ." He took a step toward her.

"Stay back! How can I trust you? You've lied, haven't you?" Oh, Lord, her heart was breaking, sundering in two from an anguish so intense her knees threatened to buckle. He'd been pretending to be a friend when in fact he was trying to do the same thing Starwalker was. And Starwalker had not only tried to get her to leave, but he'd threatened her, however indirectly. Cody was no better. Worse, even, because he had lied to her. Lied by omission. "What is Starwalker to you?"

"Lynn, you can trust me! All I've tried to do is protect you from harm! Can't you feel the threat?"

"Starwalker is the one who's threatened me! More than once. You're together somehow, aren't you? You're working together to—" She broke off abruptly as some shift of light and shadow suddenly revealed the truth. Her voice was little more than a hoarse gasp. "You *are* Starwalker."

The sense of betrayal that swamped her then was crushing. A sickening sense of loss gripped her as she felt her barely born dreams crumble.

"Lynn, listen . . ."

But she turned and fled, unable to bear the hurt that filled her, knowing only that she couldn't stand to have him touch her, couldn't stand to listen to any more of his lies.

But there was nowhere to run. She was trapped in this alcove, and if she tried to scramble down the narrow hand- and toeholds on the cliff, she would probably break her neck. Certainly she would be exposed to anything Cody might want to do to her. These cliff dwellings were highly defensible because they were so inaccessible. And now, working in reverse, one held her trapped because there was no easy way out.

"Lynn, wait! I won't hurt you!"

He wasn't moving, she realized. He wasn't chasing her. Maybe she ought to try to climb down, anyway. If she got enough of a head start . . .

Suddenly she stepped into the frigid, hateful aura around the kiva. It struck her with all the force of a punch to the solar plexus, leaving her breathless in shock. Gasping, she froze, unable to breathe, unable to move, as if trapped in ice.

"Lynn . . ."

She felt as if sheets of ice water were pouring over her, freezing her where she stood, turning her limbs into rigid icicles.

"Lynn!"

A hand, stunningly warm, reached out and grabbed her, yanking her back from the kiva. Numbed, she fell back against Cody and felt him stumble. He managed to regain his balance without falling, then swept her right up into his arms and carried her away from the kiva.

"God, Lynn!" he said huskily. "My God!"

She was cold, so very, very cold, and he was so incredibly warm that the touch of his fingers against her arm felt like fire. He lowered her gently to the alcove floor on the silvery survival blanket and wrapped her snugly in it. Then he lay beside her and drew her into his arms, wrapping himself protectively around her.

She shivered wildly, colder than she had ever been in her entire life. It was as if the aura around the kiva had sucked all the heat from her body, and she felt deeply, internally cold. It was a long, long time before the shivers slowed.

All of a sudden she found herself staring into a pair of very dark, very intense eyes. "Damn it, Lynn, you don't have any idea what you're fooling with! Give it up!"

Another shiver ripped through her, making her teeth chatter helplessly, but finally she managed to say, "Why don't you tell me what's going on?"

He shook his head, just a short, negative movement. "Damn, you don't quit! Can't you tell there are things here beyond your comprehension? Powers that defy explanation?''

"You must have some idea what's happening here! You told me to leave so no one would get hurt! What are you doing running around pretending to be Starwalker?''

He turned his head sharply, looking away from her. The afternoon was waning into evening, and the shadows were becoming deep again, this time naturally so. "I'm not pretending to be Starwalker. I *am* Starwalker. That's my real birth name. Cody Starwalker. I go by Walker as a ranger because it causes less comment."

"Why didn't you tell me that was you? Why did you pretend to be two different people? Why did you *lie?*"

He compressed his lips for a moment, then shook his head as if dismissing an unpleasant thought. "I didn't think it would matter. It never has before. But park ranger Cody Walker can't be scaring people away from this alcove or forbidding them to come here. I'd lose my job, and then protecting this place would become really difficult. Hell, if it became known I'm driving people away from here, there'd be a federal investigation—the real thing—and I can't allow that! Don't you understand, Lynn? I wasn't kidding when I said people would die if the seal is broken!"

"What seal? Damn it, Cody, what the hell is going on here? What's your part in it? And what are you going to do with me?''

His dark eyes bored into hers. "I'm going to get you out of here in one piece—if there's any way now possible. You've stirred things up so much that I don't know...." His voice trailed away slowly, and then, like a swooping hawk, his head lowered and his mouth covered hers, stealing the breath from her in a fiery kiss.

She was trapped in the cocoon of the Mylar blanket, her arms wrapped around her waist and unable to move. There was an instant when she resented that, wanting nothing more than to be free to embrace him, but a moment later the resentment died and everything inside her seemed to go warm and weak. Utter surrender overtook her.

His mouth was so soft and so hot, his tongue a rough contrast to the velvet of his lips. She opened her mouth to him with a readiness that betrayed her heart to him, taking him inside her in the only way she could at that moment. She was his. It was branded on her soul and had been since before time. For such feelings there was no rational explanation. She belonged to Cody Starwalker.

She had stopped shivering, and somehow the blanket was gone, leaving her open to his marauding hands. The tremors that passed through her were of purely sensual delight, and completely silenced her last doubt...for now.

Her shirt disappeared, and with it the bra she didn't really need. Small breasts, pale and tipped in coral, were exposed to the light of the dying day and to the gaze of the dark-eyed man who hovered over her. She had always been self-conscious about her smallness, but not now. Suddenly it didn't matter, as if his soft smile was a benediction. When he bent to take one hardening nipple into his mouth, she knew she was woman enough for him.

The world spun away. Night settled over the land, and the stars made their appearance in the black velvet sky. With soft touches of lips and tongue, Cody taught her what pleasure could be. Liquid murmurs escaped her as her body began a dance older than time, an undulation that pressed her to him and enticed him closer... and closer....

Her torso and breasts felt as if they were bathed in the fire of his mouth and hands. Inwardly she pulsed in rhythmic contractions such as she had never felt in her life before. She was helpless against the feelings this man evoked in her, and she loved it.

Dimly she sensed things swirling in the shadows just beyond the edge of consciousness. Vaguely she was aware of whispered urgings and promptings that were never quite audible. Her entire attention, however, was given over to the magic Cody Starwalker was weaving for her, a glistening, glittering, diamond-dust web of sensation that left her breathless, eager and aching.

The button of her slacks gave way, the zipper slipped down. Momentary consciousness of her scarred leg intruded, then faded away. It was dark, he couldn't see much... and she wanted him too much to shatter the spell in any way.

Fabric slipped softly over her legs, shoes fell from her feet, panties vanished. Her breath caught in her throat as his fingers found the soft hair between her thighs and brushed lightly, so lightly, the merest hint of sensation sent rivers of fire streaking straight to her womb. And helplessly her thighs parted, begging for more.

Then his fingers found the scar on her thigh. Time stood still, the breath jammed in her throat and her eyes flew open. Night had fallen, and Cody was nothing but a pale shadow hovering above her.

"Don't," she whispered, choking. "Don't."

"Shh...it's all right, sweetheart. It's okay. You told me it was here...."

Bending, he robbed her of breath by the simple act of kissing the hideous scar. She never doubted he could feel the indentation or the puckered skin, could feel the way her thigh muscle was so deformed. But she could tell he didn't mind, and something inside her, something long held tight and close against hurt, relaxed in a way that seemed to reach her soul.

"You're so brave...so determined...." His whispers soothed her, coaxed her, drove away the fear and allowed the desire to return. Carried away on a soft, warm tide of feeling, she lost track of everything.

Until her hands found bare skin. A long, tremulous sigh escaped her as her palms slid over the smooth, muscled flesh of Cody's back. The intimacy was incredible, the sensation one of the most delightful she had ever experienced. Skin on skin with nothing in between.

In her mind she saw their lovemaking as a candle flame brilliant in the night, holding the cold, threatening shadows at bay with the strength of passion and love. The dangers lay beyond the circle of light, lurking in the shadows, awaiting their opportunity, but unable to break the magic circle that surrounded the lovers.

"So pretty," he whispered roughly. His hand slid between her legs again, and a finger gently slipped within her, testing her readiness. A shudder of sheer delight ran through her, and she arched up helplessly.

Moments later he was between her legs. A moment of pure lucidity caught her between one breath and the next, opening her eyes and making her acutely aware of what she was about to do. And then, with a sigh as soft as down, she took him within her.

Heaven, she thought, could not be so sweet. Then waves of intense pleasure gripped her and carried her far, far beyond thought.

Wrapped in Mylar, they sheltered in each other's arms. The night had grown bitterly cold, carrying a scent that Lynn associated with snow. A late storm wasn't out of the question, and she wondered if they would awake to a wonderland in the morning.

She felt safe in Cody's arms, so safe that she refused to think about his lie. She could understand his reasoning and was ready to forgive him for that much. What she was not ready to forgive him for was keeping his secret after they had begun to become involved. She was not ready to forgive him for attempting to scare her just a few hours ago. And she couldn't help but wonder if he had somehow rigged that rock to fall.

She had questions, so many questions, but his hand was gently kneading her breast, and she really didn't want to think about them. Besides, the cold and the dark seemed to have strengthened whatever lurked in this alcove. She could feel it hovering at the edges of her mind, a frigid threat. Somehow Cody's touch seemed to hold it back, keep it from springing. It was certainly keeping her from wanting to think about those things.

And perhaps he knew that. Perhaps he was using seduction to keep her from questioning him and demanding explanations.

She tried immediately to dismiss the thought, but once planted, the seed insisted on growing. Perhaps he was just manipulating her. How could she possibly believe he found her attractive, anyway? She'd been rejected often enough because of her gimpy leg, too often to readily believe that any man could really want her.

But wasn't that what she had just done? Believe that Cody wanted her despite her leg? Hadn't she just believed the whispered words of a man who had lied to her?

God, how much of a fool could she be?

She must have stiffened, because at once Cody's hand paused on her breast. After a moment he raised his head and tried to see her face by the dim starshine. "Lynn?"

She didn't answer. Her throat had grown painfully tight with tears she didn't dare weep, and her mind, hurled suddenly back into cold reality, served up questions she was afraid to ask.

"Lynn? Talk to me. What's wrong?"

She honestly didn't think she could force a sound past her locked throat, and she didn't know if she really wanted to. What if he told her more lies, lies crafted so they would be easier to believe? How could she trust him now, knowing he had deceived her about who he was and what he was trying to do?

But what had his deception really been? another corner of her mind asked. What had he really done that was so awful? He had kept his identity secret so as not to risk his job. That was perfectly understandable. And once they became involved ... well ... that had made it even more difficult to tell her the truth, hadn't it? He must have known she would be upset.

"Tell me the truth!" She blurted the words, and they sounded harsh and unnaturally loud in the absolute silence of the canyon.

He answered quietly. "What truth? Or should I ask, which truth?"

"What's going on here, Cody? Why do you have to lie to people and pretend to be someone else? What are you protecting? And what are you going to do about me? Kill me?"

The question hung in the air, a stark accusation. When Cody stiffened, Lynn was sure he was going to pull away and leave her. She had to force herself not to reach out to stop him, reminding herself that all she was asking for was honesty, and she had every right to that.

But then the stiffness left him and his arms tightened around her, holding her close again. A small, helpless sigh of relief escaped her. She ought to despise herself for this, she thought, for being so weak, but love seemed to know no shame.

"I'm the Guardian," he said finally. "I protect the Seal. So far I haven't had to kill anyone, and you're not going to be the first. But I'm not the only power here,

Lynn, and that's why I'm worried about your safety. You've felt the touch of the Ancient One. He could seriously hurt you!''

"Who made you a guardian? What does that mean? Who's the Ancient One? What's the Seal? And why do you have to protect it? Cody, I need to understand! That's only fair!''

"Fair doesn't play any part in this.'' He shook his head and sighed heavily. In the ensuing silence, Lynn thought it was possible to hear the seconds creep past. "The role of the Guardian passes from father to son and has for over seven hundred years. I was raised from birth to protect the Seal, and when my father died ten years ago, I took my place here.''

Lynn was awed. Other than a few European monarchs, she didn't know of anyone who could trace his lineage in such a way. Seven hundred years!

"There was a village in the alcove once,'' Cody continued. "A group of outsiders settled here and built the first village on the cliffs. It was the model for all the cliff dwellings that came after, I understand.''

That, thought Lynn, would explain the sudden burst of dwellings on the canyon walls that had sprung up and then disappeared in the relatively short time of about seventy or eighty years. If it were true.

"Anyway,'' Cody continued, "there was a clash between two powerful shamans. I told you about that. The soul of the evil one was imprisoned here, and the village was destroyed. The Seal is the ward that holds the Ancient One prisoner, and it's my job to make sure no one breaks that seal.''

"What if someone does?''

Cody shook his head. "Then thousands will die."

"Of what?"

"I don't know. The legend is just that thousands will die a horrible death if the Ancient One is released. Could be disease. I just don't know."

Well, disease was a possibility, she found herself thinking. Smallpox bacteria could survive two hundred years in the grave of a victim, unless she'd been misinformed. There were probably other diseases that could live that way, as well. Assuming, of course, that there was any truth to this legend and the threat.

"Archaeologically speaking," Cody continued, "there's absolutely nothing to be gained by disturbing this site. Look at it, Lynn! Everything was destroyed, torn down, moved away, centuries ago. What could you possibly hope to discover here that could justify running the risk that something horrible will happen? And you've felt the evil yourself. I know you have. It's nothing to be fooled with."

She nodded slowly, remembering the hatred, the rage, the terrifying chill, she had found in the shadows. He was right; that was nothing to fool with.

But she still couldn't be sure he wasn't manipulating her for his own ends. Despite all that had happened between them, despite the fact that she had trusted him with her body and her heart, she couldn't quite shake the last niggling doubts. This man, as Starwalker, had threatened her. He had warned her away from here. His life was dedicated to protecting the Seal, whatever that was. Cody had a lot of excuses for wanting her out of here, and she had only his word that his reasons were altruistic. Or that they were even valid.

"Maybe you're right," she hedged. "I'll sleep on it."

That seemed to satisfy him, and he settled in more comfortably beside her, cradling her close. "I didn't want to lie to you," he said quietly. "Never. And I'll never lie to you again."

She hardly heard him. Her mind was running over what he had told her, and over the vision she had seen earlier. What if Cody had it wrong?

There was only one way to find out. On that thought, she let sleep creep up. And just beyond the edges of her dreams, she heard lost voices whispering of doom.

CHAPTER ELEVEN

Dreams filled her sleep, vivid and disturbing. More than once she awoke and opened her eyes to find herself staring into the night with only the faint glimmer of starshine to illuminate the alcove. Cody slept behind her, wrapped around her protectively. Funny, she thought drowsily, to feel he was protecting her when she couldn't even be sure he was telling her the truth.

And each time she awoke, she heard the nearly soundless whispers from the shadows deeper in the alcove. Each time she roused, she felt as if invisible fingers had been plucking at her, trying to get her attention, as if a legion of voices had murmured pleas she couldn't quite hear.

The experience was so real that each time she opened her eyes, she expected to see faces gathered around her in the dark, but when her eyes fluttered open, she saw only the starlit night. Then sleep claimed her again, soft dark wings that swept her up and carried her off into the twilight mists of dreams. . . .

She sat by the stone beehive oven, watching wisps of smoke curl up through the hole in the top. Somehow the fire, which she had so carefully banked the night before, had all but gone out, and now it would take hours to get the oven hot enough to fire clay. Beside her, in tidy rows, were the cups, bowls and jars she and her sisters had painstakingly formed. The designs painted on them, geometric patterns in red and black, were hers and hers alone. She found it soothing, somehow, to paint the careful, repetitive patterns.

A group of children dashed by, laughing and shrieking, and one of them bumped her shoulder. She winced, but didn't cry out, as an old injury twinged. Everyone here had old injuries. Pain was a constant companion.

But so was the laughter, and she laughed now as the child paused and looked doubtfully at her, as if expecting punishment. When he saw her smile, he smiled back and dashed off to rejoin his friends.

The men were gathering at the kiva again, she saw. They needed to decide what the village should do about the witch from a neighboring village who kept stirring up trouble.

It was true that they were different from the other inhabitants of the canyon and liked to keep to themselves, but they weren't trying to cause any trouble.

But the Ancient One from the other village claimed they were demons, and threatened them with various spells and magic. So far their own shaman had been able to protect them, but worry was growing. How long could they withstand this onslaught?

Tilting her head, she leaned toward the oven and felt the blast of heat against her cheeks. Not yet.

"That cup is pretty."

She looked up at once and smiled as she saw the village shaman looking down at the pottery. He squatted and indicated the cup she had painted with a cross-

hatched black pattern that looked like a woven basket.

"Save that one for me," he said, and gave her a warm smile.

She watched him walk away and thought about how nice he was. Oh, he had a temper and could be unreasonable sometimes, but overall he looked after everyone in the village as if they were his children, always finding a moment to stop and speak with them, to notice what they were doing, to admire their children.

And most of all he stood against the outsiders who would harm them.

There was a darkening in the day, an abrupt change of light like the one that presaged a coming thunderstorm. She looked up and around, surprised, for there hadn't been any clouds in the sky earlier. Not that a storm was a problem. Here in the protection of the alcove they wouldn't even get very damp.

But there was no cloud to be seen in the sky beyond. There was only the strange darkening, more like twilight had overtaken the world, though it was a long time until dusk.

"The sun is gone!" someone cried.

Shock held her rigid; then she joined the others hurrying to the edge of the cliff to look up at the sun. There she saw only a black disk, a hole in the sky where once there had been the blinding light of the life-giving sun. The shaman, too, came to the cliff's edge to look up at the wonder, and as he stood there, a lightning bolt streaked out of a clear sky and wrapped him in blue light.

It was over, she thought. They would all die now, at the hands of the witch....

Lynn's eyes snapped open, and she found herself staring into the dark. The faint sheen of starlight gave her only the dimmest view, just enough to make out the alcove. Cody still slept behind her, but he had removed his arm from around her waist and tucked it between them. The blanket had lifted, letting the wind nip at her knee.

And it was a cold wind blowing. The silent night held the restless sound of the lonely wind as it whipped through the alcove. Lynn, caught in the grip of her dream, remembered the darkening of the sun and the blue fire that had caught the shaman in its grip.

And she knew what she had to do.

Slipping quietly from beneath the Mylar, she reached for her clothes and tugged them on, trying to suppress shivers born of the cold and the late hour. It was dark; she would need some light. Being as quiet as she could, she reached into her pack and felt around for the disposable penlights she carried everywhere. Instead she found her light sticks and decided to settle for them. Bending one briskly, she unleashed a shower of yellow light into the alcove.

Then, moving as quietly as possible, she tried to creep away without waking Cody. With only the light stick to guide her, she couldn't see very far in any direction. The shadows seemed to press inward, and the air grew even colder. The Ancient One was stirring, she thought. Getting ready to protect the Seal.

As she reached the back of the alcove, she hesitated. Turning, she looked back to see if Cody still slept and she gasped when she realized the village was once more appearing in the shadows, looking as if it was washed in moonlight. And this time the shadowy figures of its occupants were visible, moving around slowly in the narrow streets.

And down the street came the man from her dream, the one who had wanted her to keep the cup for him. He walked as if he had all the time in the world, pausing to speak to nearly everyone he passed, including the smallest children. Lynn watched as he drew closer, then caught her breath as his eyes focused on her. Dark eyes, hypnotic yet kind, stared at her out of an illusion.

"Free us," he said.

In an instant the village and the people vanished and she stood alone on a windswept rock ledge in a pool of yellow light.

Free us.

She had to find that Seal. She had to set that shaman free. Something was terribly, terribly wrong here, but the evil she had felt did not emanate from the spirit who wanted her to set him free.

Galvanized, she turned and hurried toward the back of the alcove, determined to find the Seal, whatever it was. It was back there, though. She had felt the pressure of opposing forces as one had tried to guide her there and the other had tried to prevent her from going. At the back of the alcove. Perhaps near the kiva? Yes, near the kiva. Why else did that aura of evil hang there all the time?

Yes, the old shaman that Cody served was probably protecting something over there. There could be no other reason for that aura. But even in the midst of her determination to settle matters and free the shaman with the kindly eyes, she felt a terrible pang at how Cody had been deluded and misled over the years. He thought he was protecting the world from the evil shaman, when in fact he was helping imprison the kindly one. He would feel so awful once he discovered the truth!

She hurried toward the kiva, pulling out more light sticks and activating them. Truth was all that mattered here, she told herself. The truth had to be uncovered, even if it hurt Cody. She couldn't allow him to spend the rest of his life committed to a servitude that wasn't necessary. Once he saw that the shaman had been freed, his duty would be over, and he would be free to live a normal life.

And not once, not *once,* did she question her own reasoning. She hardly noticed that she moved as if guided, hardly cared that something or someone was urging her forward. She had looked into the kindly eyes of the shaman and was convinced of the rightness of her actions.

When she reached the depression that marked the kiva, she was astonished to find the evil aura gone. For a fleeting instant some corner of her mind shrieked a warning, telling her that the feeling hadn't vanished, couldn't vanish, that it was being masked. That it was being masked for a purpose. The good shaman would have no reason to mask the aura, and the evil sha-man—

The thought was truncated abruptly, gone almost before she was aware of it. Her purpose grew firmer, and she forgot her doubts as she set the light sticks around the perimeter, casting a soft yellow glow over the entire bowl. The Seal had to be somewhere in there.

But how was she to find it? She didn't even know what it looked like!

Almost as soon as she thought of the question, something misty began to stir in the center of the depression, like whirling smoke, and an image began to form. A carved stone tablet, perhaps, though it was hard to be sure.

Yes! Break the Seal. Smash the stone. All she had to do was find it, but after seven hundred years, it could be buried almost anywhere.

She shivered, suddenly realizing that the cold hatred around the kiva seemed to have intensified, as if trying to drive her away. But she was not going to be driven away this time. Not this time.

She wasn't willing to believe that her dream had misled her, that the eyes she had looked into moments ago were a deception. Evil imprisoned the Ancient One. She could feel it surrounding the kiva.

"Lynn, no!"

She heard Cody call from the other end of the alcove, but she refused to listen. She wasn't going to let this evil stop her. No way. Whatever had been imprisoned deserved to be free.

"Lynn!"

Cody was getting closer, and there wasn't a doubt in her mind that he'd risk his own neck to yank her away from the kiva. She didn't want him to do that. She wouldn't be able to stand it if anything happened to him. She loved him. Oh, God, she loved him, and she didn't doubt for a single moment that he believed in what he was doing, believed he was on the side of right...and would willingly sacrifice himself to protect others, whether her or the faceless people he believed would be threatened by the shaman's release.

Cody Walker was a good man. He had been misled and misguided, used remorselessly by the evil shaman. He believed he was on the side of good when he was actually on the side of evil. She dreaded how the truth was going to wound him, wished desperately that there was some way to spare him...short of sacrificing the truth.

He would recover, she told herself. He would be hurt initially to discover he had been duped, but he would recover. He was a good man, and he would eventually be glad that the evil scheme had been defeated.

But no matter how much it hurt him to know he had been used, she couldn't let him continue in his misguided purpose. She couldn't allow him to serve evil, however unwittingly. The shaman had to be freed, and in freeing the shaman, she would also free Cody.

"Don't come in here!" she shouted over her shoulder, knowing better than to think he would stop. He was getting closer, and between his duty to protect the Seal and his desire to protect her, he was going to dive in with her....

And suddenly she saw the Seal. It lay in the dirt, covered by reddish yellow dust, a triangular shape softened by years of windblown dirt. She hurried forward, never doubting that this was what she had come here for.

Dropping to her knees, she bent forward and began to brush away the accumulated dirt of the ages. The lightning struck closer, and the cold deepened until she felt as if she were kneeling in a frigid arctic wasteland. Her fingers were turning numb, and she wondered for a fleeting instant if she might not freeze to death before she could uncover the Seal.

Hurry.

Cody's rapid approach, the threat of the lightning and the cold, urged her to move as quickly as she could. Her nose was numb now, her cheeks and ears aching, her fingers beginning to fumble as hypothermia rapidly debilitated her.

Hurry.

She winced as her nail jammed and pulled against one edge of the Seal. The pain seemed to shoot all the way up her arm, and she jerked her hand back just in time to avoid a fork of lightning that struck at the edge of the Seal.

"Lynn..."

The sound of Cody's voice so close was the final goad. Now, before he could prevent her. Bending forward, she forced her fingers into the dirt until she could feel the bottom edge of the Seal, and then, with all her might, she leaned backward and pulled.

And up it came. About a foot high and nine inches wide at the base, it was a triangular stone slab on which were carved strange symbols that resembled nothing she had ever before seen. Oh, how she wished she could preserve it! The knowledge here...

Hurry!

Time was running out. If the lightning didn't get her, Cody would.

Forcing herself to her feet, she staggered against the unexpected weight of air that seemed to have turned to lead. She had to get this away from the kiva, throw it over the edge. Staggering, nearly stumbling as the frigid air resisted her, she headed toward the edge of the circle, toward the dimly seen edge of the alcove beyond which the moonless night waited.

Suddenly she burst free of the cold miasma surrounding the kiva and met the warmer, lighter night air. Suddenly energized, she dashed toward the cliff edge, determined to hurl the Seal over and smash it forever.

"Lynn, no!"

Her feet hardly seemed to touch the ground. She had to get there before Cody caught her. Behind her, the hammering of his feet on the rock was getting louder as he neared.

Suddenly the edge was there, the canyon bathed in starlight visible beyond. She stopped so quickly that she nearly stumbled. Giving the Seal one last look, she lifted it and hurled it outward over the edge with all her might.

"Lynn, no!"

But even as Cody shouted, the Seal was spinning through the air away from them, beyond recovery. In some strange way it seemed almost to glow, as if emitting light of some kind, and then it disappeared into the shadows below.

Cody reached her and drew to a sharp halt, breathing heavily. "God, Lynn," he whispered. "Oh, God, what you've unleashed . . ."

"No. No. You'll see." Even now she couldn't doubt that she'd done the right thing. The evil that surrounded the kiva had to be destroyed.

Abruptly Cody reached out and gathered her against him, her cheek on his chest so that she could still see out across the canyon, and beneath her ear she could hear his heartbeat. "I thought you'd be killed," he said gruffly.

Before she could respond in any way, they heard the crash as the Seal shattered on the rocks below.

Instantaneously a blinding light filled the entire canyon, so brilliant it washed out the night sky and branded an afterimage on Lynn's eyes. When it faded, she felt blinded by the night, her dark adaptation gone.

There was a silence so profound that Lynn's ears seemed to ring, and she blinked desperately, trying to see something, anything.

"Lynn," he whispered. "Lynn, look!" He turned her head so that she was looking into the alcove.

There, over the kiva, a black whirlwind appeared to be growing. Inky, icy, it swelled in size, reaching up toward the overhang. Deep in its depths, red lightning sizzled and crackled, as if seeking to escape. Tendrils of black smoke reached out from its base, creeping across the floor in all directions in a threatening, serpentine movement.

Instinctively, Lynn tried to step backward, but Cody's arm stopped her.

"Don't move," he said harshly. "We've got to stop it."

In that instant she realized that it was she who had been duped, that Cody had been right all along. Evil had been imprisoned here, and she had been used as a tool to free it.

A gut-wrenching, revolting odor accompanied the growing strength of the black whirlwind, worse even than rotting meat. It spread outward until it reached the very edge of the alcove, making Lynn gag helplessly.

"Stay with me," Cody commanded. "Whatever happens, don't let go of me."

He tucked her fingers around his belt and then lifted both his arms. As he had the night on the mesa top, when she had first seen him, he began to chant in a powerful voice. At first his words echoed off the rock walls and overhang, seeming to bounce back at them from every direction, but as the black whirlwind grew, it began to absorb the sound, muffling Cody's chant until it seemed to come from miles away.

And in the depths of the whirlwind, Lynn began to see something forming. Little by little, as if coalescing out of dark smoke, a man took shape, at first seeming small and distant. But as he watched, he grew in size and stature until he towered over them, stretching from floor to overhang.

It was the shaman of her dreams, she realized, except that now he didn't look at all kindly or friendly. His smile was a satisfied sneer, and his eyes held the cold, dark emptiness of hell.

Oh God, what had she done?

Cody's chanting changed tenor, growing more forceful despite the muffling presence of the black whirlwind. Lowering his arms a little, he cupped his hands as if to receive something. And in his hands a soft golden light appeared. At first it was little more than a candle flame, but as Cody chanted, it grew to fill his hands and then spill over in amber radiance. Lynn caught her breath in awe.

The black whirlwind intensified, filling the alcove with the enraged howl. Blown sand and dust stung Lynn's cheeks and made her squint, but she didn't dare close her eyes. The golden light was growing, spilling over Cody's hands like a glowing waterfall as he chanted.

The shriek of the wind nearly drowned him out, but he kept right on, narrowing his eyes and staring into the punishing gale. Golden light pooled at his feet and spread like a gentle tide toward the threatening fingers of oily smoke. When they met, red and blue sparks sizzled and popped angrily. Golden light fountained upward and splattered over black smoke; black smoke curled around golden light and tried to swallow it.

And Cody continued to chant.

The whirlwind shrieked furiously, and from within its depths the arms of the evil shaman reached out toward Cody, threatening to close around him.

Cody spread his own arms as if to embrace something and pointed his fingers toward the whirlwind. Lynn gasped desperately for air as the foul stench grew thicker, then gasped again in disbelief as golden fire poured along Cody's arms, threatening to consume him in tongues of flame. Before she could cry out, the fire leaped from his arms to the golden puddle on the floor.

A silent explosion of light filled the alcove, a light so blinding and brilliant that its afterimage flared whitely in Lynn's eyes and prevented her from seeing what happened next. Cody's continual chanting was all she had to cling to as the wind shrieked and buffeted them with sand and dust and the foul stench.

Then her vision cleared, and she gaped in astonished awe and fright. Two whirlwinds were facing one another now, one as golden as warm sunlight, the other as black as the depths of a tarpit. And the image of a man was visible in each. The two shamans faced each other again after seven hundred years, still locked in their mortal combat.

"Lynn! Lynn!"

Cody tugged on her, drawing her away from the edge of the ledge, away from the towering columns of light and dark, back deeper into the alcove.

"Cody..." She dragged her eyes away from the warring shamans as she stumbled after Cody. "What's happening? What—"

"Let's just get into the tunnel," he said sharply. "I want you in a protected place before those two start fighting!"

She looked at him, his face a harsh mask in the light from the column. "Tunnel? Fight?" But even as she formed the uncomprehending words, the wind howled furiously and a fireball flew through the air, crashing on the alcove floor with a burst of blue fire. She stopped questioning and hurried with Cody toward the rear of the alcove.

There, hidden cunningly behind a boulder, was the mouth of a tunnel. This was how Starwalker had made his mysterious appearances and disappearances, she realized, as Cody urged her behind the boulder and into the protection of the tunnel.

From their safe position, they stopped to look back into the alcove over the lip of the concealing boulder. The two columns, one golden, one black, were reaching out toward each other, extending tentacles as if to consume one another.

"I'm sorry," Lynn heard herself say helplessly. "Cody, I'm sorry! He was manipulating me! I thought..." She couldn't even remember now what she had thought. She knew she had been manipulated by the dark thing that was even now trying to kill the golden shaman, but she couldn't remember how. Or why she had believed it. She knew only that she had unleashed that black evil onto the world, and the awareness left her feeling sick to her soul. "I'm sorry...."

"Shh." He wrapped an arm snugly around her shoulders and tucked her up against his side. "It would have happened sooner or later. Sooner or later I wouldn't have been able to keep someone out of here, and he would have manipulated them into freeing him. Lynn, I'm the one who's sorry. If I'd guessed there was more than just your normal curiosity driving you..."

"What could you have done? He controlled me, Cody! He *controlled* me!"

Before he could reply, a roar filled the alcove, deafening her. Fountaining fire seemed to rise up from the very ground, sinister red and blue flames. Lynn cried out as they threatened to consume the golden shaman, but her cry was lost in the howl of the wind and the roar of the flames. For an instant, just an instant, it seemed that the golden light was about to be snuffed out by the red and blue fire.

Then, quicker than the eye could see, the golden light expanded, filling the entire alcove, surrounding the black whirlwind, swallowing the fountaining fire. Consuming them all.

Silence filled the night, as did a gentle golden light. The abruptness of the change was almost stunning, and nearly a minute passed before either she or Cody moved. When they did, it was to straighten and look out into the peaceful alcove.

The light slowly shrank, drawing back from the walls of the alcove and gradually resolving into the figure of a man.

"It is done," he said. "The Evil One is gone. Go in peace, Starwalker. Your guardianship is at an end."

Then the man dissolved into the golden light, before fading away into nothing. The night was once again broken only by the faint yellow glow of Lynn's light sticks.

Cody's arms had grown so tight around her that she could barely breathe, but she didn't mind. Oh, no, she didn't mind at all. Words were locked in her tear-constricted throat as the night's events crashed in on her. She hadn't listened to Cody, had doubted him and allowed herself to be manipulated by some evil thing.... Would he ever be able to forgive her?

"It's over." He spoke the words almost reverently, and with his finger tipped her face up so he could see her in the faint glow from the light sticks. "It's over."

Slowly he released her and took her hand. With the gentlest of tugs, he guided her out of the tunnel and back into the alcove to where the light sticks lined the depression of the kiva. They needed to know for certain that the cold, evil feeling was gone, she realized.

When they got there, they both hesitated, and then together they stepped over the faint scuff marks Lynn had made yesterday to delineate the aura.

It was gone.

Slowly Cody turned his head and looked down at her. "It's done," he said. "It really *is* done."

"Does . . . that bother you?"

He shook his head, and a smile gradually curved his mouth. "Oh, no. Not at all. I've been freed, too."

"Freed to do what?"

His smile deepened, and a soft laugh escaped him. "Chase you all the way back to your home and persuade you to marry me."

And in that instant Lynn, too, was set free. A laugh bubbled up from deep inside her and spilled out into the quiet night. He had forgiven her. She didn't even have to ask. He had forgiven her!

"But first," Cody said, "I'm going to help you finish your survey of this canyon. I think we're going to make a great team."

She was still laughing with joy when he laid her back on the blankets and showed her how to walk among the stars with him.

* * * * *

Dear Reader,

It is impossible for me to stand among Anasazi ruins and not hear the whispers of the past. There is nothing eerier than to walk through the neatly constructed cliff dwellings and wonder what ever happened to the people who built them. At times I almost hear the laughter of the children who lived there so long ago, and each time I turn a corner I expect to see a woman grinding maize or painting a design on a piece of pottery.

Cody Starwalker came to me in the Aztec, New Mexico, ruins as I sat on the bench in the reconstructed Great Kiva and listened to the wind whistle through the slit windows. There's so much we'll never know about the Anasazi, so much we can only speculate about. They are a people who built a great culture and left behind a thousand unanswered questions.

But Cody had a story to tell, and he whispered it to me on the wind.

I hope you enjoy it as much as I did.

Rachel Lee

ETERNAL LIFE, ETERNAL LOVE

Twilight Memories
MAGGIE SHAYNE

Darkly handsome Roland de Courtemanche had rejected Rhiannon's affections for centuries, banishing her to exist alone for all eternity. Yet now that the man she loved and the boy in his care were in danger, Rhiannon knew staying away was impossible.

Discover the dark side of love in *Twilight Memories* by Maggie Shayne, book two of WINGS IN THE NIGHT, available in April from Shadows.

**And now for something
completely different
from Silhouette....**

SPELLBOUND
R O M A N C E

**In May, look for
MIRANDA'S VIKING (IM #568)
by Maggie Shayne**

Yesterday, Rolf Magnusson had been frozen
solid, his body perfectly preserved in the
glacial cave where scientist Miranda O'Shea
had discovered him. Today, the Viking warrior
sat sipping coffee in her living room, all six feet
seven inches of him hot to the touch. His heart,
however, remained as ice-cold as the rest of him
had been for nine hundred years. But Miranda
knew a very unscientific way to thaw it out....

Don't miss MIRANDA'S VIKING by
Maggie Shayne, available this May,
only from

Fifty red-blooded, white-hot, true-blue hunks
from every State in the Union!

Look for MEN MADE IN AMERICA! Written by some of
our most popular authors, these stories feature fifty of
the strongest, sexiest men, each from a different state in
the union!

Two titles available every other month at your favorite
retail outlet.

In May, look for:

KISS YESTERDAY GOODBYE by Leigh Michaels (Iowa)
A TIME TO KEEP by Curtiss Ann Matlock (Kansas)

In June, look for:

ONE PALE, FAWN GLOVE by Linda Shaw (Kentucky)
BAYOU MIDNIGHT by Emilie Richards (Louisiana)

You won't be able to resist MEN MADE IN AMERICA!